D1806426

HMS NIGHTINGALE

ALEXIS CAREW #4

J A SUTHERLAND

HMS Nightingale

by J.A. Sutherland

© Copyright 2016 Sutherland. All rights reserved.

 Created with Vellum

For Lieutenant Alexis Carew, it should be the perfect assignment — a command of her own and a chance to return to her home star system.

What she finds is a surly crew, the dregs of every frigate and ship of the line to pass through on the way to the war's front, a first officer who thinks the command should have been his, and colonial worlds where they believe a girl's place is somewhere very different than command of a Queen's starship. Add to that the mysterious disappearances of ships vital to the war effort and an old enemy who seems intent on convincing her he's changed.

Then there's the mongoose with an unnatural affinity for her boots.

For Mom & Dad, If I could choose the childhood I'd most like to have had, it would be the one you gave me. The variety, the adventures, the freedom to explore ... I wouldn't trade those memories for anything. Today's Child Protective Services might disagree, but they shouldn't have joined if they can't take a joke. :) Thank you.

PART ONE

identify the ship. Zariah orbital was busy and the station's quay was so full that many ships were being forced to simply orbit the planet and transfer supplies to and from the station by boat. The pilot had notified *Nightingale* of their imminent arrival and they wanted to know who was aboard in order to arrange for the appropriate side-party at the entry lock.

"Who should I say, miss?"

Alexis took a deep breath and calmed her excitement. There were many firsts about to happen and she wanted to remember them all. So much so that she could even forgive the civilian pilot for calling her "miss" instead of the Navy's preferred "sir" for all officers, regardless of gender. He was likely a former Navy man himself, older and having left the Service to make his way as a boatman, and should know better, but this event was too important to be bothered by something so trivial.

"*Nightingale*," she said.

The pilot glanced at her with raised eyebrows and Alexis nodded to him, at least trying to portray a calm she didn't feel. He grinned, nodded once, and turned back to his control board. He reached forward and keyed the boat's radio to the cockpit's speakers, instead of his earpiece, so that she could hear.

"What boat?" sounded from the speakers. Probably the midshipman of the watch, Alexis presumed, and a bit irritated that he'd had to ask again.

"*Nightingale*," the pilot said.

There was the briefest pause, then, "Aye, aye," and the connection was cut off.

Alexis shivered at the tingle of pleasure that went through her. A ship's commander announced herself by the name of her ship. Right now that midshipman would be scrambling to assemble a side-party and all of *Nightingale's* crew to gather at the lock in order to greet their new commander, sole master of a Queen's ship after God.

"First command, miss?" the pilot asked.

Alexis nodded, ignoring his use of "miss" again. "First I've been appointed into." She caught her lower lip between her teeth. "It's different than taking command of a prize."

The pilot nodded, giving her an appraising glance. Alexis couldn't really blame him; she didn't much look the part of a Royal Navy officer, much less a ship's commander. She was young, just eighteen, though she'd been in the Service a little over three years, and her height, or lack thereof as it was a bare meter and a half, made her look younger.

"You've commanded a prize, then?" the pilot asked.

Alexis nodded absently, still searching the space ahead of them for some sight of *Nightingale*.

"*Grapple*, a pirate my first ship took," she said, absently. She thought she might be able to make out the shape of a fore-and-aft rigged vessel ahead of them. "The pirates retook her during a storm, but we prevailed later and returned safely. Then my division took a Hanoverese ship, *Sittich*, from our ship's boat. Our frigate had left the system already and we were forced to sail her back from Hanover ourselves." She frowned. "*Trau Wunsch*, but she was just a scow of a merchant ship we took to escape imprisonment in the Berry March." She paused and her throat tightened along with her chest. "And there was a ship at Giron, of course —" She swallowed hard as her throat tightened more. "I suppose I was appointed into her, at least temporarily, but she was never properly bought-in to the Service ..."

She trailed off. Speaking of that ship brought up too many memories of that last, desperate action with a Hanoverese frigate when so many, virtually all, of her crew had perished — to say nothing of the refugees she'd been carrying. Women and children fleeing Giron and the reprisals of the Hanoverese. Women and children she'd brought aboard, promising them she'd keep them safe.

She caught the pilot staring at her. She thought for a moment that she could see similar feelings in his eyes — too many actions, too many ships shot to lifeless hulks floating in the emptiness of *darkspace*, and too many mates floating just as lifeless aboard them. Then she shook herself, forcing those thoughts and memories aside as she found herself doing more and more often these days — and made herself look forward instead, to her new command.

"But this is to be my first official command," she said with a small smile. "It's different." She peered forward. "Do you suppose you could circle her once or twice? Before docking, I mean. So that I might get a good look before going aboard?"

The pilot gave her another look before turning back to his console.

"Aye, sir."

<hr />

ALEXIS SWALLOWED and licked her lips as she waited for the lock to cycle. The boat had made fast to *Nightingale's* port side and the ship had extended its plastic boarding tube to the boat. As soon as the tube was aired she'd be able to board *Nightingale*. She spared a quick glance to Isom, the spacer who'd attached himself to her some time ago as a personal servant. He was ready behind her with their baggage. Not very much of it, just his spacer's bag and her two chests and bag of belongings. Her personal stores, food, and wine to supplement the poor ship's offerings of recycled water and vat-grown beef, could be sent for later.

Perched atop her pallet of belongings, though, was a covered, vacuum-safe cage containing the damned, bloody creature given to her by the smuggler and former pirate Avrel Dansby. The irony of her current orders being to put a stop to smugglers after being partnered with one by the Foreign Office in her last posting wasn't lost on her. Still, he hadn't turned out to be a half-bad sort at the end, though the gift was a dig at her.

When they'd first been introduced by Mister Eades of the Foreign Office, they'd taken an immediate, strong dislike for each other, even before she knew he was a former pirate. Eades had looked them over and commented that it was much like sitting down to sup with a mongoose and a cobra. Alexis had quickly named Dansby the serpent and he'd just as quickly replied that, of course, she was the "cute, cuddly one". At the end of that mission, he'd sailed out of the system leaving Alexis saddled with his gift of a mongoose. She'd been entirely unsure what to do with it, not wanting to turn it loose to some horrible fate, but certainly not wanting to keep it. She hadn't even named the thing yet and was unsure she ever would.

Perhaps my grandfather will want it when we stop at Dalthus. Don't they sometimes turn things like that loose on colonies to control the vermin?

She reached down and touched her pocket to ensure her tablet was there, but resisted the urge to pull it out and see that her orders were still displayed. She probably wouldn't need the tablet to read herself in — she'd fairly memorized the orders on her trip to Zariah system — but this was, as she'd told the boat's pilot, very different from taking command of a prize.

There was no ceremony involved in leading a prize crew, one simply went aboard with the assigned crew and started giving orders. Moreover, at least two of the ships she'd commanded she'd taken herself.

Certainly no time for ceremony when you're overpowering the crew and having to prepare to run for your life.

It seemed to her that an undue amount of her time in the Navy had been spent doing exactly that.

But taking command of a proper Royal Navy ship had a ceremony attached to it, one that Alexis had studied on the trip here just as diligently as she'd read and reread her orders. She'd run through it in her head over and over again, wanting to be sure she got it right and that she did things perfectly, for she'd have the eyes of her new crew upon her and they'd be judging her from the start — and she knew that she'd have to overcome their first impressions when they saw her, before she'd had even the chance to speak.

More than that, though, she wanted it perfect for herself. She was proud, perhaps inordinately so, of what she'd accomplished in the Navy so far, and she believed Admiral Cammack when he said that her appointment into *Nightingale,* even when the ship was so far from the border and the war with Hanover, was a recognition of those accomplishments.

There are few enough lieutenants given even so small a command at just eighteen.

The lock seemed to be taking forever to pressurize, or perhaps it was just that her thoughts were racing. She ran through the steps once more in her head.

Pause at the hatch and get a foot aboard carefully, so as not to stumble at the change from the boarding tube to the ship's artificial gravity. The ensign will be on the aft wall and I'm boarding the port side, so turn to my right — don't want to be looking about unsure of where to turn. Then doff my beret to the ensign and face the senior officer there to greet me — that'll likely be Midshipman Villar.

She'd read the copy of *Nightingale's* muster book on the way, as well. At least the most current one in the records on Lesser Ichthorpe where Admiral Cammack had given her the commission. *Nightingale* was a small ship, just a revenue cutter, tasked with inspecting merchants in the sector for contraband or untaxed goods. Other than the lieutenant who commanded her, she rated only two other officers, both midshipmen.

Wait for him to doff his beret, then mine in turn, and when he informs me that the crew is properly assembled I read my orders out. Simple, really.

She touched her pocket again to see that the tablet was still there and wondered why the bloody lock was taking so long. The orders were simple and brief, leaving a great deal to Alexis' interpretation — and responsibility.

By the hand of Admiral Westley Johnathon Cammack, Lord Firdale, by and for the Commissioners for executing the Office of the Lord High Admiral of New London and New Edinburgh &c and of all Her Majesty's Colonies and Affiliated Worlds &c.

To Lieutenant Alexis Arleen Carew hereby appointed Lieutenant, Master and Commander of Her Majesty's Ship the Nightingale.

By Virtue of the Power and Authority to us given We do hereby constitute and appoint you Lieutenant, Master and Commander of Her Majesty's Ship the Nightingale *willing and requiring you forthwith to go on board and take upon you the Charge and Command of Lieutenant, Master and Commander in her accordingly. Strictly Charging and Commanding all the Officers and Company belonging to the said ship subordinate to you to behave themselves jointly and severally in their respective Employments with all the Respect and Obedience unto you their said Lieutenant, Master and Commander; And you likewise to observe and execute as well the General printed Instructions as what Orders and Directions you shall from time to time receive from your Superiors or any other your superior Officers for Her Majesty's service.*

Hereof nor you nor any of you may fail as you will Answer the Contrary at your Peril.

And for so doing this shall be your Warrant. Given under our hands and the Seal of the Office Admiralty this eighth day of October, 2968 in the fortieth Year of Her Majesty's Reign.

By Command of their Lordships and by the Hand of Admiral Westley Johnathon Cammack, Lord Firdale.

(his signature and devices)

The light on the airlock turned green, indicating that there was a good seal between the boat and *Nightingale*, and Alexis reached to pull the hatch open. She took a deep breath, made an effort to keep her face from breaking out in a wide grin of joy, squared her shoulders, and launched herself out of the boat's artificial gravity and down the boarding tube toward her new ship.

My ship, my command, and earned on my own bottom.

She caught the grab bar at the end of the boarding tube and swung her feet into *Nightingale's* lock, then slid the exterior hatch shut — Isom would follow behind her after she'd boarded. She gave her jacket a tug, slid the interior hatch open and stepped aboard, turning sharply to her right and saluting the ensign hanging on the aft bulkhead.

She turned her attention to the waiting men, surprised to see that it didn't appear the full ship's company was present on the main deck, at least not near the lock. There were the two midshipmen she expected, but they were in common ship's jumpsuits, not their dress uniforms as she'd expect them to be to meet *Nightingale's* new commander. Nor was the full complement of Marines turned out, only the one who'd normally be left to guard the lock.

The eldest and tallest of the officers stepped forward.

That'll be Villar, if I read the muster book properly. Twenty-four — a bit old to have not passed for lieutenant himself, but not unheard of.

Then she noted that the man's rank insignia was that of a lieutenant, not a midshipman. The man was tall, almost a full two meters so, and seemed to tower over her. His face twisted in a scowl as he stepped toward Alexis and looked down at her.

"Who the bloody hell are you then?" he asked.

TWO

Alexis drew her head back, shocked by the lieutenant's aggression. Her first thought was that someone had made a mistake and appointed another officer into *Nightingale* without knowing that Admiral Cammack had appointed her. Still it was no cause for such an attack. She glanced around and saw that everyone within earshot, which included most of the crew, had stopped working and were watching the drama.

And certainly not cause to address a fellow officer that way in front of the crew.

"I'm Lieutenant Carew," she said. "Ordered aboard by Admiral Cammack. And you, lieutenant?"

"Villar," the man said. "*Nightingale's* commander, and none too pleased at your little joke."

Alexis frowned. So this *was* Villar, but he was a lieutenant and not a midshipman? Her copy of the ship's muster book could well be out of date, but surely Admiral Cammack would have been aware that Villar had received his commission.

"Joke?"

"Calling 'Nightingale' from the boat, as though she were yours." He looked her over and sneered. "What are you? Twelve?" He shook his head. "Nightingale's a small ship and a smaller crew, we don't have time for some snotty's pranks. Now if you're sent aboard to fill out my gunroom, you'd best get a proper uniform and insignia on and be about it."

Alexis flushed. Did he really think any midshipman would play such a prank coming aboard a new ship? She looked young, yes, but she was properly commissioned lieutenant, not playing at it for a lark.

"I'm no 'snotty', Lieutenant Villar, but a properly commissioned lieutenant. There's clearly some mistake and I think if we —"

"Aye, a mistake and it's yours." Villar tapped his rank insignia. "We've our full complement of lieutenants, as you can see, and we've no need of some hopped-up, coreward bint, in any case." He pointed at the hatch. "Now if you're not here for my gunroom, get off my ship."

Alexis clenched her jaw and drew in a slow, deep breath. Regardless of any mix up, and she had to admit she'd be a bit put out if some other officer approached her ship that way, it was no excuse to speak so to a fellow officer. Especially as she'd been a lieutenant nearly two years now and certainly had seniority over Villar, given the date of the muster book she'd reviewed.

"May I ask the date of your commission, Lieutenant Villar? My own is February ninth, some twenty-one months past."

Villar's face flushed.

Alexis leaned toward him, kept her voice low, and forced herself to remain calm. What she wished to do was call for the bosun and have the arrogant prat placed in irons, but there was the possibility he was in the right and properly in command, despite his attitude.

"Lieutenant Villar, it's clear we have conflicting orders. Only one of us is commander of Nightingale." She held up a hand as Villar started to speak. "Should that be you, I will wish you joy and luck in your command, sir, but should Admiralty confirm it is me ..." She let her voice trail off, hoping Villar would see the right of it without her having to state it bluntly. If her orders were valid and he refused to accept them, then his actions could be considered mutiny — at best, it would be an inauspicious start with his new commander. Villar's nostrils flared and the muscles in his jaw bunched. "Perhaps we should retire to the master's cabin and speak privately?"

Villar looked uncertain for a moment, then sighed and nodded sharply. He turned and walked away.

Alexis waited a moment before following. She noted the expressions on the crew's faces. The other officer — Midshipman Spindler, she assumed, though nothing seemed certain at this point — looked confused. As for the crew, they seemed to be divided between shooting her dark looks and looking amused at the exchange they'd just witnessed.

"Wait for me here, Isom," she said. He'd come through the boarding tube with their baggage during her exchange with Villar. "And tell the pilot to remain alongside until we have this mess sorted out."

She followed after Villar on the short walk to the master's cabin. Villar left the hatch open and she nodded to the Marine standing guard beside it as she passed. She slid the hatch shut behind her and looked around.

Nightingale's master's cabin was small, as she'd expected. The whole of it was less than three meters to a side and a single compartment, not divided into a sleeping- and day-cabin as it would be on a larger ship. A cot, larger than the narrow cots found in the junior officers' cabins, but still not very large, was still folded down against the far bulkhead. The part of the cabin nearest the hatch was taken up by a table, small as well, but still large in the cabin's space, and a few chairs. Villar was busily clearing the table of wine bottles and plates. The rest of the cabin was no better kept — the bedclothes on the cot in disarray and uniform bits strewn about.

Alexis pulled her tablet from her pocket. "Perhaps if we compare our orders, Lieutenant Villar, we can determine where the error is and how best to go about clearing it up."

Villar sat down abruptly and gestured. "Yes, let me see yours then and we'll see where you've gone wrong."

Alexis shook her head. It was clear that Villar was trying to maintain his position as commander of *Nightingale* by acting the role. She wasn't at all interested in his petty power games, she simply wanted to determine whose orders took precedent and should remain. She wished that Zariah warranted a Port Admiral they could appeal to or even that there was another, larger, Naval ship in the system.

One with a proper captain ... we could go running to like children to resolve who'll be allowed to play with the favorite toy next. She snorted. *For that's how he's acting, at least.*

"Something amusing ... Carew, was it?"

"Merely the absurdity of the situation."

"Yes, it is absurd. The war's set everything all a-kilter." He leaned back in his chair. "Look, then, it's clear someone in the Core sent you out here without considering the circumstances and consequences, but it's unthinkable for you to command *Nightingale* in this sector." He ran a finger over the tabletop's screen to bring up a document and slid it in front of Alexis. "Lieutenant Bensley received leave to return home for a family matter and left me in command. He even gave me an acting commission as lieutenant. Now, I'm sure they didn't know about this when you set out and appear to have forgotten that we don't *have* girls aboard our ships in the Fringe Fleet, so, I'm sure you see, it's quite impossible for you to remain here at all, much less command *Nightingale*."

So that's it, Alexis thought. Villar was Fringe Fleet through and through apparently. He was likely from a Fringe world himself and hadn't shed the attitudes of whatever planet he'd been born on in the slightest. *Which would be why he keeps mentioning the Core worlds and assumes that's where I'm from. But what's this nonsense of a lieutenant giving him command?*

A captain could make a midshipman an acting lieutenant, certainly, and it would most likely be confirmed by Admiralty, but a lieutenant had no such power. Villar's "command" of *Nightingale* was looking more and more suspect to her.

She frowned and looked up to meet Villar's eyes with a raised brow. "'Acting'?"

Villar flushed.

Alexis slid her own orders from her tablet to the tabletop screen and pushed them in front of Villar.

"My own orders come directly from Admiral Cammack," she said.

"I've commanded *Nightingale* for eight weeks now on Lieutenant Bensley's orders. We've no Port Admiral at Zariah and few enough other ships even passing through. *Nightingale* is the Navy in this sector — *I* am the Navy in this sector."

Alexis read over the two documents Villar had presented her. They were truly nothing more than notes from Bensley in *Nightingale's* order book for Villar to continue *Nightingale's* regular patrols in Bensley's absence. There was a copy of a message Bensley had sent along with his request for leave to the effect that he was giving Villar an acting commission, but that was something he simply hadn't had the power to do, and Alexis wondered that he'd even tried.

With the war and being so isolated, have they just gone power-mad here?

She reread the documents just to be sure she hadn't missed something, but she found that she hadn't and it only made her angrier. Angry at Villar and at the system that had created him. Now she'd not only have to deal with his disappointment at not having the command, but his resentment that she was a woman, as well.

His and how much of the crew's?

She hadn't thought to check the muster book for the crew's home planets. Of a certainty they'd be from Fringe worlds, but some were more hidebound than others. If the crew was all like Villar ... She sighed.

And first I've him to deal with, and find some way I'm to rely on him as my first officer?

15

Villar sat back and stared at Alexis for a moment.

"They can't mean to do this," he said finally. "It'll never work."

Alexis fought down the urge to grasp Villar by the ear, drag him to *Nightingale's* gundeck, and set the gunner to introducing Villar to his daughter. "Kissing the gunner's daughter", or being bent over a gun and caned by the gunner, was the traditional chastisement for an impertinent midshipman, and though Villar might be a number of years too old for it, Alexis could still wish to see it done.

She took a deep breath and restrained her temper, something she found herself having to do more and more often of late.

"Do you accept Admiral Cammack's orders, Mister Villar?"

"I —"

Alexis could see the struggle in Villar's face and felt a sudden surge of sympathy for him instead of anger. She could well imagine how he was feeling. At twenty-four he'd have few opportunities to advance to lieutenant. A captains' board, no matter how well he might perform, would wonder at his age and be influenced by it. Likely his one chance for advancement was to be made acting-lieutenant by his captain. A thing which simply couldn't occur aboard a cutter commanded by a mere lieutenant.

Bensley's decision to overstep himself must have seemed like a godsend, and Villar must have spent these many weeks thinking his position was secure.

Now I've come to bollox it all up proper. I could almost feel sympathy for him.

"This is a mistake," Villar said, his face still.

"It's no mistake." Alexis shook her head gently. "I had the orders directly from Admiral Cammack's hand. Surely part of you knew that Lieutenant Bensley could not do such a thing?"

"Oh, not that." Villar waved his hand. He sighed. "I did. I suppose I did. I mean, I hoped, but ... no." He met Alexis' eyes. "I meant a mistake to send you here."

Alexis took a deep breath to settle herself. She'd never met anyone who could so quickly send her from anger to sympathy and back again.

"Mister Villar, I assure you I'm quite capable of commanding a Queen's ship."

Villar rubbed his face with his hands.

"I know Core Fleet's come out for the war," Villar said. "You and Admiral Cammack and the rest, you look down on the Fringe, but these worlds out here won't accept you. Look, then —" He leaned forward. "— there's a *reason* for the way ships in the Fringe Fleet are crewed. Yes, Zariah here's just asked for a Crown Magistrate to be appointed, but this system is quite near the Core now — they're five generations in. There was a time, though, that they'd have nothing to do with you. It wasn't but a generation or two ago that they'd have stoned you for being in that uniform — what with trousers on and your face uncovered."

"I'm from the Fringe, Mister Villar, not the Core. I was born on Dalthus."

Villar snorted. "Dalthus? That's a corporate system. What's the worst that's happened there? I'm talking about those settlers on Man's Fall who think *darkspace* is Heaven and proves God doesn't want us using electricity? Or Al Jadiq, where the hardliners from Zariah went off to? They'll, neither one of them, deal with a woman, you know? Lord knows Bensley and I both had enough trouble doing so ourselves — what with being *kāfir* to one and technology worshiping devils to the other."

Alexis frowned. She'd read of both worlds on the packet to Zariah, as she'd tried to familiarize herself with *Nightingale's* duties. To tell the truth, she had no idea yet how she'd deal with the more political and religious worlds of the Fringe, those peoples who'd been so outcast in the Core Worlds that they'd banded together and bought their own star systems, so that they might practice their ideologies in peace.

The New London Crown overlooked most of their practices, so long as the worlds allowed free emigration to any who wished it.

Never mind that most inhabitants had no means to do so, save signing on as indentures and mortgaging years of labor for the cost of the transport.

"Dealing with those worlds is my concern, Mister Villar." Alexis couldn't very well tell him she really had no idea how to go about it. Perhaps if she'd come aboard to find a first officer she felt she could rely on she might, but not as things stood with Villar now.

"I suppose so," Villar said. He glanced around as though waking from a trance and stood hurriedly. "I suppose, as well, I should move my things back to the midshipmen's berth." He frowned as he looked around the cabin.

Alexis stood as well, watching him closely. He seemed to have resigned himself to it, but that wouldn't mean he'd not come to resent her.

"I'll have my man take your things to you in your berth." She could save him that further embarrassment, at least.

"Thank you." Villar cleared his throat. He glanced around, his face showing every bit of disappointment Alexis knew he must be feeling, then he stood. "Thank you, sir."

Alexis nodded. It was a start, she supposed, that he'd at least called her "sir". Now she only had to make a better start with the crew.

"I'll spend an hour's time here reviewing the logs," she said, "that should give you time to have *Nightingale* put to rights and assemble the crew for me to read myself in." She sighed. It wouldn't be at all as she'd imagined it. "After which, I'll meet with you properly, as well as Mister Spindler and the warrants."

"Aye, sir."

Villar made his way to the cabin's hatchway. He paused and turned back to her.

"Lieutenant Carew, sir?"

"Yes?"

"About what I said ... when you came aboard, I mean ... I —"

"Mister Villar," Alexis said quickly, "I really must apologize."

Alexis suspected what Villar was talking about and thought the least said about it the better. She hadn't read herself in yet, so hadn't been his commanding officer when he'd called her ...

What was it? "A hopped-up bint"?

Not the first time she'd been called that, and she suspected it was closer to Villar's true feelings than he'd admit now, but it was still better if they didn't mention it again.

Villar looked confused.

"Apologize, sir?"

"Yes, Mister Villar. I'm afraid the events of my coming aboard have gone right out of my head. It's a complete blank." She smiled slightly and shrugged. "The excitement of a first command, I'm sure. If anything said was at all important, I trust you'll bring it up again after I've read myself in properly?"

Villar swallowed and nodded.

"Yes, sir. Thank you, sir."

"As for this ... misunderstanding about *Nightingale*, Mister Villar, let us simply put it about the crew that there were conflicting orders and we've worked out what was intended. Put the whole of the fault on Admiralty, I think — they're quick enough to take the credit for things, surely they can shoulder a bit of blame?"

THREE

7 September, aboard *HMS Nightingale, Zariah System*

Alexis stretched her back and grimaced. She'd been sitting for what seemed like hours as she met with *Nightingale's* warrant officers. At least there was only the one left, Wileman, the purser, and then a second meeting with Villar.

She'd originally planned to meet with him first — that was what was typically done. A new commander come aboard would meet with her first officer and get his opinion of the ship and crew. But after her initial meeting with the man, Alexis decided she didn't entirely trust his judgment. She wanted to form her own opinion of the others before hearing his.

The ceremony of reading herself in had, indeed, been nothing like she'd imagined. Villar might have struggled a bit to keep his own disappointment off his face, but he hadn't succeeded. The assembled men had been respectful, but she'd seen their looks cut from her to Villar — some amused at his discomfiture and others angry. It appeared Villar was well-liked by some the crew and they already resented her presence.

Isom cleared the opposite side of her table of a wineglass and replaced it with a fresh one in preparation for her next visitor.

The last meeting had been with Corporal Brace of *Nightingale's* Marine complement — only six of them and not rating a sergeant to command them. Brace was a typical Marine for a Queen's ship, bluff and confident, but appeared a bit unsure when Alexis informed him that she intended to continue her practice of working out with the ship's Marines in their unarmed combat drills. It wasn't until she informed him that she'd been doing so since her first ship that he seemed to believe she was serious.

Before Brace, she'd met with *Nightingale's* bosun, gunner, and carpenter — *Nightingale* did not rate a sailing master, and the ship's surgeon, Poulter, was off on Zariah station for some business of his own. All three were very much what she'd expect of warrants in a small ship. Young yet, but still experienced enough to gain their place, and a bit standoffish in their first meeting with their new commander. Wary of how open they could be, she surmised.

She'd done her best to reassure them and hoped her decision to inspect *Nightingale* after meeting with them might go further toward that end. Some captains would inspect their new ship immediately after coming aboard, hoping to find things amiss or slack. By waiting, she hoped it was clear she expected *Nightingale* to be well-kept, but wasn't going out of her way to catch them in some laxity.

"You'll need another bottle opened," Isom said.

Alexis nodded and rubbed her eyes. The courtesy of a glass, or more, of wine with each of her new officers was wearing on her as well. She'd not tried to match them glass-for-glass by any means, but she was still feeling the effects of so much wine in so little time.

"Pussar, sar!" the Marine sentry at her hatchway called out with a rap on the hatch's surface.

Alexis fought a smile. That particular Marine's accent was going to take a bit of getting used to.

"Come through," she answered.

Wileman entered and Alexis suppressed her initial dislike. She thought little of ship's pursers in general, who seemed to all be cut of the same tricksy, cheating cloth. She supposed it had something to do with the nature of the position attracting a certain sort of man.

Unlike the other warrants, who were appointed on merit and received pay in excess of a common spacer, ship's pursers were not only unpaid, but bought their positions. Some port admirals, faced with an open position on a newly-built or refitted ship, were even known to set the place up for auction to the highest bidder.

Why anyone would turn over good coin to take a job which paid nothing became clear once one understood the nature of the purser's duties. *Nightingale's* accounts received a certain sum from Admiralty each month, out of which the purser was to see to the needs of the ship and crew. As such, the funds for everything aboard ship passed through the purser's hands — from the last drop of nutrient solution in the beef vats to the ship's commissary that supplied the crew.

And with every transaction, a bit was certain to stick to the purser's fingers.

Whether it was the "purser's grams" of his weights and measures — the difference between the half kilo of beef the men were promised each day and the few grams less the purser, by tradition, doled out — or the markup on necessities and luxuries from the ship's commissary — where the purser had a captive customer base on long cruises with little off-ship liberty given — or even the illegal but still common practice of carrying a dead man on the ship's books for a time and pocketing his pay, there were countless ways to turn a bit of profit from the position.

Of course, if the ship's books turned out showing a loss, then the purser would be responsible for making up the difference when the ship paid off at the end of her commission. It was a rare thing, but pursers were known to have been ruined or taken up for debt at the end of a poor cruise. Still, it was widely thought that any man who couldn't turn a tidy profit from a purser's warrant aboard a Queen's ship was one who probably should be indentured for debt and sent to toil on some colony world — for he was clearly incompetent for any other task.

"G'afternoon, captain, g'afternoon," Wileman said, ducking his head repeatedly as he entered the cabin.

"Good afternoon, Mister Wileman." Alexis gestured for him to sit. "May I offer you some wine?"

"Aye, please, and thank y', captain." Wileman settled himself into the chair and nodded to her. He seemed to nod to everything, come to that, his head bobbing up and down continuously as though it were on a spring.

Isom filled Wileman's glass and Alexis raised her own to drink with him.

Once the courtesies were complete, she consulted her tablet.

"I've been reviewing *Nightingale's* accounts, Mister Wileman."

"All in order, captain, all in order, sure."

Alexis made a noncommittal sound. Her perusal of *Nightingale's* accounts wasn't an idle one. In another bit of Naval lunacy she was certain she'd never understand, a captain was also held responsible for the ship's accounts at the end of a commission. Never mind that the purser handled the accounts, or that a ship might pay off with a commander different from the one who'd started the commission in command, as was the case with *Nightingale*, with Alexis taking command from Bensley midway through.

That accounting wouldn't be nearly so dire as the purser's, but she'd still have to account for and justify every bit of expenditure and missing equipment. Why shot canisters might have gone missing after an action, the cost of repairing damage from an action or a storm, even recruitment bonuses, were she to need additional crew. All of it would be gone over by Admiralty clerks when *Nightingale* paid off at some point in the future.

"All in order," Wileman repeated yet again.

"Yes, it appears so," Alexis said finally. She'd ask Isom to go over the accounts once more to be sure, but her first glance through them led her to believe that Wileman might be no worse than the typical nip-cheese, as the hands referred to his position.

Wileman fairly beamed at her acceptance, head bobbing rapidly.

"I do, however, have some changes, some minor changes, mind you, in procedure which I'd like you to look into."

The corners of Wileman's mouth turned downward the tiniest bit and his head-bobbing slowed almost imperceptibly.

"Changes to procedure, captain? Changes?"

"Yes, *Nightingale* has a rather easy patrol schedule — no more than a month between systems. I'd like you to see to it that there's fresh meat brought aboard at each of our port calls, rather than relying solely on what's grown in the vats."

"Fresh, captain? Fresh meat, you say?"

"Yes. It doesn't have to be beef," Alexis went on to reassure him. "Whatever might be least expensive in the system. Chicken, pork, lamb, what have you."

Wileman's head bobbing had slowed further and now he added a shake, so that his head was moving in a sort of undulating, sideways figure-eight.

"Oh, the men'll not like that, captain, not like that at all. Good beef, straight from the vat, that's what spacers want, captain. That's what they was promised. Half kilo a day's what they likes." His head shaking grew more pronounced, stretching the ends of the eight out almost to his shoulders. "Not no chickens nor wee lambs, they don't."

There was a long silence.

"Captain?"

Alexis shook herself. Wileman's head weaving was almost hypnotic and she dragged herself back to the conversation.

"Right, well, as may be, Mister Wileman, this is what I would like aboard *Nightingale*. If any of the men find themselves distraught at the idea of fresh pork in place of their half kilo from the vat, I'm sure I'll be made aware of it and we may speak again. Fair enough?"

Wileman's lips pursed and Alexis could see him calculating both the cut to his profits and how he might get around it.

"As well, I should like fresh fruits and vegetables brought aboard at each stop along the way. Whatever happens to be in season when we put down and might, therefore, least impinge upon the ship's accounts."

"For the officers, captain, yes? For you and Mister Villar and Mister Spindler? Why, yes, captain, that's no trouble."

"For the entire crew, Mister Wileman."

Wileman swallowed heavily and his eyes grew wide.

"Just enough of all so that the men may have single fresh meal — something not from the vats or freezers." She met his eyes as well as she could with his head in constant motion and smiled. "I'm certain you can manage this for me, Mister Wileman."

"I ... aye, sir."

"And as for those vats ..."

Wileman's shoulders slumped. "Yes, sir?"

"I note in the logs that it's been some time since the vats themselves were emptied and cleaned. Is this an oversight?"

Wileman grimaced and looked away. "Well, sir, it's as needed and they've not —"

"The regulations state the vats should be cleaned every six months, is this not the case?"

"At the purser's discretion, it says, sir. At the purser's discretion."

Alexis remained silent and stared at him calmly.

"Discretion, sir, is like ... an option, isn't it?"

"A bit more than that, I think."

Wileman sighed. "So it's clean the vats, is it?"

Alexis nodded.

"Takes time, you know, sir? Have to empty the solution and any beef what's grown — have to store that somewheres and —"

"Space it."

"Sir?" Wileman's eyes grew wide.

"Mister Wileman," Alexis said, leaning forward and resting her hands on her table, "I've read your logs. We both know, then, how long it's been since the vats were cleaned and how long since the nutrient solutions were replaced, not just added to. Too bloody long, yes?"

Slowly and reluctantly Wileman nodded. "It may be there's been some delays —"

"I'll not have beef served at my table that's been grown from three-year's edge-scrapings in your vats."

"Your table, sir?" He looked down. "This table, sir?"

Alexis nodded. "Yes, Mister Wileman. I'll not be eating from my own stores every day. Periodically and without — well, let's call it on a whim, shall we — I'll have the same beef from the same vat as the crew is served."

Wileman's shoulders slumped even more and he hung his head.

"Clean vats, sir, and new solution. Aye, sir."

"Very good. And lastly, Mister Wileman, there's the matter of breakfast."

"Lastly, sir? Breakfast, sir?"

"Yes. Now I do understand the difficulty of ship's stores and the regulation banyan days when there's no meat served, but on those days when the men are allowed more than a porridge of a morning I've always noticed something missing aboard ship."

"Missing, sir? At breakfast, missing?"

"Bacon, Mister Wileman. There's no proper breakfast without bacon, now is there?"

FOUR

"Pass the word for Mister Villar, sir?" Isom asked after Wileman left.

"Give me a moment, Isom."

Alexis rubbed at her forehead again while Isom exchanged Wileman's glass for a fresh one in preparation for Villar's arrival. She'd been aboard *Nightingale* no more than a single watch and already she was astounded at the number of things she was finding to juggle in her head all at once.

Not only were there *Nightingale's* accounts to familiarize herself with, but also the ship's log, the punishment book, recording those spacers having committed some offense which couldn't be corrected by the bosun — Alexis was pleased to see that neither the departed Lieutenant Bensley nor Villar had been at all liberal with the cat. More than those, there was the muster book itself which listed all of *Nightingale's* crew — Alexis was determined to have their names and faces memorized in short order. Not too ambitious a task, since the ship had only fifty-four souls aboard, including Alexis herself.

Next would be the ship's log, so that she could familiarize herself with how Bensley and Villar had gone about their patrols. That would take more study than she had time for without keeping Villar waiting too long; and there were other things to think of as well. The myriad little details of command she'd never before considered. Some of them seemingly trivial, but nonetheless important.

"I suppose I'll need a cook, Isom," she said. "Would you ask amongst the men for someone who might have a bit of skill?"

"I will, sir, and you'll be needing a coxswain, as well."

Alexis nodded. She'd be just as happy to share a cook with the gunroom, there being only the two midshipmen and a handful of warrants aboard, but it was traditional for a ship's captain to have her own. As for a coxswain, the spacer who would be in charge of her boat crew, she thought *Nightingale* was far too small to bother with that formality. And it was a new crew to her — a coxswain was generally a trusted man who'd follow along with his captain from ship to ship.

"Just the cook for now, Isom, until I've learned enough of this crew to choose someone properly."

"Aye, sir. I'll ask around a bit."

Alexis nodded her thanks. Isom's position was a new one as well. He'd followed her from ship to ship since *Hermione,* but as a sort of unofficial servant, lieutenants without an official command being generally not able to have personal servants aboard ship. Alexis had never asked how the man wrangled his transfers along with her, though she suspected he'd simply shown up with her baggage and followed her, then put his name down in each new ship's muster book. What captain would turn away a fresh pair of hands, after all?

And it's not as though we've left previous ships in any semblance of good repair.

Hermione had been turned over to the Hanoverese, after all, and the crew members Alexis had brought out of captivity with her had been disbursed throughout the fleet. *Shrewsbury,* her last official ship where she'd been a very junior lieutenant, was still missing. Off with

Admiral Chipley's fleet somewhere in Hanoverese space and no word on their fate. Her last ship, a temporary command of a captured barque, had been destroyed delaying a Hanoverese frigate from catching up with the unarmed transports carrying troops and refugees from the aborted invasion of Giron.

Now, though, she had a proper command and Isom was officially her cabin servant and clerk. A much more appropriate position for the former legal clerk caught up by the Impressment Service and thrown into life aboard a Queen's ship, as he'd no longer have to work the ship's sails or berth with the crew. He'd have a cot in the captain's pantry and his sole duties would be to Alexis.

Alexis closed her eyes for a moment and offered a silent prayer as she always did when her thoughts turned to Giron. First for the dead, especially those who'd stood with her on that ship, then for those left behind on Giron or with Admiral Chipley's fleet, and lastly, but most ardently, for Delaine Theibaud, a lieutenant in the French fleet which had sailed with Chipley off in pursuit of the Hanoverese.

Please, Delaine, stay safe and come back to me.

A clank of bottles behind her drew her attention back to Isom. He'd finished clearing another pile of the mess Villar had left behind.

And if the man had to play at being commander these last few weeks, could he not have had one of the men keep his quarters clean?

Alexis eyed the cabin's cot with sudden distaste.

"I'll want fresh bedding, I think, Isom."

"Of course, sir. I was thinking to have some hands in and scrub the whole lot down to the hull soon as you were off to the quarterdeck."

Alexis nodded. "Yes, good thought. Thank you."

She looked down at the table's surface again and closed the logs and accounts. It was time to speak with Villar again, she supposed, and get his take on the state of *Nightingale*. She truly didn't want to, though it was likely unfair to him. The warrants and Spindler hadn't expressed any distaste or disdain for her, she thought it possible they, and the crew, thought the same as Villar did. Perhaps more so, as surely some of the crew would have come to like Villar and be more put out at his not receiving *Nightingale* than the man himself was. Villar had just had the bad judgment to express it to her.

Nothing for it but to move on, though.

She tapped the table's display to summon him. He must have been waiting nearby, because it was just a few seconds before the Marine at the hatch announced him.

"Midshupmon Villar, sar!"

"Send him in, please." The hatch slid open and Villar entered. "It'll be First officer, if you please, Clanly," she called to the Marine. She could give Villar that distinction at least.

"Oye, sar!"

Villar sat when she gestured to the chair across from her. He was seated stiffly, but not still. Alexis could see a bit of a twitch in his leg and he was rubbing the knuckles of one hand with his thumb, clearly nervous.

"So, Mister Villar," Alexis started, "I've met with Mister Spindler and the warrants. They seem a decent lot."

Silence dragged on. Alexis had hoped that would prompt Villar to offer his opinion of them, but he remained silent. That told her more about Villar and how he was feeling at the moment than anything else.

If there's no question before you and you have no wish to muck things up worse than you have, keep your bloody mouth shut.

She'd found herself keeping silent on the other side of a captain's desk more than once, so she could sympathize with him on that point.

"Your opinion, Mister Villar?"

Villar cleared his throat and frowned. "Mister Spindler's young, sir, but he shows promise," he said tentatively.

Alexis nodded encouragement.

"The warrants are all steady men. They've experience in other ships before *Nightingale*, but they've been here with her quite a while now. All of us ... them, sir, since the start of the war." Villar paused and then went on. "All except Mister Poulter, that is, he's new come aboard just before our last patrol — eight weeks now."

Just about the time Alexis had left the border to take her place aboard *Nightingale*. Villar's voice changed slightly as he spoke of *Nightingale's* surgeon, whom Alexis had not yet met.

"When is he expected back aboard?" she asked.

Villar took a deep breath. "I couldn't say, sir, it's ... Mister Poulter appears to prefer going his own way, if I may be so bold as to say so."

Alexis frowned. "Despite our, shall we say, rocky start, I shall be relying on you heavily, Mister Villar. *Nightingale's* is a small crew and you know them well. I should prefer it if you were as bold as you deem necessary, at least when we are in private conference."

Villar's eyebrows rose at that. "Thank you, sir."

She'd just given him a great deal of leeway in speaking to her, more than many captains would. Perhaps it would turn out to be a mistake, but she'd rather he spoke his mind to her than keep something important to himself for fear of reprisal. If it did turn out to be a mistake she could attempt to correct it later, but for now she wanted Villar's honesty more than propriety.

"About Poulter?"

Villar's mouth quirked and his brow furrowed as though he were searching for the correct words.

"He's private, not commissioned," Villar said. Alexis had assumed that from the fact that he was listed on *Nightingale's* books as "Mister" and not by rank. "The Sick and Hurt Board appointed him, of course, but he has a low opinion of the Navy in general and the Fringe in particular. Not that he's said so outright, but he's from the Core, you can tell." He looked to Alexis as though wondering if he should truly go on and seemed relieved when she nodded. "Very ... modern. Seems more interested in talking than in fixing up injuries. Goes on and on about the workings of men's minds, and ... well, in the gunroom he's constantly asking us about ... well, our *feelings*, if you can believe it."

"Oh ..." Alexis had felt growing dismay as Villar had gone on.

She'd rather liked most of the ship's surgeons she'd dealt with. Even aboard *Hermione*, the surgeon, though a bit cowardly, had been a decent hand at patching up the crew, and what more could one ask, really? But what Villar described was quite a bit more like ... "Oh, dear."

"You understand what I mean, sir?"

"Yes. Yes, I think I do. I had dealings with someone very like that just before being posted here." The thought of her sessions with Lieutenant Curtice of the Sick and Hurt Board after Giron came to mind. Endless questions about how she'd slept and how she felt, as though that had any bearing on her duty and the tasks at hand. Endless appointments to be kept, and idle all the rest of the time — as though dwelling on all that happened could somehow make it better, rather than moving on and keeping busy as she preferred to do. She could well imagine how Fringe Fleet officers and men would take to that.

"Well," she said firmly. "We'll just see if we can't get this Mister Poulter to stick to bodies and leave minds alone, shall we? Between the two of us, we should be able to come up with something."

Villar straightened in his chair. "Thank you, sir. The men, and especially the gunroom, will be quite happy if you can manage that."

"Careful, Mister Villar. If Poulter hears that he'll be after you about exactly how happy you are and it's a short hop from that to what you dreamt last night."

Villar actually laughed at that. "Oh, aye, sir, it's to the point we can't talk about sleep before he's on about our dreams ... and forever tapping at his tablet as though he's taking down every word we —"

"Shup's carepentar, sar!"

The sentry's announcement cut Villar off.

"Yes, come through," Alexis called. "I apologize for the interruption, Mister Villar. We'll just be a moment."

Robnett, *Nightingale's* carpenter, and two hands entered.

"You mentioned some work you wished done, sir?" Robnett said.

"Yes." In their meeting earlier, Alexis had asked him to come back and see to some temporary modifications of *Nightingale's* cabin. "I just need ..."

Alexis trailed off. What she had in mind wasn't forbidden, but it was frowned upon to a certain extent. Captains often took their wives and families aboard ship on the sail to a remote station. Some had additional servants, even their own clergy, brought aboard. Still, the Royal Navy wasn't a passenger service, after all.

Alexis cleared her throat and fought not to flush.

"There'll be a ... young lady traveling with us when we leave Zariah." Alexis felt herself flush despite her efforts not to and glanced down at her tabletop. There was no reason for her to be embarrassed, she told herself, ship's commanders did this sort of thing frequently. Still, Marie Autin and her infant son, Ferrau, were neither her family nor servants. They were simply ... well, she wasn't at all certain what they were to her.

Marie had been a young girl in Courboin, the town on Giron in the Hanoverese sector known as the Berry March, where Alexis was held prisoner after the crew of *Hermione* mutinied. Alexis had hardly known her then, not even her name, she'd simply been one of the girls the other midshipmen of *Hermione* had some relationship with. Whether Marie was a prostitute or just a young girl taking up with *Hermione's* paroled officers staying in the town, Alexis still didn't know for certain and had never asked.

Alexis next met Marie when she returned to Giron as part of the ill-fated attempt to free the worlds of the Berry March from Hanoverese rule. Those worlds, once part of the French Republic, then conquered and taken by Hanover long ago. Still, after generations of Hanoverese rule, they thought of themselves as French. Marie had a child in the time between Alexis' escape and return — the child of one of *Hermione's* midshipmen, Penn Timpson, a vile little toad if ever there was one, in Alexis' opinion. As well as irresponsible, to have not taken precautions in his dalliance with Marie.

In the flight, abject rout to be truthful, from Giron, Alexis took Marie, Ferrau, and thirty other refugees aboard her ship. Marie and

Ferrau were two of only seven of those to survive the encounter with a Hanoverese frigate that destroyed her ship.

For some reason, Alexis continued to feel responsible for the pair. Rather than leave them on Lesser Ichthorpe with the rest of the refugees, she'd offered Marie a place on her grandfather's holdings on Dalthus. She supposed the proper thing to do would have been for Marie to contact Timpson, but the girl seemed to have no interest in doing so. She loved Ferrau, but thought little of the child's father.

That might have something to do with seeing me slap him and call him a coward and a bully for that trick he pulled with my messages aboard Hermione, Alexis thought.

In any case, Alexis brought the two with her. Thankfully, the lieutenant commanding the fast packet that brought Alexis from Lesser Ichthorpe to Zariah was willing to bring them along as well. Alexis thought that probably had more to do with the opportunity to host a beautiful, young French girl at his table for supper each night than any general kindness on his part, but it did get the three of them to Zariah together.

Now all she had to do was get the pair to Dalthus and her grandfather's holdings.

Where he'll likely chide me for bringing in more strays, what with the number of Hermione's *dependents who've made their way there.*

After the mutiny on that ship, Alexis had told the mutineers that their families would have a place there, should their lives become too hard. The mutineers themselves would have to flee and keep fleeing, for they'd been convicted *in absentia* for their actions and would be executed if ever the Royal Navy caught up with them again.

"A young lady?" Villar was asking, drawing Alexis' attention back to him.

"Yes." Alexis was watching Robnett as the carpenter studied the compartment's bulkheads. The tiny cabin was going to be quite crowded with Marie and Ferrau ... and Ferrau had an annoying tendency to cry at all hours. She'd thought to give them a cabin of their own, but *Nightingale* was so small there were no spares. It would mean displacing both Villar and Spindler, as the midshipmen shared a berth, into one of the warrants' cabins and sending that worthy to berth with the crew. It was only a matter of a few weeks, but Alexis didn't want to cause any more disruption to *Nightingale's* routine than she already had.

"A, ah, particular friend of yours, then?" Villar asked.

"I suppose so," Alexis said. Well, come to that, she'd grown quite close to Marie on the journey and the girl was now one of only a few people Alexis felt she could call a friend at all, certainly the only female in that company. "Yes, I suppose you could say that."

"No room to put a cot on t'other bulkhead, sir, as the quarter gallery's hatch'll not allow it," Robnett was saying, distracting Alexis again. "It's either over yours or make yours wider."

Alexis frowned. No, she could see that her original thought to put another cot folding down from the bulkhead opposite her own would never work. The hatchway to her quarter gallery — the commander's private head and something Alexis thought the largest benefit of commanding a Queen's ship — took up too much of the space.

Neither could she see putting Marie or herself in an upper bunk — the girl was up and about at all hours tending to Ferrau. They'd tried that in the cabin they shared aboard the packet and ended with Alexis in the top bunk, a thing she'd had quite enough of as a midshipman. Her lack of height, at only a meter and a half tall, made such things annoying to say the least.

"Doubling mine will do quite nicely, Mister Robnett," she said. "It'll be no hardship for us to share. I don't take up much space, after all."

Robnett glanced at her as though unsure if she was joking, then grinned as he saw her smile.

"Aye, sir."

Alexis turned back to Villar.

"It's only until we reach home, Dalthus, so we'll make do."

"So, you're, ah ..."

Alexis noted that Villar seemed quite uncomfortable suddenly.

His eyes were darting about and his brow was furrowed. She tried to think what might have put him off, but the last of their discussion had been about Poulter, and she thought he'd been growing more comfortable speaking to her, not less.

"Ah, just taking the lady home to meet your family, is it?" Villar asked.

FIVE

"Well done, Isom," Alexis whispered as the plate was set in front of her. "Please tell Garcia it was a wonderful meal."

"Aye, sir."

After her disaster of boarding *Nightingale*, she'd thought not to dine her officers in, as was traditional, especially as she had no cook, but Isom had managed to find someone in the crew who was not only eager for the position, but qualified as well. That the captain's cook became mostly answerable only to the captain and was relieved of other duties aboard ship had more than a little to do with the eagerness, she suspected — there were no end of hands aboard ship who were willing to make that change. Qualified, on the other hand, was more difficult to find.

Garcia's family had emigrated all the way from *Nuevo Opportunidad* to a Fringe colony world and spent three generations owning their own restaurants. Garcia hated the business and took the Queen's shilling when the recruiters came about, only to discover that sailing the Dark wasn't quite as glamorous and adventure-filled as the lieutenant leading the recruiting party made it out to be. He jumped at the opportunity Isom offered him to avoid the heavy, dangerous work of hauling on sail lines outside *Nightingale's* hull and spend his days cooking for her captain instead.

If the food was a bit more heavily spiced than Alexis typically preferred, well, it was tasty enough and she felt certain they could come to some arrangement on the spices.

The other diners at table with her, Villar, Spindler, the freshly returned surgeon, Poulter, and Marie, all seemed to enjoy it as well. The dessert now in front of her gave her a bit of pause, though. It was quite similar to the boiled puddings typically prepared for the crew — those weren't bad at all, but she'd expected something more after the meal itself. This was just a jiggly blob turned out on the plate with some sort of brown sauce over the top of it.

A quick taste, though, proved that this dish was every bit as good as Garcia's previous offerings.

Alexis vowed to let her new cook have as free a rein as possible in ordering stores brought aboard. She'd discovered since joining the Navy and traveling more widely that colonies tended to become quite limited in their cuisine, partly due to the culture of those settling and partly due to fewer resources during the early days. One simply couldn't bring all of humanity's preferred spices and herbs to every world — both for the cost of shipping them and that some things simply wouldn't flourish on certain worlds.

A pleasant side-effect of that, though, was discovering new cuisines and dishes as she traveled.

Or not — I'm still glad Dansby warned me off that currywurst *when we were in Hanover.*

Marie's giggling drew Alexis' attention. She'd seated Marie and Villar along one side of the table, Spindler at the far end, as befitted the junior officer present, and Poulter on the other side.

Marie was caught up in giggling as she shook Villar's plate, making his dessert jiggle in turn. Villar, for his part, was watching as though it were the most fascinating thing he'd ever seen.

Alexis sighed. She'd found Marie to be a quite pleasant traveling companion in the weeks they'd been aboard the packet, save for two things: Ferrau, who was, thankfully, asleep at the moment, and the other girl's tendency to put on the appearance of a vapid coquette in the presence of any reasonably handsome young man.

The young lieutenant commanding the fast packet had found it enchanting at dinners aboard. Every night. Alexis, however, had found it teeth-itchingly irritating. It was as though the presence of a handsome young man caused Marie to behave as though her brains had been removed with a soup ladle, despite her otherwise good sense.

Alexis watched Villar smile and laugh with the girl in turn.

Or perhaps both their brains are siphoned at the same time.

Villar looked up from his jiggling dessert and caught Alexis' eye. His smile fell and he flushed. He straightened in his seat, shoulders back and averting his eyes from both Marie and Alexis, despite the fact that Marie was now playing at sneaking bites of his dessert. After a few moments of this, Marie gave a little frown and sat back herself.

This had played out several times over the meal. Villar seemed to respond to Marie's flirtations, then he'd glance at Alexis and sit stiffly until Marie managed to captivate his attention again. Alexis found it perplexing. Marie was traveling with her, yes, but the girl was older than Alexis and her own person. Villar seemed to be acting as though Alexis had some say in it or would disapprove of.

If there's one thing I've learned about Marie it's that she's generally no fool, despite appearances. She must see some good character in him, so if she chooses to flirt with him, why should I object?

As Villar's captain, she supposed she could, but what would be the point?

The dessert was soon finished and plates cleared, followed by Isom refreshing their wine glasses. As Spindler's, the last of them and the junior officer, was filled, he raised it and others looked to him expectantly. Even Marie had enough suppers aboard ship to know what was to come.

Spindler opened his mouth, then closed it with a quick glance at Marie and then Alexis, then spoke.

"Gentlemen, lady, sir," Spindler raised his glass, "the Queen!"

"The Queen!" the rest of them echoed, raising their glasses in the Loyal Toast that marked the end of the meal aboard ship.

The lad's quick, to address us each so, and being unused to a female officer aboard, much less female passengers.

Even Marie raised her glass, calling, *"La Reine,"* with the rest of them.

Alexis had to wonder at that, when it was New London's aborted attempt at freeing the Berry March worlds that had cost Marie her family and home to begin with. After the evacuation of Giron, it had appeared for a time that refugees might be taken to the French Republic and resettled there, but those talks had dragged on and on, all the while those refugees had been housed in nothing more than rough tents and cots in empty buildings on Lesser Ichthorpe.

"If you'll pardon my saying, Miss Autin," Poulter said, "I don't recognize your accent. May I ask where in the Republic it is you're from?"

Alexis glanced at *Nightingale's* surgeon in surprise. Poulter had remained mostly silent throughout the supper, only responding to direct questions, and he'd arrived back aboard so close to the meal being served that she'd had no time to speak to him privately.

"Non, Monsieur Poulter," Marie said, "I am not born in *La Republique."*

"Really?" Poulter said. "Some border world on New London's side, then?"

Marie shot a glance to Alexis. They'd been through this many times before with ships' captains on the trip to Zariah. The answer to Poulter's question would only lead to more questions about the evacuation, and that was painful for both of them. There was no getting around it, though.

Alexis nodded.

Marie took a deep breath.

"Giron," she said.

"Giron!" Spindler fairly shouted in excitement. "Were you part of the evacuation?"

Alexis couldn't fault his enthusiasm, difficult though it was for her. The invasion and subsequent evacuation of Giron had filled the Naval Gazette and other news sources for weeks. Even captains of frigates and ships of the line they'd met in transit had been eager as boys to hear a firsthand account.

"*Excusez-moi.*" Marie rose and made her way to where Ferrau was sleeping on the cot.

"Did I say something wrong?" Spindler asked, watching her go.

"It was a difficult time, Mister Spindler," Alexis said, "but, yes, we were part of the evacuation." She looked at her wine glass, concentrating on the way the light played in the wine while she waited for the next question. Marie at least had the excuse of Ferrau to leave the conversation, while Alexis was stuck with it.

"What ship, sir?"

Yes, that's always the next question, isn't it?

Alexis felt it might be easier if the Gazette had made more mention of her, as it had of Admirals Chipley and Cammack, and the captains in their respective fleets. The captains of the evacuation fleet, the civilian craft that had sailed off into the Dark to bring New London's soldiers home, were made much of, as well. Her, they'd mentioned once, and only as Lieutenant Carew — not even her full name. Admiral Cammack had explained it to her. If they'd used her full name as they did for the other ships' commanders, well, Lieutenant Alexis Arleen Carew might offend the sensibilities of some worlds in the Fringe.

And they're beginning to offend my *own sensibilities, not least because of this.*

It wasn't that she wanted the credit or more notoriety at all. It was that the repetition of this conversation was becoming tiresome.

And if they knew already, then I wouldn't have to say it.

The answer to Spindler's question pained her. She tried to not even think the ship's name, it was too soon and too tied to the men she'd lost aboard. Alexis grasped her wine glass, careful not to do so too hard and break another one as she had aboard a ship on the journey here.

"I had command of *Belial*."

She raised her gaze to find the others staring at her as she expected.

Villar's brow furrowed, then his eyes widened.

"You're *that* Carew?" He frowned. "I thought you'd be a ..."

Alexis raised an eyebrow. She'd heard that from more than one captain on her journey as well.

"Yes, Mister Villar? You thought I'd be what?"

Villar flushed and cleared his throat, then squared his shoulders and met Alexis' gaze.

"Thought you'd be taller, sir," he said finally.

SIX

"You're a hero!"

Alexis tore her gaze away from Villar to look at Spindler.

Her instant of amusement at Villar's comment, and his look of consternation, faded as she saw the look on Spindler's face. First the look of shock and adulation, followed quickly by embarrassment at his outburst.

Spindler winced visibly and looked down at the table, but for a moment, it was another midshipman entirely looking back at her. A midshipman who'd followed her to Giron.

Don't look at me like that.

She wanted to take Spindler by the shoulders and shake him.

Don't look at any officer like that. We'll use you up. The Service will use you up. Don't you understand?

But she couldn't, wouldn't. For, hard as it was and as young as Spindler was, she also knew that the Navy needed him — needed the young officers who'd one day command ships, no matter the sacrifices they made to get there. The thought of Midshipman Artley and his loss aboard *Belial* was like something inside her had been ripped apart.

Those who survive, at least.

Spindler flushed and looked away. Perhaps because of his outburst or perhaps because of the look on Alexis' face. The moment passed and she tried to relax her expression into something less stern.

"I wouldn't say that, Mister Spindler," she said. "If anyone in the Fleet was a hero at Giron, it was a midshipman not much older than yourself. He brought the fleet of civilian ships that made the evacuation possible."

Spindler's eyes widened.

"Really?"

Alexis nodded had to restrain a wince. What she'd said to honor Midshipman Artley's memory had spawned that same look on Spindler's face again. A look of wonder and almost hope — and she knew his thoughts were turning to some grand deed he might do that would earn him the same description one day.

They'll use that too, your yearning to do great things. I'll do it myself, if duty demands it. God forgive me.

"Could you describe the action for us, Lieutenant?" Poulter asked.

Alexis turned toward the surgeon, glad for the interruption. Even describing that action and the loss of *Belial* would be a relief from thoughts about Artley. She was used enough to doing so after her time aboard the packet.

"Certainly, Mister Poulter." She set her tablet on the tabletop and transferred her data on the engagement to the table's display. The Naval Gazette had published much of the ship movements from the action, reconstructed from the ships' logs that were available, but she'd augmented her own copy with her recollections and notations.

"Isom," she called. "We'll have a bit of port now, but clear the center of the table."

"Aye, sir."

She examined the others' faces while Isom and another spacer cleared the table and set glasses before them.

Once everyone was served, she started the display, beginning with *Belial's* transition to *darkspace*.

"The last of the transports were away with what troops and civilians could be carried by them," she said. "*Belial* was the last to transition and our orders were to simply play herd on the civilian convoy back to New London space. The two fleets, Hanover's and our own under Admiral Chipley, were near — quite near —"

She indicated on the display.

"They had already formed their lines, in fact, and were close to beginning their own engagement. By all rights we, *Belial* and the convoy, should have made it to Giron's shoals and been on our way before any Hanoverese could break through the New London lines."

Those shoals, the halo of dark matter that surrounded systems, marked the point where the dark energy winds became more variable. No longer blowing directly toward the system's center, but changing somewhat.

She let the display continue for a moment, accelerated to pass the time. On the tabletop the two fleets edged ever closer. Massive line-of-battle ships preparing to come into firing range with each other, some edging up or down in relation to the other line, hoping to encircle their target, their smaller consorts, frigates and sloops, behind the respective lines to relay signals.

Communication in *darkspace* being limited to messages passed via lights on a ship's masts and hull, as no electronics or radios would work with so much dark energy permeating the space. Not even lasers could be used for communications, as the dark matter, which made up most of the mass in the universe, permeated everything and the gravitational effects changed how even light behaved. The coarse, steady light of a beacon on a ship's mast would be distorted, but still visible, while a thin communications laser would be warped and bent. Likely never finding its target receiver and, if it did, the timing would be so off that no message would be decipherable.

"That's him, then?" Villar asked pointing to a Hanoverese frigate which had begun falling back and above the opposing fleets.

Alexis nodded. It wasn't a particularly perceptive comment on Villar's part. What they were watching now had been included in the accounts of the battle in the Gazette, so he would have seen which frigate had bypassed the lines and fallen in amongst the unarmed transports from other reports.

"Yes," Alexis agreed. "If we'd spotted him right then, perhaps we might have signaled another ship to cut him off."

It was the one thing she'd found in her own endless reviews of the action. She'd watched the action a hundred times after her return to New London space, and the only thing she'd ever found that could have gone differently was to identify what the frigate was doing earlier than she had.

"They'd not have been looking toward the convoy for signals," Villar said absently, his brow furrowed as he watched the action unfold. "Their attention would have been on the fleets."

Alexis nodded again.

"It was. This is where we noticed him," she said softly, marking the time display. "We made those signals, requested assistance, but, as you say, no one was looking toward us."

Villar was silent, and Alexis took up her narrative, describing every bit of the action — *Belial's* orders to the convoy, her own course changes, and those of the Hanoverese frigate. On the display, symbols for ships in the convoy disappeared, one by one, as the frigate passed them and fired on them, *Belial* unable to bring the other ship to action. *Belial* turned her stern to the enemy and emptied her guns into space — an expression of contempt. Then the frigate turned, the enemy captain's pride finally pricked enough by *Belial's* actions for him to acknowledge it.

Alexis described the battle as best she could remember it, for there was a large gap in the logs for most of the rest. Admiral Chipley's fleet had eventually sailed off after the Hanoverese, taking their logs with them. *Belial's* log had stopped recording due to damage, and it was only the arrival of Admiral Cammack's fleet on the scene which resumed the recording.

By then, both *Belial* and the frigate were battered hulks. Mastless, mostly gunless, but still firing into each other.

"How?" Villar asked. "However did you manage it?"

"The frigate outgunned us, but *Belial's* crew ..." Alexis had to pause. "They'd been drilled beyond all reason during our wait at Giron. I believe at one point our guns were firing four broadsides in three minutes to the frigate's two. They were outmatched and ... while their casualties were not near *Belial's*, they lost heart and became even more so."

"Most of the crew were killed, were they not, lieutenant?"

Alexis looked up from the tabletop in surprise. She'd almost forgotten that Poulter was at the table.

"Yes, Mister Poulter. Only a few of the crew and myself survived the action."

Poulter cocked his head to one side. "How does that affect one? As their commander?"

Alexis caught her breath. Poulter's words echoed those of the Sick and Hurt Board's Lieutenant Curtice, who'd been tasked to evaluate her after the action. She had not liked Curtice's questions at the time, and didn't like Poulter's now.

"I suppose such a thing affects everyone differently," she said.

Poulter raised his glass and took a casual drink.

"And how were you af — *Ow! Bloody* —"

A streak of brown fur raced up Poulter's chest from beneath the table, knocked the surgeon's glass from his hand to spill into his lap, then circled his neck once before diving beneath the table again.

Poulter leapt to his feet, eyes wide. *"What!"*

"Isom!" Alexis called. "That damned creature's loose again!"

Isom rushed from the pantry.

"I'm sorry, sir! I had his cage latched, I'm certain — I can't see how he does it."

"What *is* that?" Poulter demanded.

The creature in question rushed from under the table as Isom crouched to retrieve it. Long, lithe, and covered in brown fur, tail bottle-brush thick, it leapt onto the edge of Alexis' cot, which was folded upright and latched to the cabin's wall to provide more space, somehow managing to trip the latches as it scurried along the edge and sent the cot crashing down.

The cot swung open just as Isom arrived to make a grab for the creature, but it darted out of reach and began burrowing in the bedclothes.

"What is it?" Poulter demanded again, examining his clothes and touching a tentative hand to a scratch on his neck.

"A vile creature which will find itself put out the bloody airlock if it so much as messes once in my bedclothes," Alexis said. She turned toward Marie who was covering her mouth with one hand in an effort to control her laughter. "It is *not* funny."

"*Non,*" Marie said, lips twitching.

"I apologize, Mister Poulter," Alexis said, though to a certain extent she wasn't sorry. The creature's antics had at least interrupted Poulter's questions. "Are you badly hurt?"

"Not hurt, no." Poulter examined a rent in his uniform jacket. "Just a scratch, though I'll have to see a tailor about this."

"Is it some sort of cat?" Villar asked.

"No." Alexis sighed. "It's a mongoose. An acquaintance's idea of a joke, I suppose, before I left Lesser Ichthorpe for Zariah. The thing was delivered to my rooms and I've no real idea what to do with it. Perhaps I'll see if my grandfather wishes it for vermin control on the home farms, once we arrive on Dalthus."

"That's what some colonies imported them for," Villar said, "but it rarely works. We have a few on Chorthampton still, but those who brought them along found they had a much stronger taste for the chickens' eggs than any vermin."

"You must not abandon him, Alexis," Marie added. "He would be so alone if there are no more of his kind on your world."

"There are no more of its kind aboard ship, either." Alexis

grimaced. "And damned if I'll bring another aboard to accommodate the thing."

"Here he has you," Marie said.

Alexis watched as Isom gathered up a struggling bundle of bedclothes and made his way back to the pantry.

"I'll have a better lock on his cage before morning, sir," he said over the sounds of chittering outrage from his bundle. "Don't know what could've got into him to do such a thing."

"See that you do." Alexis turned to Poulter. "My apologies again, Mister Poulter, but Isom's correct. The creature is a bit of an escape artist, but it's never been violent or scratched anyone before. I hope you're not too badly injured."

"I see." Poulter touched his neck again. "No, it's not serious, but I do think the excitement has gotten the better of me and I will retire."

"Of course." Alexis glanced at the others. "Perhaps this would be the time for all of us to retire in preparation for sailing in the morning."

Villar and Spindler rose at this, correctly interpreting her suggestion as an order.

SEVEN

8 September, aboard *HMS Nightingale*, Zariah System

"Take us out, Mister Villar."

Alexis clasped her hands at the small of her back and stared straight ahead. *Nightingale's* quarterdeck was small, smaller than any of the ships she'd commanded, short of *Grapple*, the pirate pinnace she'd gone aboard on her first cruise.

The little cutter's navigation plot was barely a meter across, half the size of that on the last ship she'd commanded and only a quarter of the massive plot on a ship of the line. Besides the small plot, the other stations were similarly cramped. The signals and tactical stations were side-by-side and the spacers stationed there were practically sitting on top of each other.

"Aye, sir." Villar turned to the helmsman and began issuing the orders necessary to get *Nightingale* under way and moving from Zariah Station.

This will take some time to get used to.

Unlike the other ships she'd been in command of, which had been either prizes or ships she'd effectively stolen, she had a full command crew aboard *Nightingale* in the persons of Midshipmen

Villar and Spindler. In addition to their watch standing, they had other duties, one of which was Villar's position as her first officer. As such, it was her responsibility to give general orders about what she wanted and Villar's to deal with the specific orders to the crew in order to achieve it.

True, it was Alexis' prerogative as commander to give as detailed an order as she liked. She could even bypass Villar entirely if she wished, but she'd have to sleep sometime and then Villar, and even young Spindler, would be taking watches in command of her ship. Alexis wanted to have the man's measure sooner rather than later.

For Alexis, who was still a bit unsure of Villar, the experience was not only new but more than a little nerve-wracking. She watched as Villar began giving orders and couldn't help judging him against the orders she would have given. She also keenly felt the fact that she had yet to serve as a first lieutenant aboard any ship, so had never been in Villar's position herself.

Also there was her unfamiliarity with the crew as a whole. In previous commands she'd had men she could trust and whose skills she'd known she could rely on. *Nightingale's* crew was entirely unknown to her. She made a sudden decision.

"Mister Villar, I'd admire it did you utilize the lunar L1 point for our transition. And that the mast be stepped during our travels, if you please, so that we may leave orbit as soon as possible. One quarter speed on the drive, if you will, until the mast is stepped."

Villar was silent for a moment and Alexis felt as though the others on the quarterdeck had paused as well.

"Aye, sir," he said finally.

Alexis frowned as Villar resumed giving orders, wondering at the reaction. True, most ships transitioned to *darkspace* at the planetary/solar Lagrangian points, those spots in space where the gravitational pull of any two orbiting bodies created a relatively stable orbit around the point. The lunar points were considerably smaller and required more precise positioning to transition within them, but nothing a Naval crew couldn't handle.

And how this crew handled it was exactly what she wanted to see, which was why she'd chosen L1, the Lagrangian point between an orbiting body and the mass it orbited. L4 and L5, which preceded and followed the orbiting body in its path were the norm for transitions, as they were larger. L1, which lay midway between the two bodies was closer to the planet for the lunar pairing, but was smaller yet.

She placed a video feed from the hull cameras on the navigation plot so she could watch the mast being stepped, raised from its position flush against the hull and with yards and sails attached and ready for use in *darkspace*. It was possible the reaction was from her ordering only one quarter speed on the conventional drive — other ships she'd been aboard would step the masts and raise the rigging while under half or even full acceleration in an emergency. For the crew outside the hull, outside the artificial gravity and inertial compensators they enjoyed here on the quarterdeck, the tasks would be more difficult under acceleration. They'd have to brace themselves and apply force to those parts not directly attached to the ship. She'd thought to make it somewhat easier for them by ordering the lower acceleration, but had they taken it as a lack of confidence in their abilities?

Alexis pulled her tablet from her thigh pocket and ran her own calculations. She could have done it on the navigation plot itself, but didn't want Villar or the others to realize she was checking them.

Under the conventional drive's normal acceleration, it would take a bit under seven hours for *Nightingale* to arrive at rest in the center of the L1 point. Running at one quarter power until the masts were up would increase that, but not appreciably, she thought, as once the mast was stepped and the crew back inside, *Nightingale* could accelerate well beyond that speed.

Or I'm entirely wrong ...

She watched in growing irritation as the minutes dragged on and work outside the hull continued.

First, the mast went up, unfolded from its resting place against the hull. Then it was lowered partway, as no one had pulled the pin which would lock it in its upright position and it was blocked from settling into place. Once the pin was out and the mainmast fully upright, a pair of men went to its top and began extending the telescoping segments which made up the upper masts ... until the ship's momentum outstripped that of the mast and the whole lot began a slow topple backward as no one had replaced the bloody pins to hold it in place.

Alexis turned her head to look at Villar, who flushed. She could see the muscles working in his neck as his jaw clenched and unclenched, much as she felt her own doing.

In defense of the men working outside, she supposed, was the fact that the helmsman appeared to be constantly adjusting *Nightingale's* acceleration, so that the thrust the men must adjust to was forever changing. More than that, the ship's course was constantly changing as well.

It's a straight bloody line and one bloody button — what *is he doing?*

There was a flurry of activity on the hull and Alexis turned her attention from Villar and the helmsman to the images on the navigation plot. The mast's fore and backstays had somehow become tangled, forcing the men to walk round and round each other in an effort to untwist them.

"They're dancing a bloody maypole on my hull," Alexis muttered.

HER COMPARTMENT'S hatch was barely closed behind her before Alexis was stripping off her uniform and flinging the pieces toward her cot.

"Of all the cack-handed, cunny-thumbed, bloody *lubberly* bits of —"

She stormed into her head and slid the hatch shut with a loud *thump*, then turned her shower on with the water set as hot as she could stand it. As commander, she had a much larger water ration than the crew or even the midshipmen. It was still limited aboard a ship as small as *Nightingale*, but it was a luxury she intended to make full use of.

She let the pounding of the water and the heat work on her until she could feel her muscles relax a bit. She'd likely go over her water ration, generous as it might be, with this shower, but it was either that or strangle someone, and she felt that might set the wrong tone this early in her command.

"Or it might be just what's needed," she muttered.

She'd managed to stay on the quarterdeck until *Nightingale* transitioned to *darkspace*. And managed to remain silent throughout. Through the bit where a pair of hands had rushed in from the hull to retrieve new lines when it was discovered that fully half the running rigging for the mainsail was missing from the sail locker. Then again through the bit where those same hands returned the lines as the missing rigging was discovered to be, inexplicably, bound up in the headsail itself.

Through it all, the helmsman — Alexis didn't yet know his name and hadn't asked, as she'd have not a single encouraging word for the man after watching that display — had continued to adjust and readjust both the ship's acceleration and course.

The final straw, which had sent Alexis to her quarters with a terse, "Set us a course out of system toward Dalthus," had been the transition itself.

A full twenty minutes of work by the helmsman to position and keep them within the Lagrangian point long enough to trigger the transition to *darkspace*. The ship's safety overrides were tripped time and again as it was determined *Nightingale* was drifting too much to make transition — or not entirely within the Lagrangian point to begin with.

Alexis had never seen those overrides trip aboard a Naval vessel. They were there to keep a ship from attempting to transition outside of a Lagrangian point, something which would have dire results. Whether from *darkspace* or to it, ships that tried to transition outside of a Lagrangian point simply disappeared and were neither seen nor heard from again. There were a multitude of superstitions built up in spacers' lore about the fate of such ships, but no scientific data, as there'd never been any trace of them found.

Finished with the shower and feeling at least somewhat more relaxed and human than when she'd entered, Alexis returned to her compartment. Isom had been in while she showered and tidied up the bits of uniform she'd flung around, leaving them neatly folded on her cot.

She grimaced. She hated that she'd let her temper get the better of her and made extra work for him with her tantrum. That was happening more and more lately. She regretted it after, but seemed to have little control in the moment. She dressed, this time in a worn ship's jumpsuit, as she planned to tour the nether reaches of *Nightingale* while they sailed toward the system's edge and the more variable *darkspace* winds there.

While the winds were sometimes unpredictable far between star systems, they rather consistently blew directly toward a system the nearer one got to it. This was what made the dark energy the winds consisted of drive those systems, and even galaxies, faster and faster as part of the ever expanding universe.

Alexis sat down on the cot's edge and picked up a boot. She froze as it seemed to shudder in her hand, then a small, bewhiskered face appeared in the boot top, which explained its unexpected weight.

Before she could draw breath to yell for Isom, the creature was out of her boot and streaking across the floor for whatever cover it could find, leaving behind an unmistakable scent wafting from Alexis' boot.

EIGHT

13 SEPTEMBER, ABOARD *HMS NIGHTINGALE, DARKSPACE* NEAR Zariah System

Nightingale's quarterdeck was silent save for the occasional rustling of the crew's jumpsuits as they shifted positions at their stations.

Alexis' jaw muscles ached more than before. She'd returned to the quarterdeck to observe the simple act of sailing from their entry into *darkspace* at Zariah toward the system's outer edges, and found even that simple task quite beyond her new crew's ability to perform satisfactorily. As the *darkspace* winds blew directly toward the system's center here, leaving meant either a series of long tacks or an ever growing spiral to keep *Nightingale* as close to the winds as she could sail.

Or as close as this crew can put her.

Nightingale was a fore-and-aft rig, simpler than the larger, square-rigged frigates or ships of the line, and also able to sail closer to the wind than those other ships. Or should have been. As it was, the helmsman and crew seemed unable to keep a course and set a sail trim which would allow that. The ship was now sailing a full point to windward *less* than the typical frigate could, zagging and bobbing about to such a degree that the far off features of *darkspace* storms visible on the plot's monitors were in constant motion as the helmsman constantly adjusted his course in one way or another.

Alexis glanced at Villar for perhaps the thousandth time and the midshipman flushed and swallowed hard.

"Steady on, Busbey," Villar murmured to the helmsman.

"Aye, sir."

Alexis closed her eyes and tried to keep her composure — as well as her stomach in the face of the swirling images from outside. She wanted to offer some words of encouragement or advice, but could think of nothing to say, neither to Villar, nor Busbey, nor the rest of the crew, most of whom were back on the main deck at their midday meal after hours of hauling sail and pulling lines outside the hull.

There's not even a joke to be made of this nightmare.

The soft chimes of the ship's bell sounded over the speakers, interrupting her thoughts. The men would be nearly finished with their meal and ready for their daily tot, not that she thought they deserved it after this performance. Another captain might stop the spirits ration altogether until the crew improved, but she'd just come aboard and didn't want to be thought a Tartar before she understood the reason for their seeming incompetence.

Surely, there must be a reason ...

She sighed. "Pipe *Up Spirits*, Mister Ousley."

The bosun straightened in his position at the hatch to the main deck and pulled out his tablet. "Aye, sir."

The trill of bosun's pipes replaced the ship's bell on the speakers.

"Mister Villar, you have the deck," Alexis said quietly. "I believe I'll observe the spirits issue and gain some feel for the crew."

"Aye, sir."

NIGHTINGALE'S main deck was mostly her only deck, given her size. Just aft of the quarterdeck, which took up a quarter of the ship's length forward, it was where the men ate, slept, sat at leisure, and fought the guns. The only other deck, below, held Alexis' quarters, the gunroom where the midshipmen and warrants berthed, as well as the purser's and carpenter's compartments, and below that was the hold, full of stores, the ship's magazine, and the well-protected fusion plant fully aft.

Alexis found the main deck gloomy and oppressive. It was crowded, obviously, with all of *Nightingale's* crew, as well as the Marine complement, berthed in the one space. Their bunks were folded up against the bulkheads now, but when they came down at night there'd be barely room to walk sideways between them.

The guns were tightly clamped to the deck, crystalline barrels covered with protective shrouds, and the crew's mess tables lowered from overhead to sit atop them. Unlike the rest of the ship, which maintained the naturally light color of the thermoplastic from which the ship was constructed, the main deck was darkly colored, the better to absorb and not reflect enemy shot during an action.

Alexis took a place near the hatch back to the quarterdeck and settled in to observe. The compartment echoed with the clatter of dishes and cutlery as the crew cleared away their meals.

Shortly the purser appeared with his spirits barrel and there were some muted cheers. Less, she suspected, than there would have been if she had not been present.

One man from each mess lined up before the barrel and Wileman, the purser, began doling out the portions. Each mess' representative took the ration back to their messmates where it was further divided.

Alexis' brow furrowed as she watched the crew. This was the first time she'd really had the chance to look at them all assembled in one place. They'd been present when she'd read herself in, but the confrontation with Villar and her own nervousness at a first real command had kept her from really noticing the men. Now she did, and she was growing more and more perplexed at what she saw.

All ships might have a man or two who seemed unsuited to the life and work aboard ship, whether too old or too unfit, especially with the war on and the Impressment Service growing ever less discerning in their quest to feed the Navy's ever growing demand for more crews. Isom had been one of those — a legal clerk with neither the strength nor temperament to survive in the Navy for long, but still taken up by the Press and sent aboard ship before he could protest.

Nightingale, though, seemed to have a greatly disproportionate number of these sorts. Most of her crew, in fact, were not men Alexis would think suitable for service aboard ship. Old, clearly unfit, and in some cases even too young. Those who were fit had the look about them of men who'd gone to the Navy as the alternative to the gallows on some world, and, more so, looked as though the near miss hadn't led them to consider changing their ways.

Four of these drew Alexis' attention immediately. One of them was first in line at the spirits barrel and once he returned to his messmates the four stood and left their rum ration on their table. They began circulating around the room from mess to mess collecting a bit more in the way of rum from each.

This wasn't unusual in itself. With the men paid so little, they generally had nothing in the way of coin to use in commerce amongst themselves, so *Up Spirits* was the time when debts for gaming or services were settled by giving the man owed 'sippers' or 'gulpers' from the rum ration, depending on the size of the debt. No, it was not unusual for men to circulate amongst the other messes settling such things at this time.

It was, however, for there to seemingly be so much owed to one mess.

"Mister Ousley?" Alexis called, just loudly enough for the bosun to hear in his position near the cask. She waited until he approached her before continuing, then low enough that she felt no one could overhear, "Without being too obvious in my pointing them out, but those four men there, now approaching the number three gun?" She paused, wondering now how best to ask her question.

"I've no need of a look to know who it is you're asking after, sir," Ousley said, also keeping his voice low. "It'll be Scarborough, Carras, Chivington, and Monks, if I'm not mistaken."

Alexis frowned. "There is something, then?"

Ousley nodded. "Oh, aye, something." He took a deep breath and raised an eyebrow toward the quarterdeck hatch. "Perhaps?"

"Yes, let's do."

Alexis led the way back to the quarterdeck and then down to her quarters.

"Isom, a glass for Mister Ousley, if you please. Wine, Mister Ousley? Or will you take a bit of rum yourself?"

"Beer, thank you, sir, if you've a bit. It sits better with me."

Alexis caught Isom's nod that he did store a bit of beer in her pantry. Marie caught Alexis' look as well and took Ferrau into the quarter gallery to offer her some privacy.

"Of course. Wine for me, Isom."

Once they were settled and Isom had filled the glasses, Alexis took a sip.

"So, these four men?"

Ousley drained half his mug.

"Scarborough, Carras, Chivington, and Monks," he repeated their names. "Come aboard, oh, it'll be three or more weeks now, I think. Off of *Cambrian* ... forty guns, out of Pavv on her way to the border in escort to a convoy."

Alexis nodded. "I had noticed in reading *Nightingale's* muster book a remarkable number of transfers from other ships."

"Aye, remarkable's a word for it, I'd say." Ousley drained the rest of his beer and Alexis nodded for Isom to refill the mug. "Seems every frigate and liner what crosses our path has a man or two to trade, 'for the good of the Service'."

"I see," Alexis said, and she thought she did. The reason for a captain to trade a man could only be that the man was trouble or incompetent in some way. "A great many of these trades, you say?"

"Oh, aye. There's only us as have warrants left of *Nightingale's* original crew. All the rest been taken off by some ship or another, and us left with those what can't pull a line nor wipe their own ..." He paused. "Begging your pardon, sir."

"It's quite all right, Mister Ousley."

"Well, there's those that ain't proper fit for the Navy, see, then there's those that are trouble no matter where they go."

Ousley raised his mug, then set it down when he found it empty. Alexis nodded to Isom. If more beer might put Ousley in a talkative mood, she'd empty her pantry of it. The more she could learn of *Nightingale* and her new crew, the better.

"I'm saying not a word against Mister Villar nor Lieutenant Bensley before him, you understand," Ousley went on. "A full post-captain says, 'This man for that man,' and a lieutenant's to say no? A midshipman's to say no?" He snorted. "Not if he wants a commission or to be made post himself one day — not in this Navy."

Alexis nodded, both in agreement and to keep Ousley talking. She could well see his point, though. Technically one captain could not loot the crew of another as seemed to have occurred with *Nightingale*, but in reality the positions of a lieutenant versus a full post captain were so different that who would oppose the senior offi-cer? Such a slight would be remembered and the senior officer would always be senior, and often in a position to do damage to a junior's career and prospects.

Still if other captains were unloading the old and unfit onto her ship, why had these four been sent? They were young and strong. Were they such troublemakers that their former captain would truly rather take a chance on random replacements off *Nightingale*?

"So what is it these four are up to?" Alexis asked.

"Oh, it's outright extortion, sir," Ousley said. "Nothing clever about it."

"What?"

She'd suspected some sort of gambling operation for them to be collecting from so many of the others, but this?

Ousley nodded. "Aye. There's nary a man who'll complain or call it what it is, mind you. Ask and it's payment for this debt or that favor, you'll be told, but the *favor's* the foregoing of a beating, I've no doubt."

Alexis frowned.

"I know what you'll ask next, sir," Ousley said, "but there's little me and my mates can do without someone coming forward to complain." He shrugged. "They're careful — leave alone those who might fight them for their own bits. Most ships'd have a few among the crew who'll stand up for their mates, but *Nightingale* ... hadn't been any aboard with that heart for months. They're careful, as I said — give no cause to be sent to a captain's mast, nor really any cause for complaint from me or my mates. They get a man alone, though, and he's moving stiff the next day — ask him, and it's a terrible fall he took, being as clumsy as he is and all."

"I see," Alexis said.

Ousley frowned. "I'd not have you thinking I can't keep order, sir." He raised a hand and scratched at his neck. "But my mates and I ... well, if we see nothing and there's no complaint — we can't beat the men for no reason. The crew'd not stand for it."

"No, I see that."

Even if the four men were hated, the bosun — or Alexis and the other officers — would need some proof before acting, else the rest of the crew would feel the punishments were unfair. It might seem an odd thing, but the men would often see their own troubles with someone as secondary to fair treatment by the officers. After all, if one man could be punished without proof then anyone could be, and they'd not stand for that.

"Very well, Mister Ousley. Do keep an eye out, though. I'd like it dealt with as soon as we do have some sort of proof — or anyone to step forward as an accuser, whether that be to you or at mast."

"Aye, sir."

Ousley rose and made his way to the hatch.

"Isom," Alexis said after the hatch shut behind Ousley, "have you heard any rumblings amongst the crew about all this?"

"A bit," Isom said.

Alexis raised an eyebrow.

"And did you not feel it prudent to pass the information on to me?" she asked. A captain's clerk, after all, was her ears amongst the crew.

"Not 'til there's need, no," Isom said, moving to refill her glass. "Nor a thing you can do about it, and with all the rest you've to deal with." He nodded toward her desktop, where the myriad reports required by Admiralty seemed to be continuously displayed and updated, then sighed. "But now it's out ... you might as well know the whole of it. There's more than spirits those four are taking from the other hands."

Alexis raised an eyebrow. "Really? Why didn't Ousley mention that, do you suppose?"

"He doesn't know." Isom glanced at the hatchway. "The bosun only knows what he can see or hear, and those four have the crew so scared there's nary a peep as to what's happening. Ousley can see the spirits well enough, as it happens right in front of him, no matter the excuses the men might make, but the coin those four take from the hands each port call's done in secret. Then there's the gambling — none of it straight, mind you. Those four could fleece a bald sheep, it seems."

"And the crew will tell you all this but not the bosun?"

"I'm your clerk, or near as never-mind to it — not proper crew, but not an officer neither. There's looser talk around me." He looked at her pointedly. "The clerk's a captain's ears ... and the coxswain's her fists, which I've said you've need of already."

"So you've said, but do you see anyone likely aboard *Nightingale?*"

Isom pondered that for a moment. "Well ... Ruse and Sinkey aren't a bad sort, really. They're healthy, know their way about a ship, and keep their own messmates clear of those four bastards easily enough."

"Yes, they're strong enough to fend for themselves and their mates, but do they have the judgment and discretion to act as coxswain?"

She could tell from Isom's look that he didn't think either of those two truly suitable, which left Alexis no closer to filling that role than she had been before. The captain's coxswain would lead her boat crew and, as Isom had said, act as her fists below decks where even the boson and his mates didn't have eyes. Judging when and how to act, though, without bringing it to the captain's official attention, which was a delicate balancing act.

Bloody byzantine, the politics aboard a proper ship.

NINE

23 SEPTEMBER, ABOARD *HMS NIGHTINGALE*, DARKSPACE NEAR the Remada Straits

The sheer amount of records to review in properly taking command of a ship surprised Alexis. She'd known there'd be more to it than just going aboard and meeting the crew, but there were simply too many documents to keep straight. She'd stayed up late, all the nights since they'd left Zariah, pouring over the records.

First there were the purser's records, which she'd looked at, but really required more study if she wanted to ensure herself they were entirely accurate.

An accountant wouldn't go amiss there, either — one of those fellows they bring in to untangle it all when a confidence artist's on his way to a stretched neck.

Though Isom would take a closer look at those — he was acting as her clerk, after all.

Then *Nightingale's* log, at least for the last few months, to familiarize herself with what the ship had done in that time. This showed her that *Nightingale* had kept a regular patrol schedule amongst the systems she was supposed to visit.

Quite regular — perhaps too much so.

Nightingale had kept to the same route over and over again, so far as Alexis could tell, never varying the order of destinations. That would have to be one of the first things she changed — a regular route might make things easy on the crew, but to be so predictable when the ship was supposed to be on the lookout for smuggling and piracy?

Nightingale had also stopped fewer ships for inspection than Alexis would have expected, and taken far fewer smugglers, much less any ship engaged in piracy. That gave her cause to wonder what Villar, and Bensley before him, had been about out here all this time.

As well, she must review the standing orders entered by both Villar and Bensley, so that she knew how the ship had been run and what she might like changed.

The ship's current muster book gave her some sense of the crew and she found it much changed since the copy Admiral Cammack had supplied her on Lesser Ichthorpe along with her orders. *Nightingale*, it seemed, had been used as a veritable employment service by nearly every other Naval ship she'd encountered. Captains, all superior to Villar or Bensley, of course, had both taken and traded hands when they encountered *Nightingale*.

As a result, Alexis' new ship was both shorthanded, she only had two thirds of her expected complement, and had a mix of crew who'd really spent very little time together.

Her review of the punishment log, the list of those in the crew who'd been sent to captain's mast for discipline over some offense that couldn't be handled by a petty officer's fist told another story of the crew.

Her first review of it upon coming aboard had been to determine if Villar or Bensley had acted the Tartar, being too free with the lash. She'd been aboard one ship with an abusive captain and wanted no officer under her who might have similar predilections. She was happy to find that wasn't the case with Villar, but when Alexis plotted the number of men appearing at each captain's mast on a graph and saw a steady increase in incidents, it told a different story. She doubted Bensley or Villar had changed their own ways over time, so suspected that the crew those other ships had "traded" into *Nightingale* had not been their best or most well-behaved.

She was happy to note, though, that neither Bensley nor Villar after him appeared to have been too free with the lash. There were floggings in the log, of course, but none too severe nor for offenses that didn't warrant it. Much as she hated the practice, and she'd been subjected to it herself, she understood the need.

Nightingale, at her farthest, would be ten weeks' sail from the nearest permanent Naval authority — and that she'd have to leave her patrol area entirely to reach. Any discipline for infractions must be handled aboard ship, and with an immediacy that didn't leave *Nightingale* even more shorthanded than she already was. The ship did have a brig, of sorts — a single locking compartment in the Marines' berth, but that was more for keeping a man segregated from the crew until a proper punishment could be performed, not at all for long-term imprisonment.

Lastly, she had her own orders, the ship's orders, to review.

And what a tangle those are.

Nightingale, it seemed, was to be everywhere and do everything all at once.

She was to:

Inspect and Identify all Ships engaged in the Avoidance of Due Custom amongst and between the Systems of the Patrol Area, Destroying or Taking those Ships and Cargoes for the use of the Crown.

Harass, Take, Drive off, or Destroy any and all ships engaged in acts of Piracy amongst and between the Systems of the Patrol Area.

Harass, Take, Drive off, or Destroy any and all ships of Powers with whom a State of War exists amongst and between the Systems of the Patrol Area.

That last she doubted she'd have cause to concern herself with, as these systems were far from the border with Hanover and she didn't think any enemy ships would turn up. Of somewhat more worry to her, were the orders regarding the star systems themselves. On the one hand, she was ordered to visit each system and ensure that the terms of their colonial charters, with regard to the Kingdom at large, were being properly carried out. On the other hand, she was to *"make no action with regard to Colonial Worlds which shall incur Offense or Slights toward Their Customs and Beliefs."*

And all with the admonition that I succeed in all of it or I "shall Answer the Contrary at my Peril."

Alexis rubbed her eyes. She didn't see how one undermanned revenue cutter could conceivably accomplish all of that, especially given the size of her patrol area. When she'd first joined the Navy, this area had been served by a sloop-of-war, and that was before the newly settled systems of Al Jadiq and Man's Fall were added. Nor did she see how she herself could both carry out her orders to enforce the colonial charters on those worlds and avoid giving offense to their customs and beliefs.

With at least two of the worlds in her patrol area, Man's Fall and Al Jadiq, her very presence in a Naval uniform would likely give offense. Zariah would be no problem; despite their origins they'd recently requested a Crown Magistrate be appointed and were rapidly bringing their own laws into full accord with the Kingdom at large. Eidera as well, for she'd visited that system aboard her first ship and they were an incorporated world, where the settlers mostly just wanted to be left alone. As was Dalthus, her own home — oh, there might be a few who remembered her as no more than the teenager she was when she'd left, but she doubted there'd be much in the way of offense at her turning up in charge of a Queen's ship.

The last two, though, and the newest colonized, were both cultural worlds, settled by religious sects who found the constraints of the Core worlds — or in Al Jadiq's case, even Zariah — too much to bear.

Villar was not exaggerating when he said that those two would balk at her being in command of *Nightingale*. The briefing material on both told her that they had very definite and constrained ideas about the proper place of women — and none of those places included command of a Queen's ship.

It made her wonder, a bit, about Admiral Cammack's intent in giving her command of *Nightingale*. He'd had the same information available to him when he'd made the appointment, and the Navy was generally quite accommodating of Fringe World attitudes. Even going so far as to shuffle entire crews about to accommodate the beliefs and prejudices of the worlds that ship might visit.

Cammack must have known that Alexis would unwelcome on those worlds, yet he'd appointed her anyway.

Of course, Cammack was from Core Fleet and certainly not used to the ways of the Fringe. It was entirely possible he'd made a mistake and not even considered Fringe Fleet's practices. On the other hand, Cammack had not struck her as a man who made decisions without understanding the circumstances ... and he *was* Core Fleet. Had not Captain Euell, of her last ship, *Shrewsbury*, mentioned to her that many officers in Core Fleet found this particular practice distasteful? He'd even gone so far as to say that Core Fleet officers felt it was well past time Her Majesty told the Fringe Worlds to "suck it up" and accept the men and women of both fleets as they were.

Would an admiral from Core Fleet go so far as to deliberately ignore that custom? Was Cammack using her as some sort of cat's paw to force the issue?

She rubbed her eyes again then looked up as there was a rustle of bedclothes from the rear of the cabin.

"You work too long," Marie said softly so as not to wake Ferrau. "How will you do the works tomorrow, if you do not sleep tonight?"

Alexis took a deep breath, then closed the documents.

"You're right. Time enough tomorrow." She rose and stretched. "I'll have a bit of bourbon before bed, Isom."

She ignored the looks both of them gave her at that and made her way to the head to change. Neither Isom nor Marie approved of her nightly tot, she knew, but she felt it did help her sleep and avoid the nightmares which had been plaguing her more and more often since Giron.

It's not as though I drink so much as anyone else in the Navy.

TEN

24 September, aboard *HMS Nightingale*, darkspace, the Remada Straits

Alexis came awake to a whispered, "Sir?" and a light touch on her shoulder. Isom was bent over her cot, leaning across Marie who, Alexis had discovered, was extraordinarily grabby in her sleep and had somehow draped herself over Alexis.

"Mister Villar's at the hatch for you, sir," Isom continued. "Three bells of the middle."

Alexis groaned, only an hour and a half past midnight.

"Let him in," she said. It must be important for him to interrupt her sleep.

Isom nodded and Alexis began the process of extricating herself from a sleeping Marie. She'd realized the first night that her thought to simply share a larger bunk instead of mounting an upper bunk on the bulkhead was not, perhaps, her finest. True, she didn't have to climb in and out of an upper bunk, but Marie had a tendency to drape herself over all of the available space and anything else that might be in it, trapping Alexis against the bulkhead and underneath an astonishing variety of limbs. Unfortunately, to have an upper bunk mounted now would likely hurt the girl's feelings and Alexis didn't want to do that.

She eased Marie's arms and legs off her and slid from under the bedclothes on the bulkhead side, then crawled to the end of the bunk. Marie let loose a rattling snore and settled back to sleep.

Isom had turned the compartment lights on to a dim glow, so she could see Villar standing near her dining table. His eyes were wide and kept darting between her and Marie. He met Alexis' eyes, then cleared his throat and looked pointedly at the bulkhead.

Is he embarrassed to see Marie abed? She glanced back, but Marie's form was nothing more than a lump of bedclothes with hair, not even her face was visible. *It certainly can't be me.*

Despite the protestations of Delaine Theibaud, her French ...

Well, whatever it is Delaine and I are to each other. And I do wish there'd be some word from him or about the fleet.

In any case, despite what Delaine had to say about it, Alexis had no illusions about how she looked getting out of bed in her Naval issue boxer shorts and undershirt. With her small frame and figure, she looked like nothing more than a young midshipman who'd let his hair grow halfway down his back.

Perhaps he's from one of those worlds where seeing a girl's knees and elbows is right out. Lord knows there's enough of them. Or where wrists and ankles are all over shocking, come to that.

Well, both Mister Villar and the rest of the crew would have to get over that, as she had no plans to wear a full uniform whilst exercising or sparring with the Marines — something she reminded herself to begin the very next day, as she was already feeling out of sorts from lack of activity.

"Your report, Mister Villar?" Alexis prompted quietly.

"Ah, yes, sir, my apologies for waking you." Villar continued to stare at the far bulkhead. "A sail's been sighted. Lieutenant Bensley's standing order was to be wakened for such. I kept that when I ... well, before you took command, that is, and you've not changed it, so ..."

"Quite right," Alexis said. She'd reviewed Bensley's standing orders and let them be for the time being. "I'll be up to the quarter-deck presently."

Villar left and Alexis found that Isom was already quietly laying out her uniform for her. She whispered her thanks to him, neither of them wanting to wake Ferrau, though if Alexis chose to close with the spotted sail, both Ferrau and Marie would soon be wakened by *Nightingale's* call to quarters.

Alexis briefly visited the head and splashed a bit of water on her face, then ran a brush through her hair before capturing it in a tight ponytail. She dressed and made her way to the quarterdeck.

"Where away, Mister Villar?" she called as she stepped through the hatch.

"Fine on the starboard bow, sir, a fair distance, but looks to be two-masted," Villar said. "We're midway through the Remada Straits. The sail was in the Straits when we spotted her, but now she's running fully downwind toward Greater Remada."

Alexis scanned the navigation plot as Villar described the situation. Two masts would most likely make it a sloop or barque. Larger than *Nightingale*, and better armed if it wasn't a merchant ship. The location and course were odd, though.

Nightingale was in the Remada Straits, an area of space named for its proximity to three uninhabited star systems, Deltiri and Greater and Lesser Remada. It was an oddity of *darkspace* navigation that a ship's travel time was affected by normal-space masses such as planets and stars. The closer one was to a star system, the slower, or less distance, one traveled relative to normal-space.

Whether *darkspace* itself expanded and contracted in an exponential relation to normal-space masses wasn't fully clear, only that it might take a ship a day or more to sail between Lagrangian points within a star system, but only a week or a fortnight to cover the light years between different systems — provided that ship avoided the slowing effects of any normal-space masses in between.

The shortest time between Zariah and Dalthus, then, wasn't a straight line. It was a curving course that wended its way around intervening systems, trading distance in *darkspace* for faster travel relative to normal-space.

In this instance, the Remada Straits were the best-time course between those three systems, a sort of S-like curve which maintained as much distance from all three as possible.

The spotted sail, though, was not in the Straits. Its path on the plot showed it starting there, but sailing for the Greater Remada system and leaving the variable winds of open *darkspace* for the system winds that blew steadily toward that system's star.

It was possible the ship was a research vessel. The sailing notes said there were still such ships being sent to the Straits, even with the war against Hanover on, to study the nature of *darkspace* here. The currently popular theory being that, much as mass in normal-space warped space-time, it had an almost reversed, mirror-like effect on *darkspace*. If *darkspace's* normal state was greatly compressed, accounting for short travel time between systems, and if the effect of normal-space mass were to stretch things, it would account for the greater distance/travel-time encountered in or near star systems.

Those research voyages were well known to the Navy, however, and Alexis had no notes of one in her logs or dispatches. They were also, generally, more than one ship and accompanied by a Naval vessel for protection against the pirates who sometimes thought the relatively narrow channel of the Straits a fine hunting ground.

Still, it could well be a research vessel or there could be some new find in one of the systems resulting in a settlement.

"Has there been some development in Greater Remada I'm unaware of, Mister Villar?" Alexis asked.

"No, sir, all three are uninhabited. We'd have had word if that were changing."

Alexis frowned. It would take *Nightingale* some time to catch up with the strange sail, and when they did she suspected they'd find the stranger was up to no good. She'd encountered ships frequenting uninhabited systems before — aboard her first ship, *Merlin* — and there were few legitimate purposes for it.

"Bring us three points to starboard, Mister Villar," she said, "and send the hands to an early breakfast. I have a feeling we'll have business for the guns this morning."

Villar snorted, but said, "Aye, sir," and passed along her orders. *Nightingale* began to sound with activity as the crew was wakened.

Alexis ignored the sound. Villar might think her overly cautious, but even were the other ship entirely innocent, a bit of drill at going to quarters wouldn't do the crew any harm.

The helmsman changed their course and the ship eased onto a new tack, bound to intercept the strange sail ahead of them.

The quarterdeck hatch chimed and Alexis turned from the plot to find Poulter. The surgeon raised his brow inquiringly.

"If you don't mind, captain, I'd rather like to observe the approach from the quarterdeck."

Alexis frowned, but couldn't think of a reason to deny the request, other than her own discomfort with his presence. That might be enough for some captains, but refusing for that reason alone felt too much like acting the Tartar for her to be entirely comfortable with.

"I suppose that will be all right, Mister Poulter," she said, "but I'll want you on the orlop if there's any shooting done."

"Of course," Poulter agreed. He took a place to the side, as unobtrusively as possible, given *Nightingale's* small quarterdeck. "Do you suppose that will be necessary?"

"I suppose, Mister Poulter, that will be up to those aboard our chase."

Poulter merely nodded and faded back against the quarterdeck bulkhead. From the corner of her eye, Alexis could see him working on his tablet and felt she could almost hear the tapping of his fingers as he took some sort of note. She forced down her irritation and turned her attention back to the plot and the ship they were pursuing, though not before wondering at Poulter and the similarity of his attitude to that of the lieutenant who'd questioned her after Giron. She wondered at the difference between those two and the other ship's surgeons she'd encountered, and whether they might be some further evidence of some sort of split within Admiralty's hierarchy — the "two Navies" she'd encountered aboard *HMS Hermione*.

Isom appeared at her elbow with a tray containing a plate of eggs, rolls, and, Wileman being true to her orders, a full rasher of crisp bacon. Alexis ate and sipped the accompanying coffee until she thought they'd closed enough with the other ship to identify signals.

"Put up our colors, Creasy," Alexis said to the spacer on the signals console, "along with *Heave-to* and *Inspection*."

"Aye, sir."

Alexis waited, giving time for the requested signals to begin lighting and flashing on *Nightingale's* hull and mast. Then more time to allow for the other ship to sight those signals and respond.

She expected the other ship to either douse her sails and return a signal with her name and purpose, if she were a legitimate craft, or turn and run from *Nightingale*, if she were a smuggler or pirate.

What Alexis did not expect was to be ignored.

ELEVEN

24 September, aboard *HMS Nightingale*, darkspace, the Remada Straits

"Anything at all?"

Alexis could see well enough on the navigation plot that there'd been no change in the other ship's course or signals during the time *Nightingale* had closed on it, but she asked anyway. Perhaps others on the quarterdeck had noticed something she hadn't.

"No signals, sir," Creasy, on the signals console, said.

"Course changes a bit as she goes, sir," Dorsett, on the tactical console, informed her, "but it's consistent with the winds. Not a soul out on her hull."

The image of the chase, not referred to as sail now that *Nightingale* had beat to quarters and prepared for a fight, remained unchanged. Remarkably unchanged. Suspiciously unchanged, in fact, for the other ship had altered neither course nor speed throughout the entire time *Nightingale* tracked it. There was a slight arc to its path represented on the navigation plot, but that was explained by its travels farther into the Greater Remada system where the winds shifted to blow straighter and stronger toward the system center.

Alexis frowned and narrowed her eyes at the sight. They were close enough now that the features of the other ship were clear in the image. Not a barque at all, but a massive, four-masted ore carrier, though with only main and mizzen masts having sail bent on. That was what had led to the mistaken identity, as the lack of sail made the ship seem smaller at a distance.

The spare use of sail was not the only oddity they noticed as they grew closer, though. Not only did the ship show no signs of life via signals, but there was no sign of a crew working those few sails. No spacers worked on its hull and the other ship hadn't responded to any of *Nightingale's* signals, which now included the demand *Imperative* along with *Heave-to* and *Inspection*.

"Let us have a shot across their bow, Mister Villar," she said. "Perhaps that will engender a response."

"Aye, sir."

She waited a moment as the order was relayed and a bolt of laser shot lanced out from *Nightingale's* bow chaser to pass far ahead of the other ship.

There was still no reaction at all. The other ship maintained its course, oblivious to *Nightingale's* shot and its masts and hull remained dark of any signal in return.

The ship itself appeared ill-kept, even from the outside. Two loose lines trailed from the unused masts and the spars on those masts held the sagging rolls of hastily furled sails. The hull was pocked and scarred, dirty where that damage hadn't cut through the grime to the raw thermoplastic beneath.

"An ore carrier out of Dalthus, I'll wager," Villar said. "They pick up such dust in the space around the refineries and get knocked about by debris at the mines."

Alexis nodded absently, still studying the image.

"Can you make out her name at all?" she asked.

The ship's bow and transom were so caked in grime that there was no trace of a painted name to be found.

"Some of the carriers don't' bother," Villar said, "as it's so difficult to keep them clean." He frowned. "The lack of any hands on the sails is disturbing."

Alexis nodded again.

Some ruse? Or is there truly no one aboard?

They'd be within a good range for the guns soon, and then the wait would be over. That was how chases always seemed to Alexis, long hours of the chase with the other ship out of range, then suddenly it was there and the distance closing too fast to even think as the shot flew.

"Put us a point to port of their course," she ordered, "and close slowly."

"Point to port o' the chase's course, aye," the helmsman echoed.

Now they were closely paralleling the other ship's course, sailing toward it by only a few degrees. *Nightingale* was the faster ship, so she was also pulling ahead a bit. Alexis eyed the plot, judging the other ship's speed.

"Take in two reefs of the main courses and cut the particle projector by a third."

"Two reefs of the mains, aye," Creasy echoed from the signals console as he relayed the order to those working the sails outside the hull. Their suit radios wouldn't work in the radiations of the *dark-space* winds, the dark energy that permeated everything not enclosed in gallenium, so the order was sent via the ship's fiber optics to a display panel at the bow. With the sails reefed, pulled up and tied so that they had less surface area to catch the dark energy flowing past the ship, and the particle charge to what sail area was left lessened as well, *Nightingale* should match the other ship's speed more closely.

"Another across their bow, sir?" Villar asked.

Alexis shook her head. "I can't see what good that will do. They can surely see us and know who we are. It's as though no one is home at all over there."

"Bloody Dutchman," Creasy muttered from the signals console.

"Silence on the quarterdeck!" Villar snapped and Creasy hunched over his console.

Alexis laid a hand on Villar's arm and shook her head slightly when he looked at her. She wouldn't be a captain who demanded silence from her crew and wanted Villar to know it, but she wouldn't correct him in front of the hands either. Especially in something like this. Many of the hands were superstitious — the Dark seemed to be made for fashioning legends and stories, after all. If the hands began to think this was a Dutchman, a ghost ship of some sort set to plying the shipping lanes and ensnaring the crews of other ships, then there could be trouble from them. She'd rather that thought was out in the open, rather than whispered in secret.

"Oh, I doubt it's that, Creasy," Alexis said. "Aren't a Dutchman's sails said to glow green with eldritch energy? This ship's are as blue as ours ... though flickering a bit ... it's a poor spirit who can't tune his projectors, don't you think?"

That drew a laugh from most of the quarterdeck crew, but Creasy still looked unnerved.

"Still, it is very odd, and that's enough to make me wary." Alexis tapped the navigation plot, then turned to the tactical console. "Dorsett, when you first spotted him in the Straits, was this one coming through and then turned? Or was he sailing across from Lesser Remada?"

"Hard to say, sir." Dorsett ran fingers over his console, bringing up several images. "More like he just ... appeared like. He were far off when I sighted him, but not so far as I'd have missed him coming, if you understand."

"Dutchman," Creasy muttered.

Alexis ignored him and went to the tactical console.

"Show me."

Dorsett played the recordings of his first sight of the chase for her, then again. A dark, featureless expanse of *darkspace* at first, then lit suddenly with the pinprick of light that would become the ship they now chased.

"You see, sir? As though he were layin' doggo there, then charged his sails all at once like."

"Yes, I see, very like he was lying there quiet. We'd not see a ship with uncharged sails and a darkened hull at that distance, and far better explanation for his sudden appearance than some ghost story," she said loud enough for Creasy to hear. "The question is, why do that?"

"Ambush, sir?" Villar asked. "Lie silent and invisible in the Straits until some fat merchantman's in range, then pop up after her? But it's us instead, so he takes off at a run?"

Alexis raised an eyebrow and saw that Villar had the good grace to flush a bit. He might have scoffed at her calling the hands to quarters with no cause to think the sail an enemy, but could now see there was something decidedly odd about the other ship.

"Perhaps," Alexis allowed, "but a bulk hauler isn't the sort of ship one thinks of when piracy's the goal. Too slow and ill-armed." She frowned. "Still ... alert the guncrews to stay ready, Mister Villar, perhaps this chase isn't as toothless as we've been thinking."

"Aye, sir." Then after passing along the order, "Q-ship, do you think, sir?"

"It's possible," Alexis nodded.

A Q-ship, or a ship that ostensibly resembled a merchantman of some sort but was really a heavily armed warship, was a possibility. Either for piracy, as most pirate ships would have started as innocent merchantmen, or by Hanover if they'd chosen to attack this deep into New London space. The question was what to do about it and how to approach the other ship, which was still not deviating from its course or responding to any signals.

If it were a trap or a Q-ship of some sort, then the smart thing to do would be to lay off and fire into it. On the other hand, the other ship could be an innocent, fallen to some calamity. Perhaps the crew was sick and unable to work the ship. If that were the case, then firing on the ship and opening the hull to vacuum could kill dozens of innocent men.

Another three quarters of an hour passed, with *Nightingale* drawing ever closer and still no sign of life from the other ship. To Alexis' mind the time had long passed for the other ship's crew to take some action if their intents were nefarious.

"We'll close further with them. See that the guns are kept manned, Mister Villar, but assemble a boarding party. We'll ease up on her starboard side and board. Once we've taken in her sails we'll see what this is all about." She paused. "I think if they intended us harm they've had ample opportunity to begin their game."

"Aye, sir."

Creasy muttered something, but Alexis didn't catch what it was.

Odd, yes, but I think they'd have fired on us by now if she were secretly armed.

"Dorsett, run that appearance for me again, will you?" She leaned over the spacer's shoulder to better see his console. "Let's see if we can find an answer to this."

Behind her there was a bustle of activity as her orders were carried out. Villar gave instructions to the helmsman to take *Nightingale* in beside the other ship until, with several false starts and the need to sheer away and begin again, the two hulls were almost touching. It was closer even than they should be, and Alexis noticed Villar tense, as she herself did, to wave the helmsman off again, but the man had made it work this time. All still with no sign of movement or life aboard, even with the extended time it took for her crew to carry out those orders and *Nightingale* giving all appearances of ramming the other ship at the end.

No one can say we didn't give them time to acknowledge us, at least.

Spacers leaped across the small space, carrying lines to attach to the other ship, then tied them off tight and made for the masts. Sails on both ships were furled and with nothing to harness the dark energy winds of *darkspace* and overcome the pull of dark matter that permeated everything, the two ships slowed to a stop.

Alexis spared a thought to note again that Villar was, indeed, a quite competent ship handler. His orders were crisp and timely. It was the first time she'd truly had someone as her second when commanding a ship, and she found that she quite liked it. She could give an order and move on to the next decision, confident in the knowledge that Villar would see it carried out properly, despite his sometimes sullen attitude and the crew's difficulties.

"Boarding team's ready to breach the hatch, sir," Villar said.

"Have them wait a moment. Arrange the boarding tube so that *Nightingale's* sealed. If there is a crew aboard that ship and the cause of all this is some sickness, we'll not want to bring it back aboard."

"Aye, sir."

"Go back, Dorsett," she said suddenly. There was something odd in the images – just a bit of a flash, as though the other ship's sails had received a sudden surge of power after they were initially charged. It was different than an increase in the particle charge, though.

Dorsett repeated the recording from the first appearance of the other ship's sails.

"That flash, just there," she said, "what is that?"

On the screen, the other ship's sails started dim, then brightened and stayed that way for some time, but finally began to dim more as *Nightingale* drew nearer.

"Projector acting up?" Dorsett suggested. "Sails brighten for a time, then go dimmer."

Alexis caught her lower lip between her teeth. The other ship's sails did brighten, but not the whole of them, only part. There was a shape there, it seemed, but at the distance they'd first spotted the other ship the image was blurry and indistinct.

"Mister Villar, you've fresh eyes. See what you can make of this."

Villar leaned over Dorsett's other shoulder. He frowned.

"Looks like sails," he said.

"Well, yes, Mister Villar, that is what we're looking at, after all."

"No, sir," Villar said, pointing to the brighter portion. "Other sails, behind these."

Alexis looked again and now that he'd said it the pattern was unmistakable.

"A second ship?" She glanced over and met Villar's eyes.

He nodded. "Smaller, and behind this one. Dorsett, play it forward at high speed."

At the higher speed, Alexis could make out what hadn't been clear before. The brighter spot, another ship's sails, grew smaller and smaller over time until only the first ship's remained.

"Kept that ship between us and them until they were well away," Alexis said. "Fancy bit of ship-handling, that."

"I think Dorsett had the way of it — lying doggo in ambush, only it wasn't our chase here that was doing it."

Alexis thought it through. "Some pirate lying in wait, here in the Straits where merchant shipping funnels through a relatively small area. They take this fat prize, but aren't away with it before we come on the scene."

"So they send the prize off toward Greater Remada as a decoy and escape out of sight behind it." Villar straightened.

Alexis did as well and nodded Villar toward the navigation plot.

"They're well away, whoever they were." Alexis started to order the locks on the other ship breached in case the merchant crew was still aboard, but paused. "Decoy. Do you suppose that's all?"

"All?"

"I've had some dealings with pirates, Mister Villar, most are straight-forward brutes, but some —" She thought of Avrel Dansby, the "former" pirate in whose ship she'd sailed into Hanover space to find Commodore Balestra and the Berry March fleet. "Some are quite clever." She paused. "We'll have to enter that ship, but I think it might be wise if we were to avoid using the airlocks to do so."

"You fear a trap of some kind?"

"An abundance of caution, let's call it."

TWELVE

24 September, aboard *HMS Nightingale*, darkspace, the Remada Straits

It took only a short time for the crew to rig a boarding shelter over a blank portion of the other ship's hull, clamber inside the shelter, and set off a breaching charge. Air rushed out, filling the mostly deflated shelter, and debris forced out by the escaping air was caught by the shelter's tough fabric. The crew surged through the breach, weapons ready, but soon reported that there appeared to be no one aboard, not even bodies.

This news caused another muttering of "Dutchman" from the quarterdeck crew and Alexis replayed the images she believed were a second ship leaving this one in an attempt to calm the crew.

Talk of spectral Dutchmen-ships ended, though, when further reports were brought back.

"Rigged like I've never seen, sir," Corporal Brace said. He shook his head in amazement, sending drops of sweat from his face before he wiped at it again with a rag. His hair was matted to his head with sweat from the exertions of searching the other ship in a full vacsuit, as Alexis had ordered no one take their helmet off until they were certain there was no contagion responsible for the other ship's silence. "A quick job, but thorough — all the exterior hatches had lines run to explosives around the fusion plant. Come in through one and the whole ship would have gone, and *Nightingale* as well."

"And no one aboard at all?" Alexis asked.

"Not a soul," Brace said. "Some signs of a scuffle, but no bodies. Only those booby-traps to show there ever was ..." He paused and frowned. "Those and the helm, that is."

"The helm?"

Brace nodded. "Odd, that, sir. The helm's disassembled — looks as though someone was trying to repair it, then stopped in the midst."

Alexis frowned. "That is odd. Is the ship safe to board? I'd like to see this for myself. And one of the engineers, I think."

"Aye, sir," Brace said. "We've found just the hatches rigged, and that's all cleared."

ALEXIS SEALED her helmet and made her way through the airlock onto *Nightingale's* hull. The disparity in size between her ship and the much larger merchant vessel was quite clear when viewed from this perspective. The other ship's masts towered nearly twice as high as *Nightingale's* and the stern stretched well past even *Nightingale's* rudder and planes. Though only two of the ship's decks were for her crew, the hull housed a hold fully as deep as all of the little revenue cutter — possibly more so.

Because they'd breached the hull on the upper deck, away from any hatches, there was no boarding tube rigged from *Nightingale* to the other ship's side, only a series of lines strung between them.

Alexis attached one of her safety lines and began pulling herself across. Even the short span between hulls gave her a bit of a chill, as she could look aft and see that there'd be nothing for her to catch onto if the line gave way. That both ships were at rest, sails uncharged, didn't alleviate the feelings of dread at the thought of being left behind to the effects of *darkspace.*

Once on the other ship's hull, she made her way to the breach, into the breaching chamber, and then lowered herself through the hull into the ship's interior. As her legs passed the edges of the hull, they came within the ship's gravity field and she felt the pull increase the more of herself she lowered inside, until finally she hung by her fingertips before letting go and dropping to the deck.

The breach was on an upper deck, into what was the captain's pantry. Both hatches to the tiny space were kept closed so that any sudden damage to the breaching chamber outside wouldn't cause the entire ship to de-air. It would also keep the radiations of *darkspace* from moving through the ship and rendering its electronics useless. Alexis moved aside so that Villar could lower himself into the ship, then they eased the aft hatch open and stepped into the ship's main deck.

"The quarterdeck's just down this companionway, sir," Villar said as they eased their vacsuit helmets off.

Alexis looked around the abandoned compartment that would have been the living space of the ship's crew. There were no signs of a struggle or disaster of any sort.

The bunks were rigged, swung down from the compartment bulkheads. Some bedding trailed over the edge of bunks, as though the occupants had been hurriedly called from their sleep. Here and there a chest was left open. But, all in all, it looked like nothing so much as though the entire crew had been picked up and carried off somewhere without warning.

"Yes," Villar said, nodding in the direction of her gaze. "There was some more muttering of Dutchmen amongst those who first came aboard, but it mostly quieted down when we saw the traps rigged — the men generally accept that ghosts aren't too involved in engineering."

"'Generally?'"

Villar shrugged. "There's some, sir, who'll take more convincing." He opened the companionway hatch. "Quarterdeck's this way, sir."

The scene on the quarterdeck was less surreal than the empty, abandoned berthing deck above. At least here there were some signs of a struggle. A splash of blood across the navigation plot and the air still held an acrid scent despite the ship's ventilation systems.

Alexis sniffed. "Neither do ghosts use firearms, I should hope has been pointed out to the crew."

Villar nodded. "Nor disassemble consoles, sir, at least in those fairy stories my grandmother read to me."

Alexis looked at the console in question, where an engineer from *Nightingale* was busy examining the exposed systems. All of the helm's maintenance panels had been removed, exposing the inner circuits and wiring. Several circuit boards were hanging loose, and there appeared to be more than the usual number of jury-rigged components, as well.

All ships made do with what components and repairs could be fabricated by their onboard printers when away from more sophisticated planetary resources, frequently resulting in a mishmash of technologies in their systems. Especially for merchantmen, where repair costs ate into a voyage's profits, if a system, ugly as it might be, was still working, why spend the coin to repair it or replace it with something more modern?

"Show the captain what you've found, Cottier," Villar said.

The engineer glanced up from his prone position on the deck, only half his face visible behind the tangle of cables and circuits.

"Aye, sir, this —" He separated a circuit board from the others and swung it to the side. "— and this here —" He pointed to an oddly shaped chip on another. "— don't belong at all, you see? And there's wire runs I don't understand."

"Is it some sort of additional sabotage?" Alexis asked. Though why someone would bother to sabotage the helm when they'd also rigged the ship to explode, she couldn't fathom. Or ... she recalled the encrypted navigation plot she'd encountered on the pirate ship

Grapple during her first cruise. "Or something so only the pirates could pilot the ship?"

The half of Cottier's head she could see shook back and forth. "No, sir, at least not as makes any sense at all. The modifications are all on the transition controls — rest of the helm's as normal and plain as can be."

Alexis pondered that. The transition controls were what detected when a ship was inside of a Lagrangian point, where the normal-space gravitational fields of two bodies canceled each other out enough for a ship to transition from normal-space to *darkspace* and back again. Outside of those points, moving between the two realms wasn't possible.

"What modifications?"

"Can't tell, sir — those aren't circuits we generally modify, you understand? What's the point, after all? You're either in a Lagrangian point and able to transition or not."

Alexis ran her fingers over the navigation plot, but the system appeared to have been wiped clean, showing only the plot since just before *Nightingale* had spotted the ship and nothing of her course before that. She tried to bring up the ship's log, but that was also empty.

"We may be able to recover something, sir," Villar said, "but it's all been wiped. Captain's personal files, as well."

"There'll be a copy of the log in the ship owner's core, they won't have been able to wipe that, but it'll also be encrypted so we can't get at it." Alexis sighed. "We'll likely not know what happened aboard her until we can have that unlocked at Zariah and find out who owned her."

The quarterdeck hatch slid open and a Marine, out of breath and clearly excited, rushed in.

"Corporal Brace's compliments, sir, and he'd admire it did you join him in the hold!"

TWO OTHER MARINES blocked the open hatch to the aft companionway leading down to the hold. A dozen or more spacers, seemingly all who'd come aboard from *Nightingale*, surrounded them in a half circle, craning their necks and muttering.

"Make a lane!" Villar bellowed, stepping ahead, clearing a path for Alexis, and stopping before the Marines.

Alexis paused there as well and glanced at the assembled hands.

"What's this about, Angers?" she asked one of the Marines.

"Don't rightly know, sir. Corporal Brace went into the hold with Vibert, then come out and told us to secure the hatch and send for you — next we know, this lot showed up."

Alexis turned to the watching hands. "I'm certain you lads have tasks in securing the ship so we can sail her on to Dalthus with us, so what's this about, then?"

Some of the crew took a step back, looking down at the deck, but a few looked defiant. Defiant and no little afraid, she thought.

"Some'ats not right on this ship, sir."

"Not right."

"Bloody Dutchman."

"Oh, for the love of —" Alexis caught herself and restrained her temper. "Look, you —" She singled out the hands who seemed most concerned. "Rhone, Dicker, Summersett — there're no bloody Dutchmen, lads. This ship was taken by pirates, nothing more — what business would some spook have rigging the hatches like that or disassembling the helm?"

"Crew could've done it!" Rhone exclaimed. "T'at other ship bein' the Dutchman and this un's crew rigged her all up afore she's took! To protect 'emselves, like!"

Dicker and Summersett, along with one or two of the others muttered, "Aye."

"Lads, this ship was taken by pirates, nothing more. There's blood on the quarterdeck and the smell of gunfire — it's an odd sort of spirit who shoots his victim, isn't it?"

Some of the crew frowned, but others looked stubborn. Alexis could understand their feelings — this ship made her uneasy as well — and the Dark itself lent itself to odd tales, with so much about it not understood.

"Who's to say who shot, eh?"

"Aye, crew shoots at the Dutchman spirits come aboard, then get all tore apart and there's your blood, right?"

"An' where's the bodies, then?" Rhone asked. "Pirates don't take no crew what don't join 'em! Never heard a whole merchant's crew join up — most're either offed or left to drift!"

And Alexis had to concede that was true. With the pirates interrupted by *Nightingale's* arrival, the absence of any bodies or the merchant's crew itself was, indeed, quite odd. Most pirates wouldn't kill a crew outright if the merchant surrendered quickly, else why would the next not fight harder? Instead, they'd dump the crew on some colony world without much in the way of air vehicles, or leave them aboard a ship's boat near a major shipping lane. That these had apparently taken all of this ship's crew with them in their flight from *Nightingale* was worth questioning — but not the questions running through her crew's heads now.

"Et 'em!" a voice called. "Dutchman spirits et 'em whole!"

"Ghosts and spirits do not eat people," Alexis said firmly.

"Ghoulies do, me mam said!"

Alexis clenched her jaw and cast a stern look at Villar who was hiding a grin behind one hand. Of all the times for the stiff-necked man to show a sense of humor, it had to be when what was needed was calming the crew.

"As I recall," she said, forcing calm into her voice, "the ghoulies come to eat small children who misbehave or won't eat their vegetables. Are you placing yourself in that company, Rhone?"

"Well, me mam dint say *when* the ghoulies'd come, an' I were a right bloody —"

"Lads, there're any number of explanations. Perhaps the crew was already aboard the pirate ship, under guard, before we arrived and there was neither time nor inclination to put them back with

Nightingale approaching. We'll likely be finding them drifting in a ship's boat along with the crew of the pirate's next victim."

"What's so secret in the hold, then?" Dicker demanded.

Alexis felt as though she were losing control of things — the situation, this conversation, to name only two. She understood the crew was disturbed by the state of this ship, no doubt it was out of the ordinary, but that was no excuse for this degree of questioning their officers. The first thing that needed dealing with, though, was the tone.

She stepped away from the Marines to face Dicker.

"Who is it you think you're addressing in that manner, Dicker?" she asked, keeping her voice level and calm.

"I —" He looked away, glanced at the others, then down at the deck. "Sorry, sir ... it's just this ship — it's all over willyfying."

Alexis nodded, then ran her eyes over the others, meeting each man's eye until he looked away and at least muttered something she could take for an apology and appropriate recognition of her rank.

"I understand we've found this ship in odd circumstances, lads, but there's nothing more than common piracy here." She raised her eyebrows and smiled. "And now we have her, that's prize money, right?"

The men brightened at that. With no crew aboard, the ship was theirs. It wouldn't be bought into the Navy, like an enemy warship might be, and the Prize Court would likely award the crew a fraction of its value after selling it back to its owners, but *Nightingale* had such a small crew that any amount would make for a nice windfall.

"Aye," Alexis said, "too busy cringing at every creak and rattle aboard to think of that, weren't you." She nodded to them. "So back to work, lads, and let's get this tub spaceworthy and underway. Sail her back to Zariah and see what she'll bring us."

There were more mutters as the men left and returned to their work, but these were more cheerful and expectant than fearful.

Alexis took a deep breath, shared a look with Villar, and started down the companionway.

In the hold she found Corporal Brace and the engineer who'd

assisted him in opening the hold. Hopkins, the engineer, was standing near the hatch, eyes wide, while Brace was farther into the hold near a sealed crate. The hold was mostly empty except for those stores one would expect for a long journey and perhaps two dozen crates. The crates were clearly the merchantman's primary cargo, but there were far fewer of them than could fill the hold and they were evenly spaced fore and aft. Each was nearly a meter on each side and sealed with digital locks.

"Well, Brace, what is it you wanted me to see?"

Brace swallowed. "You asked me to secure the hold and see what the cargo was, sir ..."

"I did," Alexis prompted as Brace trailed off. She eyed the crate next to him — its lock was cut through with the plasma torch the engineer carried. She shared a glance with Villar, who seemed no more knowledgeable than she about why the two men might seem so nervous, nor what this ship might be carrying. "What's this all about, Brace? There'll be no trouble for opening the crate, lock or no — we have to know what's aboard, after all."

Brace nodded, but swallowed again. He gestured to the crate. "Yes, sir, but ... well ..."

Villar stepped forward and grasped the crate's lid.

"Move aside, man, there're but a dozen of these from what I see. What could —" Villar broke off as he lifted the lid and stared inside, eyes wide. "Sweet mother —"

Alexis stepped up to the crate and found herself as shocked as Villar seemed. As speechless as Brace and Hopkins.

Inside the crate were bars of metal. Dull grey for the most part, but with flecks of azure here and there.

"Gallenium," Villar whispered. He glanced at Alexis. "This ship must be out of Dalthus and the new mines there, bound for processing."

Alexis nodded, still staring at the bars filling the crate.

Gallenium was certainly the most valuable substance there was, gram for gram. It was the only thing that could insulate a ship from the ravages of *darkspace* radiation. It offset the pull of the dark matter that permeated *darkspace,* allowing ships to slide through it, and it made up the sails which harnessed that energy to propel ships from system to system. It, quite literally, made trade and expansion amongst the stars possible.

Rare and valuable though it was, only a little was truly necessary for those purposes. A ship's hull was primarily a tough thermoplastic with just enough gallenium powder infused throughout to keep the *darkspace* radiations at bay. The sails and nets for the gunports were all alloyed with other metals. Only the shot casings contained more than was strictly necessary, being over engineered so as not to fail to fire in action.

"How much?" Villar whispered.

Alexis was already figuring that. The top layer of the meter cubed crate held fifteen rows of four long bars. Tentatively she reached out and lifted one from its place, needing both hands and surprised at how heavy it was.

"Each is different, sir," Brace said. "Weight's stamped on the side, just there."

Alexis examined the side of the brick.

"One thousand four grams," she said. "It can't be pure, can it?"

Villar shook his head. "No, the gallenium's the blue bits mostly, but the refining's difficult." He reached into the crate and tilted another brick to view its side. "Twenty-five percent. Still ..."

Alexis stared at the crate. The bar in her hand was perhaps half its width, which would mean ...

Eighteen hundred bars, nearly two tonnes per crate.

"Does anyone know the market price of gallenium?" she asked, voice sounding a bit shaky to her ears.

Brace cleared his throat. "I ... may have looked that up on my tablet while waiting for you to arrive, sir."

Alexis raised an eyebrow.

Brace flushed. "Just curious, you understand, sir."

"As am I, corporal — what did you find?"

"As of we left Zariah, sir, it was five shillings the gram, fully refined."

"And this has further to go for that." Alexis returned her gaze to the open crate, then stared at each of the others in turn. "Did your curiosity take you so far as the maths, Brace?"

Brace cleared his throat. "Well, sir, figuring at all the bars being twenty-five percent purity, then it seems like a bit over a hundred thousand pounds per crate. Twelve of them that I can see."

Villar shook his head in wonder. "Over a million pounds value."

"There's all sorts of refiners and processors take a piece along the way, sir," Brace said.

"No doubt." Alexis set the bar she held back in the crate. "See that's sealed up again, Mister Villar."

"Aye, sir."

"And we'll have a pair of Marines full time at the hatch." Alexis frowned. "I'll want you aboard as part of the prize crew, yourself, Brace, to watch over things."

"Aye, sir."

She sighed. "And we must seek to manage the crew's expectations, gentlemen — both the spacers and Marines alike. With this much involved there'll be complications, no doubt, and I'll not have them dividing a million by the crew's two eighths and planning their lives on it."

THIRTEEN

7 OCTOBER, ABOARD *HMS NIGHTINGALE*, DARKSPACE, ENROUTE to Zariah System

"Boosun, sar!" Clanly, the Marine outside Alexis' quarters, called to her.

She looked up from her desk and frowned, wondering just what the man had said. After a moment she deciphered it, though she did begin to wonder if that was indeed Clanly's accent or if the man was somehow playing tricks on her.

"Send him in, Clanly." Alexis waited until the hatch was shut again. "Yes, Mister Ousley?"

The bosun grimaced, cast his eyes to the deck, and took a large breath.

"More, is it?" Alexis asked.

Ousley's breath left him and he seemed to deflate.

"Afraid it is, sir."

Alexis sighed. They were three days from Zariah, sailing back from the Remada Straits with their prize — the *Greenaway*, as some unpurged files and documents aboard the ship had revealed.

Under normal circumstances, she'd have sent a prize crew aboard under Midshipman Spindler and have him sail *Greenaway* back to Zariah then wait there for *Nightingale's* return after patrolling the rest of the systems she was responsible for.

A million and more pounds worth of gallenium was not normal circumstances.

Instead, Villar was in command of the prize with a crew of *Nightingale's* most reliable hands, such as they were, along with Corporal Brace and half the Marines to keep watch over the hold, and both ships were returning to Zariah together. Though she longed to finally get to Dalthus and see her home and family again, *Greenaway's* cargo was one she felt she had to oversee herself.

Unfortunately, Villar's absence left a hole she hadn't expected. It was usually the first lieutenant's task to deal with any issues amongst the crew which couldn't be dealt with by a kick or cuff from the bosun and didn't rise to the level of a formal captain's mast. Truly serious matters would rise to the captain's attention and be dealt with at mast, but that was official, and it was far better to handle minor issues unofficially. Without the captain's official notice.

With Villar gone, though, she didn't feel she could pass that responsibility on to Spindler. Though neither midshipman was yet a commissioned officer, at least Villar had the benefit of age and having, at least temporarily, commanded *Nightingale* himself. The crew would accept things from him that they wouldn't from the far younger Spindler. Which left Alexis in the position of having to deal with some matters without officially noticing them.

"What is it this time?"

"Fighting, sir," Ousley said. "Cosgrove and Scarborough."

Alexis frowned. Cosgrove was a weedy, middle-aged man, barely suited to life aboard ship, while Scarborough was one of the harder men. It seemed odd that Cosgrove would stand up to the larger, tougher man at all, much less fight him long enough for Ousley to find out about it.

"Over what, do you know?"

Ousley nodded. "Gambling, sir." He shrugged. "My mates and

me, we're trying to keep it down, but there's more games going since we took that ship, and more fights over them. This one ... well, sir, it's that Cosgrove had a knife in hand when I come across them."

"A knife? That's cause for a captain's mast, Mister Ousley, not something I can overlook. What brought that on?"

Most fights aboard ship, where rough, hard men were thrust into close quarters with one another, were still simple things. A scuffle, a blow or two exchanged, a bruise or bloodied nose, and then done with. Fights over gambling tended to be more serious, and the gambling itself was discouraged, but for one combatant to have a knife in hand made it far more serious. That rose to attempted murder, which under the Articles, like so many other things, was punishable by death if the captain chose.

The physical punishments aboard ship, such as flogging or the rare hanging, might seem harsh or cruel to those in the Core worlds, but many Fringe worlds had similar consequences built into their charters. For a new colony with few settlers and virtually no infrastructure, devoting time, manpower, and resources to imprisonment or rehabilitation simply wasn't possible. Even older, more settled worlds lacked the necessary resources to devote to such things and would frequently resort to transporting offenders as indentures, shifting their problem to some other world.

Alexis didn't even have that option. *Nightingale's* patrols would take her days or weeks of sailing from any world at all, and none of the worlds she'd frequent had a permanent Naval presence. The most developed was Zariah, and that with only a civilian prize court, entirely unrelated to Naval discipline. Even Zariah was a month's sail from the nearest system with a port admiral and the Navy wouldn't tolerate her leaving her patrol area for so long just for a problem of discipline amongst the crew.

No, it was expected that Alexis, as the ship's commander, would deal with it herself, and they'd given her the power to do so. In a strict reading of the regulations, a captain couldn't order more than two dozen lashes for an offense, nor hang a man without assembling a full court martial of three captains, but with the war on and the fleet stretched so thin, even those protections had been relaxed. That some captains might abuse the power was generally overlooked, unless the offenses were particularly egregious.

She closed her eyes and rubbed her temples for a moment.

"Bring them in."

Ousley returned to the hatch and motioned two men through. A pair of his mates came along, holding the men's arms, despite their hands being bound before them. Both came to stand by Alexis' desk, Cosgrove with a nervous manner, looking down at the deck and refusing to meet Alexis' gaze, Scarborough more confident, shoulders straight, though he, too, kept his eyes downcast.

"Cosgrove and Scarborough, sir," Ousley announced.

The two men stood on the other side of her table, eyes downcast.

"What was this all about then?" Alexis asked.

Cosgrove muttered something and Ousley cuffed the back of his head.

"Speak up, so the captain can hear you!"

"He's a cheat! A bloody cheat!" Cosgrove pointed at Scarborough.

Alexis sighed. Well, of course he would be — it was a small step from extorter to gambling cheat, and likely the one preceded the other. She'd like to have taken this opportunity to punish Scarborough for all he was involved with, but couldn't when the other man had drawn a knife.

"I ain't no cheat!" Scarborough put in. "He owes fair and square!"

"Lads, there're games enough going on aboard ship, I know, this can't be —"

"Took ten thousand pound off'n me!" Cosgrove yelled, trying to lash out at Scarborough, despite cuffs around his wrists and the master's mate holding his arms.

Alexis' eyes widened, as did Ousley's and his mates'. Gambling amongst the crew was common, but usually for very small sums, if there was actual coin involved at all — for the most part, the stakes were a share of the spirits issue or trades of the more onerous duties aboard ship. Ten thousand pounds was, well, it was a ridiculous sum for a common spacer to even speak of, much less wager.

"Bloody gallenium." Alexis rubbed her temples where she felt yet another headache forming. "Mister Ousley, assemble the crew, if you will. It appears I'll have to explain some things to them."

"LADS," Alexis began once the men were assembled, "there're rumors running rampant about the cargo on that ship and we need to set them to rest now."

"Gallenium!" one of the men yelled.

"Bloody fortune!"

"Have y'eard what we'll get fer it? That why we're here?"

"Quiet down!" Ousley bellowed.

When they were quiet again, Alexis wasn't quite sure what to say. Of course there'd been rumors about the cargo, that sort of thing couldn't be stopped — so she couldn't tell them there was no gallenium aboard the other ship, they'd know that to be a lie. Nor could she tell them how much the Prize Court would award, for she didn't know herself. She did know it would be far less than the value and far less than these men were dreaming of — and gambling on.

That, at least, she could address.

"First of all, we've no idea what the Prize Court on Zariah will award for that ship. Most likely the numbers in your head are phantoms — no more tied to reality than Creasy's Dutchman, eh?"

That at least got a chuckle for the crew.

"You've all seen the prize court at work — they're not the most efficient, are they?" That got mutters and nods of agreement. "It could be months or more before they render a judgment, and the sums involved —"

No, she couldn't make the argument that there was so much they'd be getting that they should risk the prize agents on Zariah and sell their certificates before the final judgment was rendered. That would start them speculating all over again.

"We don't know what the sums involved are. The ship's not even a proper prize, more likely salvage, and you know how the Prize Court has its fingers into everything. The gallenium's raw, not properly processed like what the prices are quoted for. It'll have to go through a lot of hands before it can be sold at that price, and you know what that means from other prize cargoes, right?"

"Hands full of sticky bloody fingers!" one of the men yelled.

"Yes," Alexis agreed. "They'll all take a piece, so the ore's worth less than those numbers you've all been thinking. Much less, I'd wager."

There were at least a few nods in the crowd.

"And as for wagering, I'll not have it. Not for these sums and not on my ship." She nodded to Brace, who had his Marines warned and at the ready. This next bit wouldn't sit well with some. "Some of you have been wagering outrageous sums based on this phantom — well, no more. I'm telling you now, that all wagers, won or lost, since we found that ship are void." Many of the crew looked up at that, slow grins starting to grow on their faces. "All of them — large or small — and no more gambling until we've left Zariah and have at least some idea of the sums involved.

"And no payments for past debts, either," she said, going one better. If she could use this to hurt Scarborough and his band further, then she would. "No sippers or gulpers at *Up Spirits*, until we've transitioned from Zariah space again. Those debts, those *legitimate* debts, you'll still owe once we leave, but there'll be no collecting until then."

Most, if not all, of the crew looked quite happy at that, only the cohort of extorters looked displeased. Perhaps, if the crew got a taste of their full spirits ration, they'd not allow those four to go back to their ways.

At least she'd have a more orderly crew until they reached Zariah. After that ... well, with the sums involved, even with all the sticky fingers, she'd be lucky if she had a crew at all. If the payout on that cargo was half what she suspected it really would be, most of the crew would run as soon as they had their prize certificates in hand.

Sell those for a fraction, which'll still be a fortune, and bribe some merchantman sailing for far, far away from New London. The risk of running was high, they'd be severely punished if taken up by a Royal Navy ship again, but the reward ...

Why risk death or injury aboard ship when you've a life's fortune in hand?

FOURTEEN

"Nine hundred pounds?" Alexis stared at the Prize Court's agent, Edric Bramley, in astonishment. She shook her head. "There must be some mistake."

Bramley frowned. He was a fat, florid man, with little hair and hooded eyes. His offices were large and busy, with a number of clerks all hunched over their desks. He acted as factor for several merchants, in addition to being agent for the Prize Court.

"In what way, Lieutenant ... Carew, was it?"

"Yes, sir. Carew."

Bramley's frown deepened. "Why do I know that name? Have we met before, lieutenant?"

"I don't believe so, sir, no."

"No matter, I suppose." He shook his head. "In any case, I did think you'd be pleased that the Court would act so quickly." He ran his finger over his desktop. "Barely three hours' time since you filed your claim and we already have a resolution — a firm resolution, I might add."

"Yes, sir, the speed with which you've resolved this is indeed gratifying, but the amount —"

"I assure you it's all in order, lieutenant. The ship's not a war prize, after all, merely retrieved salvage. Luckily for you and your crew, the shipping company has a factor right here on Zariah who was quick enough to approve a standard settlement." He slid a list of figures across his desktop to Alexis. "The ship's valuation is clear — insured at some four thousand six hundred eighty-two pounds. A salvaged return to the owner at twenty-five percent ... less the Prize Courts twenty percent cost for adjudicating salvage ... leaves a net of nine hundred thirty-six pounds for you and your crew." Bramley smiled. "Not a bad bit of business for the few weeks you've been gone from Zariah, eh, lieutenant?"

"Yes, Mister Bramley, the matter of the ship itself seems in order," Alexis said. It was less than they'd receive from a warship or pirate, taken in action, but she'd expected that, "but is there not still the matter of the *cargo?*"

Bramley looked perplexed.

"Cargo?"

Alexis nodded. "Yes — some eighteen hundred kilograms of gallenium aboard *Greenaway?*"

Bramley stared at her for a moment, then his eyes widened.

"Oh! Oh, yes, I do see ..." He paused. A long pause through which Alexis resisted the urge to hurry him along. "You're unaware, then?"

"It would appear so." Alexis had a sinking feeling in her stomach. She'd warned the crew there might be some difficulty, what with the huge value of the cargo, but this sounded like far more than a difficulty.

"Well, it was made easier to determine this by the shipowner's factor being on station, you understand."

"I still do not, Mister Bramley."

Bramley pursed his lips. "The cargo ... the gallenium ... you see, was under contract by the Crown. From the mines themselves, you understand. *Greenaway*, the ship you salvaged, was merely the conveyance, the shipowner was not the owner of the cargo, you see?"

"The owner of the gallenium ..." Alexis closed her eyes and taking a deep breath as she saw Bramley's meaning.

"Is the Crown, yes. So you do see?"

Alexis nodded, shoulders slumping. "And there being no rights of salvage for a Queen's ship, nor for the Queen's property."

Bramley smiled and nodded. "Not for getting Her Majesty Her own property back, no."

Alexis stared at him for a moment, then covered her face with her hands.

"Bloody bollocks."

THE LONG WALK back to the station's quayside seemed funereal. Alexis was at a loss for what to tell the crew — she'd tried to prepare them for far less than the rumors aboard *Nightingale* suggested, but this?

She took a boat from there, rather than calling for one of *Nightingale's*, and was surprised to find that the pilot was the same who'd first carried her to *Nightingale*, though she shouldn't have been, as there was not so much traffic in the system that more than a few private boatmen could make a living at it.

The man remembered Alexis, too, and tried to strike up a conversation while they made their way to the ship — ships, as *Greenaway* was still at rest very near *Nightingale* — but she couldn't remember a moment later what he asked or what, if anything, she answered. Her thoughts were wholly on her crew and how she could possibly explain the Prize Court's decision.

Once aboard ship, she went immediately to her quarters and called for Villar, Spindler, Brace, and Ousley. They assembled around her table, at first with expectant looks on their faces while Isom served wine, then with troubled looks as Alexis said nothing and they took in the expression on her face. When the wine was served, Alexis raised her glass, drained it in one gulp to fortify herself, and broke the news.

"Gentlemen ... the gallenium is property of the Crown, purchased directly at the mines, and is neither a prize nor salvageable. As a Queen's ship, it was *Nightingale's* duty to recover it ... I suppose we shall have a note or two in our files ensuring Her Majesty's gratitude and such ..." She drew a deep breath, "... but there's not a single pence in the lot of it for us. Only a bit over nine hundred pounds for the ship itself."

There was silence for a moment.

"Bloody bollocks," Ousley muttered. His eyes widened. "Begging your pardon, sir."

"My own sentiments exactly, Mister Ousley." Alexis heard voices from the hatch to her pantry. "Isom, Garcia, not a bloody word of this to the crew before we've sorted out how to tell them, do you hear? I know how word of everything gets about aboard ship, but I'll have none of it with this."

A muffled, "Aye, sir" came from the pantry before Isom appeared with a tray of spirits bottles and glasses. Alexis watched as her officers drained their glasses and set them aside without another word. Isom had rightly determined that they'd all require something stronger to deal with the news.

If we splice the mainbrace on the bell for the next fortnight, perhaps we can keep the crew drunk enough to accept it.

"I am open to suggestions, gentlemen," Alexis said.

"So there's really to be no money?" Spindler asked.

Alexis shook her head. "Little. None for the gallenium at all."

"You'll do alright," Villar muttered.

"I beg your pardon, Mister Villar?"

Villar hunched his shoulders and set his glass down as though he'd already had too much to drink. "I'm sorry, sir, I just meant that the captain's share of this isn't nothing."

Alexis watched him for a moment. Perhaps he'd been counting

on the windfall as well — even a midshipman's portion of what they'd thought the prize might be worth would set a man up for life. Villar wouldn't have had to worry about making lieutenant, he could simply leave the Navy and do whatever he liked. Or perhaps he was simply irked that it was Alexis, not himself, who commanded *Nightingale* at the time the *Greenaway* was taken.

"No, it's not," Alexis agreed, "nor is what you and Mister Spindler and the warrants will share, but we're speaking of the men now, not our own fortunes. They were expecting ... well, lord knows what they were expecting, but it certainly wasn't the two hundred pounds or so their two eighths of this will bring — what will it be for each man? Four pounds?"

"A bit more, but not so much," Ousley said, "enough for a few good drunks in our next ports."

"They wished for more than that," Villar said.

"'If wishes were fishes we'd all have twelve blokes following us about writing down our every word,' as my mum said." Ousley scratched his neck. "They'll forget, given time, as they never had the coin in hand." He nodded to Alexis. "Tell 'em, set sail, and work 'em at the sails and guns until they're too tired to think of it. A fortnight of that, a bit of grumbling, and they'll forget it."

FIFTEEN

31 October, aboard *HMS Nightingale, darkspace,* Dalthus System

"Pilot boat's signaling that we're in the transition zone, sir."

"Thank you, Mister Spindler."

Alexis swallowed and took a deep breath, clenching her hands behind her back. She shouldn't be nervous. This was simply a return home, after all.

A return after nearly three years away.

She'd been just fifteen when she'd gone aboard *Merlin* and still fifteen when she'd sailed off aboard *Hermione* from this very system. Now she was eighteen, and so much had happened to her in that time. Much had happened on Dalthus, as well, and she wondered if it would still feel like her home after so much time away.

"Make transition," she ordered.

Inside the quarterdeck, there was no sense of the change other than the sudden appearance of new activity on the monitors. Even before the spacer at the helm responsible for transitioning the ship to normal-space could announce that it was complete, *Nightingale's* sensors woke after their long sleep in *darkspace* and began receiving signals from around the system. The navigation plot changed from its display of only the ship's course and an estimation of Lagrangian points near them to a plot of the Dalthus system itself.

Alexis almost gasped in shock. When she'd left home it had been rare to have two ships in-system at the same time — a half dozen at most. Now there were dozens. Not all of them were for sailing the Dark, but there were still more contacts on the navigation plot than she'd ever thought to see in Dalthus.

The biggest change was the partially assembled station in orbit around the planet. Two merchant vessels were docked to it, probably delivering more materials for its construction. Another three merchantmen — big, wallowing ore carriers such as they'd encountered in the straits — were in orbit around one of the moons. Her grandfather had written her that they'd decided to use that moon for the transshipment of gallenium mined in the system's asteroid belt.

There'd be a second station going into orbit there soon. Small, with just enough space to house a proper customs house to deal with the gallenium shipments. Loading merchantmen there instead of directly in the belt would avoid some of the smuggling, since several of Dalthus' first settlers had already proven themselves willing to do that.

The majority of the ships were small miners, made for intrasystem work and not intended to sail the Dark at all. They'd be owned by the miners themselves, broken down to fit in the holds of ships capable of traversing *darkspace*, then reassembled here as their owners hoped to make their fortunes.

A few of these were enroute from the belt to the moon with loads of gallenium ore, or on their way back to the belt from dropping one off. Still there were plenty of them in the belt itself. Enough even to make the empty sections of the belt stand out — those claimed by the families who'd been involved with Daviel Coalson in the secret mining of gallenium. Aside from the punishments handed out to those who were proved to be involved in that scheme, the families had been banned from mining their claims for five years.

"Make for orbit," Alexis ordered, still staring at the plot.

"Aye, sir."

"And I'll have the mast unstepped as we make our way."

A barely perceptible pause before Villar's "Aye, sir," let her know that he was as weary of that sort of order as Alexis. Unstepping the mast, taking in all sail, and laying the mast down flat against the hull, wasn't strictly necessary in-system, nor were the frequent sail changes she'd ordered on their way here from Zariah, but it did exercise the crew's sail handling skills, and lord knew they needed it.

She caught Villar's eye and he flushed, looking away. They both knew the faults in the crew's handling of the ship's sails and guns, but Alexis wished there was a way to correct them that wasn't seen as a constant criticism of Villar's time in command. She felt that every drill she ordered increased the tension between her and her first officer.

"Signals away, sir," Creasy said from the signals console.

"Thank you, Creasy." Alexis nodded absently.

Nightingale's signals computer would have sent off its messages automatically as they transitioned. With no other way to communicate across light-years, the messages had to be carried by ships. Automatically loaded into the ship's secure storage by Zariah Station, any bound for Dalthus or for ships known to be in-system would soon be delivered. Those bound for other destinations might have copies sent to those merchantmen in system who were advertising their own destinations or at least the direction of their future travels. At any moment, the same message might be aboard a dozen or more different ships, to be delivered by whichever arrived at a destination first — and then further notices sent out to reach and delete-as-delivered as many of those copies as possible.

Her own message to her grandfather would be among those just sent, informing him that she was finally back and would be home soon. She wondered what might have changed there, as well.

"Will you be granting leave, sir?" Villar asked. "Or allowing boats to come alongside, at least?"

Alexis noted the quarterdeck's crew's sudden attention at Villar's question and suppressed a smile. The entire crew was tired after the long trek from Zariah, made more so by the drills Alexis had set them along the way.

Near daily gun drills and sudden, random calls to change sail or tack the ship, had worn heavily on them. They'd improved — a bit — but were still the sorriest lot of spacers she'd ever laid eyes on. Some slow of body, due to age or weakness, others slow of mind — and those who weren't either of those were often simply the laziest sods she could wish to encounter.

The extortionists were in the latter category, holding back, both she and Ousley were certain, but never more than the others. Instead of setting an example, they were taking advantage of the others weaknesses to lay off their own efforts.

Still, most of the crew had worked hard, despite the poor results, and deserved a bit of a break. There was just something missing that she couldn't put her finger on — some spark that would drive them to more than their best, as she'd gotten from crews on other ships.

She examined the unexpectedly crowded navigation plot. She'd been planning to allow the men leave in Port Arthur, thinking it would be much the same as when she'd left home, but there was so much new traffic in the system that she feared some of the men would run.

"Half a day for each watch," she said, making a decision. "At my grandfather's holding, not in port." She sensed shoulders slump in disappointment all around her. "There'll be good, fresh food and the village pub, but no … livelier establishments."

Villar nodded.

"And no outbound merchantmen with a suddenly filled cot," he murmured.

"Exactly."

ALEXIS FOUND the surface of Dalthus as much changed as the system's space. She stopped at the bottom of *Nightingale's* boat's ramp to stare around her in wonder. She'd seen far more advanced systems in her travels, and Dalthus was still far from advanced, but this was home, and the changes were ... disconcerting.

When she'd left, Dalthus had boasted of three antigrav transporters to ferry goods and people about the planet's surface. Those and the two small craft attached to the system's pilot boat were the only permanent aircraft.

Now there were a dozen or more craft in the skies above Port Arthur, and more ships' boats on the landing field than she'd ever imagined she'd see on her home world. Motorized, wheeled, and antigrav ground vehicles were more numerous as well, scurrying about the field and off down the town's streets, most making to and from the nearby chandlery, but others merging with the traffic of the town itself.

She moved away from the ramp so that Villar could step onto the field. Ousley and the hands exited via the boat's rear ramp and were already forming up to visit the chandlery for *Nightingale's* resupply.

"It's much changed since I left," Alexis said to explain her gawking to Villar.

"How long ago was that, if you don't mind me asking, sir?"

"Just a bit over three years." She looked around again, taking in the bustle of activity and noting that the town itself had expanded to encircle more of the landing field and with more new construction visible at the edges. "It's much changed," she repeated.

"Much changed in the year or more I've been aboard *Nightingale*, as well," Villar noted. He pointed to some of the new buildings encircling the field. "Chandlery's put a second warehouse off over there some six months past, and with it came more pubs and br ... er, establishments of interest to the spacers and miners."

"I'm familiar with the sorts of establishments frequented by spacers, Mister Villar."

"I ... er, see, sir."

Alexis glanced over to see what had discomfited him further and her lips twitched.

"That is," she said, "I am *aware* of such establishments, if not familiar with them."

Villar cleared his throat. "Of course, sir. I didn't wish to imply that you'd ... well ..."

Now Alexis flushed, remembering more than one visit to such a place on Penduli Station while awaiting the return of her second ship, *HMS Hermione*. It had only been a bit of comfort and talking to a willing listener during a very difficult time, but the visit itself would likely not improve Villar's opinion of her.

"So the chandlery has two warehouses now?" she asked quickly.

"It does, sir," Villar confirmed, just as quickly. "Though the Naval stores are still served out of just one."

"May I presume that's where I'll find Mister Doakes still?"

Alexis wasn't looking forward to seeing the colony's chandler and Crown representative again. When she'd last met the man just before joining her first ship he'd been not only been rude and dismissive of the idea that she might become a midshipman, but he'd outfitted her in the most ridiculously oversized kit she could imagine.

The spacers aboard Merlin *could have made a whole other uniform from the material left after they tailored mine down to size.*

She smiled at the memory of her first day aboard ship, jumpsuit sleeves and legs rolled up to fit while she waited for others to be altered. Her uniforms now had been tailored to order, specifically made up for her small frame on Lesser Ichthorpe while she'd awaited her next assignment.

Still, the memory of Doakes' dismissive attitude burned a bit and she wondered if even properly fitting uniforms and command of a Queen's ship would change it. If it weren't necessary, she wouldn't meet with the man at all, but he was the Crown representative, such as it was, on Dalthus.

When visiting other systems she might meet with a planetary governor or some other official, but Dalthus' government, what there was of it, was quite decentralized. Most decisions were made by the three thousand original settlers, or their heirs, by vote of shares in the colony corporation, and within certain limitations each settler ran his own lands as he saw fit.

The few areas that were considered the property of the colony as a whole, such as Port Arthur itself, had government councils for internal matters; but trade and relations with the Crown went through the Doakes family, by virtue of the few colony shares they'd used to purchase the ninety-nine-year chandlery lease when the planet was settled.

Alexis took a deep breath. Ousley was already leading the men toward the chandlery warehouse to begin loading *Nightingale's* supplies.

"Let us make our courtesy call upon the Crown representative, Mister Villar," she said, starting toward the edge of the landing field and the street which led to the chandlery's front entrance, then continued under her breath, "And see if his opinion of me has improved at all."

SIXTEEN

31 October, Port Arthur, Dalthus System

"Miss Alexis!"

Alexis stopped, eyebrows rising. She was a bare two steps through the chandlery's door, Villar was still in the doorway behind her, and the chimes of the door's arrival bell still rang in her ears, yet Doakes was already around his counter and heading her way, a wide, tooth-filled grin on his pinched, narrow face.

The chandlery itself was much as she remembered it, though now as busy as the town outside, with merchant spacers and more roughly dressed men Alexis took for miners milling about its aisles of shelves piled high with goods. This smiling, enthusiastic Doakes, though, was far different from the chandler she'd last had dealings with.

"Miss Alexis!" Doakes cried again, coming toward her with one hand outstretched to shake hers and the other raised as though to pull her into an embrace. "Been waiting for this since I read of your appointment in dispatches and the pilot boat announced you'd arrived!"

Alexis was about to pull back in alarm, regardless of Villar being immediately behind her in the doorway, when Doakes came to an abrupt halt. He squared his shoulders, head and neck straight and rigid, and lowered his hands to his side. His expression turned serious.

"Or should it be 'Captain Carew', now, eh? What with a ship of your own and all?" he asked, then his grin broke out again and he reached forward to grasp her hand in both of his before she could even think more about turning and running down Villar to escape. "No, no, it'll always be 'Miss Alexis' to old Talmadge Doakes, it will."

His beady eyes darted about the room and he spoke again, loudly.

"Known you since you were a wee lass, have I not, Miss Alexis?" Most of the shoppers had stopped what they were doing and were now looking toward Alexis. Doakes raised his voice even further. "Now you're a grand Naval officer, and just imagine it was me what gave you your first midshipman's uniform. Right in this very chandlery, it was — not three years past, I think."

"Gave" is not exactly how I'd desc — but even her thought was cut off as Doakes continued. Nearly all the shoppers were watching curiously now.

"Read your doings in that dustup in those fruity French worlds in the Naval Gazette, I did."

"The Berry March, Mister Doakes," Alexis said.

Doakes waved a hand. "Called your grandfather straightaway I read it. Said to him, I said, 'I knew that girl would do great things, ever since she brought in those little bushels of wheat from a field she'd sown all by her lonesome.'" He looked past Alexis to Villar, still not releasing her hand. "No more than knee-high, she was, and already working at what she put her mind to."

Alexis flushed and cleared her throat, pulling against Doakes' grip to retrieve her hand. She was having a great deal of trouble reconciling this Doakes with the one who'd threatened to put her over his knee when he believed she was playing a game with him by asking for a midshipman's kit. The change in his attitude had her torn between amusement and irritation with the man.

"Thank you, Mister Doakes, that's very kind of you to —"

"And look at you all grown up now," Doakes went on. He looked down at her and his brow furrowed. "Well, older, as may be, at least." He nodded to Villar. "With a bright, young midshipman of your own, I see. Not that you weren't doing a fine job yourself, Mister Villar, since Lieutenant Bensley left us, but, well ..." He reached past Alexis to pat Villar on the shoulder. "You just watch our Miss Alexis, young man, and she'll show you how it's done proper, I'm sure."

Villar raised an eyebrow and Alexis flushed further.

"Mister Doakes, we really should —"

"Lo, but you've come a long way! Why, I remember how you looked coming out of my office in that first uniform, sleeves and cuffs rolled up to fit and beret sliding down —"

"Mister Doakes! We have the business of my ship and the port to discuss, if I'm not mistaken."

Doakes broke off, then nodded sharply and spun to walk back toward his counter.

"Oh, indeed! Straight to business — you must be busy, what with your ship patrolling from Zariah on out." He called loudly toward the back of the shop. "Thomas! Watch the counter, boy, I've Naval matters to discuss with these officers!" Then louder to the shoppers. "This girl'll be Admiral of the Fleet one day, you lot mark my words and remember it was me what sold her her first beret, it was!"

ALEXIS FOLLOWED Doakes into the chandlery's rear, to a small office near the warehouse and store yard that backed up to the landing field. Once out of sight of the shoppers, at least his pronouncements seemed to be at an end.

"I've wine, if you like," Doakes said once they were settled. "Bit early here in port for it, but your ship's time may be different. Or Thomas can bring tea, if you like."

"Tea, if it's not too much trouble," Alexis said. Doakes' weasely, pointed nose was twitching and she wanted her wits about her. In fact, she noted, there was a remarkable resemblance between Doakes and the damned creature sharing her cabin aboard *Nightingale*.

Perhaps I could give him ... no, that would be cruel to the creature.

Alexis and Villar settled into their chairs, accepted tea from the harried Thomas, who Doakes then sent scurrying back to wait on customers in the chandlery, and began reviewing a rather long list of complaints Doakes had compiled. Alexis glanced at Villar to gauge his reaction, it being her first time meeting with a colonial representative. Villar, for his part, seemed to find Doakes' list quite ordinary.

"Four ships gone missing in this last year," Doakes said. "Five with that *Greenaway*, and now we've reason to suspect piracy and not misfortune."

Alexis blinked. For Doakes to know about *Greenaway*, he'd have to have read all of her dispatches in the few hours' time it had taken *Nightingale* to reach orbit and send a boat down. As she pondered that, Doakes went on, briefing her on news of Dalthus and the surrounding *darkspace* in a surprisingly efficient manner. It was, admittedly, her first such briefing by a colonial representative, but what she found most astonishing was that Doakes managed without ... well, being Doakes. It was as though he were an entirely different person in this capacity.

Perhaps he takes his duties as Crown representative more seriously than his personal stake in the chandlery.

"Is five an unusually high number?" Alexis asked, as Doakes seemed to be winding down his report.

"It may not be so many, sir," Villar put in. "Other than *Greenaway*, the others are only missing or overdue."

"Oh, true enough," Doakes said. "A storm, poor winds — chance of a cargo off his normal route."

"So it can't be certain piracy was involved — or that they're even truly missing at all," Villar maintained. "Other than *Greenaway*, I mean, sir."

"You listen to Miss Alexis when it comes to pirates," Doakes said. "She's seen her share and more, she has."

Villar flushed. "I didn't mean to —"

"It's quite all right, Mister Villar," Alexis said. "I do take your meaning. The only thing we know for certain is that *Greenaway* was attacked — these other ships might well have gone out of touch for other reasons. Still, we've had piracy in this area before."

"Since the founding, off and on," Doakes said, nodding. "Miss Alexis knows all about that — put paid to some of the bastards her very own self, she did."

"Do you suppose it might be some of the same band, Mister Doakes?" Alexis asked, hoping to get the conversation back on track.

Doakes straightened and squared his shoulders, as though happy she'd sought his opinion. "Could be, could be indeed." Then he paused. "Or some new blokes, of course."

Alexis frowned. There was nothing, really, in all Doakes had said which they didn't already know. Some indeterminate number of ships gone missing, and *Greenaway* had proven there was at least one pirate operating in the area.

If it were more of the same band, then there could be a further connection to families on Dalthus. The Coalsons and others had ties to such criminals, as she'd found before. Investigating this now might mean having to deal with them — something Alexis didn't relish.

If I never breathe the same air as another Coalson, I shall be quite happy.

"You mentioned difficulties with the miners — something you thought *Nightingale* might assist with. What was that?"

"Well, now," Doakes said, "most of those lads are all right, you see. They're rowdy, sure, and not from Dalthus, but they have coin and they're free with it — something there's no shop or pub in Port Arthur you'll find objecting to.

"Two, though, there's been more than a spot of trouble with," he went on. "They run claims in the belt together and cause no end of trouble here in Port Arthur." He took a large gulp of tea. "The town's told them they're not welcome no more, but they turn up again. No place to lock them up for more than a few nights and no way to stop them at the field, what with it being so open."

Alexis frowned. "So they've been told to leave the system and refused?"

"Ignored's more like. They nod and take off back to their ship, then do their mining and return as though we'd said nothing. It's only when there's trouble that we — meanin' the town — even know they're back. Not the first we've had trouble with, neither, but they're the worst." He raised an eyebrow and nodded to Villar.

"I remember, Mister Doakes," Villar said, then to Alexis, "The miners who've come are an independent lot and they know Dalthus has no ships of its own to patrol the system's space. So there's no way for the government here, what there is of it —" He cleared his throat. "Meaning no offense, sir, you being from here, but the, shall we say, casual structure of governance on Dalthus does make things a bit difficult."

"No offense taken, Mister Villar," Alexis assured him. "If these miners are something *Nightingale* must deal with, then I'll find it useful to understand your frustrations." She shrugged. "I am forced to admit my own understanding of our government here never got much past that there'd be a conclave of holders every five years."

"Not much more to it than that, Miss Alexis," Doakes said. "And there's the problem. The holders run their lands, Port Arthur and the few other towns not on held lands have a bit of a council, but dealings with off system bits, visiting ships and such, it's always been just the chandlery's job." He straightened. "Proud to say my family and I've done well at that since founding, but ..." He shrugged and gestured in the direction of the landing field. "A visiting merchant or indenture ship at a time's far different than that ... that gaggle out there."

Alexis nodded. Much as she might still not think too kindly of Doakes, she could see his point. "It's just you then? To deal with all visiting ships?"

"Visiting, *and* the miners who take residence in the belt, *and* the construction crews for the stations who come down for leave, *everything* in and out of Port Arthur." Doakes shook his head sadly. "There's contraband come in and out, no doubt. Untaxed goods and more."

"It almost sounds as though it's time for a proper customs house, as other worlds have," Alexis said.

"And haven't I said that these two years past?" Doakes said. "But the holders, those with lands and not just us who had a few shares and made a life in Port Arthur, they only see the expense and, well, there's some don't like it on principle. 'Start of a bloody bureaucracy,' they call it."

"I sent messages to these two miners when last *Nightingale* was in system, sir," Villar put in. "They weren't planetside, but out in the belt at their claim. Made it clear they were to tear down their ships and have them packed aboard the first available transport for some other system."

"And they have not?" Alexis asked Doakes.

"Headed right in from the belt as soon as *Nightingale* cleared the Lagrangian point and left last time," Doakes said. "Near burned poor Neil Grayson's pub to the bloody ground, they did."

Villar flushed.

"What consequences did you state they'd incur for staying?" Alexis asked.

Villar flushed more. "Consequences, sir?"

"Well, yes, you ordered them to leave, so what were they told would happen if they didn't?"

"I —" Villar frowned. "Well, it was a Queen's officer telling them to clear out, I —" He broke off and looked away.

"If they've no regard for Mister Doakes and the leaders of Port Arthur telling them the same, it's no wonder they ignored a Queen's ship on her way out of the system. Especially if there's nothing concrete for them to be afraid of."

"There's little we can do to them, sir," Villar said. "*Nightingale's* writ is smuggling and piracy, which they've not engaged in. I don't know what consequences we could impose, come to that. The belt's huge and if they turn off their transponders they could play hide-and-seek for months with *Nightingale* never sighting them. We'd have to resume our patrol some time. And, even caught, we can't transport them ourselves."

"Well, there must be something we can do. Perhaps we can come up with it before these troublemakers return and —"

"Oh, they're here now, and if it's a talking-to you'd like to give them, Miss Alexis, that can be arranged."

"It can?"

"Oh, aye, tore up a broth ... er, a ladies' house, that is. Tore it up something fierce just two nights past."

"And they're still on planet, then?"

Doakes nodded.

"Right at the back of the chandlery here," he said. "There's a bonding cage I keep them as gives us trouble in if there's no cargoes for it. Have to let 'em out after no more than seventy-two hours, as that's the most the Conclave's voted a man may be boxed up for unless he's slated for the transports — and I can't send 'em on those, as they've not signed the Charter, see?"

SEVENTEEN

Doakes led them from his office deeper into the chandlery's warehouse. Stacks of incoming and outgoing goods filled the space, along with a mélange of scents. Alexis spotted tall stacks of *varrenwood* boards awaiting export, most of which might well have come from her grandfather's lands. Beyond those were piles of bulk grains from Dalthus' fields, headed for far hungrier worlds.

Nearest the doors leading to the chandlery's outdoor storage and then the landing field were a series of large wire cages used for bonded goods or those too valuable to leave loose in the warehouse while waiting to be picked up.

All during the walk, Alexis wracked her brain for what she'd do with the two miners. She'd spoken quickly enough to Villar about consequences, but in truth there was little she could do. They'd broken none of the Kingdom's laws in the space around Dalthus, nor certainly in *darkspace*, where *Nightingale's* true authority lie. It was up to the colonies themselves to make laws and enforce them on the surface, but only for citizens. The sudden influx of miners and construction workers for the stations, none of whom had signed the colonial charter and agreed to be bound by it, made for a difficult situation.

Many other worlds did impose their laws on visitors, but Dalthus had been founded by an independent-minded lot who felt the best thing they could do with those who didn't wish their governance was to ask them to move along — with, apparently, little thought for those who might simply refuse to do so.

As they neared the cage the two miners were locked up in, she was no closer to a solution. She doubted any, as Doakes had put it, "talking to", would at all move the men.

The cage the two were in was a mere three meters square with walls of wire mesh and a single locking door. It was in the middle of a row of similar cages, those stuffed full of valuable goods. Theirs, though, was empty save for a pair of cots, a jug of water, and a bucket.

"It not being a proper cell," Doakes said as they drew near, "there was still a need for the necessaries, you understand?" He nodded to the bucket.

"Of course."

The two men were lying on the cots. They eyed the approaching group — one with both eyes, though they were hooded with sleep and the after effects of drink, the other with the one good eye which wasn't swollen shut by a livid, purple bruise — but didn't rise.

Doakes led Alexis and Villar up to the cage's door and gestured.

"Iveson and Spracklen, Miss Carew," he said, pointing at each in turn. "For whatever good it might do you to have them named."

Alexis stared at them for a moment, saying nothing.

The man with two good eyes rose and approached the cage's door.

"Time for us to go already, Doakes? We was just settled in for a good rest, seems like."

"Past time for you to go, Iveson," Doakes said. "You've fines and damages to settle, as well."

Iveson shrugged. "Send the reckoning. We've enough coin, what with our strike." He grinned. "See you next load, eh, Doakes?"

"You're not welcome here."

"Our coin's welcome enough." Iveson turned his gaze to Villar and squinted. "You that bloke what squawked at us back a few weeks?"

Villar straightened and his eyes narrowed. "Midshipman Villar, then commander of Her Majesty's Ship *Nightingale* — and you, sir, were instructed to leave the Dalthus system forthwith."

Iveson's drooping eyelids lowered further and he pursed his lips.

"For what?"

"Forth*with*, sir!"

"With what?"

"Bloody —"

"A moment, Mister Villar," Alexis said, laying a hand on Villar's arm. She wasn't certain, but believed Iveson was playing with Villar, winding him up a bit, and even if not, there was nothing useful to be gained in continuing down that path.

"Brought yer lil' sister?" Iveson asked.

Villar made to answer, but Alexis squeezed his arm and he broke off.

"Mister Iveson, it's been requested that you leave the Dalthus system," Alexis said, "and yet you —"

"Who're you again?"

"Lieutenant Alexis Carew, commander of Her Majesty's Ship *Nightingale*, and senior Naval officer in-system. It's been requested that you —"

"Thought he was captain o' that glorified rowboat," Iveson interrupted, looking at Villar. Then he looked at Alexis and back to Villar. His face broke in a wide grin. "Oh, that must gall, lad."

Villar's face flushed and Alexis took a deep breath.

"Mister Iveson, will you leave the Dalthus system?"

Iveson inhaled deeply through his nose then made a rattling noise in his throat before spitting on the floor near Alexis' feet. He turned his back on them and threw himself down on his cot, fingers laced behind his head.

"We like it here, Spracklen and me. Don't you worry, Doakes, nor you, neither, little girl. We'll off to the belt soon as we've rested and not trouble you for a fortnight or more."

Alexis felt her fingers twitch and forced her hand to remain at her side despite the sudden desire to pull her small flechette pistol from its hidden pocket at the back of her uniform jacket. She'd felt the urge to deal with things through violence more and more often of late and that disturbed her — despite its having been effective at times.

It's not as though I can simply shoot everyone who annoys me and
—

"You bugger off, too, Mister Midshipman Squawky Man," Iveson said, "and let us sleep." He frowned and raised his head, running his eyes over Alexis. "Leave your sister, if you like, we've a bit of coin left."

It is not *as though I can simply shoot everyone.*

Alexis gripped Villar's arm tighter as he started to speak and Doakes stared at the floor as though he'd like to sink into it.

"Sorry, Miss Alexis, they're —"

"It's all right, Mister Doakes," she said quietly, not taking her eyes from Iveson, who'd laid back down and closed his own eyes. The other one, Spracklen, seemed to be seeking sleep as well. "Though I do see your difficulty."

Doakes nodded. "The Charter never imagined these miners and such coming temporary-like."

Alexis took a deep breath and let it out slowly, then gestured for Doakes and Villar to follow her a few steps away from the cage.

"The further difficulty," Alexis went on once out of earshot of the two miners, "is that I'm unsure of what use *Nightingale* might be to you in this regard." She frowned. "I've no authority on the planet's surface, save over my own crew, and little enough in the system's space — if they were engaging in piracy or smuggling, perhaps." She raised an eyebrow in query to Doakes.

"No, Miss Alexis, nothing like that. They work their own claim and bring their gallenium in to sell the lot all legal-like. It's only in the pubs and houses where they cause trouble."

Alexis sighed. "Then I'm not at all sure what use I can be, Mister Doakes, much as I might like to be. Their little mining rigs aren't *darkspace* capable, so *Nightingale* can't escort them to some other system — even had I cause. I suppose we could inspect their ships and hold them up a bit in being about their business, but even at that they've only to wait us out. *Nightingale* must continue her patrol and they'll be free to do as they please again."

Doakes sighed and hung his head. "I understand, Miss Alexis — it's no more than Mister Villar and Lieutenant Bensley have said before." He glanced back at the cage. "Folks in the pubs and houses are fed up, though. If they refuse service those two go on a tear, or get drunk and wreck the place anyways. Girls're afraid to say yes or no to the bastards."

Alexis grimaced. She wished there was something she could do, but it wasn't as though she could simply pack the pair up and —

She paused, frowned, and caught her lower lip between her teeth.

"Mister Villar, would you be so kind as to summon Mister Ousley — and some few of the hands as he can spare from loading the boat. Sturdy, reliable hands, if you please."

"Aye, sir."

Alexis ignored his questioning looks while they waited for the bosun to make his way across the landing field from *Nightingale's* boat. She spent the time waiting in thought about whether this was a wise course of action or not.

Certainly not ... these two are trouble, no matter where they go, I imagine, and I've enough of that sort. She glanced over at Doakes. *But Port Arthur has no means at all of handling them.*

Ousley and two of his mates arrived. Iveson opened his eyes and looked up at the approaching footsteps, then furrowed his brow and sat. He slapped a hand into Spracklen's leg and they both stood, eyeing bosun warily.

"Sir?" Ousley asked.

"Stand by, Mister Ousley, we'll have need of you in a moment."

"Aye, sir."

Alexis led the way back to the caged miners.

"Mister Iveson, Mister Spracklen, your presence is unwelcome in the Dalthus system and Port Arthur. I'll ask you one last time if you're willing to leave of your own accord."

"Or what? You'll have your bully-boys give us a beating?" Iveson rolled his shoulders and twisted his neck from side to side, cracking it. Spracklen said nothing, but pressed his fists into opposite palms, cracking his knuckles. "A bit of a dustup's a good night for us." He nodded to Ousley. "All at once or one at a time, then?"

"Sir?" Ousley asked, keeping his eyes on the two miners.

"Very well, then." Alexis sighed. She hadn't really expected the bosun's presence to make a difference, but it had been worth a try to give the two men a last chance. She pulled out her tablet and searched it quickly. "Mister Doakes, you are the Crown representative on Dalthus?"

"I am, Miss Alexis, you know that."

"And are you familiar with Article Thirty-Four of the Crown representative's duties?"

Doakes frowned and scratched his neck. "Well, we've not had cause to be taking on all of the —"

Alexis handed her tablet to Doakes, who scanned it for a moment, then his eyes widened and he looked at the two miners, face breaking out in a wide grin.

"Oh, I'm bloody well familiar with it now, I am."

"What are you on about, little girl?" Iveson asked.

Alexis ignored him. "Mister Doakes, do you agree that these two are able-bodied, experienced spacers?"

"I do indeed."

"And that the exigencies of the current conflict with Hanover and the needs of Her Majesty's Naval Service outweigh any benefit these two represent to Dalthus?"

"Worthless pair of buggers, aye."

Iveson's eyes grew wide. "Wait —"

"I believe the third paragraph is what you need, Mister Doakes," Alexis prompted.

Doakes scanned down the tablet and nodded. "Oh, aye." He cleared his throat and grinned at the pair in the cage as he read. "Iveson and Spracklen, the needs of Her Majesty being paramount, do you wish to voluntarily enter into Her Naval Service at this time?"

"I bloody well don't!" Iveson yelled.

Alexis reached into a pouch at her belt and pulled out two coins, holding them up for the pair to see.

"The joining bounty's a full guinea," she said, "the Service is a far better life as a volunteer, gentlemen, I assure you."

"You can't!"

"My dear Mister Iveson, the Impressment Article is quite clear. A Crown representative may impress spacers to the benefit of the Service virtually at will."

"We're not spacers, we're miners!"

Alexis frowned. "Mister Villar?"

She found Villar staring at her open-mouthed, but he quickly closed it as she turned to him.

"Sir?"

"You're familiar with the Dalthus system, I believe?"

"Ah ... I am, sir, somewhat, I suppose."

"Sailed to the belt here, have you?"

Villar nodded. "I have, sir."

Alexis furrowed her brow. "Enlighten me, then, if you will. In the belt, that rather large void between all of the rocks, what is that called?"

"Ah ... that would be called space, sir." He cleared his throat and pursed his lips, seeming to finally find the situation amusing instead of shocking and trying not to show it.

"And what would one call those who spend the majority of their time in such a place?"

"I believe the term for one such as that would be *spacer*, sir."

Alexis turned to the men in the cage and smiled pleasantly.

"There, now, we've settled that, haven't we?"

"Bloody —" Spracklen muttered, speaking for the first time.

"You can't do this! We'll file suit, we will!"

Alexis nodded. "I'm sure you will, just as soon as you're allowed off *Nightingale*. At Zariah station. Some ten or so weeks from today — provided we have decent winds." She held up the two coins again. "Now, will you be signing on as volunteers and taking the joining bounty?" She rubbed the coins together, two guineas, one for each of the men. "Or will it be the Impressment Articles for you?"

Spracklen sighed, shrugged, and held out his hand. "I'll sign." Iveson glared at him. "It's not as though we've a choice — and a guinea's a guinea."

EIGHTEEN

"Those two'll be trouble," Villar said as he and Alexis made their way back to the chandlery's front.

Ousley and his mates left with *Nightingale's* new recruits between them — each of the men's arms tightly clasped by a bosun's mate, while Doakes gleefully led Alexis and Villar out of the warehouse to the shop floor. As they came around the counter into the shop proper, the chandlery's door opened.

Alexis glanced that way, then froze, struggling to keep her face impassive as she saw the man in the doorway.

The last time she'd seen Edmon Coalson she'd been threatening to have him hung for striking her in her role as a Queen's officer if he didn't tell her where his father, Daviel, had run to — and that after she'd dumped a pot of tea over his head when he'd come courting her.

More than that she'd later fired a broadside of *HMS Merlin's* guns into the father's fleeing boat, destroying it and horribly maiming the man. In fact, for years she'd thought him dead, until encountering him again in Hanoverese space — where she'd rectified the oversight by setting him adrift in *darkspace* after he confessed to his and his own father's roles in the deaths of Alexis' grandmother and parents.

She still had nightmares about that act. Being lost in *darkspace*, where everything, even one's thoughts, was slowed by the effects of so much dark matter, was a fate spacers feared beyond all else. Many would dump the air from their vacsuits if they suspected their ship would not turn around to retrieve them, rather than suffer longer.

But cruel as that fate was, and much as it made her sick to have done it, Alexis forced herself not to regret it.

If ever a man deserved that and more, it was Daviel Coalson. I only wish I could have sent his father, Rashae, to join him for his role in grandmother's death. She sighed. *And now comes Edmon.*

Alexis braced herself as the son of the man she'd killed sighted her and strode forward. Four others entered behind him and she regretted not moving to immediately put her back to something. She stiffened her shoulders, settling her uniform jacket and grateful for the weight of the tiny flechette pistol she kept tucked in a hidden pocket at the small of her back. She didn't think Coalson would attack her openly, that really wasn't his family's way, but she wanted to be prepared.

Coalson strode toward her, the men following him spread out to either side.

Beside her Villar stiffened, as though he sensed something of her tension.

"Sir," he whispered, "should I call for Mister Ousley and some hands?"

Alexis shook her head minutely — grateful for Villar's support, but knowing whatever happened would be over before the bosun could arrive back from *Nightingale's* boat. Instead she watched Coalson approach.

Neither time nor the disgrace and death of his father appeared to have either diminished the Coalson's family fortunes or improved Edmon's taste in clothing. Alexis was certain everything he wore was both expensive and imported — from the shiny material of his trousers to the garish, orange and blue pattern of his jacket. Likely someone, somewhere thought it the height of fashion, as the four men with Coalson were dressed similarly.

They were all of an age with Coalson and Alexis recognized two of them, sons and younger sons of families the Coalsons had been allied with since the colony's founding.

Coalson stopped a bare pace from Alexis.

"Carew."

"Mister Coalson," she answered, nodding politely. Inside, her stomach clenched.

"I wasn't sure it was you, when the notice of your ship's arrival was signaled." He took a deep breath and raised his hand midway between them. "I'm happy I was in town to greet you."

Alexis stared at the hand for a moment, then blinked.

Coalson cleared his throat. "Ah ... is that not the proper greeting for a Naval officer?" he asked. "I don't suppose I should salute, not being one myself and all."

Alexis blinked again and looked from his hand to his face. His expression was bland, perhaps slightly amused, but not at all antagonistic. His hand appeared to hold no weapon, though she wasn't sure she could rule out some sort of contact poison when dealing with the Coalsons. She reached out tentatively and took it.

"No," she said, hesitating. "No saluting — this is quite proper." Her brow furrowed. She released his hand and resisted the urge to wipe it on her trousers just in case.

The very best *encounter I've ever had with Edmon Coalson ended with my pouring a pot of tea over his head. Cordiality is ... quite unexpected.*

"It would be lieutenant," Villar said from beside her, "as a form of address, Mister Coalson, or captain, as she commands a ship."

Coalson turned his gaze to Villar and Alexis thought she detected the slightest tightening around his eyes.

"Both lieutenant and captain?" He laughed. "The things the Navy manages." Coalson looked Villar up and down. "Is that why your own insignia's changed, young man? Weren't you a lieutenant as well, last you were here? What is it now?"

Villar flushed and tensed, whether from the reminder of his reversion in rank or at being called "young man" by someone younger than him.

"Midshipman."

"I see." Coalson returned his attention to Alexis. "I'll not keep you long ... lieutenant, I expect you'll be visiting your home holding soon, but will you be returning to Port Arthur before you sail on?"

Alexis hesitated — she was uncomfortable saying anything about her plans to a Coalson, but couldn't think of a way to put him off without being rude. A quick glance around the chandlery showed that the conversation had attracted more attention from those shopping. Coalson himself was being nothing but polite and proper, so any rudeness on her part would only reflect poorly on the Navy and the Crown.

"As soon as my ship has taken on supplies, yes."

Coalson glanced around the chandlery as well.

"I have a dinner party scheduled in five days' time." He nodded toward the men who accompanied him. "Myself and some other younger holders." He squared his shoulders. "Or holders' sons — they've not all come into their lands as I have, but they will one day." He smiled. "The future of Dalthus, as it were."

"We'd be honored did you attend. There've been many changes on Dalthus these past years, with more to come, and we'd value your insights — as a Naval officer and representative of the Crown, so to speak."

Doakes cleared his throat.

"Meaning no diminishment of Mister Doakes here and the service his family's offered the colony as Crown representative since the founding, of course. Only that so much is now happening off-planet and, perhaps, a bit of Naval insight might do us good."

Alexis studied Coalson's face, which now held what seemed to be a genuine smile. Much as she loathed the family, she couldn't find a way to beg off. They might be prohibited from mining in the belt due to Daviel Coalson's actions, but the family was still a powerful force on Dalthus — and her orders required her to provide such assistance and advice as might be requested by the colonial governments. Perhaps if Edmon were just another heir as his friends seemed to be she might decline, but he was head of his family now and held the colonial shares in his own right.

Nor could she claim the exigencies of *Nightingale's* patrol and leave system before the dinner. She'd told Doakes she'd be in-system for several days, and if she changed that now without some emergency to call her ship away Coalson and others would surely hear of it and feel slighted.

She suppressed a sigh.

"Yes, Mister Coalson, I'd be happy to attend."

Coalson's smile widened.

"Wonderful! I'm so glad I was able to catch you here, then," he said. "I'll just forward an invitation to you and let you and your ... midshipman, Mister Villar here, get on with your business." He nodded politely, smile never leaving his face. "Good day, Lieutenant Carew."

Alexis watched him leave, trailed by his companions, and waited as the shoppers in the chandlery returned to their errands — finally she turned to Doakes.

"Thank you for your time, Mister Doakes. Your thoughts on the challenges facing Port Arthur were most enlightening."

"And I thank you for listening, Miss Carew, and for ridding us of those troublemakers, I do."

"Perhaps we'll have more to speak of on those matters before *Nightingale* sails — I do plan on asking my grandfather about all we discussed."

Doakes nodded. "Not to speak out of turn, Miss Carew, but that Mister Coalson's settled down a might since you were last here." He shrugged. "Blood's been bad 'twixt your families, I know, but he's not been the rake he was before you ..." Doakes paused and scratched at his neck. "Before his father passed."

"Thank you, Mister Doakes." Alexis assumed Doakes meant the first time, when she'd fired into Daviel Coalson's boat here in the Dalthus system. That he'd survived, run to Hanover space, and subsequently been killed by her there wouldn't be common knowledge.

Doakes nodded again and returned to his counter.

Alexis frowned as she left the chandlery, trailed by Villar, though she was barely aware of his presence. Her mind was still on Coalson and what his game might be, for she was certain he had one. The blood between their two families had been too bad for too long for her to believe his seeming cordiality.

"If you'll pardon me asking, sir," Villar said, "should I know the nature of the tension between you and Mister Coalson?"

Alexis ignored his question and asked her own. "Have you met him before, Mister Villar?"

"Lieutenant Bensley met with him and his group a time or two — he seemed to make a point to meet me after Bensley left and I took command, but no more than to say hello."

"I see." She pondered it more, wondering what Coalson's goal might be, then decided Villar deserved at least a partial answer to his question. "Edmon Coalson thought himself a suitor before I joined the Navy and left Dalthus." Let Villar think it was a mere personal grudge and not so serious — she was still unsure of Villar's own loyalty at this point and didn't want him to view Coalson as a potential ally against her. "Childish, really. Some words were exchanged ... the misuse of a teapot may have been involved in our parting."

NINETEEN

Alexis had always loved seeing her home from the air, and this arrival was no different. Foregoing the passenger compartment, she seated herself in the cockpit next to the pilot for the trip from Port Arthur to her home.

There were changes — only to be expected after three years away. The farmstead itself was much the same, but the nearby village was larger. There was a new bridge across the river, just upstream of the fishing docks, and new buildings on the far bank.

As Rasch, the boat's pilot, circled to find a spot to land, she saw that there had been one change at least to the farmstead. One of the home fields, just past the outbuildings, had a section carved out of it, leveled and cobbled, and with new trees planted at the edges — just large enough for a ship's boat to put down in.

The crowd of people there, far more than she'd expected, made that space's purpose even more clear.

"I'm given to understand we're the first boat to set down on that space, Rasch," Alexis said. "Please do the Service proud, will you?"

"Aye, sir," Rasch said, tensing.

Alexis repressed a sigh.

Nightingale's crew seemed made up of different sorts when it came to their duties. Those who did the least they could, not caring at all how well they performed — and those who tried, but through age, infirmity, or some other cause, never quite measured up. Rasch was in the latter group. The best pilot aboard, though that was faint praise, and seeming to constantly question what skills he had.

The boat dipped, settled, and finally came to rest on the field. If it wasn't quite centered in the space, and if there happened to be more than a little of the surrounding shrubbery entangled in the landing struts, Alexis was at least satisfied that they hadn't crushed any of the crowd approaching from the farmstead.

"That was ..." Alexis paused, then patted Rasch's shoulder. "A solid landing, Rasch."

"Thank you, sir."

Aye, the thumps of each landing strut coming down independently had a solid tone, at least.

She made her way back to the passenger compartment. Isom was there, trying to chivy the boat crew into some semblance of order. Alexis knew he was correct that she should pick a coxswain to deal with that, but there were none aboard *Nightingale* who seemed right for the task.

The ramp was lowered, Alexis walked down, smelling the fresh air that seemed, in some way she couldn't place, different than that on other planets, different even than Port Arthur. The scent of home.

Suddenly, she was no longer eighteen and a ship's commander, she was fifteen, too long from home, and witness to far too much.

Throwing any thought of decorum to the winds, she dashed from the shadow of the boat toward the crowd, threw her arms around the figure at its fore, and buried her face in her grandfather's chest.

"Lexi-girl."

The next moments were a blur. A babble of voices surrounded her and she could never say afterward what words were spoken. More embraces and greetings — Julia, her grandfather's housekeeper,

Brandon, the foreman, old friends from the village and seemingly every worker on the lands who'd had a hand in raising her.

When the whirl subsided a bit and she had a moment to think, she turned back to *Nightingale's* boat, ashamed at having forgotten her crew in the joy of seeing everyone here again. The boat crew, though, was well in hand. Villar caught her look and nodded, indicating the men grouped at the bottom of the ramp — some stacking the few packages of belongings Marie and Ferrau had accumulated since Giron. Marie herself, babe in her arms, waited patiently midway between the boat and the crowd.

Alexis gestured for her to join them. Marie walked over, a tentative look on her face for the first time since Alexis had known her. It couldn't be an easy thing for her. She'd lost her home and family on Giron when the Hanoverese retook the planet. Since then, though, there had been mad rushes from place to place aboard ship, then weeks in what poor housing was available to the refugees once they arrived in New London space, then back aboard ship with Alexis for the trip to Dalthus. What must she think to be at the journey's end, so far from home and among strangers, knowing that Alexis, her one friend, would be here only a short time before setting off again?

"Grandfather, this is Marie Autin and Ferrau — I wrote you about them."

Her grandfather held out his hand and Marie shifted Ferrau to the other arm to take it.

"Denholm Carew," he said. "You're welcome here — you and the babe."

"*Merci, Monsieur* Carew — I hope to ..."

Marie trailed off uncertainly, as though searching for the correct words.

"La! Come along, girl," Julia said, stepping forward and wrapping an arm around Marie. "You've seen too much and come too far to have need of these crowds."

With a nod to Alexis and Denholm, Julia ushered the now wide-eyed girl off through the parting crowd to the farmhouse.

Denholm put a hand on her shoulder.

"She'll see the girl settled, don't you worry," he said, then nodded in toward the other side of the crowd. "Much as she did your other lost lambs."

Alexis looked that way and found a small group set apart from the rest of the crowd. Mostly women and small children, a few older, there were perhaps two dozen all told in the group. She frowned for a moment, then realization struck.

"*Hermiones*," she whispered. "You said some had come, but not so many."

She looked back to Denholm, suddenly flushing at what she'd asked him to take on. The farmstead wasn't poor, far from it, as the Carews were one of the five or so wealthiest landholders on Dalthus, but that was the wealth of land and property, not hard coin, and even with the influx of additional wealth from the gallenium, the transport and support costs for so many were an ill-afforded expense. And now she'd added Marie and Ferrau to that, without even asking — simply sent a message that she was coming and there'd be two more mouths to feed.

"I'm sorry," Alexis said. "I didn't mean for —"

"Shush, Lexi-girl. You said you had a debt to them — lord knows you've your grandmother's sense of obligation to your clan ..." He eyed the group, then the still visible Marie making her way to the farmhouse with Julia, then the cluster of spacers around the boat's ramp and smiled. "Eclectic as that clan may be."

"Thank you."

Alexis made her way to the other group, wondering why they hadn't joined the others from the village in greeting her, though she supposed it made a bit of sense for them to be reserved. The villagers and farmhands she'd known all her life, while these she'd never met.

After the mutiny on *Hermione*, most of those she was closest to, her division, had held back from participating and become captives of the Hanoverese with her and the ship's officers. The rest of the crew, the mutineers who'd had to flee from New London space for fear of being taken up and hanged as mutineers, despite the revelations of how brutal and deranged that ship's captain had been, Alexis had known only a little.

One face, though, stood out in the group. A tall, broad shouldered lad, perhaps in his twenties — though, Alexis didn't think his father was so old for that. Perhaps it was only his size that suggested it — as he was as broad-shouldered as he was tall. The lad's face was so like his father's that Alexis had to steel herself as she approached.

"Mistress Nabb," Alexis said to the woman next to the lad with a hand on his shoulder, then looked up — far up, as the lad had to be close to two meters tall and Alexis' bare meter and a half didn't quite match up. "Thomas."

The pair nodded to her. This was no joyous homecoming. The Nabbs, and the other families of the *Hermiones,* were only on Dalthus because they had nowhere else to go — because their old homes had cast them out or shunned them after word of the mutiny arrived.

Wallis Nabb had been the only man of Alexis' division to join the mutineers, and he'd not done so for any desire on his part. Instead, he'd done it because she'd asked her division to keep clear of revolt. When Captain Neals, of that ill-fated ship, ordered her flogged, she'd been unconscious as the mutiny occurred and some of her lads had thought to join — mostly so they'd have a say in the outcome and could protect Alexis, no matter the fate of the other officers.

Nabb convinced them to hold back, not join, that he'd do so himself and report back, calling them to step forward if their voices were needed.

He'd saved them, the rest of her lads who were left free to return to New London and their families with Alexis, but Nabb himself was forced to flee with the other mutineers. Alexis had told him that if the repercussions for his family were too great, they should make their way to Dalthus and her grandfather's lands where they'd be given a place — then expanded that, telling him to pass the offer on to the other mutineers as well. If they could never come home, it was little enough she could do to give them the knowledge that their families were safe and cared for after all they'd endured aboard *Hermione*.

"Your father was a brave man," she said, taking the lad's hand in hers. "He helped a great many men be able to come home again."

It might be small comfort for him given that his own father had sacrificed that right, but Alexis was heartened that he squared his shoulders and nodded.

"Aye, miss."

"Do you hear from him at all?" Alexis asked the woman.

"A'times," she said, nodding. "Short and rare, but a'times ... hard to respond, knowing the messages'll be traced and he's had to move on." She shrugged. "Last I heard he's off in Hissie space." She laid a hand on Alexis' arm. "Sends his regards to you, miss, every letter, though — and his thanks for our place here."

Alexis smiled.

"Send my own well-wishes in return, if you will."

Though if Wallis Nabb was off in *Hso-His*, far past Hanover, the French Republic, and even *Deutschsterne*, then it would be months, if ever, before a message caught up with him.

And if he's any sense, he'll have moved on even farther before then. Perhaps even far around the Core worlds to the other side.

Hso-Hsi might be far away, but the New London Navy traveled far in its task to protect the Kingdom's shipping and merchant interests. Any of the *Hermiones* found were liable to be hanged outright.

As though Alexis' words with the Nabbs showed her as more accessible, the other *Hermione* families pressed closer, each wanting a word. Alexis didn't recognize any others, but once they'd said a name she found that she did remember the man from the ship and was able to speak to those memories.

"Rockwell? Yes, he was a dab hand at the guns — my division had a chore trying to outshoot him ... Grays? Topman, wasn't he? A fine hand ... Aye, Hepburn — set for master's mate before the ... troubles. I hope he's doing as well aboard a new ship somewhere safe ..."

TWENTY

Though the space around Dalthus was much changed, and Port Arthur, and even her home's village, with its new bridge and buildings, those changes stopped at the farmhouse door.

The kitchen held the same sights and scents as when Alexis was last in it. The same *varrenwood* table and cabinets, the same neat order to the canisters and baskets on Julia's counters, the same odd, cycling rattle from the refrigeration unit that Julia wouldn't let her grandfather replace, saying it would make do quite well and there was always something someone in the village might need more.

From the smell, Alexis could tell there was a chicken or two set to roasting for their dinner, and baked yams — something she'd always loved, though her grandfather refused to eat the yams for some reason she never quite understood.

It was new to have a crib of *varrenwood* bars in the kitchen's corner, Ferrau standing in it, little fists clutching at the cream-colored wood shot through with purple streaks, but the crib itself was the one she remembered from her own childhood, and had been first built for her father, she knew. Any doubts she might have had that her family would make Marie feel welcome were put to rest at that sight.

Marie herself was seated at the table, Julia to her right. Tea and a platter of small cakes in front of them. As Alexis and Denholm entered, the girl looked up, smiling.

"Ah, Alexis," she said, "*Madame* Julia is telling me there is a place here in the house, if I wish it."

"For a time," Julia said, "until you're settled and decide what it is you'd like to do more."

She rose and crossed to the oven to check on the cooking food, then returned with more tea and replenished the platter of cakes.

Alexis settled into a seat at the table, suddenly feeling as though she'd never left home. Talk drifted from topic to topic — settling Marie and Ferrau in place, news of the farm and village which Denholm hadn't yet sent on to Alexis in a message, Alexis' astonishment at the growth and changes in system and in Port Arthur, as she felt her grandfather's descriptions hadn't done them justice, especially the amount of traffic and construction in orbit and beyond.

"And it's not as though I have my own personal ship to go gallivanting about in," he said with a grin.

"I do not gallivant," Alexis answered with a grin of her own.

"You're likely missing some of the point to having a ship of your own then."

Alexis laughed and hugged him again. It had been too long since she'd had the good-natured teasing she'd grown up with.

"Will you be staying long?" Julia asked.

"No." Alexis noted the disappointment in everyone's eyes, even Marie, who must be dreading being left alone in a new place amongst strangers, no matter how welcome they might make her. "I've one day here, then more visiting other holders — showing the flag, so to speak, as Dalthus has no central government for me to visit — and finally back to Port Arthur before *Nightingale* must move on to the next system ..."

She paused as she saw her grandfather looking at her oddly.

"What?"

"Only that you've grown so damned much."

Alexis frowned. "I'd not think so — I still fit the uniforms from when I first joined."

Denholm shook his head. "Not what I meant, Lexi-girl."

Alexis flushed and Denholm cleared his throat.

"More personal matters, though," he said, "and something your visits to the other holders might help with, as they'll see how much you've changed — this damned vote."

Alexis nodded. Since she'd left Dalthus her grandfather had been working to convince the first settlers, those who owned shares in the Dalthus Colonization Company, which owned all of the system, to change the colony's charter back to its original form. In that, unlike the current laws, a holder's eldest child, not the eldest son, inherited the lands. It was that law, which prohibited her from inheriting her grandfather's lands, that had triggered her flight into the Navy.

"There're enough shares in favor to get it onto the agenda for the next Conclave," Denholm said. "There may not be the votes to pass, though, and that's what concerns me. It's a simple majority to make the ballot, but two-thirds to pass."

Alexis sighed. "Could we not just wait until a Crown magistrate's requested and deal with it then? Surely the other holders wouldn't wish to hold up closer relations with the Crown over this? Or risk having it declared void? And with the gallenium mining and stations being built, it must be time for closer ties to the Kingdom at large."

The colony's law, as Alexis understood it, was invalid under New London's laws. Only the long-standing policy of leaving colonies to their own devices and letting them run their systems as they saw fit until they specifically requested more services and closer ties to the Kingdom allowed it to stand.

Denholm shook his head.

"No, we were cleverer than that when we set up the Charter." He pursed his lips. "Cleverer by far. The lands, all of them, are really still held by the Company — it's my shares which allow me to do with them as I see fit. So it's not the lands themselves to be inherited, but the shares — and those are what have the restriction on them. There's little say the Crown has in how the shares of a private company are traded or transferred — we can thank Marchant and the like for that."

Alexis hurriedly swallowed the cake she was eating and washed it down with a bit of tea.

"How so?" she asked, not seeing what the giant shipper had to do with Dalthus. "Marchant has little to do with Dalthus, doesn't it?"

Denholm shook his head. "No, little more than shipping, but they like their secrecy more than profit at times. As a private company themselves, they've lobbied the Crown and Parliament for ages to leave all such alone. How a private company runs itself is as a man runs his home, they've said, and made it so by law. A private company could vote to have its shares held only by purple marmots in the future, and there's nothing the Crown could do about it."

He took a sip of tea.

"Come to that, if the Crown did object to the Dalthus Company's Charter, then we'd likely find Marchant involved to stop them. Wouldn't want the precedent set for any intervention in a company's private affairs." He pursed his lips. "Mind you I do think that's best, in general. We, all of us first settlers, formed the company charter freely and agreed to be bound by its terms. No one was forced. I only never saw how this change would affect you."

"Well, I wasn't even born yet, was I?"

"No, but there were others it hurt at the time. I should have fought it harder — should have fought it at all."

Alexis laid a hand on his arm.

"Still, there's hope," he said. "We have until thirty days before the Conclave to place it on the agenda. The main opposition's Edmon Coalson and his group — they and a few others hold enough shares to keep the measure from the two-thirds needed to alter the Charter."

"Of course it would be the Coalsons," Alexis said.

"When Daviel was taken down by your ship in the belt I thought things might go differently — that Edmon was a prat, but he never seemed as insane as his father and Rashae before him. Little changed — though this last half a year or more he's seemed more easy-going. Less angry than his family's wont to be."

This was a direction Alexis didn't want the conversation steered. The less said about the Coalsons, the better, in her opinion. Her grandfather had no knowledge of the role that family had played in the deaths of her grandmother and parents, and she didn't think he could bear it.

"Alexis," Marie said, "when you return to Port Arthur for this party, I may come with you, *oui?*"

"Party?" Denholm asked.

Alexis grimaced. This was one of the things she hadn't wanted to speak to her grandfather about.

"The ... Edmon Coalson spoke to me at the chandlery, grandfather. He's hosting some sort of dinner and invited me — in my capacity as *Nightingale's* commander."

Denholm frowned. "The boy might be less angry than his forebears, but I'd still not trust him."

"Trust isn't in it, believe me, but I can't ignore his invitation, much as I might like to." Alexis had more reason to despise the Coalsons than her grandfather did, knowing far more about what that family had done to hers. "It would be seen as the Navy snubbing a major colonist, wouldn't it? Or more evidence that I'm petty and troublesome, as the rumors were before I left, and therefore more fuel for those against changing the inheritance laws."

"Rumors started by the Coalsons, remember," Denholm said, "and an opposition led by Edmon still."

Alexis sighed. "I know, grandfather, but this is my work now. I must deal with him."

"I should not have spoke?" Marie asked, looking from Denholm to Alexis.

"You did nothing wrong, Marie — I'm simply not looking forward to the event myself." Alexis pursed her lips. "I doubt any of those attending will be the sort I'd prefer to sit down to a meal with. You may find it quite tedious."

"Ah." Marie flushed and glanced at the door. "But *Aspirant* Villar will attend with you?"

Alexis' lips twitched.

"You've not given up on him then?"

Marie flushed more, then took a deep breath. "Perhaps I should." She pouted. "He has the interest — I can tell this thing, but then *pft!*" She waved her fingers. "He — how do you say — goes away?"

"Pulls back," Alexis agreed. "Yes, I've noticed that."

"And always he looks to you as he ... pulls back, yes? But it is not that he pursues you instead."

"I should hope not." *That* would be more awkward than she'd like to deal with, if her first officer were to have such an interest in her.

"It has seemed to me that he fears you," Marie said, frowning.

"Perhaps my disapproval," Alexis mused. "It's not quite proper for him to pursue you aboard *Nightingale,* after all, where he has other duties."

"Hmph." Marie pouted again.

Denholm shared a look with Julia. "I gather we're missing a bit of information about this conversation."

Julia stood and snorted. "You might be, but I followed it well enough." She patted Marie on the shoulder. "Give it time, girl. Some men take longer to get through to than others ..." She frowned, lifted the teapot and filled Denholm's cup. "'course then there're those dense as any stone."

TWENTY-ONE

The evening was pleasantly cool with the slightest hint of a breeze — just the perfect evening Alexis remembered from her childhood. The afternoon had been pleasant as well — sunny and clear. Tomorrow *Nightingale's* watches would come down for leave, port in the morning and starboard in the afternoon, but for tonight it was still only Alexis and the boat crew visiting her home.

That boat crew was making the most of it. The Carew farmstead and village might not be a Naval station or frequent liberty port, but the people were friendly, the food was plentiful, and, if Alexis had cautioned them with regard to drink and how they conducted themselves here, there was more than one bottle being shared.

Quite a few more than one, if the shouts and laughter from the indenture barracks were any indication; but both were still friendly, so Alexis had no worries. No worries about that at least.

Without a word she rose and eased away from the group on the farmhouse's porch. Her grandfather, Julia, and Marie were discussing something — likely some embarrassing event from Alexis' childhood, as her grandfather liked to share — and she felt a sudden need for solitude.

She settled herself onto the rough seat of a rope and board swing hanging from a tree midway between the farmhouse and indenture barracks. It seemed as stable as it had been before she left home, though perhaps the tree had grown some.

She took a drink from the bourbon bottle Isom had brought down with her things and closed her eyes as the liquor burned its way down her throat. There'd been wine with dinner, but she felt the need for something more — glad as she was to see home again, the familiar, peaceful surroundings seemed to only remind her of the darkness she'd both witnessed and been part of since leaving.

"Will you need anything else, captain?"

Alexis turned to find Isom near the tree's trunk. Behind him, she could see the others still on the porch. Villar had joined them for dinner and she could see him engrossed in conversation with Marie.

"No, thank you, Isom," she said. "Why don't you go and bed down for the night?"

Isom nodded, his eyes darted toward the bottle in her hand and he seemed about to say something, but then he nodded again.

"Good night, then, sir."

"Good night."

Alexis turned away again to look out over the fields. Marie's laughter rang through the night and Alexis felt her jaw and stomach clench. She drank from the bottle again to ease both.

Villar's pattern had continued through the evening. He was clearly taken with Marie, but would suddenly break off and become stiff and formal with worried glances at Alexis. It clearly frustrated the French girl, and, for Alexis' part, she wished the man would get over whatever it was that was bothering him.

Marie's laughter rang again and Alexis tensed. She had to admit that when the two were enjoying each other's company it did bother her. Not because she had any designs on Villar herself, or begrudged

Marie a moment's happiness, but because it reminded her too much of her own worries.

With still no word from the fleet which had torn off into Hanoverese space under Admiral Chipley, there was no word either from the Berry March fleet or Delaine Theibaud. No word — and as time went on, less and less hope that the fleet, and all those manning it, hadn't been taken or killed by the enemy.

She drank again and stared up at the stars through the tree's leaves. Somewhere out there, possibly in dire straits, was the man who could make her laugh as Marie was, and there was nothing she could do to find him or keep him safe.

"Do you have any orders for the men, sir?"

Alexis turned again, this time to find Villar by the tree trunk. She must have been staring at the sky far longer than she thought.

"Orders?"

"I thought I'd check on them — head off any trouble as the night wears on."

"I'm sure Mister Ousley and his mates have things in hand," Alexis said. "You should enjoy yourself and rest. Lord knows we've little enough opportunity for such things."

Villar cleared his throat. He glanced back at the porch, then at Alexis.

"I think it's best if I check on them, sir, if you don't mind."

Alexis shrugged.

"As you will, Mister Villar."

"Thank you. Good night, sir."

"Good night."

She sighed and drank again. The bottle had grown lighter and she felt as though she might just have a dreamless sleep tonight. That was easiest when there was work to do — when she could concentrate on the ship's business until her eyes grew so heavy she could barely keep them open, then drop onto her cot. Barring that, the bourbon helped.

"Alexis? Are you well?"

Marie passed the tree trunk and moved to the swing's side.

"As well as may be," Alexis said. "Are you?"

She could imagine the girl would be anxious at the thought of Alexis leaving her in this new place.

Marie sighed. "The *aspirant*, he ... to say, confuses?"

Alexis nodded. "Yes, confuses would describe it well, I think."

"He makes to me the confuses," Marie said firmly.

Alexis hid a smile. "To me, as well, though likely for different reasons. I'm not at all sure what you see in him to begin with."

As she said it, Alexis realized it was none of her business, really, and wished she could recall the words, but Marie didn't seem to take offense.

"'e is a good man," Marie said, her accent becoming a bit more pronounced.

"I suppose."

"'is family has little wealth and he has joined your Navy to make 'is way. The brother will inherit what there is and this world he is from 'as little else for him."

Alexis raised an eyebrow. That was more than she herself knew of Villar's past — and it explained a great deal. Without family wealth and connections, advancement in the Navy was difficult — she herself had advanced only for having been in the right, or wrong, places for significant events to occur. For others ... well, the wardroom toast "to a bloody war or a sickly season" quite summed up what those without connections needed for advancement.

It explained both Villar's still being a midshipman at his age and his initial, perhaps ongoing, resentment of Alexis.

"How do you know all that?"

Marie shrugged and frowned. "I speak with 'im," she said.

Alexis felt a twinge of guilt at that. Despite dining her officers in quite often on the sail from Zariah, she'd spent little time simply speaking with either Villar or Spindler — she didn't include Poulter in that number, as the surgeon spoke with her quite a bit more than she'd otherwise prefer. He seemed as intent on speaking to her about her past as Lieutenant Curtice had been back on Lesser Ichthorpe, and she dearly wished to avoid him for that.

Nevertheless, she should get to know her two midshipmen better — as more than simply two cogs in the machine which was *HMS Nightingale*. It wouldn't do to become overly friendly or personal, that wasn't done, but she should have been aware of what had brought Villar to the Navy, at least.

The most basic thing I think my first captain ever taught me — I can't imagine how I've forgotten that.

Marie yawned. "I will go to my bed, I think." She raised her eyebrows. *"Tú?"*

"I'll sit a bit longer," Alexis said. "Until I'm more tired."

Marie pursed her lips, eyed the bottle in Alexis' hand, then sighed and walked back to the farmhouse.

It was some time later, Alexis had lost track of how long again, before she heard footsteps behind her once more. She sighed and took another drink from the bottle's neck, resisting the urge to turn and snap at whoever it was to just leave her be so that she could find a way to get through the night.

"It's a lovely night, Lexi-girl."

Alexis sighed, more glad that she hadn't turned and snapped, as her grandfather didn't deserve that.

Sir, Captain, Lieutenant, Miss, Lexi-girl — I'm having to be far too many people to fit it all in my head. A bit of space to get it all sorted out for once wouldn't do me any harm.

Before she could say anything, her grandfather was behind her, rough hands grasping the swing's rope and gently pulling it back. Alexis tucked the bottle between her legs and grasped the ropes herself as she had so many times when she was a child.

Well, without the bourbon then, at least.

He pushed the swing in gentle silence for a time, then said, "I missed this even before you went away."

"I did too, I think," Alexis said. The motion was somehow settling and peaceful. *Perhaps I should have a hammock mounted in my cabin, it might ease my nights.* "But I'd stopped being a child, even then."

"Oh, aye," Denholm said. "There's times I wonder if you ever were a proper child, what with my dragging you about the holding every day."

"I learned a great deal, grandfather."

Alexis' head was spinning a bit now. She thought she was speaking clearly, but her lips were numb. She took a deep breath. She didn't want her grandfather to know how very much she'd had to drink — tonight or any of the other nights.

He's not Navy — he wouldn't understand that it's a part of our life, a bit of a wet is.

"It's late, the others have all gone in." Her grandfather let the swing slow and offered her a hand.

Alexis took it and stood, suddenly quite grateful for the hand as her head spun more and her legs wobbled. She'd been sitting for so long that she hadn't felt the full effects of the liquor and it came on her all of a sudden. So much so that she almost dropped the bottle she grasped in her other hand.

Her vision swum and she reached out to take hold of one of the swing's ropes in order to steady herself more, but missed it and staggered. She might have fallen if someone — Isom she saw — hadn't appeared at her other side to take her arm and help prop her up.

"Thank you, Isom," Alexis said, feeling very proud of herself for managing it after she realized just how difficult it suddenly was to form words.

"Of course, sir. To bed, is it?"

Alexis nodded, then regretted what it did to make her head spin more. She clenched her jaw and swallowed hard — the last thing she wanted was to spew in the farmyard on her first night home. Her grandfather might worry and certainly wouldn't understand.

He's not Navy — he wouldn't understand how very much a part of our life a bit of a wet is, she thought again.

"Just a bit of a wet," she said out loud for her grandfather's benefit. "Missed *Up Spirits* while I was pressing those two miners in Port Arthur."

"This way, sir," Isom said, "there're steps to the house and stairs, but no challenge after a ship's companionways, eh?"

"No, no challenge at all," Alexis said, allowing Isom to lead her.

"Is she often like this?" her grandfather asked.

Alexis heard the concern in his voice and felt both guilt that he worried for her and annoyance.

As though three years in the Navy haven't taught me to handle my drink!

"Just a bit of a wet," she repeated. She thought to pat his arm reassuringly, but couldn't raise a hand, both arms still being held as the two men helped her back to the house.

"More often since Giron, Mister Carew," Isom was saying. "Better since she went aboard *Nightingale* — there're troubles enough to keep her busy well into the night."

"I see," Denholm said.

Far too worried, Alexis thought. Isom wasn't at all reassuring, but he wasn't entirely a spacer himself. Just a pressed clerk who she'd been unable to get out of the Service despite her best efforts. *I should write to Mister Grandy again and see if there's a solicitor he recommends on Zariah — get Isom released so he can go home.*

"I shall write to Mister Grandy, Isom," Alexis said, turning her head toward Isom so he'd know she was speaking to him. Her foot caught on a tree root and she stumbled, but Isom and her grandfather kept her upright. "Reverse your impressment, if we can."

"No need, sir, as I've said before. I'm satisfied."

Alexis shook her head. "No, no, it's dangerous aboard ship for you — I should like to keep you safe."

"Thank you, sir, perhaps we'll discuss it in the morning, then?"

"Yes, very well. Remind me, shall you?"

"I will, sir, thank you."

Alexis resumed moving toward the farmhouse, eyes alternating between her feet and the upcoming steps. She didn't want to stumble again and worry her grandfather further.

"Safe?" Denholm asked.

"Thinks my safety's on her, Mister Carew," Isom said. "Mine, those lads from *Hermione*, their families, Miss Marie —" He grunted as they eased Alexis up the first step. "Well, you've seen how it is, sir."

Denholm sighed. "Too like her grandmother in protecting her own."

"If the lady was like to gut a man who threatens them and blame herself for every hurt and fault, aye," Isom said.

"I do not — *ow!*"

"Watch your shins, Lexi-girl," Denholm said, "the stairs're steep."

"Up another, sir," Isom said.

Alexis frowned, working her way up the steps to the farmhouse. They'd been saying something she wanted to correct them on, but the what of it had run right out of her head.

They entered the farmhouse and Alexis eyed the suddenly imposing staircase leading up to the bedrooms.

No, it wasn't so steep as a ship's companionway, but neither had she been required to negotiate one of those after an evening's drinking. Even without her own cabin as commander, her berth and bunk had been just a few steps from the wardroom or gunroom.

She twisted to look past Isom.

"Perhaps we shouldn't disturb Marie," Alexis offered. The farmhouse had only the two bedrooms upstairs and a small room off the kitchen for Julia. She frowned. "Did Julia ever get the tea out of the rug?"

"For the most part," her grandfather said, urging her toward the stairs. "But up you go, there's no fair place to lie down here."

"I am sorry about that, grandfather," she said, "but I was quite put out with that Edmon Coalson."

"It's all past, Lexi-girl."

"I put his father down," she said, "for what they did to us."

"Did to us?"

Alexis regretted the words as soon as she'd said them. *Oh, bugger — he's not to know about that.* She wracked her brain for what to say — her grandfather was already worried about her and she didn't want that, nor for him to suspect a thing about what the Coalsons' true involvement in her grandmother's and parents' deaths had been.

"Bit of a wet?" she offered, hoping to explain things away and let him see that her condition was simply the natural state of a Naval officer, especially one off the ship and effectively on a bit of leave.

"What did you mean, 'did to us'?"

Well, that didn't work at all — what would make him forget it and think I'm just a lieutenant blowing off steam with a good bit of drink? What do the hands do when they're drunk?

There were several things — though, a brawl was unlikely to improve matters and there were no port-wives come aboard for her to sport with, not that she would.

Which leaves ... I suppose ...

"*Farewell an' adieu to you fair* Hso-Hsi *ladies,*" Alexis sang, trying to keep a cheerful look on her face.

"What?"

"Up the stairs, sir," Isom prodded, "a nice soft bed'll do you right."

Alexis worked her way up the steps, grandfather and Isom assisting, and working her way through the shanty all the while.

"*We'll rant an' we'll roar, like New London sailors!*"

"Do you have any idea what she meant by that?" Denholm asked.

"She don't talk about that Coalson much, sir," Isom said. "And I wasn't with her when she went into Hanover with pirate Dansby."

"What?"

"*From Penduli to Ichthorpe is ...*" Alexis tried, louder. Her grandfather wasn't supposed to know about that, either. All that bloody sneaking about business of Mister Eades of the Foreign Office was to remain as hushed as possible. But she never could remember this verse because she was forever thinking she should calculate the proper distance and make it fit, "*... is ....* Is too bloody far," she muttered before moving on to the next verse.

"There's more to what she's done than's in the Gazette or letters home, Mister Carew," Isom was saying. "More than I know, even."

Alexis reached out a hand to cover his mouth, but missed and stumbled toward the wall before they righted her.

"Which is why she needs such taking care of."

"Dear lord," Denholm muttered.

They reached the top of the stairs and eased open the door to Alexis' room.

"We stood by our stoppers, we brailed in our spankers!"

Alexis thought she should probably quit singing now, before she woke Marie or, worse, Ferrau, but she'd started this to distract her grandfather and must see it through. Besides, having started, she suddenly realized she had quite a nice singing voice. And, she saw as they entered her room, she needn't have worried.

Marie was already out of bed and Ferrau, though awake, wasn't crying. He'd worked his way over to the bars of his crib and was staring at Alexis with wide eyes, a string of drool running down his pudgy chin, and no more sound than the occasional giggle.

Quite the thing, my singing.

"Let every man here drink up his full bumper!"

"You've managed that, sir, no doubt. Just give me the bottle then," Isom said.

Alexis let him take the bourbon from her hand, it was nearly empty as it was and she was quite ready for bed.

"Let every man here drink up his full bowl!"

"Again?" Marie asked.

She and Isom began working at removing Alexis' uniform.

Alexis thought she should object to that. Her grandfather was here and she didn't think he understood the sort of close quarters spacers lived and worked in. The breath went out of her in a loud *oof* that interrupted her singing as the two sat her down and pushed her back onto the bed to remove her boots and trousers.

At least my boots will be clean in the morning, with that vile creature locked up back aboard Nightingale.

"And let us be jolly and drown melancholy!"

"And you say this is common?" Denholm asked.

Alexis felt she wasn't quite able to get the proper volume to do the song justice as her bed was wonderfully soft and warm. As soon as her trousers were off she rolled away from the others, burrowing into that warm softness, and felt blessed darkness come over her.

"Drink a health to each jovial an' true-hearted soul," the last verse came out in a whispered murmur.

Isom said. "Not the worst she's been and not the best." He paused. "The singing's a new bit, though."

TWENTY-TWO

1 November, Carew Farmstead, Dalthus System / 5 November, Port Arthur, Dalthus System

The next morning was not as Alexis had envisioned her homecoming would be.

Her head and stomach rebelled against the treatment of the night before, and she was forced to admit to herself that she'd taken on more drink than was usual.

No one said a word, but the raised eyebrows and silent questions in those glances made her flush whenever her grandfather or Julia looked her way. She was used to such things from Isom, less so from Marie, but to receive them from her family gave her pause.

It's the idleness. Too much time for thoughts of the past.

She told herself that, as she was aware she'd felt the same aboard the packet from Lesser Ichthorpe to Zariah. *Nightingale* had given her a welcome set of tasks, keeping her days and thoughts full enough that she didn't feel the need to dull them in other ways — at least not so much as she did when idle.

That made her planned stay at the family holdings more difficult, though, as she'd be nothing but idle here, and she made a sudden decision over breakfast to avoid that.

The looks on her grandfather's and Julia's faces when she announced that she wouldn't be staying after all were painful, but she thought it best.

She and her crew would leave that very day and be about *Nightingale's* business of visiting the other settlers.

Isom gave her a look also — reproving, she thought, but her mind was made up. More so as she saw Isom and her grandfather in some discussions as the boat was being loaded with supplies. She couldn't think what they might have to talk about but her and wished to be away before any more secrets were shared.

The crew grumbled at the news, as they'd been looking forward to a bit of leave, but they brightened when Alexis said she'd bring a new boat crew down from *Nightingale* with each visit to a farmstead. Just the chance to breathe fresh air that didn't smell of half-a-hundred men crammed together in too little space was a treat and most of Dalthus' holdings were willing to put on a meal in exchange for news and the sight of fresh faces.

She only needed a bit of time, she thought, to busy herself with *Nightingale's* business and settle all those thoughts which had disturbed her the night before firmly in their place. Then she could come back and enjoy a visit, perhaps even explain to her grandfather that her behavior wasn't so bad as he might think.

For now, though, it was on to the other settlers, then a final night in Port Arthur and Edmon Coalson's promised dinner.

LAVISH.

That was the only description Alexis felt worthy of Edmon Coalson's Port Arthur home and dinner party.

From the house itself — set back from the newly cobbled street in growing Port Arthur and surrounded on all sides by a high, spike-topped wall — to the meal set before her in the dining room, all was lavish.

So lavish, that Alexis wondered at the expense and how Coalson, who had no access to the vast sums pouring into Dalthus from the gallenium mines, could afford it.

His family's banned from the most profitable export we have, yet he can spend like this?

The table was local — made from *varrenwood*, she noted wryly, as the Coalsons had no tracts of the wood and would have had to purchase it from her grandfather or one of his friends — but the tableware was all imported. China plates and dishes beyond the means of Dalthus' current craftsmen. Cutlery of gold, which no one on Dalthus bothered to mine, as it had little local use yet and wasn't worth exporting.

No fewer than seven servants waited on the twenty guests seated around the table, one of whose purpose seemed to be solely standing to the side and glaring at the others.

He can have his indentures do as he likes, I suppose, but it does seem an extravagance.

Alexis glanced at Coalson from the corner of her eye as one of the servants removed her finished plate. The food, at least, had been locally grown — Dalthus had been colonized long enough for full variety to take root in gardens and fields.

She was seated to Coalson's right. Villar was seated near the table's far end, as befit his rank, though he'd looked unhappy about it until Marie was seated across from him.

Across from Alexis was Lilian Scudder, who Coalson seemed to be wooing, or at least escorting for the dinner. Or possibly it was Coalson's younger brother Herne, seated to her left, who was doing the wooing — Alexis had a bit of trouble keeping it straight, as the woman appeared to be flirting with both men equally.

To her own right was Charles Warriner, heir to a family suspected of being involved with the Coalsons in their illegal gallenium mining, but never proven so.

With Marie and Villar seated so far away, Alexis felt as though she was treading waters filled with sharks.

Sharks and a particularly vapid remora, she thought, as Scudder tittered at something Herne Coalson whispered too low for Alexis to hear.

While she'd grown quite used to Marie playing the coquette, she knew the girl was still very bright and only playing at it. With Scudder, she wasn't entirely certain — and the dinner conversation had done nothing to inform her. Though Coalson had said he invited Alexis to discuss matters to do with the colony, they'd stayed with the convention of not discussing business over the meal.

Instead Alexis now had a more thorough knowledge of the Port Arthur social set than she ever thought she'd need — though the knowledge that the town now had a decent theatre company was good to hear. She'd picked up an interest in live theatre on her last commission, but most of the shows performed on Naval stations were aimed at the tastes of the common hands — rough, bawdy bits — so she'd had little chance to indulge.

That kept her from engaging in much of the conversation, as well, for she was certain a description of the sorts of shows Penduli Station put on for the common spacers would give Miss Scudder the vapors.

The sound of pleased gasps drew her attention back to the table, where Coalson was grinning widely at his guests' reactions.

What they were impressed by was a levitating disk which had just entered the room. It slowly made its way down the table, starting with Coalson, and deposited a fresh glass in front of each guest, then filled it with wine.

Alexis had seen these servers before in her travels, but it was new on Dalthus. Perhaps one or two of the others had traveled far enough coreward to have seen such things, but the others hadn't, and the display of wealth and ostentation for Coalson to have had the serving unit shipped here was impressive to everyone.

The looks on the faces of the indentures who'd served the meal were another thing entirely, and Alexis could tell they were none too pleased to see the technology enter their realm.

It was odd, really. On Dalthus, and other worlds with lower technology bases, the human servants were the norm and the mechanical was a sign of wealth — while on worlds like Penduli, where the machines could readily be manufactured, it was the opposite, with clubs like Dorchester's employing exclusively humans to serve their wealthy clientele.

"Ah! It's arrived, Edmon, good for you!" Warriner exclaimed as his glass was filled and the device moved on. He waited until everyone was served then raised his glass to Coalson. "First on Dalthus, a real coup for you."

Coalson beamed and nodded as the other guests raised their glasses in turn. Alexis sipped politely, though she really didn't see what honor there might be in ordering a device and having it shipped to you.

"I was the one told Edmon about these, you know?" Warriner went on. He sat straighter and took a deep breath. "After my last visit, to Tunstead, it was. Quite the thing there. Dinners at Dorchester's every night — family's a member, you know —" He waved a hand dismissively. "Distant cousin, but family all the same, yes?" The hand now waved wildly about his head, causing Alexis to edge away for fear of being struck. "Bloody things buzzing all about — could hardly straighten in one's seat for fear of being struck."

I quite know how that must have felt, Alexis thought, edging farther away while trying not to appear rude, as Warriner's fingertips brushed past her face.

"In any case, I told Edmon about that and straightaway he determined he was to have the very first on Dalthus for himself. Good show, man!" Warriner raised his glass again and drained half of it. "Honored you invited me to its debut!"

Alexis raised her glass to sip again, unable to keep the amusement from her face.

"Do you not find the device impressive, Miss Carew?" Warriner asked.

In truth, Alexis didn't — well, she had when she'd first seen one, so she supposed she couldn't fault the guests for feeling the same, but she didn't recall being quite as impressed as the others made out. Nor did she find it at all impressive that there was now one on Dalthus, what with there being an entire space station being built above their heads at this very moment.

"It is a fine device, Mister Warriner." She nodded to Coalson, giving him that at least. "And an impressive feat to bring one to Dalthus only two generations after our founding, I'm sure, Mister Coalson."

Coalson nodded back and Alexis supposed she should leave it at that, but it was the third time during the meal that Warriner had referred to her as "Miss Carew", entirely ignoring her Naval rank. Even Coalson had used her rank and Warriner's failure to do so, despite hearing it from others, irked her more than it really should for some reason. Possibly more because it seemed to indicate a dismissal of the Service itself, rather than any slight to her personally.

Her jaw tightened and she tapped her collar where her lieutenant's insignia, parallel bars crossed with the fouled anchor of New London's Navy, were pinned.

"And it's 'lieutenant', if you please, sir," she said, keeping her voice pleasant with an effort. "Or 'captain', if I'm acting in my capacity as commander of *Nightingale*, come to that."

Warriner raised an eyebrow.

"Lieutenant and captain?" he asked, then laughed and ran his eyes over her. "Seems that would be too many people to stuff into so slight a package."

"Charles," Coalson said, a bit of sternness in his voice.

Warriner drank again and the floating device came over to refill his glass as he set it down.

"Oh, just a bit of a joke, Edmon." He nodded to Alexis. "I'm sure

Miss ... I mean, Lieutenant ... that is, *Captain* Carew has thick enough skin, what with her time in the Navy and all."

"Quite," Alexis said quietly, taking a much smaller sip of her own wine. "I've heard the like from the impressed hands, or even a bosun, aboard ship often enough."

Alexis set her glass down in the sudden silence, not looking at Warriner, but instead catching Coalson's eye. If she wasn't mistaken, she saw his lip twitch a bit, and when she ran her eyes down the table she definitely caught Villar covering his mouth with a hand. She didn't need to look at Warriner, as she could see his face redden from the corner of her eye.

While she'd agreed with him, she'd also compared his comment, and effectively himself, to not only the common hands aboard ship, but those caught up by the Impress Service — drunks and criminals from the gaols, mostly — and not the officers who were gentlemen.

She let the silence build for a moment, then, as she saw Warriner's mouth open, she spoke again before he could.

"Now when I was at Dorchester's on Penduli, the dinner was served by an entirely human staff with nary a robotic server in sight. Odd how the more developed worlds like that have eschewed the robotics in the finer establishments, while the younger ones, such as Tunstead where you visited, Mister Warriner, have them all the rage."

Alexis raised her glass to Coalson, not wanting to take from his pride in bringing the device to Dalthus with her dig at Warriner. He was her host, after all, and had really been quite proper since she'd returned home. Perhaps he was changed from when she'd last encountered him — it had been three years, after all.

"I do find it lovely how Mister Coalson has merged both fashions," she said, waving her glass at the device and the human servants along the wall. "Quite innovative, don't you think, Miss Scudder?"

Across from her, Scudder jumped as though suddenly shocked. Her eyes widened.

"Yes," she said. "Oh, yes. Best of both worlds, yes!"

"So your family is a member of Dorchester's, *lieutenant?*" Warriner asked.

Alexis repressed a sigh. She'd rather suspected a man like Warriner wouldn't like being one-upped like that and almost felt sorry for him, because she'd prepared her response to the question she'd known would come at the same time she'd mentioned the exclusive club. It galled her to play this game, but damned if she'd let the man insult the Navy and get away with it. If he wanted to wade farther in, she'd let him.

"Oh, no, Mister Warriner. Not the Carews here on Dalthus, at least." She supposed the families her grandparents had left behind on New London when they'd come to found the colony might be members — they were quite wealthy, after all — but she knew little of them other than that they hadn't approved of her grandparent's choice to colonize and they'd become estranged.

She turned her attention back to Warriner. "No, I was a mere midshipman at the time — a 'snotty' in the parlance of the Navy." She smiled tolerantly. "One more persona stuffed into my package, I suppose."

Warriner flushed.

"So some Naval function then?" he asked, his tone dismissive.

Alexis raised her glass to sip again. *If you'd only stop the questions, it would end, Mister Warriner,* she thought, then aloud, "No, sir, I was dining with Lord Atworth."

The silence, as she'd expected, enveloped the table. While there were one or two families on Dalthus, like Warriner, who were distant branches of some peerage, most had simply acquired enough wealth to buy into the colony corporation at its start. For the younger generations here, who'd likely never leave the planet, much less the system — though that might be changing with the growing gallenium processing in orbit — the lords and ladies coreward were like some untouchable myth. Despite his family's relation, Warriner had not likely met anyone with an actual title when he traveled.

"You dined with a peer?" Lilian Scudder asked, awe fairly dripping from her voice.

"Only a baron," Alexis said, then frowned, "though I did read in the Gazette that his father, the Earl, was ill."

Alexis didn't feel the need to tell them that she considered Lieutenant Williard, Lord Atworth, a bit of a whingey prat. The second lieutenant aboard *Hermione* had done nothing to offset the vile Captain Neal's treatment of her or the crew, nor bothered to stand up for them during their trial for mutiny upon returning to New London space. The best she could say of him, in fact, was that he hadn't joined that captain and other officers in their lies and attempts to paint Alexis as an enemy provocateur who'd instigated the mutiny.

"Well," Coalson said with a sharp look at Warriner, "perhaps I'll now set a fashion of having both and we'll see that make its way back to the Core!"

Several of the guests laughed at that, far more than the jest warranted as it was clear Coalson simply wanted to head off further confrontation, and Warriner glared at Alexis.

If you had ever told me Edmon Coalson would not be the most offensive person at a table, I'd have scorned you for a liar — yet here he's met his match and more.

As the laughter faded, Lilian Scudder stood, one of the servants pulling her chair back.

"At that, ladies," she said, "I believe it's time for us to withdraw and let the men get on with their tedious discussions of business matters. If you'll —"

She broke off and frowned, looking at Alexis.

"That is, we ... um ..."

Alexis looked from Scudder to Coalson, who was frowning with consternation as well. It might be the norm on Dalthus now for the women to withdraw to another room for a time after dinner, allowing the men time with their port and business conversation about their lands, but that didn't take into account what to do when the one you wanted to discuss business with was one of the women.

Alexis fought back a smile. It was Coalson and his ilk who were blocking her grandfather's efforts to change the inheritance laws so that she could inherit his lands, yet he wanted to discuss business with her as a commander of a Queen's ship?

Well, let him be hoist on his own petard, then — it is a silly custom.

"Why, yes, Miss Scudder, let's," Alexis said, rising. After a moment the other ladies at the table rose as well. "Mister Coalson, gentlemen —" She nodded to them and strode toward the door, forcing Scudder to scurry ahead of her or lose her place of precedence.

TWENTY-THREE

Hoist by my own bloody petard.

Alexis fought back the urge to groan aloud as one of the women in the drawing room, she couldn't keep them straight as they all spoke the same inane things over and over again, went on about ... something. It was lace ... or doilies ... or lace doilies ... or ... something. Marie, Alexis noted, was having no trouble at all inserting herself into the conversation and she felt a bit of envy at that. More than inserted, really, as the other girls seemed to find her Frenchness quite exotic and interesting.

"Do you find it so aboard ship ... lieutenant, is it?"

Alexis jerked her attention back to the conversation and found herself the focus of it.

"I'm sorry," she said, "my mind was elsewhere."

Scudder smiled and Alexis felt there wasn't so very much friendliness in it as anticipation.

"We were speaking of the difficulties in training decent help," Scudder said. "It's my understanding that ship captains have their own servants, is that true?"

"It is," Alexis allowed. "Even aboard so small a ship as *Nightingale*, I have a cook and a clerk who doubles as my steward. A coxswain also, if I were to choose so. There are more aboard larger ships —"

"A what?" Scudder asked.

"A coxswain," Alexis said. "He would command my boat crew."

"I ... see. And do you find it as difficult to find competent people for those positions as we do?" Scudder rolled her eyes. "Why some of these indentures have not the slightest idea of how things are done. It simply *must* be more difficult for you aboard your ship."

"Not that I've noticed," Alexis said. She actually had a feeling where this was going, it was something she'd heard murmured about at gatherings before joining the Navy. Her grandfather was one of those who didn't see the need for numerous house servants, preferring to live simply despite the large number of shares he owned in the colony. "Of course, we've always had only the one person to help around the house — been with us for so many years, it's hard to call her a servant. More like family."

"I see," Scudder said. "I suppose if one isn't used to a full household staff, it's far easier to make do with less." She squinted at Alexis as though seeing her for the first time. "Isn't it your family who's making such a kerfuffle over inheritance or some such?"

"It is," Alexis allowed.

"What was that about again?" one of the other girls asked.

"I heard I'd be forced to go down in the mines like my brothers do," another said. "Can you imagine?"

"Ah ... no," Alexis said, "I don't believe there's to be any force involved."

"Then what is it all about."

"Honestly just to change the Charter back to the way it was at the start, where the eldest child, son or daughter, inherits the colony shares." From Alexis' view, that wasn't nearly far enough. She could understand the desire to keep the colony's power in the hands of those who founded it and not dilute the voting shares over and over with each generation, so stipulating they went to only one person made a bit of sense, but what if the eldest was a blithering idiot.

"Good lord, that means I'd inherit instead of my brother!" The girl, Alexis had forgot her name, glared at Alexis. "Why on earth would you want that? Running a household's difficult enough, by far!"

Alexis eyed the girl, who seemed near tears, and felt her point that the proposal needed to go further might just be proved by this single room.

"But as it stands," she said, "someone who wants to is prohibited, just because she's a girl."

"That may be fine for you," Scudder said, "with your trousers and spending all your time in space locked up with a bunch of common men and your coxswain —" There were a few titters from the group. Marie, who'd been in the midst of it, rose and made her way to Alexis' side. "— but the rest of us certainly have no interest. Perhaps you ought to just leave well enough alone."

"It does seem a bit selfish," said the girl who'd spoken before.

"Selfish?" Alexis' skin felt hot. "Selfish is not allowing someone to do what they're good at — or worse, stealing a family's lands because they've no son to carry on."

"Well, isn't that exactly what you want to do with this new law? Force us to inherit if we're the eldest?"

Alexis drew breath to speak, but one of the other girls broke in.

"Oh, look at you all — you've ventured into *politics*," she fairly whispered the word, as though it were somehow obscene. "You'll be calling for cigars and brandy next."

And with that, and no more than a guilty glance or two, the conversation abruptly veered back toward servants and lace-cleaning, as though they were all programmed the same way and someone had flipped the switch. Alexis edged away from the group to a table of after-dinner sweets and stuffed a small cake into her mouth, not caring at all that it was an act far removed from the dainty way the others ate.

Good lord, is that what I missed becoming?

If it was, she might have to thank her grandfather even more for the way she was raised.

Marie raised a cake of her own to her lips and offered Alexis a small smile.

The girl who'd said politics like a dirty word approached them with a smile. She took a plate with two cakes and took a bite of one of them.

"You very nearly set them all against you, you know?"

Alexis bristled. "I rather felt that was the starting point."

"They've been raised a certain way, told they'd become a certain thing, and seen their futures quite clearly. If one feels one's life is set — and quite comfortably, come to that — can you imagine change being a welcome thing for them?"

"For them?"

"Your grandfather's proposal is not without supporters. If it were, there's be no chance for it to even be on the ballot."

Alexis raised an eyebrow.

"And you're one of those supporters?"

"Of course, if I weren't, my aunt's spirit would likely haunt my dreams."

"Your aunt?"

The girl cocked her head then bit her lip to keep from smiling. "You didn't catch my name?"

Alexis flushed. "There were so many, and ..."

She looked back at the other girls, not wanting to say that they all looked the same. The same ridiculous dresses, the same entirely unpractical hair ... assemblies, was the only way Alexis could think to describe it. And, in her defense, there had been a great many names all thrown at her at once, and she'd never really gotten to know too many of the other settlers on Dalthus.

"Alexis," Marie chided. "We spend weeks on ship together and you name to me every bit — four thousands of ropes and you tell me what each does."

"That's different!" She saw Marie and the girl exchange a look and grin. "It is! First of all, they're lines, not ropes, a different thing entirely, and there are *not* four 'thousands'. It's not as though *Nightingale* was a frigate, she has no more than —" She thought for a moment. "— fourteen in the standing rigging and thirty-two in the running. Unless we're storm-rigged and then it would be —" She caught the other two grinning at her. "It's different, I tell you."

"Lauryn Arundel," the girl said, chuckling.

Alexis flushed. Arundel, her mother's maiden name — though she'd had little contact with the family as her grandfather avoided them as he did most of the other colonists. Nevertheless, she'd not only failed to recognize her own cousin, she'd ignored her all entire even when introduced at dinner. She closed her eyes and groaned.

Just as she did so, the door opened and the servants began rearranging the room to face four chairs at the far end.

"It appears it's time for music," Lauryn said, laying a hand on Alexis' arm. "I hope we can get to know each other more, but simply know there are those who welcome the change your grandfather's championing." She nodded to the other women in the room. "There are those who don't, of course, but you're certainly not alone."

———

THE GENTLEMEN MADE their way in from the dining room, the scent of brandy and cigars coming along with them. Alexis caught Villar's eye, wondering what had been discussed and what he'd had to say on it. It was, perhaps, a mistake on her part to have tweaked Coalson and the others by withdrawing with the ladies and leaving Villar there. There was no telling what he might have committed *Nightingale* to and it might have reinforced to Coalson and the others that Alexis wasn't to be taken seriously as the ship's commander.

It was a bit petty, I suppose.

She had no immediate chance to speak with Villar, though, as Coalson hurried to unveil his next extravagance. A full quartet of musicians, instruments shipped in from the Core, he assured them, and with no other duties but to play for Coalson and his guests.

Alexis grimaced. It was one thing to enjoy music, quite another to use it as a display of one's wealth — and again she wondered at Coalson's spending. The cost of four indentures and the shipping for those instruments was no trivial matter, and she wondered more where the coin had come from. With the family locked out of the gallenium trade, the Coalson estates had little other than bulk grains for export. Her thoughts turned toward *Greenaway* and the other ships Doakes had mentioned were missing or overdue.

The family's been involved in piracy before, why not still?

The music went on for some time, Alexis' thoughts whirling all the while. In a short break between numbers, she excused herself from her seat and made her way to the back of the room, liberating a glass of something from a passing tray. She remained there as the music started again, studying the back of Coalson's head and those of each of his coterie in turn.

Villar glanced back, caught her eye, and excused himself from his seat to make his own way back to her.

"Your Mister Coalson does like his luxuries, sir," Villar said, sipping appreciatively at his glass. "This is imported from Chuisnes, if I'm not mistaken." He sipped again. "And I'm not, because the fellow mentioned it three bloody times over the brandy and port."

"Was aught else mentioned?"

Villar glanced around to see if anyone might overhear and chuckled. "Your leaving left them rather flummoxed. Kept trying to start with me over *Nightingale's* deployment and intentions."

"And your reply?"

Villar looked at her oddly. "Told them they should take it up with the ship's commander, sir." He cleared his throat and looked away. "As it's no longer my place to say."

Some tension in Alexis' shoulders eased and she felt a sudden guilt at putting Villar in that position. It couldn't be easy for the man to return to these worlds as a subordinate after commanding *Nightingale* himself, however briefly.

"My apologies, Mister Villar, I fear I left you in an awkward position."

Villar grinned. "Not at all, sir. That lot was always a bit haughty and demanding of Lieutenant Bensley and myself — nice to see them put out themselves."

Movement caught her eye and Alexis saw Coalson making his way toward them.

"Are you enjoying the music, lieutenant?"

"It's lovely."

Alexis still couldn't understand Coalson's attitude. She decided to address it straight-on, in the hope that he might give something away that would help her understand what game he might be playing.

"If you'll pardon my saying so, Mister Coalson, I wasn't expecting you to extend such hospitality to me. Our past meetings have not been so very cordial, after all."

Coalson smiled. "Yes, I remember the tea."

Alexis flushed. "I was, perhaps, not at my very best on that day."

"Nor was I," Coalson said. "I was rather callow and entitled, if I remember correctly." His face sobered. "Coming to head the family has taught me a great deal." He nodded to her and his lip twitched. "As you may have by withdrawing with the other ladies — my colleagues were quite put out."

"Your colleagues, but not yourself?"

Coalson smiled broadly. "I've learned a great deal, as I said. Not least of which is examine *why* I'm put out by something — the feeling generally means I've been in error, I find." He sobered. "Still, there were those in attendance who feel differently."

"I won't apologize, Mister Coalson."

"Nor should you, I suppose. You made your point quite eloquently." He sighed. "Will you agree to a proper meeting?"

Alexis shook her head. "I'm afraid I have no more time on this visit. *Nightingale* must sail and resume her patrol."

"When next you return?" Coalson looked as though he honestly wished for such a meeting. "There are issues facing Dalthus for which we need — desperately need, in some men's minds — the assistance of the Crown. The influx of coin and outsiders, ships gone missing — all of it. It's not urgent, mind you, but all of these men are young. We're thinking of the future and how best to reach it."

Coalson drained his glass and signaled a waiter for another, refreshing Alexis' and Villar's at the same time.

"Mister Doakes is the Crown representative," Alexis reminded Coalson.

"Doakes does a fine job as chandler. These issues are more complex."

"Yet you'd speak to me about them?"

"Why not?" Coalson's brow furrowed. "Short of a Crown magistrate — and there's little likelihood the holders will ask for one of those anytime soon — the commander of whatever ship the Navy sees fit to send us is the most influential party we may speak to on these concerns. Oh, we could hope there was a frigate and a full post-captain assigned, but with the war on ..."

He shrugged.

"We do have a history, your family and mine, Mister Coalson," Alexis said. She closely, wondering if he'd give some sign he knew what his father and grandfather had done. "One of more than a bit of tea."

"Because you killed my father," Coalson stated flatly.

Alexis nodded. Beside her she felt Villar stiffen and glance from her to Coalson and back again.

Coalson took a deep breath and looked at the floor, clearly uncomfortable.

"You met my father, Lieutenant Carew, more than once. I think it was you, or perhaps your grandfather, who suggested he might be mad, as my grandfather, Rashae, surely was." He looked up and met her eyes. "Can you imagine spending your every waking moment in a house ruled by such a man? Being raised by him?" He looked away again.

Alexis blinked. She'd entered Coalson's house with the expectation that the son was much like the father, and his father before him.

"Daviel Coalson ruled his house with an iron fist, lieutenant. Much as his father, my grandfather Rashae, did before him. When his gallenium-mining enterprise in the belt was discovered and his boat destroyed, I thought I was free of him. But then word came from his ... associates — you know the ones I mean, those pirates and smugglers he dealt with — that he'd survived and was in hiding amongst the Hanoverese.

"Even from so far away he ruled us. I did what he said still, for fear of those associates and what they'd do to me — or my mother and brothers." He cleared his throat. "To hear that he'd encountered you again there, and was presumed dead, was almost too much to hope for ... but we've not heard from those associates since."

Coalson met her eyes and Alexis thought she could see both pain and hope in them.

"Is he truly gone this time?"

Alexis nodded.

"How exactly did he ..." Coalson shook his head. "No, never mind, I don't want to know. Hung, I suppose, as a common pirate."

Alexis was just as glad he didn't want to know. She hadn't hung Daviel Coalson, despite that being her plan. Instead she'd spaced him in *darkspace* with his hands bound so he couldn't dump his air and die quickly. Instead he'd spent hours experiencing the ever-increasing effects of being unprotected in *darkspace*, feeling his blood and thoughts slowed by the press of dark matter.

Coalson took a deep breath.

"I'm free now. My family's free. I won't thank you for it. I'm not oblivious to his faults — and they were ... many — but, whatever else he was, Daviel Coalson was still my father. Though his actions had consequences which he reaped. In all, I'd prefer to put the matter well behind me — and us."

Coalson squared his shoulders and looked her in the eye.

"I spent my childhood with my every action being judged by him ... I'd rather my adulthood wasn't spent with others judging me by his."

Alexis nodded.

"I can well understand that, Mister Coalson."

Coalson smiled tightly.

"Well, then, that's enough of this for now, I think." He nodded to Alexis and to Villar. "I'll take my leave and return to my other guests. Do enjoy the party."

Alexis watched him go.

"Did you really kill his father?"

She turned to regard Villar. His brow was furrowed. She grimaced.

"Twice."

It would certainly feel that way to Coalson. She couldn't imagine what he must have thought, first receiving word that his father had been killed by her in command of *Merlin*, then the certain word that Daviel Coalson was still alive and in hiding amongst smugglers, and finally that she'd encountered him once again and this time he was presumed dead.

She wondered if she should take Coalson at his word. Surely being raised by such a man as Daviel Coalson couldn't have been easy for Edmon — but neither could she accept a man would look on his father's death so calmly.

Or perhaps I'm prejudiced against the Coalsons for what they've done. For Grandmother and my parents.

Before she'd spaced him — the reason she'd spaced him — Daviel Coalson had told her the truth. That it was his father Rashae who'd purposefully had the colony's only air transport damaged the night of her father's birth, resulting in her grandmother's death, then Daviel himself who'd driven that same transport at her parent's buggy, driving them off the road to their own deaths years later.

Truth to tell, she wished she could truly kill the man twice. A dozen times. A thousand, and Rashae Coalson along with him, for what they'd done to her family.

But other than being rude and callow, Edmon had done nothing to her. Perhaps he truly was different. On the other hand, could anyone good ever truly come out of so vile a family?

She looked over at Villar to find him staring at her in shock, and realized what he must be thinking of her answer.

Alexis shrugged.

"The first time didn't take."

TWENTY-FOUR

12 November, aboard *HMS Nightingale, darkspace, near* the Dalthus System shoals

"Beat to quarters, Mister Ousley."

Alexis kept her eyes on the navigation plot, though she could see the quarterdeck crew's reaction in the corner of her eyes. No doubt they were all tired after the long, tack upon tack journey out of the Dalthus system. The system winds were particularly strong, blowing directly into its center, and it had taken several long days of calling all hands to the sails before they reached the system periphery and more variable winds — too many days, which should have been fewer if the crew weren't so terribly apt at throwing the sails and rigging into disarray at the most inopportune moments.

For Alexis' part, she was oddly happy to be back aboard *Nightingale* and leaving home again. It had been nice to visit, but she'd felt strangely out of place.

"Sir?"

"You heard me, Mister Ousley. Beat to quarters. We shall exercise the guns, now that we're in more favorable winds and can keep a steady course for a time."

"Aye, sir."

Villar edged closer and spoke quietly, "The men are likely tired, sir."

Alexis nodded. "Aye. And they'll be tired some day when an enemy appears after we've fought the winds for days, or after a *darkspace* storm. I'd rather, when that day comes, they were tired than dead, and imagine they would as well. So we'll exercise the guns, tired or no, until their performance is sufficient. For I assure you, Mister Villar, the least of those few enemies I've encountered in my short Naval career would make still shorter work of *Nightingale* in her current state."

"Aye, sir."

The sound of the call to quarters echoed from the ship's speakers while they'd been talking. Alexis nodded to Isom, who arrived with her vacsuit held out for her, already in his own, and started changing. At least the quarterdeck crews seemed to have become more used to her and her ways, as they showed little reaction to her, concentrating on donning their own vacsuits instead.

Once her vacsuit was on, she watched the video feeds on the navigation plot, gauging the state of the guns and preparation for action against the timer running along the plot's edge. Tired though they were, the crew was on its way to at least meeting their best time for bringing the ship to action, perhaps even bettering it, and that gave Alexis some optimism.

The shot garlands lining the center of the gundeck, really *Nightingale's* only deck, were all full, gleaming with the charged canisters which held the capacitors and lasing tubes. The guns themselves were well back from the still closed ports, but ready to be run out as soon as those ports were opened. The crews on the guns were in their vacsuits, helmets donned and waiting for the deck to be de-aired.

All in all, Alexis thought it might be her crew's best performance to date ...

Right up until the moment there was a call for the bosun over the suit radios, a minute's pause, then Ousley's voice raised in a string of curses that shocked even Alexis.

"*Belay vacuum!*" Ousley yelled when his outburst was done. "Belay vacuum and keep the ship sealed! And you, damn your eyes, on your feet and come with me to the captain!"

"WHY?"

Alexis buried her face in her hands as she awaited the answer to her question. The vacsuit gloves were rough on her face, but she rubbed her forehead anyway — she felt the distinct onset of a headache beginning there. A physical one to match the metaphorical standing on the other side of her desk flanked by Ousley and Corporal Brace, both of whom looked, by turns, furious and chagrined.

She raised her eyes, skewering Thomas Nabb with what she hoped was a piercing gaze.

Unfortunately, the man — boy, perhaps, as she didn't rightly know his age — returned her gaze calmly, appearing not the least unsettled by her or the two older men who flanked him.

"Answer the captain!" Ousley barked, cuffing Nabb on the back of the head.

Nabb showed no outward sign of emotion at the blow.

"Followin' my da', miss," he said, calmly.

Alexis sighed, was the boy that dense that he didn't understand his father was halfway across settled space, in *Hso-Hsi* or farther?

"Nabb," Alexis said, "your father's not aboard this ship, nor even in the Royal Navy any longer, do you understand that? You'll not find him this way."

Nabb's brow furrowed. "No, not *findin'* him, *followin'*."

"Do you understand what he means, Mister Ousley?"

Ousley shook his head. "Not a bit, sir. Dense as bricks, this one, and twice as silent. That's the most he's said since we found him in the hold."

Nabb turned to look at Ousley. "Not stupid — just nothing to say to you."

"Why you sodding —"

"Belay that, Mister Ousley," Alexis ordered, thinking another cuff to the head was unlikely to improve Nabb's communication. Not that she hadn't a mind to strike him herself. His stowing away on *Nightingale* — and how'd he managed that? — complicated her life immensely.

She couldn't just turn back to Dalthus — that would mean days of sail to return, then more days beating back against the winds the men had just managed to get out of. Nor did she feel she could just carry him along as a passenger.

First there'd be where to put him — it was one thing for Marie to have shared her cabin from Zariah to Dalthus, but even if she were comfortable with it the crew would look askance if she did so with Nabb. Nor did she feel it right to put him in one of the few other private compartments *Nightingale* had — doing so would displace either one of the midshipmen or warrants. While she might do that for a true passenger, she wouldn't for a stowaway. Housing him with the crew, while he wasn't part of the crew, would likely cause other trouble and resentment, something she felt she could ill afford with *Nightingale's* already strained relations.

"Come aboard to join, miss," Nabb said, finally.

Alexis stared at him for a moment.

"What? To join the Navy?"

Nabb nodded.

"Of all the ..." Ousley shook his head in disbelief. "I seen your holding, sir, and how your folk are treated." He cuffed Nabb's head again. "Leave that to join the sodding Navy? Dense as bloody bricks!"

Alexis regarded Ousley for a moment, mouth quirked in a

repressed grin. The bosun glanced at her, then colored as he realized she'd done exactly that herself.

"Nabb," Alexis said, "if you wanted to join, why didn't you say something while we were on Dalthus?" At least then she'd have been able to tell him no, regardless of how desperately *Nightingale* needed crew, and leave him safely at home.

Nabb shrugged. "Mum wouldn't like it, miss."

"Oh, aye," Ousley said, rolling his eyes. "Come to join the Navy, but won't cross your mum? We're a fighting ship, boy!"

"Cross your own mum at home, do you?"

Ousley's eyes widened and his mouth worked silently for a moment. "Now, look, you ... that's ... that's not the bloody point, now is it?"

Alexis rubbed her mouth to keep her sudden grin from showing. The thought of the fierce bosun confronting his, presumably, quite a bit fiercer mum almost made her laugh. If the situation weren't so serious, she might have, but the Navy — and Alexis herself, through his loyalty to her — had already destroyed Wallis Nabb's life. She didn't want the same to happen to his son — though if he were determined to join, she didn't see how she could stop it. If *Nightingale* wouldn't take him, he could ship out of Port Arthur on some merchant and sign aboard a Royal Navy ship at some other port.

Moreover, she had enough potential trouble to deal with, having pressed the two miners aboard. *Nightingale's* crew was small enough that every addition could drastically change the men's attitudes. Iveson and Spracklen, the miners, had quickly joined up with the four extorters already aboard, as though they were old mates reunited.

Like does flock to like.

Alexis sighed and grasped at a straw. "How old are you, Nabb?"

"Seventeen, miss."

Well, that was out then. She'd known he was younger than he looked, but had hoped he'd be younger still. If he'd been but fifteen, she'd be on firmer ground keeping him as a passenger. At seventeen he could sign aboard whatever Naval ship happened by, and another captain might not be so lenient for him having stowed away first. Which did bring up the question of how he'd managed that to begin with.

"He was in a stores locker, you say, Mister Ousley? I'd expect Mister Wileman to keep those well locked."

"Aye, he does, sir, but there's space in this one for the mess-kits and a few chests when we're at quarters. When Wileman opens it for all that to be struck below, he finds this one looking back at him. Swears it were locked tight, though."

Alexis frowned. "So how did you manage it, Nabb? That and getting aboard in the first place?"

Nabb reached into his pocket. "Weren't hard," he said, holding out fistful of circuits and wires along with a small tablet. He examined the lot and then picked one with his other hand. "Caught the signal from that man's tablet — the one who opens them rooms?"

"Mister Wileman? The purser? You recorded the signal from his tablet when he opened the stores lockers?"

Nabb shrugged. "Maybe him, don't rightly know." He held up the wires and circuitry. "Code don't change, though, miss."

Alexis raised an eyebrow. "I trust you'll have a word with Mister Wileman about security, corporal?"

"Oh, aye," Brace said, "a word and more, sir."

"And did you find our ship's boat similarly vulnerable, Nabb?"

"Oh, no, miss." Nabb shook his head. "I just helped to load things and stayed in a corner, like. Those folks in the red suits weren't countin' us come out or nothing."

Brace flushed as Alexis caught his eye again. He cleared his throat. "And quite a few words with my lads, sir."

"Yes," Alexis said. "See that you do."

She couldn't fault that security had missed Nabb, she supposed. After all, the norm was to ensure the boat lifted without having *fewer* men aboard than when they landed, what with those having a taste of the Navy so often finding it less to their liking than they'd expected.

Which might, after all, be the solution to this particular problem, as well. She couldn't turn the ship back to Dalthus, so if Nabb was going to be aboard, it might be possible to put him off this idea entirely.

"Very well, then. You want to join; you'll join — at least until we reach Dalthus again. See he's listed in the muster book as temporary crew, Mister Ousley. Ordinary spacer —" She met Ousley's eye meaningfully. "— and don't go easy on him for all he's from my home. See he understands what it means to be aboard ship."

"Oh, aye," Ousley said, "I'll see to that. Come on, then, lad, let's get you kitted up."

"Thank you, miss," Nabb said. "I'll do you and my Da' proud, I will."

"Enough of that!" Ousley cuffed him again and shoved him toward the hatchway. "It's 'sir' to an officer, not 'miss', you sodding lubber ... beggin' your pardon, sir."

"Quite all right, Mister Ousley."

Nabb frowned.

"That 'sir' bit don't make no sense."

Ousley grabbed Nabb by the scruff of the neck and steered him through the hatch.

"Welcome to the Navy, lad. You shouldn't have joined if you can't take a bloody joke, see?"

TWENTY-FIVE

1 8 November, aboard *HMS Nightingale*, Man's Fall System

Alexis raised an eyebrow as she scanned the navigation plot. *Nightingale* transitioned from *darkspace* into the Man's Fall system at the planet's L5 point and the quarterdeck's monitors came to life with their comprehensive scan of the surrounding space.

"Are we quite certain this is the place?" she asked.

Lord knows relying on my own navigation might put us somewhere else entirely.

Villar chuckled, then cleared his throat. "It is, sir."

Alexis scanned the plot. Despite *Nightingale's* navigation notes about the system and log entries from previous visits, she was still surprised. "I can understand them having no pilot boat or beacon, what with being such a young colony, but do they truly not even have a satellite constellation up?"

The plot showed ... nothing. No ships in orbit, no satellites, not even background transmissions from the planet. It was as though Man's Fall, both the system and the planet proper, had no human presence whatsoever.

"No satellites and no radio or laser coms either," Villar confirmed. "In fact, there's no way for them to even tell we're here until we land."

Alexis shook her head in wonder. It was one thing to read the navigation notes, quite another to see it for herself. A small colony might start without a satellite constellation, but to have no communication at all with ships coming into orbit?

"And they've really no contact with anyone but the Navy?" she asked.

"Not that I've seen since being here," Villar said. "There's an occasional merchant who tries, but they're sent packing and reported to us — if we see them, we're supposed to warn them from trying to trade here again, but with just *Nightingale* we're spread so thin that such a thing is unlikely."

"I see," Alexis said. "Does that happen often, the visits by merchants?"

Technically, if a merchant ship ignored the Navy's published navigation notes about the system, Alexis would be within her rights to take the offender in convoy back to Zariah for adjudication there, or send it back with one of her midshipmen and a prize crew. If the magistrate on Zariah found that the ship's captain had willfully disobeyed the navigation notes, his ship might be forfeit.

In reality, though, she suspected it would take an egregious and repeated offense to make such an effort worthwhile, what with *Nightingale* being so shorthanded and having so much space to cover.

"Not too often."

"I see." Alexis recalled another question she'd had when reading the notes and log. "And the emigration broadcast? Must our orbit cover the entire planet, as they have no constellation to rebroadcast it?"

One of the requirements of a colony's charter, if they wished to receive any services or protection at all from New London, was that anyone, colonist or indenture, be allowed to leave the planet. In return, the colonies had great latitude in their local laws and customs

— at least until they requested more in the way of services from the Crown.

Part of a Naval ship's responsibilities was to broadcast a reminder of that. The theory being that even those on-planet without a tablet to receive the message would have access, or know someone with access, to one.

What, exactly, they're to do about it — or I'm to do about it — is rather less specific in the orders.

Like many of her orders, she was told simply to "make all efforts to enforce free emigration" while simultaneously "not offend the customs and sensibilities of the colony world".

"Lieutenant Bensley always made the broadcast from just over their port city," Villar said, "there being no one who'll hear it anyway, you see."

"What?"

"They — well, you'll see, sir. I've never known quite how to explain it."

LANDING on Man's Fall was unlike any world Alexis had ever before visited.

They first overflew the town — for as Villar explained, Man's Fall had only one settlement which could be granted that name — then on to the landing field. Unlike other small colonies, Man's Fall's field was not centrally located to the town and its merchants. Instead it was nearly five kilometers away. The only structure near it was a small, rough-hewn building at its edge.

"They'll be here in an hour or so," Villar said as they exited the boat to stand on the field.

The field itself was overgrown and native grasses came several inches up the boat's landing struts.

Alexis looked around in bewilderment.

"The Navy waits on them?"

"It's part of their charter — accepted because they ask so little else, I suppose. Keep ships, pirates and merchant alike, away from the system, and land our own boats here to wait." He nodded toward the purser waiting at the boat's rear loading ramp. "Wileman likes it, though, as they'll charge us half what other systems would."

The hands were making their own way off the boat via the stern ramp, and Alexis noticed Nabb among them, laughing with one of Ousley's mates. She hoped he wasn't getting too attached to the idea of being in the Navy — or, rather, that Ousley wasn't going so easy on him as to allow him to — for she still intended to return the young man to his mum and the safety of her grandfather's holdings when next *Nightingale* stopped at Dalthus.

Her jaw tightened as Nabb turned and she caught sight of his face. A large, livid bruise covered one eye and half of the lad's cheek.

In one piece, I'd prefer.

She started to call out, then stopped — it wouldn't do for her to single him out if he was having troubles. That would likely only make the matter worse.

"Mister Ousley!" she called instead. "A moment, if you please."

The bosun approached and she gestured for him to follow her out of earshot of the others.

"Aye, sir?"

"Our young stowaway, Mister Ousley," Alexis said. "Is he well?"

Ousley pursed his lips.

"He talked back a bit at first, sir, when things wasn't to his understanding, but that ended quick. He'll do first and question later, now."

Alexis caught her lower lip between her teeth, unsure of how to phrase what she wanted to ask. Common discipline was the province of Ousley and his mates — she didn't want to undercut or question him, but neither did she want Nabb to carry marks like that back to Dalthus.

"I'm not questioning your methods, Mister Ousley," she began, "and I know it's not usual, but the lad's likely going to return to his home when we next make a call at Dalthus ..." She let herself trail off.

Ousley frowned. "Come to that, sir, young Nabb's a quick learner. If I had a deck full of him instead of these ..." It was Ousley's turn to trail off. He cleared his throat and shrugged. "He's quick as any landsman come aboard, sir, and twice as eager — I'll give him that."

"Still," Alexis said. She cleared her own throat. "I'd not have his mother think we'd abused him — when he does return home."

"Abused?" Ousley's brow furrowed, then he drew his shoulders back. "Sir! My mates've given the lad a cuff or two, sure, but them marks ain't from us."

"Then what?"

Ousley sniffed. "Watch our young Nabb's mess come next *Up Spirits*, sir, and you'll see a thing. Him and his mates, they don't give up a thing to ... well, there's no sippers or gulpers coming out of that lot to certain others, if you take my meaning."

Alexis struggled to think of who Nabb messed with and was a bit ashamed to realize she hadn't taken note. There was so much to do, and *Nightingale* in such a poor state, that it had slipped her mind to check. She was glad, though, that some of the stronger men had taken the lad in and were helping keep him safe from the predations of the likes of Scarborough and his lot.

She took a deep breath. "Well, it's a relief he's found a place with those who'll keep him safe from that, at least. I am sorry I questioned you on it, though. I should have known the blows hadn't come from you or your mates."

Ousley nodded, though he still looked puzzled. He scratched the back of his neck and pursed his lips as though considering something.

"Begging your pardon, sir, but you may not have the right of it," he said finally. "Young Nabb's taken up with Widdison's mess."

Now it was Alexis' turn to look puzzled. The men in that mess were far from young or strong — they were three of the oldest men aboard *Nightingale*.

"It's Nabb's driven the wolves off them, sir, not the other way around," Ousley said. "Scarborough's had a limp for nigh a week and that miner, Spracklen, well, there's talk his voice is a tune or two higher, if you take my meaning, sir."

Alexis looked back to the assembled men, where Nabb and one of Ousley's mates were assembling the antigrav pallets which would soon hold supplies to be loaded aboard the boat.

"I see," she said.

Ousley nodded.

"He's a likely lad, sir," the bosun said.

"Yes." Alexis paused for a moment. "Thank you, Mister Ousley."

"Aye, sir."

She watched Ousley return to the men and smiled slightly to herself. It was just like Nabb's father for him to be watching out for those he could. She only hoped he wouldn't be too disappointed when his mum came to get him on their return to Dalthus.

Alexis turned her attention back to their reason for landing on Man's Fall and scanned the horizon, frustrated at the delays. Why on earth couldn't the landing field have been adjacent to a town as on other worlds, instead of here in the middle of nowhere?

If not for a single, small building and a break in the trees beside it marking the road to town, there was no evidence of human habitation. Toward the opposite horizon, though, a tall column of smoke rose into the air.

"What do you suppose that's from?" she wondered aloud.

Villar spoke from behind her, making her jump. "Some farmstead burning debris, I imagine, sir."

Alexis frowned, continuing to stare at the distant column of smoke. Had she just seen ...

"Did you see that?"

A glint, as of reflected light, had flashed momentarily before disappearing.

"See what, sir?"

"Just there —" Alexis pointed — she thought now she could make out a darker speck in the air to the right of the smoke column, far away and moving farther, then gone from her sight.

"Something in the air just to the right of the smoke. An aircar, perhaps?"

Villar looked, frowned, then shrugged.

"I don't see it, sir. Certainly not an aircar, though. They've none of those on Man's Fall. A bird between here and there, perhaps. The perspective might make it seem farther away."

Alexis stared at the smoke column for a moment longer. The more she thought on it, the more certain she became that it had been a human craft, not some bird.

Birds do not reflect light — and she was certain she'd seen a glint in the sky.

"Everyone back aboard, Mister Villar," she said suddenly. "We're going to investigate that smoke."

"Sir? What? We can't do that —"

"We most certainly can, Mister Villar, and I intend to. If Man's Fall truly has no air vehicles at all, then what I just saw should not exist, and that's far too much smoke for a simple brush pile to be burning."

"Sir, the colony's charter doesn't allow for us to land anywhere but here, they've specifically —"

"I've reviewed the charter, Mister Villar." Alexis fixed her gaze on him. As her first lieutenant it was his prerogative to advise her, but also to carry out her orders. "See the men back to the boat — instanter!"

"Aye, sir."

Alexis made her own way back to the boat's ramp. She'd explain her reasoning to Villar once they were airborne again — it would help them both if he understood her thinking, but didn't want him in the habit of expecting to hear it before following her orders.

An aircar or ship's boat on a planet where one shouldn't be, flying *away* from a smoke column, not toward the planet's only town. Though there were no other ships in system, she knew that new colonies were often preyed upon — she'd heard her grandfather tell the story of a band who'd attacked Dalthus in its early years.

Bloody pirates.

THE SITE, when they reached it, was worse than Alexis had feared — worse than her grandfather's stories of the pirate attacks in Dalthus' early years.

Every building on the farmstead was in flames. The barn had been consumed quickly and was already collapsed, while the house was still recognizable as a structure.

To Alexis, the layout looked very much like her home on Dalthus — too much like home for her comfort, given the destruction.

Rasch, the boat's pilot, landed well away from the flames, and Alexis quickly exited along with Villar and the rest of the boat's crew. There was little sound other than the roar of the flames, and no movement around the farmstead.

Alexis looked around and frowned.

"There're no animals."

"Sir?"

"No horses, cows, nothing … not even chickens left behind. They must have taken them."

"The farmers did?"

Alexis shook her head. "What do you think happened here, Mister Villar?"

Villar looked around. "The fire got out of hand and the farmers fled to a neighbor?"

Alexis sighed. "I think not. No settler would flee like that and rounding up a farm's complement of livestock isn't so easy. No, the farmers would still be here fighting the blaze and trying to save their livelihood, if they had the chance."

She pointed to the farmhouse where flames were licking up the sides of the open doorway. The door itself was shattered and hanging from one hinge. A line of holes stitched across it from corner to the other.

"What does that look like to you, Mister Villar?"

Now it was Villar's turn to frown. "I'd say it was flechette shot, sir, but Man's Fall has no modern weapons — they barely accept chemical propellants, and those only for hunting."

"The settlers may have no modern weapons, Mister Villar, but someone does, and a ship's boat as well." She glanced back at the men gathered at the stern of *Nightingale's* boat. "Have the men break out the boat's firefighting gear. We should be able to put a stop to the burning —" She paused. "I expect we'll find the worst of it inside the buildings."

The boat crew began dousing the buildings with flame retardant, putting an end to the flames and then gaining access to the building. Despite her hopes, Alexis' worst fears were confirmed as the crew began pulling bodies from the wreckage.

Leaving them to it, Alexis turned her attention to finding those who'd done this. She contacted *Nightingale* with her tablet. With no other ships in orbit, whoever'd attacked the farmstead must have a settlement or base of some kind on the planet. Man's Fall would make a fine location for such a thing, being habitable and the colonists having no satellite tracking or modern craft of their own.

"Mister Spindler," she asked once *Nightingale* answered, "have you detected any air activity originating from our position?"

There was a long pause.

"Your position, sir?"

"Yes, the boat's position."

"Ah ... at the landing site, sir? I thought there'd just be ours, as the locals have no air vehicles."

Alexis frowned.

"Mister Spindler, is it your belief that the ship's boat is still at the designated Man's Fall landing site?"

Another pause.

"It's not, sir?"

Alexis clenched her teeth.

"Is the tactical station not scanning the planet? Did you not track our movement from the landing field?"

Yet another pause, along with muffled conversation.

"It's ... well, sir, Dorsett says as there's never anything to see here, what with them not having any kind of technology at all and never any ships visiting, well, he —"

"'Dorsett says', Mister Spindler?"

"Well, he —"

Alexis' temper broke. Her frustration with *Nightingale's* crew had been building for some time — their inability to perform even the simplest of shipboard tasks without some sort of fiasco occurring, the time it took them, and now her officers. Villar's questioning and quarrelsome looks at the start, Spindler's ...

"Mister Spindler, do the standing orders not call for the ship to monitor all traffic in the system and on the planet when in orbit?"

"They do, sir, but Dorsett —"

"Dorsett is not a ship's officer, Mister Spindler, you are!" Alexis could see the shocked look on Spindler's face and a matching one on Villar's, but she didn't care at the moment. The boy might be young, but he'd been left in command of a Queen's ship. "*Nightingale* was left in your hands, and you've failed in that duty! Dorsett's desire not to do his bloody work is no excuse for your allowing it!"

"I'm sorry, sir, I —"

Alexis could see that the boy was blinking back tears, and a part of her felt bad about it, but it also felt good to finally relieve some of the frustration which had built up in her since coming aboard *Nightingale*.

"So now you've no idea where we are in the ship's boat, Mister Spindler, and believe me I'll be having words with Rasch for not properly notifying you, but you should have had us monitored in any case! And, worse, there're dead colonists here and we've no idea where the perpetrators came from or fled to thanks to your bloody Dorsett-saids!"

TWENTY-SIX

Alexis loaded the crew back aboard *Nightingale's* boat and returned to their original landing site. Along the way, she shared some choice words with the boat's pilot for not notifying the ship when they'd moved, then settled into a row of seats away from the others. She closed her eyes, already regretting her loss of temper.

Spindler was young and hadn't yet had the benefit of serving aboard a larger ship where there were other midshipman to take him in hand. He'd had only Villar and Bensley as models and she didn't think much of either of those men, if *Nightingale's* state was anything to judge by. Still, her words had been harsh and largely uncalled for — the result of her frustration with far too many things, she knew.

"Sir? If I may?"

Alexis opened her eyes to find Villar by her row of seats. She sighed.

"Yes, Mister Villar?"

"It's about Mister Spindler, sir."

Alexis winced.

"Yes?"

"At risk of speaking out of turn, sir, it was Lieutenant Bensley's practice to leave off scanning the system here at Man's Fall. He felt —"

"I'm little concerned with what Lieutenant Bensley felt was the proper way to run things, Mister Villar."

"I ... yes, sir." He squared his shoulders. "I'm sorry to have brought it up, sir."

Villar started back down the boat's aisle and she closed her eyes. She rubbed at her temples where a sort of perpetual ache seemed to have set in these last few weeks. She'd considered seeing Poulter about it, but loathed the thought of the surgeon's probing questions more than the discomfort.

He'd likely only suggest I drink a bit less, as Isom does.

She sighed. Ache or not, discomfort or not, she couldn't shake the certainty that Villar was right — and right to have brought it to her attention. She'd snapped at Spindler out of her own frustration with not being able to follow and finish those who'd attacked the farmstead — and her certainty that they'd do the same and more once *Nightingale* sailed.

"Mister Villar," she called.

"Sir?"

"A moment more of your time, if you please?"

Villar returned and she gestured for him to sit. He did so, but stiffly, as though expecting some further reprimand, causing Alexis to sigh again. She seemed to be making a proper muck of her command, what with snapping at boys barely old enough to shave and setting her first officer to fear speaking to her. She thought about Villar's apparent fear of speaking with Marie and wondered again what she'd done to cause that.

Save for today, I'd not thought I was such a Tartar.

"You were quite right to speak to me on the matter, Mister Villar," Alexis said, "and I thank you for it."

Villar stared straight ahead, as though waiting for some other shoe to drop.

"I spoke in haste and frustration to Spindler and regret it. I'll say as much to him when we return to *Nightingale*."

Villar seemed to relax a bit.

"I'm sure he'll appreciate that, sir."

Alexis took a deep breath, wondering if that would be the case. She knew harsh words could take quite deep root in young officers. In many ways, they were far more fragile than the common crew, who seemed to shrug off harsh treatment as their due and considering such things over and done with once they were past.

"I hope so. Are there any other oddities of Man's Fall which I should be aware of?"

Villar glanced at the boat's position displayed on the forward monitor. They were now circling to put down at the planet's landing field again and a group of men on horseback waited at the field's edge. He grimaced.

"Likely more than we've time for me to acquaint you with, sir."

"IT IS AN INTERNAL MATTER, lieutenant, and we'll thank you to follow our charter agreement in the future, if you will."

Alexis clenched her teeth — it was the third time the Man's Fall representative had said the same thing, not even varying his words to any great degree. The man was older, with a full beard and white hair, dressed in the common farmer's clothes she'd expect to see on any Dalthus holding, but he spoke in a reserved, quiet manner — in an infuriatingly reserved and quiet manner, as he repeatedly denied Alexis' assertion that anything other than an accidental tragedy had occurred on the burned out farmstead.

Their meeting was taking place in an ill-lit shed assembled next to the landing field. Light crept in through gaps in the boards and the space was hot and stuffy from both the lack of windows and the flame of some sort of gas lantern on the table between them. Alexis suspected the shack, lighting, and her chair — which seemed to slant ever so slightly forward, forcing her to tense her muscles to remain in it — were all designed to make visitors as uncomfortable as possible. The better to hasten their leaving.

Sweat trickled down her face and her neck itched where strands of hair escaped her pony tail and brushed against her skin. She took a deep breath to calm herself in the face of the man's obstinacy.

"Mister Stoltzfus, I believe, again, that I did abide by your charter. The Navy is explicitly required — not allowed, Mister Stoltzfus, but *required* — to investigate and address acts of piracy. This mandate overrides all other agreements in your colonial charter, you must agree?"

"Were there any piracy, you would be correct, lieutenant, but, again, this was an int —"

"'An internal matter,' as you said before." Alexis sighed. Finding the bodies in the burned out building had been bad enough — that and loading them aboard the boat for transport back to the landing field. She'd thought the local authorities would be grateful for the Navy's assistance and provide her with some information to go about locating the men who'd slaughtered and burned an entire farmstead.

Instead Stoltzfus was infuriatingly insisting that there had been no piracy, that this was entirely an internal matter for Man's Fall's settlers to deal with, and that the Navy, in particular Alexis, should bloody well shove off and mind her own business. Moreover, he was steadfast in his insistence that Alexis was mistaken in her belief that any modern weapons or transport could have been involved.

"We saw clear evidence of modern weapons at the farmstead, Mister Stoltzfus. Flechettes and lasers, both. The bodies may have been too badly burned to demonstrate that, but there are walls still standing that bear the marks, and —"

"Moving the bodies was another sign of disrespect for our ways, lieutenant. The Yoders would have preferred to remain on their lands."

"And have their bodies burned to ash in the rubble of what they'd built?"

Stoltzfus nodded. "To remain in the place where God chose to call them home."

Alexis sighed. She couldn't comprehend that the man was so undisturbed by the deaths and the destruction of the Yoders' farmstead. Especially with the tiny size of the colony's population — the port town had barely two hundred residents and the planet as a whole had only four thousand, all within a hundred kilometers of this one town.

She pulled out her tablet.

"Sir, if you'd look at these recordings of the damage done, you'll see the marks of flechettes and lasers on the —"

"Away with the devil's devices!" Stoltzfus closed his eyes and held up a hand between his face and the tablet's screen.

"Mister Stoltzfus, I don't pretend to understand your ways —"

"We do not expect you to understand us, Lieutenant Carew, we merely ask that you leave us alone. Our group has worked for decades to purchase Man's Fall; we wish to remain here undisturbed."

"Sir, if there are pirates —"

"Pirates are your responsibility, yes, but as I said, the accident at the Yoders' farm is an internal matter and of no concern to the Navy or the Crown."

Alexis clenched her jaw. The man's tendency to cut her off would be grating at the best of times.

"There were powered weapons used, and an aircar of some sort, both of which you deny having on this world."

"Both of which are forbidden on this world by the tenets of our faith. Once landed, we have chosen not to sully ourselves with your technology and the devil's metal of those vehicles you ride in." Stoltzfus shook his head. "Regardless, we will look into your allegations when we return the Yoders to their proper place — more likely than not, we will find these marks you speak of to be entirely natural. Perhaps their ammunition caused it due to the heat of the fire — many of our holders keep a great deal on hand."

Only if your god is suddenly turning lead into lasers and gunpowder into thermoplastic flechettes.

Alexis fought down the urge to argue further, as it was clearly a lost cause. Stoltzfus either believed what he said or was hiding the truth for some reason.

"Rather than continuing to insert yourself into our internal affairs, a better use of your time might be upholding your Navy's obligations to our colony," Stoltzfus said.

"And if not putting down pirates who attack innocent farmsteads, sir, what might you suggest that be?"

"Our charter and colonial agreement call for the Navy to keep all shipping away from our system — *all* shipping, not only pirates. We are regularly visited by merchants and, thus far, our complaints to your predecessors have accomplished little."

Alexis frowned. "Most colonies welcome the arrival of a merchant ship. The goods they bring from the Core —"

"Are an abomination. The very transports which carry them are an abomination upon the face of God. One which we had hoped to avoid by coming here, and your Navy agreed to protect us from. Yet within the last fortnight one of your *merchants* alighted here, peddling all manner of the devil's temptations."

Stoltzfus frowned.

"I see that you still don't understand us. I imagine you're unfamiliar with our faith, but do you at least know the verses, lieutenant? 'And the earth was without form, and void; and darkness was upon the face of the deep. And the Spirit of God moved upon the face of the waters.'"

Alexis frowned. "I'm sorry, Mister Stoltzfus, but I don't understand what that has to do with merchant shipping."

"Are you of any particular faith at all, lieutenant?"

Alexis considered. Her family wasn't — most of the original settlers of Dalthus weren't — so it wasn't something she'd ever paid attention to. Many of the indentures were religious, she knew.

There was a sort of shared chapel in the village near her home, put up collectively by the indentures and workers. Different groups of them met there at different times, but Alexis had never paid a great deal of attention to it and had little knowledge of any religion — other than the multitude of oaths and curses she'd picked up from the men working mines, lumber camps, and, most recently, aboard ship.

She doubted that qualified as any sort of faith Stoltzfus would recognize.

"No, I'm afraid not."

Stoltzfus nodded. "It's a sad commentary on our modern times that we've fragmented as we have. That is from our holy book — the very beginning of it, in fact.

"And the earth was without form, and void; and darkness was upon the face of the deep," he said again. "Does that not sound like something you're familiar with, lieutenant? Does it not sound like your *darkspace*? The Dark, as you spacers call it?"

Alexis shook her head with growing frustration — she was trying to deal with the attack on the Yoder farmstead and a dozen dead, not receive a lecture on the man's religion.

"The Dark permeates everything, not just Earth or any one world."

Stoltzfus nodded. "Of course, yes, but we must make allowances for the words being written down by someone planet bound, long ago, without even the knowledge that the stars were more than bits of light in the nighttime sky. The most basic tenet of our faith, lieutenant, is that *darkspace* is the realm of God. It was first, always, and ever will be where God Himself resides. It is a holy realm and man's intrusions there are a sinful act of pride."

Alexis frowned and her brow furrowed.

"I mean no disrespect, Mister Stoltzfus, but you and all your people had to travel through that very realm in order to reach this planet and colonize it."

"A necessary evil, as it were." He smiled. "And one we ask forgiveness for. But having done so, we now have an entire world dedicated to living as God intended us to, unsullied with the Devil's temptations of your technology." He frowned. "Save the landing field where your Navy's boats arrive ... and now the Yoder's farmstead, thanks to your interference there."

Alexis wondered if he was saying those places were now somehow forever unclean, but was more curious about the rejection of technology.

"Our faith rejects all technology and advancements which do not function within God's realm, lieutenant. Yes, you manage to make things like your electronics work there, but only by encasing the devices in gallenium. We believe this would not be necessary if those technologies were blessed and intended for our use. Their creation, and gallenium itself, are temptations, perversions of our natural state, sent by God's enemy to lead us astray."

"I see."

Stoltzfus' face grew sad. "We were quite content here, you know, before the Jadiqi arrived."

Alexis' brow furrowed. She didn't quite understand Stoltzfus' leap from the colony's religious beliefs to this. Al Jadiq was the next inhabited system, farther out, pushing the edge of inhabited space ever more.

"Those merchants I mentioned," Stoltzfus explained, seeing her expression. "They never visited before, but the Jadiqis import a great deal. The merchant ships stop here sometimes, thinking to trade with us. They seem to feel that since they've come all this way for the Jadiqis, we're somehow obliged to welcome them as well. Many are ... quite insistent."

"If you'll name the ships, Mister Stoltzfus, I'll see what *Nightingale* may do to convince them to respect your space." That might be little, given the unlikelihood of encountering them — or that they'd listen, when she'd have to catch them at it to truly do anything.

Stoltzfus chuckled. "Do you think they tell us their true ship's name when we ask? Knowing we have no satellites or other means of confirming it?" He shook his head. "No, they land and try to entice us

— mostly our youth — with their goods." He shrugged. "Who they may be, I couldn't say."

Alexis bit down on her response, not asking just what, then, he thought she and *Nightingale* might do about it. In truth, it was the Navy's responsibility to do so, but short of a permanent blockade, something she certainly couldn't implement with her single ship, she didn't see how.

Stoltzfus smiled. "And now, lieutenant, if you have no other business on this visit?"

Alexis shook her head. "No, I suppose I don't."

"Very well." He rose and motioned toward the shack's door. "Perhaps, you and your ship should be on your way — you might even catch up with that merchant who violated our system's space and have a word with him about it."

TWENTY-SEVEN

23 November, aboard the Marchant Company ship *Dark Gale,* stopped for customs inspection, *darkspace,* enroute to Al Jadiq System

"Did you not see our colors, Lieutenant ... Carew, is it? Or did you simply choose to ignore them?"

Alexis raised an eyebrow. *Nightingale* had stopped a dozen or more merchant ships on her patrol thus far. Some captains were irritated at the delay, others friendly and welcoming *Nightingale's* news or simply the presence of a Navy ship, but all were at least polite and reasonably respectful of Alexis' position. Captain Lounds of the *Dark Gale* was ... not.

"I did see your colors, Captain Lounds." Alexis looked around his cabin. The *Dark Gale* was a large ship, as large as the 74-gun *Shrewsbury* she'd last served on, though as a merchant she was not so well-armed. The captain's quarters were similarly large, as well as lavishly outfitted. Captain Lounds, it appeared, did like his comforts and had the wealth to indulge them.

"Do you know what those colors mean, girl? Who this ship belongs to?"

Alexis narrowed her eyes.

"My orders, Captain Lounds, are quite clear, regardless of who a ship belongs to. I am to stop and examine all merchantmen, provided doing so does not unduly delay *Nightingale* in any of her other duties."

"This is a Marchant Company ship, not some common trader! Do you know what that means?"

Alexis caught herself from snapping that she supposed it meant the ship was owned by the bloody Marchant Company, as that would do little to calm Lounds.

"Are you suggesting that the Marchant Company is exempt from the Navigation Acts, Captain Lounds?"

Lounds glared at her.

No, I suppose that wasn't all that better a thing to say, was it?

"No, of course not," Lounds finally allowed.

"Well, then, let's be about it. The sooner my crew inspects your cargo, the sooner you can be on your way."

"As though a Marchant ship would stoop to smuggling."

"As you say, sir, but, again, my orders ..." Alexis let that trail off with a little shrug.

"I suppose you insist?" Lounds' nostrils flared.

"My orders provide me little leeway, sir." Alexis kept her face impassive. "I must answer the contrary at my peril, you see."

"Do you mock me, lieutenant?" Lounds asked, eyes narrowing.

"I assure you, Captain Lounds, it would not occur to me to do so."

Although it might flow quite naturally from your attitude.

The captain was silent for a moment. Alexis was certain he was weighing his ability to refuse her outright. That would be a dreadful underestimation of her, she thought, for she was already frustrated and on edge. The sail from Man's Fall had been uneventful, but the devastated farmstead there still weighed on her mind.

Nor had conditions aboard *Nightingale* improved — the crew was still barely competent at their tasks. Spindler — despite her best efforts to assure him that she'd merely been venting her frustrations and truly didn't hold him at all responsible for the events on Man's Fall — continued to jump, wide-eyed, whenever she spoke to him.

"Perhaps if you spent as much time drilling your crew as you do stopping honest merchantmen, you'd not waste half my morning with your ship's attempts to come alongside."

Alexis flushed as Lounds echoed her own thoughts, growing all the more irritated that she couldn't rightfully argue with the man on that point.

"I assure you, lieutenant," Lounds went on, "that I will inform my superiors of this delay and they will make a protest to Admiralty."

"As is your right, sir. I'll have *Nightingale's* log encrypted and sent to your secure storage for transfer to Admiralty when you do so. Or do you claim exemption from that courier service, as well as inspection?"

"I claim exemption from nothing, damn your eyes!"

"Captain Lounds —" Alexis managed to keep her voice level. "— it's clear we are at odds and unlikely to convince each other. Would it not be better to proceed with the inspection, be on our respective ways, and allow our superiors to determine the right or wrong of it?"

Lounds looked as though he might explode at any moment, and it was only the knowledge that he wanted a fight, would relish it even, that kept Alexis calm — at least outwardly. A muscle in Lounds' jaw twitched periodically, she noted with particular pleasure.

"Very well."

Lounds jerked his head to his first mate who'd been waiting at the cabin hatchway and Alexis keyed her tablet to alert Villar that he could begin the inspection soon. She resisted the urge to suggest he make it a particularly vigorous inspection, though. There was no real need to treat Lounds and the *Dark Gale* any differently than the dozen other merchantmen *Nightingale* had inspected so far on these travels. Nor would she need to oversee the inspection herself — Ousley, at least, had shown himself as competent as any bosun at rooting out the hidey-holes a smuggler might use. She supposed she might have some insight to contribute in that regard, having traveled aboard a smuggler's ship and seen such things first hand, but Ousley seemed to do a good enough job of it.

Her tablet pinged as Lounds sent her the *Gale's* log and manifest with a contemptuous flick of his fingers against his desk's surface.

"Thank you, Captain Lounds."

Lounds grunted and consumed himself with something else on his desktop. Alexis noted that she'd been offered no refreshment, despite the decanter of wine at Lounds' elbow, and watched as the captain pointedly poured himself a fresh glass without so much as a glance in her direction.

With the physical inspection underway, Alexis turned her attention to *Dark Gale's* records. The ship had left Dalthus some few days before Alexis herself had arrived there. Delivered material for the station construction, then sailed for Al Jadiq with the remainder of her cargo. She'd followed much the same path as *Nightingale* did, save for Alexis' stop at Man's Fall, and taken much the same time in transit, being spotted by *Nightingale* just short of the Al Jadiq system.

Which was somewhat odd, as Man's Fall was several days' sail off a least-time course from Dalthus to Al Jadiq. With the *Gale* having left Dalthus ahead of *Nightingale*, and *Nightingale* having detoured to Man's Fall, encountering the *Gale* here was decidedly odd.

"I do find it curious, Captain Lounds, this time for sailing between Dalthus and Al Jadiq."

"Curious?"

"It seems a great deal of time for the distance."

"The winds were against us."

"*Nightingale* did not find it so — at least where she followed the same course as is laid out here."

"Winds vary," Lounds grunted, not looking up from his desk.

"When *Nightingale* put into Man's Fall there were ... complaints."

Lounds was silent for a moment, then looked up. His eyes were narrowed and his jaw tight. "What possible matter is that to me? Benighted worlds like that are your responsibility."

"Yes, but one of those complaints was about merchant ships whose captains feel quite differently about the matter."

"You should, perhaps, address those complaints with the ships involved," Lounds said with a shrug.

Alexis nodded. "Yet without a satellite constellation or any communications gear, Man's Fall was unable to identify the ships involved."

Lounds snorted. "The difficulties of such a backward world mean little to me, lieutenant." He gestured at his desktop. "If you'll forgive me, I have a great deal of work to complete."

Alexis nodded and returned to reviewing the *Dark Gale's* manifest, becoming more and more convinced that Lounds' ship was one which had attempted to trade with Man's Fall. The manifest listing those goods shipped from Zariah to Dalthus and then those left for trade on Al Jadiq seemed to fall short of the cargo capacity for such a large ship — and Alexis doubted a captain such as Lounds would do less than squeeze every farthing of profit from each trip.

She sighed. Regardless of the truth of it, there was little she could do about the matter, unless Man's Fall was able to identify the ships which trespassed there. Perhaps she should speak to Stoltzfus about leaving at least a single satellite in orbit when next she was there?

Her tablet *pinged* and she saw that Villar and Ousley had completed their inspection without finding anything — unless she wished them to perform a more thorough search, one which would include disassembling some of *Dark Gale's* bulkheads. Much as she might wish to, in response to Lounds, she really had no reasonable cause to do so. Lounds must have received the same message from his officers, for when Alexis glanced up he was looking at her expectantly.

"If that will be all, lieutenant?" he said, gesturing toward his cabin's hatch.

Alexis nodded and stood. "Thank you for your time, captain. I'm sorry to have delayed you." She cleared her throat. There was no need to antagonize the man, she supposed, as she'd likely be encountering him again along her route. "As we're both traveling to Al Jadiq next, may *Nightingale* offer you escort?"

Lounds stared at her quizzically for a moment, then laughed outright, causing Alexis to flush.

"That's a fine jest, lieutenant, but the *Gale* is well able to protect herself," he said, rising to show her out. He paused at the hatchway. "Though, perhaps, I should offer you a bit of advice on the way of things. There are some complaints, especially from the more backward colonies, which are best left unaddressed, I think you'll find."

"Addressing the colonies' concerns is part and parcel of my Naval duties, captain."

Lounds' eyes narrowed. "There are those who would suggest the Navy's should be to *open* those worlds to trade, not assist them in remaining isolated. Trade is the lifeblood of the Kingdom. The taxes and duties on trade goods fill the Queen's coffers — coffers, I might point out, which pay your salary, girl."

TWENTY-EIGHT

enroute to Al Jadiq System

"Sail!"

Alexis glanced toward the speaker in her tabletop. She'd discovered her cabin aboard *Nightingale* had a fine relay to the quarterdeck, allowing her to hear what was said there even when not on watch. That was something she hadn't had aboard other ships, or hadn't been aware of — she flushed as she thought of the occasional thing she'd said, or muttered, while on watch that she wouldn't be entirely comfortable with her captain at the time hearing.

"Where away, Dorsett?" Villar's voice sounded from the speaker.

"One point abaft the port beam, sir, down twenty. Beating to windward, looks like."

Alexis pictured the space surrounding *Nightingale*. She could just as easily echo the quarterdeck's tactical console to her table, but it was currently covered with reports and logs of their travels since leaving Zariah and she didn't want to interrupt that work.

Nightingale was on the starboard tack, sailing almost perpendicular to the prevailing winds on her way from Man's Fall to her next stop at Al Jadiq. The other ship was downwind, one point — just a few degrees — behind the midships point on *Nightingale's* port side, and twenty degrees "below". There was no true "up" or "down" in either *darkspace* or normal-space, so all such directions were relative to *Nightingale's* keel and mast.

"Man the sails and wear to running, Mister Ousley," Villar said. "Down twenty on the planes. We'll run down to her and have a look. Notify the captain, Creasy."

The chorus of "aye, sirs" came along with the soft *ping* of Alexis' tablet.

"Yes, Creasy?"

"Sail to leeward, sir. Mister Villar's ordered us about to close."

"Thank you, Creasy," Alexis said. "Call me when we're within range to signal them. Is the *Gale* still within sight?"

"It is, sir."

Captain Lounds and the *Dark Gale* had flirted in and out of view with *Nightingale* repeatedly as they neared Al Jadiq, depending on the winds and each ship's tack, but there'd been no further communication between the ships. Lounds seemed intent on ignoring *Nightingale*, and Alexis was content to let it be so. Still, two ships owed each other a certain courtesy.

"Make a signal to Captain Lounds and the *Gale* as to our intent."

"Aye, sir."

Likely Lounds wouldn't bother to respond, but it was the thing to do.

Alexis returned to reading the logs, but was distracted about what to do about Villar and the crew.

There was now no doubt in her mind that Villar was a good officer — his orders to the crew were crisp and on point. In the interaction she'd just heard he'd followed *Nightingale's* standing orders to the letter, but still she couldn't shake the feeling of mistrust in him their first encounter had set in her. He seemed to feel it as well and it made him hesitant and seemingly unsure of himself when she was around. She'd noticed that in him mostly when they'd been around

Marie, so perhaps he was simply uncomfortable dealing with women, but it was there nevertheless.

Damn, but she need to be able to rely on her first officer, and he on her — not forever be tiptoeing around each other as though afraid to step on one another's tails.

And both of them must be able to rely on *Nightingale's* crew, something she was slowly running out of hope for.

At first she'd thought the crew's performance was something to be laid at Villar's feet, or even Bensley's before him. Perhaps a laxness in previous commanders the men had taken advantage of, but she was beyond that suspicion now.

Or all three of us, myself included, have the same failing.

Oh, there'd been a bit of improvement in the gunnery and sail handling — the extra work she'd set the men couldn't help but improve things somewhat.

And lord knows there was little room for anything but improvement when I first came aboard.

She sighed and looked over the reports again. They were still lucky to get off two broadsides in four minutes, where she'd prefer, and expect, two in three. The sail handling wasn't quite the shambles it had been when they'd left Zariah, but it was still shoddy. She was almost tempted to call the quarterdeck and have Villar pass by this latest ship without inspection, if only to avoid the half-hidden sneers and snickers of another merchant crew after they'd watched *Nightingale's* laborious attempts to put herself within range to dock with the other ship.

With our luck, the Gale *would drop back to observe and have a bit of a laugh at us as well.* She sighed. *They've no pride in themselves. They know they were cast off into this ship, so why bother?*

It was up to her — along with Villar and Spindler — to change that, to bring back the pride and sense of purpose that should exist on a Queen's ship.

But Villar seemed to lack that pride himself — or at least the confidence needed for it, if his uncertainty around Alexis were any indication — and Spindler was but a boy still, and unrecovered from Alexis' tongue-lashing as well. He should be learning that sense of pride from the experienced crew, not the other way around.

And from me, though I've mucked that up well and truly.

She sighed again and slid those reports to the side of her table, filing them to look through again at some later time when she might get some glimmer of an idea for how to fix things aboard *Nightingale*. She had other things, just as important, to think about — such as her certainty that there'd been an aircar or ship's boat and modern weapons involved on Man's Fall, the missing ore carriers, and even Edmon Coalson's seeming change in heart.

She couldn't shake the feeling that the Coalsons were rotten to the core. They'd been involved in piracy before, so if anyone on Dalthus might be in league with those who were taking ore carriers, Coalson was the first she'd suspect. And yet Edmon had seemed quite sincere in his feelings. Alexis could hardly imagine what it might be like to grow up with such a father as Daviel Coalson, and it wasn't inconceivable that Edmon would feel relief to be out from under the man's control. Still, underestimating that family had cost her own dearly over the years.

Man's Fall only added to the quandary. Stoltzfus' insistence that it was an internal matter and refusal to believe that she'd seen an air vehicle of some sort was maddening. If pirates were attacking his settlements, why wouldn't the man want the Navy's help? If it really was an internal matter, then, again, why wouldn't he want the Navy's help with what would be rebels violating the colony's charter proscriptions against technology?

Alexis rubbed her forehead. It seemed every system on this patrol added some new worry to her load — what would Al Jadiq bring?

Her tablet *pinged* and she glanced at it, surprised to find that hours had passed with her worrying and it was the quarterdeck signaling again.

"Yes, Creasy?"

"Mister Villar's compliments, sir, and we're coming close enough to signal."

"Thank you, Creasy. Fly *Heave-to* and *Inspection*, if you please, then beat to quarters. I'll be there instanter."

"Aye, sir."

As Alexis stood, Isom was there with her coat. The distinct sound of the call to quarters sounded over *Nightingale's* speakers.

"Do you expect trouble, sir?" Isom asked.

"No, I don't think so." Alexis shrugged her shoulders, settling the coat, and fastening it. "They would have run when they saw our colors if they were up to no good. I suspect they're a smaller merchantman risking the run to Al Jadiq in hopes of some profit — and'll be grateful to see us out here. Less grateful when we tell them of the *Gale* and Lounds arriving before, as no doubt the bloody Marchants will undercut some smaller carrier on the price of goods or carriage." She rose. "We'll meet them at quarters, in any case, just to be prepared."

Lord knows the men need the practice at even clearing for quarters.

"I'll just strike Boots and his cage down to the hold where he'll be safe, then," Isom said.

Alexis froze in place and turned her head to stare at Isom, who, similarly frozen in midstride, seemed unwilling to turn and meet her gaze.

"I beg your pardon?"

"Sir?" Isom asked, still not looking at her.

"What did you just call it?"

"Call what, sir?"

"The creature, Isom. The vile creature foisted on me by Avrel bloody Dansby. What did you just call it?"

Isom cleared his throat. "It may be, sir, that one or two of the crew've taken to calling him by a name." His tone turned disapproving. "Seems wrong for the poor beasty not to have one, you see."

"And what is that name?"

Isom sighed. "That would be Boots, sir."

Alexis looked down at her boots and wrinkled her nose. Isom swore he'd cleaned them thoroughly after the last incident and could detect no odor and that Garcia thought the same — though what the cook thought of being asked to sniff his captain's boots Alexis couldn't imagine — but she felt certain they still smelt of ... creature.

"I see."

Now, along with all her other troubles with *Nightingale,* the crew was aware she couldn't even keep order within her own quarters.

"So I'll seal the cage and see he's safe in the hold, shall I?" Isom asked.

"Of course, yes, do that," she said instead of suggesting they strap the vile beast's crate to the barrel of a gun and fire a warning shot, no matter if the other ship hove to as requested. "Safe in the hold."

"Poor fellow doesn't like all this rushing about and being trundled back and forth," Isom said, heading for the hatchway. "Affects his bowels, it does."

Alexis winced. Poor fellow or not, she vowed once again to insist Isom find a different home for the creature and its affected bowels, other than in her pantry. Perhaps, if the crew saw fit to name the horrible thing, they could welcome it to their berth as well. It would serve them right to find its little gifts in their own bloody boots.

She made her way from her cabin to the quarterdeck and took in the scene. Villar stepped away from the navigation plot, ceding the place to her. Through the bulkhead she could hear the muffled sounds of the crew rushing to quarters and preparing the guns — Spindler would be on the maindeck supervising and passing along her orders. Just as well they were still some distance away from the other ship and had time to spare, as the crew was none too speedy in their tasks.

Alexis took her place at the navigation plot and eyed the ships' positions and images of the other ship. She was a bit larger than *Nightingale,* but fore-and-aft rigged as well, flying New London's colors and lights flashing in response to *Nightingale's* signals.

"The *Lively Owl*, out of Grasmere," Villar said. "Says she's bound for Al Jadiq in hopes of a cargo or commission for one and would welcome sailing in consort with us."

Alexis nodded. This far into the Fringe a merchant captain would welcome any company, there was strength in numbers, but especially a Navy vessel which would provide protection without competition.

"Reply that she's welcome to sail with us, Creasy, but I note she's still on a sailing course. Repeat *Heave-to* and *Inspection*, if you please — we've tasks other than just escort to be about."

Alexis watched the plot as lights on *Nightingale's* hull and mast made the requested signals, then waited. After far more time than would be acceptable from a Naval vessel, but not too much so for a civilian merchant, the *Lively Owl's* masts flashed in acknowledgment. The other ship turned toward *Nightingale*, putting her bow into the wind, and doused her sails. Alexis nodded with satisfaction as the azure glow of the other ship's sails faded in the images on the plot.

"Bring us along her port side and extend a docking tube — and inform Mister Spindler to take a party across for inspection. This *Owl's* not too very large and the experience will do him good."

And perhaps show him I've confidence in him. Repair some of the damage I've done.

"Aye, sir," Villar said.

Alexis settled into her stance beside the navigation plot, hands clasped at the small of her back. The rest was waiting — and trying not to express her impatience at *Nightingale's* crew nor wince at the thought of what the *Owl's* captain might be thinking at her ship's antics.

The *Lively Owl* was almost directly downwind from *Nightingale* and the maneuver should be simple. Sail toward the other ship and come about, dousing sails and using what momentum she maintained as the morass of dark matter permeating *darkspace* dragged at her hull to loop about and stop — ideally just close enough to extend a boarding tube.

Instead *Nightingale* overshot, looped too late and too far, and wound up both downwind of the *Owl* and several hundred meters below the other ship.

Alexis glanced at Villar who'd just hissed yet another order to Creasy for relay to the men on the sails in some attempt to correct the latest bungle. Villar flushed, but Alexis couldn't fault his orders — it was the sloppy, lackadaisical way they'd been carried out which had put *Nightingale* in this position.

"Ah ... signal from the *Owl*, sir," Creasy said from the signals console. He squinted at his screen. "*Interrogatory,* our number, and ... ah ... *Heave-to*, sir. I think they're, ah —"

"They're bloody well asking if we'd like to sit still and have them come alongside *us*, since we're making such a cock-up of it," Alexis muttered. "Answer in the negative, Creasy — and inform Mister Spindler that I'll be taking his place in leading the inspection party."

She'd not send the lad over to face a captain and crew laughing up their sleeves at *Nightingale's* antics.

Villar's face became more and more stone-like as gave further orders. Alexis still couldn't fault his ship-handling, the orders were all the proper ones, it was only their execution that fell short. In fits and starts *Nightingale* moved once more, righting herself in relation to the *Lively Owl*, then tacking upwind, and finally the sail crew outside hauled the sail boom around via the bowsprit to take the wind and fall back slowly to come in line with the other ship.

Slowly and nearly too far away — the docking tube would be stretched to its utmost — but finally there.

"You have the deck, Mister Villar," Alexis said, "I'll be about —"

She stopped, eyeing the monitors and the images of the other ship displayed there. There'd been a hint of movement on the other ship's hull. Not their own sail handlers, who'd gathered around the *Owl's* mast to watch *Nightingale's* antics, but along the hull. A twitch of one of the gunports, which were all closed as they should be — but a gunport shouldn't move at all, unless the gundeck behind it was in vacuum, as *Nightingale's* was. And there was no reason for that unless —

"Roll to starboard — ninety degrees!" Alexis called quickly.

"What —"

Villar was staring at her, brow furrowed. The helmsman frowned, shook himself, and reached for the controls. Alexis herself flung herself at the helm, seeing he was moving too slowly. Praying she was wrong, hoping this would be just one more in *Nightingale's* long string of embarrassments this day ... and knowing if it wasn't she'd been too late.

TWENTY-NINE

23 November, aboard *HMS Nightingale*, *darkspace,* enroute to Al Jadiq System

Time seemed to slow in the next moments, like a nightmare she couldn't wake from.

"Roll ship, damn your eyes!" Alexis yelled again, stretching her hand futilely toward the helm.

Finally, the helmsman moved, hands running over the controls.

A moment later she saw the *Lively Owl's* side ripple as gunports opened and wished she'd given the order to fire first, but she couldn't have — not just on a hunch. Couldn't fire into what was possibly an innocent merchant on a reaction to seeing a single gunport twitch. And now her *Nightingale* would pay the price for that. She could still get the first shot in, but her ship was closer than she'd like to fight an action, as well as out of position for the best results.

"*Fire!*"

Nightingale's guns were already loaded and run out, the crew'd been at quarters and ready for action as they closed with the *Owl*, but undermanned as she was, that was changed as they drew closer and the *Owl* showed no signs of hostility. Most of the guncrews were either sent to the sails to help with the maneuvering, the rest to boarding tube in preparation for docking with the other ship. Only the gun captains were left at the guns.

Creasy, on the signals station, was at least well trained. He relayed Alexis' order to fire to the gundeck and the gun captains slapped their hands down on the buttons to fire.

Nightingale and *Lively Owl* were a bare twenty meters apart. *Nightingale's* shot flashed across that space, barely visible even with the compressing effects of *darkspace*. It was a pitiful thing as broadsides went — not only the number and size, being only five guns of four pound capacitors each, but for its ragged nature.

Spots along the *Owl's* hull melted and flowed as the tough thermoplastic absorbed the laser's energy, but Alexis could see that none of the shots had holed the other ship and none had struck home through the *Owl's* now open gunports.

Nightingale was not so lucky.

The *Lively Owl* fired — more guns, ten or more ports, half of which had been disguised somehow during their approach, crowded along her side, Alexis noted, and heavier than *Nightingale's*.

Eight pounders, a dispassionate part of Alexis' mind noted even as she cringed. *More than any merchant should have.*

Nightingale shook from the plastic boiling off her hull.

"Charge the sails and come about!" Alexis ordered, grasping the edges of the navigation plot. She'd been taken in, lured by the *Owl's* easy acceptance of her instructions and their request to sail in company, but there was no time for guilt about that now. "Call the men back from the boarding tube and reload the guns!"

The *Owl* had charged her sails as well and was underway — vacsuited figures were visible pulling lines to raise the already glowing sails. More figures than would be working sails on a merchantman and another sign that the *Owl* was something other than a trader.

Orders given, Alexis and the rest of those on the quarterdeck were reduced to waiting and watching. They had images from the gundeck where the crews were back from the boarding tube. Men knelt beside the guns, checking the crystalline barrels with eye and following up with instruments to detect cracks and flaws that might cause the gun to burst when next fired. Others swabbed the breech, wiping away any residue accumulating where the shot's charge met the focusing barrels. Another carried the shot — the gallenium casing which housed the capacitor and lasing tubes.

None of those crews were down, as *Nightingale* had been lucky. The hull was damaged, but not breached, and there were no injuries as yet.

She counted the seconds silently, trying to keep her face impassive so the others wouldn't realize how very worried she was. Clearly outgunned and likely outmanned, *Nightingale's* only chance was to outperform the other ship — something which would require her guncrews to act at a level she hadn't yet seen from them. If they could load and fire faster than the other ship ...

Both ships paid off the wind, turning to starboard with *Nightingale* making the tighter turn and opening some space between them.

"Roll ship," Alexis ordered. Too much time had passed — the enemy crew would almost certainly have their guns reloaded soon and *Nightingale's* guncrews were still working at the tubes and breeches. Crewmen stood by some of the guns with fresh shot, waiting to slot it home.

This time the helmsman responded immediately, working the controls to adjust the rudder and planes at *Nightingale's* stern — massive sheets with no gallenium to offset the morass of dark matter in *darkspace*, they were able to dig into that dark matter and adjust the ship's course — and send the ship in a roll to bring her keel around to face the *Owl* and protect her more vulnerable sails and sides.

The *Owl* fired, flashes of light streaking across the space between ships.

"Guns ready!" Creasy announced.

"Roll us back! Fire as you bear!" Alexis would prefer to fire in broadside and gain the stronger effect on morale that a massed impact of all *Nightingale's* guns would attain, but she had no faith in her crews' timing. Better to show them what was clearly intended to be independent gunnery than a repeat of *Nightingale's* first ragged display, which could only have given heart to the *Owl's* crew.

Two of her gun captains performed better than Alexis hoped — or were simply luckier — and sent shot into one of the *Owl's* gunports. Alexis could hope those had overset the gun, cracking its tube or damaging its breech. One shot went low, the gun captain timing *Nightingale's* roll too poorly, and wasted itself off into *darkspace* below the *Owl*, not even striking the other ship's extended keel. The others splashed against the hull, damaging but not penetrating the tough thermoplastic.

"Again, Busbey, show them our keel!"

"Sir," Villar whispered, "if —"

"I know, Mister Villar," Alexis said just as quietly.

A ship's keel board contained no gallenium to offset the effects of the dark matter in *darkspace*. It was extended and retracted to increase or reduce the drag of that dark matter on the ship, allowing *Nightingale* to do more than simply run before the dark energy winds. While the rudder and planes at the ship's stern allowed for changes in the ship's orientation, it was the keel which kept her on a track once set. If the keel were shot away, or even damaged so that its extension could not be changed, then *Nightingale* would be less able to maneuver — left to her enemy's mercy.

"I do know," Alexis said again, "but we're outgunned in both number and weight, not to mention speed. They'll batter us to nothing if we try to trade broadsides." She keyed the navigation plot to allow her to speak directly to those on the guns. The broadcast would be full of static, with the deck open to *darkspace* and the gunports hung only with the gallenium nets that kept out the worst of the radiation, but there was not so much radiation inboard that the radios would cease working altogether. "You sent a couple right through them, lads! A guinea from my own purse to each of the crews who just put shot through this bastard's gun ports, and the same to any crew who can do it again!"

Alexis shook her head at the scratchy, staticy cheers that sounded in response. They might be fighting for their lives against a stronger foe, but the chance for a bit of coin always seemed to spur a gunner. She turned her attention back to the navigation plot and the images of the other ship.

"Roll with her, Busbey, she's trying to get over on us."

"Aye, sir."

The *Owl* had started a maneuver of its own, turning toward *Nightingale* while moving above the two ships' original path and rolling as well. The result would be the *Owl* sailing in a corkscrew pattern around *Nightingale* and offsetting the latter's roll — it also meant that the *Owl* would require more sail and more frequent sail changes to maintain position with *Nightingale*, making those sails more vulnerable.

"Have guns four and five loaded with chain, Mister Villar, and target her sails. Perhaps we can draw some crew from her guns to repair damage."

"Aye, sir."

The chainshot, which channeled the gun's laser in a wide bar instead of a focused beam, could slice through sails and rigging, slowing the enemy ship and making her less maneuverable.

Alexis waited, teeth grinding, through yet another broadside from the *Owl* which crashed against *Nightingale's* keel, until word came from the guns that they were ready.

"Back, Busbey, quick as she'll come! Fire as you bear!"

Nightingale reversed her roll, quickly coming into line with the other ship as it corkscrewed around her. Lasers lashed out, stuttering from the gunports in an uneven pattern, as each gun captain chose what he thought the best time to fire. The chainshot missed, spending itself off into *darkspace* past the *Owl*, as did two of the other guns — but one struck home, miraculously, through a gunport again.

The quarterdeck speakers erupted in scratchy, echoing cheers from the suited men on the gundeck, followed by Midshipman Spindler's higher-pitched, "Belay that and reload! We're far from done!"

Alexis nodded, though she felt a bit like cheering herself for it would take many shots for *Nightingale's* shot to penetrate the other ship's hull, but a bolt through the gunport might splinter on a gun's tube or some other reflective material and cause untold havoc.

"Roll to port, Busbey."

"Aye, sir."

Back to rolling away from the other ship and back to waiting for their broadside while her own guns were slowly reloaded, Alexis gripped the edge of the navigation plot tightly.

As she expected, the *Owl* was ready to fire first and shot splashed against *Nightingale's* keel. The ship shuddered as the force of vaporizing thermoplastic shook the hull.

"A point to starboard, Busbey," Alexis said, "we'll edge up on them then turn to fire when the guns are reloaded."

"Aye, sir." Busbey frowned, running fingers over his console. "She's sluggish, sir."

Alexis nodded. "A party to the keel, Mister Villars, to determine the damage."

"Aye, sir."

Nightingale rolled more slowly this time, but eventually began to present her broadside to the other ship.

"As you bear," Alexis said, dividing her attention between scanning images of the *Owl* and those from around the ship as she examined the damage done so far. A party of men from the sails was on the keel, working to free the massive keelboard where its telescoping segments had been damaged and locked it in place.

Nightingale fired again, Alexis struggling not to snarl in frustration as most of the shot missed, though one wide line of chain cut through the *Owl's* rigging and sent the other ship's jib to streaming forward, pulled wildly by the *darkspace* winds until the crew doused its particle projector and could haul it in.

Alexis ordered *Nightingale* into another roll, but the ship's poor response was more pronounced now. She cut her eyes between the image of the *Owl* and twin timers she'd set at the edge of the navigation plot — one for *Nightingale's* gun crews and the other for the *Owl's*. The enemy ship was far too close to having fresh shot in its guns than Alexis would like.

The other ship's captain must have seen *Nightingale's* trouble with her keel as well and ordered his crews to fire as they were ready.

One after another, shot flew out from the *Owl's* side, striking well before *Nightingale* completed her roll. None made it through the ship's hull or into a gunport, but one — which Alexis thought at first would miss entirely — flew over the ship and struck the mast midway up its height.

It wasn't enough to cut through the thick pole of thermoplastic and gallenium, but the damage was visible, a pock where material vaporized and flowing distortions where the mast had partially melted and reformed.

"Fish a spar to that, Mister Villar, instanter!" Alexis ordered.

"Aye, sir —" Villar paused. "I'd best see to it myself, sir, with Mister Ousley busy on the keel."

Alexis nodded. "Go."

Villar rushed off, pulling on his vacsuit helmet.

They'd need a smaller spar from the sail locker laid over the damaged portion of the mast, then made fast with loops of line and a few welds with tools encased in gallenium to keep them operational in the face of *darkspace* radiation. With luck, such bracing would keep the mast in place and whole through the rest of the action.

Dorsett, on the tactical station and with little to do while everyone's eyes were focused on the *Owl*, sat up straighter.

"Work on her sails, sir," he called, then paused. Alexis' own eyes went to the images of the *Owl* where suited figures hauled on lines to pull on the ship's sails. "She's coming about ... no, she's falling off ... running, sir."

Alexis watched as the other ship turned, the crew hauling the long boom of her sails, and began making way on a course perpendicular to *Nightingale's*.

She thought she understood. It had never been the other captain's intention to take *Nightingale*, he'd simply wanted to escape. Faced with what he must have thought was a faster, better-crewed Navy ship, he'd lured *Nightingale* in with seeming acquiescence, then fired in the hopes of damaging her enough to allow his escape. Now, with her keel and mast damaged, he had that opportunity.

Still, whatever contraband he was hauling must be of great value for him to take such risks.

Or he's been involved in worse than smuggling — escaping the noose for an attack like that on Man's Fall would be worth the risk.

"Come about, Busbey, and after him — once Misters Ousley and Villar have the mast and keel repaired I think we'll have the legs on him." She grinned. "To run and be chased like the target of hounds will prick any feeling of pride they have at a landing a few on us, eh?"

"Aye, sir."

Busbey worked the helm, *Nightingale's* rudder turned, biting into the morass of *darkspace* and changing the ship's course. The crew on the sail responded to the orders, relayed outside the hull by lights and optics, and pulled on the lines to swing the sail's boom across the deck. The glowing azure sails swung from one side of the ship to the other, flagging and flopping as they passed in line with the winds, then billowing again. The winds caught the sails, filled them, and pulled the boom forcefully against the newly secured lines.

Then the mast, weakened midway up its length — Villar and his crew still at its base with a spar to strengthen it, but not soon enough — swayed, shivered, and began to bend.

"Douse the sails!" Alexis cried, but it was too late.

The mast bent forward, the sails spilled wind, rigging twisted into a cat's cradle of lines. Men leapt aside to avoid being caught up in the chaos.

Busbey doused the sails, cutting the particle projectors which allowed the fine mesh of gallenium to capture the *darkspace* winds. Their azure glow flickered and died.

Nightingale slowed, the pull of dark matter acting immediately now that there was no force to counteract it. On the hull, men struggled to untangle themselves from the rigging, or crept back from where they'd leapt for safety.

The *Lively Owl* showed *Nightingale* her stern and sailed on.

THIRTY

11 December, aboard *HMS Nightingale, darkspace, an* unnamed system

Nightingale limped slowly across *darkspace* with never more than half her sails set. With every increase in the wind's intensity, Alexis ordered more sail taken in, as the jury-rigged mast bent and worked against the spars fishing the two pieces together.

Some repairs could be performed in *darkspace*, but not easily. Alexis wanted a new mast, not one joined of pieces, before she encountered the *Lively Owl*, or any other foe, again. For that, they'd need to empty a good portion of *Nightingale's* hold and that was best done in normal-space where electronics would work properly.

The thought of her crew attempting to empty the massive containers in the ship's hold without radio communications chilled her.

They should, a proper crew should, be able to, but damned if I'll risk it with this lot.

Transition to normal-space, though, meant they needed a star system with Lagrangian points — and not Man's Fall, where she suspected the *Owl* had just attacked, nor Al Jadiq, where the pirate ship seemed bound.

The system she chose bore no name, just a numeric designation in the navigation notes. It had four planets, none of them habitable and none with enough mineral wealth to make visiting the system worthwhile. Still, she approached cautiously. Both because of *Nightingale's* poor handling — poorer, now, with the damaged mast — and an overabundance of caution. It wasn't unheard of for pirates to use such systems as a base, needing an uninhabited system for their own repairs, and she didn't want such an encounter.

When she finally ordered the transition to normal-space, after slowly and carefully working *Nightingale* through the system's dark matter halo of shoals to the Lagrangian point, they found it as empty as the navigation notes said.

Then the work began.

Nightingale's mast was very nearly as tall as the ship was long. Unlike a larger, square-rigged ship, where the masts were of segments which telescoped into each other, *Nightingale's* was all of a piece for strength. For the ship's carpenter to print a replacement, it meant she needed space for that mast to be extruded.

The crew not repairing other damage was set to work on other repairs set about emptying the hold, clearing space from the carpenter's shop at the rear all the way through to the forward airlock. Barrels and crates of supplies were all moved outside the ship and secured in place — anything that couldn't be exposed to vacuum was moved elsewhere in the ship. Then the pieces of the broken mast and rigging were recycled into the printer's material vats and the process of fabricating a new mast began.

Though the actual fabrication went quickly and was done in vacuum, by the end of it Alexis was certain the entire ship reeked of melted thermoplastic. Then came the equally arduous task of stepping the mast and returning all of *Nightingale's* stores to their original places.

By the time it was done, both the crew and officers were

exhausted, short tempered, and ready for a break, which Alexis couldn't give them. This tail end of *Nightingale's* patrol, first Man's Fall and then the upcoming stop at Al Jadiq, wouldn't allow for the crew to have liberty in port. Both worlds forbade it.

Nor will there be any 'wives' coming aboard at Al Jadiq.

From what she'd read and what Villar had told her, the Jadiqis forbade that practice as well — allowing merchants and any woman a man said was his wife access to the ship if the crew was to be confined there.

Near the end of the job, Alexis went out on the hull herself to observe the work. She stood on *Nightingale's* bow, looking aft to the mast jutting up three-quarters of the way back, not at the bow itself as on a ship-rigged vessel. *Nightingale's* fore-and-aft rig allowed for the sails to be worked by a smaller crew, though, and that she was grateful for.

Some of the crew were busy bringing crates and vats of stores back into the ship through the bow's sail locker. They pulled gently on the lines to bring each clump of stores, netted together to keep them from floating off, toward the ship. Slowly, so as not to gain too much momentum.

Beside her, Ousley looked on as well, keeping an eye on both the men and their task, and his own mates who were supervising each individual job.

"Handsomely, Summerset," Ousley's voice sounded over her suit radio. "Handsomely, now — else your mates'll be scraping you out of that vacsuit."

Alexis watched the spacer in question stop pulling quite so hard on the line he held, allowing others, off the ship in suits with thrusters, to slow the oncoming vat's advance.

"How long do you suppose, Mister Ousley?" Alexis asked.

"Done by the afternoon watch tomorrow, sir, but they'll need a bit of rest before sailing."

"That long?" Alexis regarded the work that seemed left and deemed it no more than a few hours. More than half the stores were returned to the hold, and all of the mast's standing rigging complete. The running rigging was left, but *Nightingale's* wasn't nearly so complicated as a ship-rigged.

Ousley grunted.

"It's longer than I'd like, sure, sir, but ..." His voice trailed off.

Alexis nodded, though he couldn't see her.

"Very well," she said. "I'll be guided by you in this."

"Thank you, sir."

Alexis sighed and returned to regarding what work was being done. Even after the drubbing they'd received from the *Owl, Nightingale's* crew was as lackadaisical as ever. If anything, she'd have thought their ship being shot to pieces would spark *something* in the men, but it hadn't.

They'd been lucky that no one was killed in the action and only a few injured. She'd not wish for worse in order to spur those remaining, but did wonder if even that would.

"Carry on, Mister Ousley. I'll be in my cabin, if you've need of me."

THIRTY-ONE

12 December, aboard *HMS Nightingale*, darkspace, an unnamed system

"Farst lieutenant, sar!" the Marine at the hatchway announced.

Alexis looked up from her table's surface where she was reviewing the lists of cargo ships that had sailed from Dalthus over the last six months, including those Doakes had told her were overdue or missing. Just because *Nightingale* was in the midst of repairing the damage inflicted by the *Lively Owl* didn't mean that was her only problem. The question of missing ships wasn't going away, though she suspected she'd find they and the *Owl* were certainly connected. There were only so many pirates who could make a living in any given volume of space, after all.

The difficulty with tracking those ships was that there were no records available for whether they'd had arrived at their destinations. Not unless they'd turned around and arrived back at Dalthus. The constraints of travel over such vast distances and the time involved made accurate records difficult, if not impossible.

"Send him in," she said.

Alexis slid the plate Isom had brought for her aside. She'd eaten half the sandwich of fine ham from her grandfather's farms without even noticing it, so absorbed in the records was she, and that seemed somehow insulting to the food.

Villar entered and stopped a meter or so from her table. He wore an old jumpsuit, wet with sweat, so must have just come in from supervising repairs. She checked the time on her tablet and found that was so — it was nearly time to call the hands in for their own meal.

"I wonder if I might speak to you for a moment, sir?"

"Of course." Alexis gestured for him to sit. "Shall I have Isom pour us something?"

"I'd ..." Villar cleared his throat. "I'd prefer to stand, sir, if I may."

Alexis frowned, suddenly wary. She'd thought she was getting on better with Villar — quite well, in fact. There were no complaints she could make about his attention to duties, and their personal interactions had even become cordial. She thought they might be developing a genuine friendship, or at least as much of one as a commander and first lieutenant could allow themselves — early times yet for that, but she did find she liked him. When he wasn't acting so stiff and formal, that is, as he was now.

"Yes?"

"This has been on my mind for some time, sir. Since the Remada Straits and that *Greenaway*, in fact. Now with the events of our encounter with the *Owl*, I feel I can no longer remain silent."

Alexis tensed. She had her own thoughts about those encounters. She should have seen the second ship behind *Greenaway* herself, and in time to pursue it. If that had been the *Owl* as well, then the current damage to *Nightingale* could have been avoided, as she'd have known the *Owl* was an enemy.

Even this last encounter left her wanting. If she'd made the decision to fire earlier, risk of firing into an innocent ship be damned, then they might have avoided all this. More, the *Owl* might not be out there right now, preying on other helpless merchantmen. There was no telling how many of the next merchant crew might die because of her oversights.

Or farmers on Man's Fall or some other world, if the Owl *was involved in that, as well.*

Still, it wasn't Villar's, or any first officer's, place to express an opinion on things like that, no matter that she thought them herself. Her leadership aboard *Nightingale* felt precarious enough already, and if Villar were to be more than critical, if he made comments as he had when she'd first come aboard, then she could no longer ignore them.

Better to warn him off that now, than let him say something she could no longer ignore.

"Mister Villar, I really don't think —"

"I'd like to offer you an apology, sir," Villar blurted.

Alexis blinked.

"For what?"

"When you first came aboard, sir, I was angry. I thought *Nightingale* should be mine — thought she was mine already, come to that." He squared his shoulders. "You said to forget all I said then, but I haven't. I still, at times — more than at times, perhaps — thought you had no business commanding. You're younger than me, for all that you were at Giron, and have fewer years in."

Villar took a deep breath.

"When we found *Greenaway* in the Straits, sir, I'd have gone right in and boarded her. I thought sure she was abandoned or her crew'd gone sick." He swallowed hard. "I'd have lost the ship to that trap, no doubt in my mind. I missed the signs with the *Lively Owl* as well — whatever you saw that had you rolling ship before they fired." He winced. "If I'd been faster to relay your order ... if I'd drilled Busbey on the helm, and all the crew, half as much as you have since coming aboard, well, we might have come out of that better, as well."

He swallowed hard.

"If I'd followed procedure in my command instead of the laxity

Lieutenant Bensley allowed, we'd have had the tracking on those who burned that farmstead on Man's Fall.

"So I wished to apologize, sir. For what I thought — for the state of the ship when you took command." He closed his eyes. "If you wish to put me off when next we encounter another Navy ship or Admiralty port, I fully understand your desire to have another first officer. One you can rely on."

Alexis regarded him for a moment, angry at herself for her ill thoughts of him when he'd started to speak. She'd misjudged him, more than once, she thought, since she'd come aboard, as he had her.

There was a bit of truth and a bit of nonsense in what he'd said — *Nightingale* had been a lamentable mess when she'd come aboard, still was in some many cases, and Villar had certainly contributed to that. She didn't like, though, the gloss he put on her own faults in those encounters. Still, nit-picking the details was likely not what he needed to hear. Best, perhaps, to put all of those misjudgments, on both sides, away and move on.

"I will say, sir," Villar went on into the silence, "that I've seen there's more to command than just the sailing orders. I do see that now."

"I think you do yourself too hard a service, Mister Villar, but I'll not argue with you."

Villar winced. "Thank you, sir. I'll see my things are packed when next we sight a Naval ship or return to Zariah. I suppose I can make my way to an Admiralty office from there…"

"No," Alexis said hurriedly, realizing she'd started it wrong. "That's not what I meant at all." She took a deep breath. "Much as I think you've been too hard on yourself, I do think that is a difficult estimation to make. More difficult yet to voice. You're a good officer and a fine ship-handler — I'd have you stay aboard, if you will. *Nightingale's* the better for your presence."

"I — thank you, sir, I will."

Alexis was glad to see his face lighten, but then it suddenly fell again.

"There is another matter, sir, on which I feel I must speak. If I'm to remain aboard, that is."

That made Alexis pause and wonder what could possibly be next. She'd had quite enough of confessions for the day and needed to get back to finding out what was going on in this space.

"Go on, Mister Villar," she said, feeling wary.

"It's regarding ... a personal matter."

"Yes?"

"It's about Miss Autin, sir."

"Marie?"

"Yes, sir."

Now Alexis understood his continued discomfort. Did he have some personal questions about Marie? Asking Alexis, as his commanding officer, was certainly inappropriate — and uncomfortable. She started to speak, to tell him that anything he had to ask about Marie should really be asked of her, but Villar spoke first.

"You may have noticed, sir, that Miss Autin and I spent some time conversing while at your family's holdings."

"I did — and before that as well."

Villar swallowed, his Adam's apple bobbing up and down dramatically.

"Sir, I wish to assure you that I have done my utmost to not ... to not encourage Miss Autin."

Alexis sighed. Why on earth would he not and why did he feel compelled to tell her so? If anything, though, this conversation, awkward as it already was, might provide some insight she could give Marie as to why Villar seemed so set against her attentions. That she'd just been thinking it was inappropriate for Villar to be asking about the girl, and then think that she might pass along anything he said, gave her a moment's pause.

They're two different things ... I think ... oh, bother.

"There is something you dislike about Marie, Mister Villar?"

"No, sir!" Villar said quickly. "I think she's quite the ..." He broke off and cleared his throat again. "Miss Autin is a quite remarkable young lady."

Alexis blinked, confused.

Damn it all, inappropriate or not, I want a bloody answer!

"Then why, Mister Villar, would you hold yourself aloof as you've done?"

Now Villar looked confused.

"I … you would not object, sir? Were I to … pursue something more than acquaintance with Miss Autin?"

"Why on earth would I object?"

"So you and Miss Autin have … an agreement, then? An arrangement?"

"Agreement?"

"An understanding?" Villar shrugged. "I'm sorry, I'm not sure what such things are called."

"What *things*, Mister Villar?" Alexis was starting to feel as though there were two very different conversations going on here.

Villar shook his head and swallowed again. "I'm sorry, sir, it doesn't matter. I … I would find myself uncomfortable with such an arrangement in any case."

"What *arrangement*? Mister Villar, I find myself entirely bewildered by your words."

"It's not that I think it's somehow wrong, mind you," Villar said hurriedly. "I'm from Chorthampton. We're somewhat conservative, but we tend to leave such things alone. Not my concern, you understand."

Now Alexis was even more confused than before.

"Mister Villar, I am at a complete loss for understanding you. What the bloody hell are you talking about?"

"You and Miss Autin, sir."

"Well what about us? For God's sake, speak plainly, man!" Alexis had to restrain herself from raising her voice. She was growing quite tired of Villar's hedging and wished he'd simply get to the point.

"Your … special friendship?" Villar ventured.

"She has become a dear friend. What of it?"

Villar flushed. "I should not wish to come between you, sir, and even if you have an understanding with her in that regard ... as I said, such is not something I could be comfortable with." He clasped his hands behind his back and squared his shoulders, staring at the far bulkhead. "Not that there's anything wrong with that — or the other either ... as I said, we don't judge such things on Chorthampton."

What on earth would he even *have* to judge her on? And what was the "other"? Good lord, he was speaking as though she and Marie were ...

Alexis stared at him as realization dawned. Her eyes widened and then she flushed herself.

"Mister Villar," she said slowly, "is it your belief, then, that Marie and I are ..." She wasn't quite sure how to put it into words, as she was quite certain this was not a normal topic of conversation between a captain and first officer, but no wonder Villar was uncomfortable and his face colored scarlet.

All this time he's thought that, and with Marie practically throwing herself at him and mostly right in front of me.

"I don't judge, sir, I assure you!"

Alexis thought of what must have been going through Villar's mind all those times he'd become engaged in conversation with Marie, then darted his gaze to Alexis, and broken off so uncomfortably. She couldn't help herself, but she started laughing.

"Sir?"

"You thought ..." She couldn't even finish the sentence for laughing so hard.

"Sir! I don't find this at all amusing!"

"Not yet you don't," Alexis said, trying to control herself.

The poor man must be driven half-mad by frustration.

Finally, she managed to control herself.

"Mister Villar, Marie and I are not ..." She paused, thinking of how to phrase it delicately. "We are not ... special friends, as you put it."

Villar's eyes widened and, if anything, he flushed redder still.

"You're not?"

"I assure you, no."

"But ..." Villar spread his hands. "But bringing her to your family's holdings, I thought?"

Oh ... good lord, he thought I was bringing my new bride home to meet the family. Alexis almost laughed again.

"Marie lost all of her family on Giron. She had nowhere to go. I simply couldn't leave her and her babe there in the refugee camps."

Villar pointed to Alexis' cot. "But ..."

"Not my best decision, perhaps," Alexis said, "but Marie had to see to Ferrau several times a night and I'm afraid my stature makes clambering in and out of an upper inconvenient."

"But I saw the two of you ... there ... I mean ..."

Alexis frowned. *Oh, yes, that night he came to report that a sail was sighted in the Straits and Marie was all draped across me.*

"As I said, the shared bunk was not my best decision. Marie is a bit ... grabby in her sleep." Alexis bit the inside of her lip to keep from laughing at the look on Villar's face. "Fair warning to anyone who would pursue her."

Villar had now lost all sense of composure and Alexis feared his eyes might pop out. She knew it was probably a bit cruel, but she couldn't help her amusement at him.

"You said your sweetheart was French!"

"Yes, French. A Frenchman. A French *man*, Mister Villar — a lieutenant in their navy."

Villar blinked and his shoulders sagged.

"Oh dear." He blinked again.

"Would you take that seat now, Mister Villar?"

Villar nodded and fairly tumbled into the seat.

"Isom! A drink for Mister Villar, if you please — something a bit stronger than wine, I think." Alexis couldn't quite keep the amusement off her face.

Isom poked his head in from the pantry and eyed Villar, who was now hunched forward and had his face in his hands, then ducked back into the pantry.

Villar looked at Alexis and she had a sudden surge of sympathy at the look on his face.

"Do you suppose I've cocked it all up, sir?"

"What, with Marie?"

Villar nodded. "What must she think of me? I've acted like ... well, I spent such effort pushing her away she must ..."

He trailed off as Isom set a glass of something amber before him. Villar grasped and drained the glass in one go, then gasped.

"Oh ... god, what is that ... it's wretched ..." He looked at Alexis and flushed more. "I'm sorry, sir, but ..."

"That's the captain's best bourbon, that." Isom's look of sympathy had changed to affront.

"It's an acquired taste, I think, Mister Villar — would you care for something else?"

"No, no." He held the glass out to Isom. "Another of those, if I may? Upon reflection I find it quite fits my mood."

Isom sniffed, but took the glass back to the pantry to refill it.

Alexis gave him a moment to settle his thoughts and have a fresh drink in hand. Villar drank, grimaced, but drank again. He took a deep breath, then groaned.

"What must I do? She must think ... oh, what must she think of me after I ..."

He looked up and Alexis found herself more sympathetic than amused as he then buried his face in his hands again. By the look on his face he had much stronger feelings for Marie than he'd admitted.

And kept them suppressed all this time for fear of offending me, his captain, the poor man.

"You should write to her immediately, Mister Villar, and explain everything. *Everything*," she emphasized as he looked up at her desperately.

"I couldn't," Villar moaned.

"You must."

Villar shook his head. "No ..."

"Better she hear it from you than from someone else," Alexis said, unable to keep her amusement in check any longer.

"But who would ..." Villar blanched, staring at her. "You wouldn't ..."

Alexis nodded.

"Oh, yes, Mister Villar. I'm afraid this is far too good a story to keep to myself."

THIRTY-TWO

The sky above the Al Jadiq landing field was overcast with low clouds and a light drizzle fell, apparently for quite some time if the state of the landing field was any indication. The field itself was sparse grass and dirt, turned into mud by the rains, save for a paved section near one end.

Alexis grimaced as she stepped off the boat's stairs into several centimeters of mud.

They'd set down near the entrance to the government buildings which, curiously, was at the opposite side of the field from the only accessible market, as well as the only paved areas. The rest of the landing field, nearly half a kilometer across, was surrounded by a high, solid wall.

"Not very welcoming," Alexis said, moving to the side and allowing Villar to step down into the mud with her. Naval precedent called for the senior officer to be last on and first off a ship's boat.

"We're *kāfir*, sir, unbelievers." Villar edged to the side as well, to allow the rest of the men to exit. "They don't really want us here at all."

259

"So they've put the government offices we must visit to one side and the market where we'll purchase supplies at the other?"

Villar nodded. "We're not all that welcome in the market, come to that — only reason it's open to us is they have to, I suspect."

"Belay that," Alexis said, holding up a hand to stop the men disembarking the boat. "Do they offer vehicles at all? For us to get the supplies across this swamp?"

"Never have before — it's tote and carry."

"I've three antigrav pallets," Ousley, the bosun, said from midway up the boat's steps. "It's multiple trips or shoulder what won't fit on them."

So slog through this muck more than once or do it carrying a load.

"That's ridiculous," Alexis said. "Mister Villar, you and two of the Marines with me. Mister Ousley, tell the pilot to move the boat to one of the paved areas by the market and load there."

"Aye —"

"Sir," Villar interrupted. "That's not how things are done here. The Jadiqis insist we put down on this side of the field. That side is for their own shipping."

Alexis frowned. "Their own? Not visiting merchantmen?"

Villar shook his head. "They discourage other merchants from coming, unless they've contracted with them for some reason. Those two ships in orbit now are Jadiqi-owned, likely waiting on some cargo to be ready."

"The colony itself owns two ships?"

"Four, I think, sir."

"However have they managed that?"

Villar shrugged. "Al Jadiq has a great deal of wealth, sir."

Alexis compared the size of the system's main town to that of Man's Fall and had to agree. Still, with all that wealth, they could have done more with their landing field.

"I'll not have my men trudging through this muck, Mister Villar. If the Jadiqis wish to object, they may do so while I meet with them."

"As you say, sir." Villar gestured to two Marines on the boat's ramp. "Raffield, Bounds, you're with us. Mister Ousley, you have your orders."

"Aye, sir."

There was a moment's confusion on the ramp as the two Marines made their way down and the rest of the men made their way back into the boat. Alexis turned and strode toward the gate in the wall nearby, Villar and the Marines following her.

"They won't like this at all, sir," Villar said, his voice low. "The only reason the market is open to us at all is that it's a part of all colonial charters that the colony must allow resupply rights to the Navy."

"Do they treat visiting merchantmen with the same lack of courtesy?"

Lounds and the *Gale* would have been here and gone in the time it took to repair *Nightingale*, and she couldn't imagine him putting up with this sort of thing.

Before Villar could answer, the gate opened at their approach, held by two guards with laser rifles slung over their shoulders. The guards looked past Alexis' group to *Nightingale's* boat and spoke rapidly to each other in a language Alexis didn't recognize.

"Through here then?" Alexis asked one of them, gesturing to the long, dimly lit corridor behind the gates.

The guard glanced once at her, then quickly turned his attention to Villar.

"Wait in the room at the end," the guard said. "You will be called."

Villar nodded and gestured for Alexis to proceed him. Alexis started to say something, but Villar widened his eyes and shook his head slightly. As he'd been here before, Alexis decided to accept his lead for the moment, waiting to speak until they were some distance down the corridor.

"What was that about then?" she asked.

Villar cleared his throat, clearly uncomfortable. "It's, well ... you're a woman, sir."

"I see." Alexis had read the briefing materials aboard *Nightingale* regarding Al Jadiq. She'd found much of it bewildering, yet the colonists had chosen to set themselves up with those rules and everyone who'd emigrated from Zariah had accepted them, so who was she to judge?

"I don't think you do, sir, not really."

Alexis glanced over at Villar and raised an eyebrow. It was a risk for a junior officer to say something like that to his commander — many wouldn't take it well. She considered it a measure of the changes in her relationship with Villar since their talk that he was willing to, though she could wish the circumstances were different.

"Go on."

"Women don't do business here, sir. I think this will be a very ... difficult interview."

They reached the end of the corridor and another pair of guards opened the doors there. Through them was an empty room.

Quite empty.

No windows, no chairs, a bare floor of some poured material. Only yet another pair of doors at the far side.

"Wait," one of the guards said before closing the doors they'd entered through and leaving them alone.

Alexis moved to stand at the room's center. "I assume we're being observed?"

Villar nodded. "I've always assumed so. Lieutenant Bensley believed so as well."

"Then we should speak no more," Alexis said, settling in to stand and wait for some time. She had a suspicion they'd be kept waiting as a sort of power play.

"Aye, sir."

The wait, though, turned out to be remarkably short as a moment later the doors at the far end of the room were flung open and a man stormed in.

"Your boat has moved!" the man yelled. "You must recall your boat to this side of the field!"

"Good day, sir, I'm —"

Alexis stepped forward and held out her hand to the man, but he swept by her without a look and approached Villar. Alexis turned to watch him, more amused than offended. The man was dressed in a modern suit, but had an odd sort of cloth over his head, held in place by a braided band. He had a neatly trimmed beard and mustache that Alexis glimpsed as he rushed by her.

"Why has your boat been moved to the market side of the field? You must return it at once!"

"Mister Khouri, sir," Villar said, gesturing toward Alexis. "May I present to you Lieutenant Carew, *Nightingale's* new commander?"

"New commander? You were to be the new commander until Lieutenant Bensley's return. Where is Lieutenant Bensley?"

Alexis stepped back to Villar's side and held out her hand again.

"Lieutenant Bensley was called away, sir," Alexis said. She gave a little shrug and smile. "Such is the way of the Navy. I'm in command of *Nightingale* now — Mister Khouri, was it?"

Khouri turned away from her, still speaking to Villar.

"Your boat!"

Alexis had to force herself not to smile at the absurdity of it. She was standing right there, and yet the man refused to even acknowledge her presence. Villar looked to her and she gave him a slight nod. She'd let him carry things a bit and at least see where it went.

"The rains, Mister Khouri," Villar said. "They've made the field quite a mess, you see."

Khouri faced Villar, apparently satisfied that he'd spoken instead of Alexis.

"You must recall it."

Villar glanced at Alexis. "Of course, sir," he said, then hesitated. "We'll have to recall the men from the market, as well, as the pilot will be with them. That will take some time, I'm afraid. I know you don't like for us to be groundside for longer than necessary."

Khouri's jaw clenched.

"And this will delay the rest of our meeting," Villar went on. "I suppose Lieutenant Carew could remain here and meet with you while I went to retrieve the men and have the boat moved."

Alexis kept her face impassive, but she was rather impressed with Villar. He was showing a streak of absolutely polite, bland-faced aggressiveness that she wouldn't have suspected.

"This once I will allow it," Khouri said finally. "As a courtesy. Due to the rains."

Villar nodded. "Of course, Mister Khouri."

"Come."

Khouri strode toward the doors he'd entered through, clearly angry. Alexis and Villar shared a look — she hoped she managed to convey her approval of how he'd handled things — and followed.

"The Marines wait here," Villar whispered to her. "It's how things are done."

Alexis nodded.

Once through the far doors, Khouri's guards closed them.

The next room was as ornate as the waiting room had been bare and Alexis assumed she'd be properly impressed if she'd been left waiting as long as she suspected was the norm. Large windows looked out on a broad square filled with people. The floor was covered in layers of rich carpets, and more colorful hangings decorated the walls. The center of the room was dominated by two chairs and a low table, the only furnishings. One chair was significantly larger and more ornate than the other and Alexis was unsurprised that Khouri seated himself in that one.

Alexis took the other and Villar stationed himself standing to her left.

Khouri's eyes narrowed briefly before he turned them to Villar.

"Tea?"

"Thank you, sir."

Khouri drew a cup of tea from a samovar on the table beside him and offered it to Villar. Villar took it and Khouri drew a second cup for himself and settled back into his chair.

Villar offered his cup to Alexis.

"Thank you, Mister Villar," Alexis said, taking it without removing her gaze from Khouri.

The Jadiqi man's nostrils flared, but he set his cup down, drew a third cup from the samovar, and offered it to Villar.

He's like a child playing at pulling the blankets over his head so the bogeyman won't get him. The image of herself as the bogeyman, all terrifying meter and a half of her, almost made her laugh out loud.

Alexis sipped her tea. It was dark, hot, and very sweet, a combination she found she quite liked.

"When will Lieutenant Bensley return?" Khouri asked Villar.

"Lieutenant Bensley may not return at all," Alexis said. "*Nightingale* is my command until I receive further orders."

From the look on Khouri's face, that time couldn't come soon enough. Alexis suspected he might be willing to make any number of sacrifices or offerings his religion allowed toward that end, in fact.

"Lieutenant Bensley shall be missed," Khouri said, still addressing Villar.

Alexis considered how long to let this go on. Her amusement with him was palling rapidly.

"Mister Villar?" she prompted.

"Sir?"

"It occurs to me that Mister Ousley might send to us with any questions he has about supplies, and that this important conference would be interrupted in that event. Would you be so kind as to wait near the doorway so that your tablet doesn't disturb us and take care of anything that comes up in that regard?"

"Absolutely, sir, I'd be delighted to." Villar spun without another word and went to stand by the door through which they'd entered, some six or so meters away, leaving Khouri with the decision of whether to continue his charade by yelling to Villar across the room or speaking directly to Alexis. She could almost feel sorry for the man.

Finally, Khouri looked at her with a scowl.

Almost sorry — if he weren't glaring at me as though I were some disobedient child he lacked the authority to discipline.

"Is it the intent of the government of New London to insult us?" he asked.

"I assure you it is not, Mister Khouri."

"It is not enough that they have driven us from our home on Zariah, but they must now send *you* here?"

Alexis frowned.

"I was under the impression your colonization here was your choice," she said.

Khouri snorted. "Choice?" He shook his head. "We move to Abhatian, then to Zariah, now here to Al Jadiq. Each time the government of New London surrounds us with other colonies, merchants bring their goods and news, our children leave our ways for your decadence." He glared at her. "Zariah was ours until too many were corrupted and took it away. It will not happen here; do you hear me?" His voice raised. "We will have our own merchants, our own protections, this time."

Alexis raised an eyebrow. It was a colony's right to cut itself off like that if they so desired. New London would only offer the services requested, though more of those services came with further requirements a colony had to comply with. Still, unless the Al Jadiqis were willing to live as subsistence farmers for generations, as those on Man's Fall seemed willing to do, it was quite an expensive proposition.

"You see our ships in orbit?" Khouri asked.

There'd been two ships in high orbit above the planet when *Nightingale* arrived and Alexis had been surprised when they'd responded to *Nightingale's* signals that they were of Jadiqi registry and not merchants from coreward.

"We have two others." Khouri's chest puffed out with pride. "They are crewed with true faithful who will not be tempted by what they see on other worlds."

Alexis had her doubts about that. The Penduli Station houses which eased a spacer's loneliness might surprise Khouri with their effect on his faithful. She tried to push those thoughts aside, as they seemed unworthy. Perhaps Khouri's faith in his faithful was well placed, she couldn't really know that.

Those thoughts also brought to mind Delaine Theibaud and the twin aches that she was so very worried for his safety and that it had been so very long since she'd seen him.

"Fully crewed, we will have the means to trade and protect ourselves without your merchants and Navy." Khouri smirked at her. "Not that your Navy has met its bargain with us. We hear of missing ships and wonder why we should keep our side of these agreements."

Alexis felt he had a point there. As she'd heard on Man's Fall, and, to a certain extent, Dalthus, the colonies were rightfully unhappy with the current situation. Even given that, though, she felt the need to defend her Service.

"There's a war on, if you hadn't heard." Alexis tried to keep her voice calm and reasonable. Now that Khouri was speaking to her directly, she had some hope for the meeting. "We're stretched quite thin to keep the Hanoverese from taking more worlds — perhaps even with an eye toward these."

The thought of Hanoverese troops and all she'd heard of their depredations on Giron arriving on Dalthus chilled her.

Khouri grunted. "So you say." He waved a hand at her dismissively. "And now they send us you, when they know our ways. What does the government of New London mean by this?"

"I was appointed into *Nightingale* because I was available."

Khouri shook his head. "There is some intent here. All things have their hidden meanings. What does the government of New London mean by doing this?"

Alexis frowned. There was something decidedly odd about the way the man referred to the government — it was usually said as … well, she supposed it would be difficult for such a man to acknowledge he was part of a star nation ruled by a queen. The rising hopes she'd had for this meeting began to fall again, and her anger grew at his dismissal of her and the implied dismissal of New London's sovereign. Alexis might never have seen Queen Annalise herself, but men she respected honored her and that was enough for Alexis.

"Her Majesty's government," Alexis said flatly. She'd had enough of this.

Khouri's jaw clenched again.

"I wish to know if the government of —"

"Her Majesty's government."

"— the government of —"

"Her Majesty's."

"What does New London mean by this?" Khouri fairly growled. "In sending you in command of a ship to our world?"

"I'm quite certain," Alexis said, "that Her Majesty, *Queen Annalise*, has not the slightest knowledge of either myself or *Nightingale*." She almost added that the Queen likely had no thoughts to give on Al Jadiq itself either, but saying so might be going a bit far. "Nor *Her* government on New London. My appointment came from an admiral here in the Fringe and I expect it's no more than an entry in some database back on New London. There is no hidden meaning or intent, Mister Khouri, I assure you. Merely the vagaries of an overworked Service in the midst of a war."

Even as she said it, Alexis had to admit she wasn't entirely sure herself. Hadn't she just been thinking that there might be something more to her appointment? Was there some hidden intent or message in giving her *Nightingale*? And if there was, was it right to do so?

"Mister Khouri," Alexis said, suddenly quite tired of the games. Her experiences since taking command of *Nightingale*, from the vapid parlor games on Dalthus to the infuriatingly obstinate Stoltzfus on Man's Fall to the ship and crew itself — and now this Khouri's attitude of dismissal and refusal to deal with her simply because of who she was. It all seemed to settle around her shoulders like a vast weight. Or, rather, it had always been there and she was only now noticing how very weary it made her. "May we settle the business of my ship's visit and both be on about other things?"

THIRTY-THREE

"That man may be one of the most infuriating I've ever met," Alexis observed once she and Villar were back at *Nightingale's* boat.

"Khouri?" Villar asked.

Alexis nodded. Khouri had, at least, provided them with transport across the landing field, as Alexis pointed out the alternative was for her to call the boat to pick them up, delaying the loading and extending the time her crew spent in and near the marketplace.

"I suppose, though the man he replaced was worse. At least Lieutenant Bensley thought so."

"I cannot imagine."

The men from the market had returned to the boat as well and were busy stowing pallets of fresh supplies. Ousley left off at their approach and walked over.

"We've a problem, sir."

Alexis sighed. "Of course we do. We've had nothing but, since arriving in this system, Mister Ousley, why should we expect our departure to be any different? What is it now?"

Ousley grimaced and rubbed at the back of his neck.

269

"Two men missing from the work party, sir. Ruse and Sinkey."

"Run?" Alexis couldn't imagine a man wanting to run from the Navy to Al Jadiq, but spacers weren't known for their thoughts about the future. If a man were fed up with life aboard ship and saw the opportunity to run, he might take it no matter where.

"I think they were took up by the coppers, sir, or whatever it is they have here," Ousley said. "Brissenden said to me they were chatting up a local girl — they was all told not to, sir, just as always here, but Ruse and Sinkey aren't ones to listen nor heed." He turned to Villar. "Come off that frigate what stopped us, sir, if you'll remember."

Villar nodded, then to Alexis, "They were part of an ... exchange with the frigate's captain, sir. One of ours for two of his."

Alexis frowned, that was an odd-sized bargain. "To what purpose? Why would —" She realized even as she was asking what the only reason for a captain to make such an exchange would be. "And they're the ones who joined up with Iveson and Spracklen, those two miners."

"They're not bad in themselves," Villar said, "but they're too eager to follow."

"And troublesome whoresons when they follow the wrong fellow," Ousley added, then quickly to Alexis, "Begging your pardon, sir."

"I've heard the same and worse, Mister Ousley," she assured him. "Besides which, I think asking a bosun to watch his language might very well be against the Articles — the unwritten ones at least. So let me hear from this Brissenden what he saw, then."

Ousley called Brissenden over and the young spacer shifted nervously from foot to foot as he described what he'd seen when asked.

"Ruse and Sinkey was slackin', sir, as they're wont to do?" He waited until Alexis nodded for him to continue. "So they's at the back o' the line fer loadin', y'see? An' there's this girl at the next stall ... well, seems she could be a girl, and it's hard to tell with 'em all bundled up as they are here and their faces covered, innit?" He hurried on. "But I didn't say nothin' to her, y'understand? Nor look too long at all. Been here before, haven't I?"

"Yes, Brissenden," Villar said. "No one's suggesting you've done anything wrong, we just wish to hear what you saw."

"Well, they was sort of lookin' at her," the man continued. "An edging toward her, y'know? An' I thought I should say some'at to Mister Ousley at the time, but then it's all 'lift this' and 'load that', an' I never thought of it no more." He paused. "'Til I heard a shout, that is."

"A shout?" Alexis asked after a moment's silence.

"Yes, sir. I heard this shout an' thought it was '*Nightingale*', which seemed odd, bein' English and all and our ship's name and us not hearin' that so much in the markets here, y'see? An' I looked around but didn't see nothing." He swallowed hard. "But then as we're startin' back an' Mister Ousley he notes that Ruse an' Sinkey's gone, y'see, it's then that I remember a bit more."

"Go on and tell it, Brissenden," Ousley prompted. "It's not getting any tastier stewing in your skull."

Brissenden nodded. "No, sir. It's like this, what I seen. There's one o' them aircars in the street, see, with two o' there coppers-like at the back door. The ones with the lasers. An' they're mostly at the gates from that market to the rest o' the city — least when I've seen 'em before."

"That would be the Jannisarian Guard, sir," Villar told Alexis. "The same who guard the government building where we met with Mister Khouri." He shook his head. "They're more of an arm of the politicians than a real police force."

Alexis frowned. "And in an aircar, you say, Brissenden?"

The spacer nodded. "Aye, sir."

Alexis scanned the sky above the town and frowned again. There were several craft visible in the air, something she'd barely noted on landing, having become used to such things in her Naval travels. Now it was brought to her attention, though, it did seem odd.

"Mister Villar, does the degree of advanced technology on Al Jadiq strike you at all odd for a colony world?"

Villar nodded. "They brought more than most do at the start, that's certain."

"Indeed," Alexis said. "Dalthus had but three antigrav haulers when I signed aboard *Merlin* and that after two generations. It's only the recent gallenium wealth that's allowed them to bring in more." She frowned again, eyeing the vehicles in the sky. "A wealthy and extravagant people."

It puzzled her how a new colony world, even one whose settlers had planned their move for years, could afford to import and maintain so much technology they were unable to produce locally, but the matter of her missing spacers took precedence.

"Where would they have been taken?" she asked.

"Ah, sir, there's no telling that, I think," Ousley said. "Play it close the vest, the Jadiqis do."

Villar nodded. "If they were taken, there's no telling where they're being kept. They'll be tried and beheaded once we've left the system."

"Beheaded?" Alexis asked. "For talking to a girl?"

"It happened once before, early in my time aboard *Nightingale*," Villar said. "A man went missing. We assumed he'd run — perhaps he did — and we heard on our next visit that he'd been executed. I was never quite sure of the charge, as we have so little contact outside the single market."

"Laws here're all fool convoluted," Ousley said. "Like Zariah was when I was a lad. All about offense to something or other and lopping off parts." He spat to the side. "Bloody barbarians."

Alexis shuddered a bit at the thought herself. "That does seem extreme for merely speaking to a girl. Still, one's no more dead from that than from a hanging."

"Least a man can be buried all of a piece if he's hung," Ousley muttered.

"Well, who do we speak to about it?" Alexis turned to Villar.

"That Mister Khouri again?"

Villar blinked. "Speak to, sir? About what?"

"About our missing men, Mister Villar, and what's needed to get them back. It's one thing if we thought they'd run, but if they were taken up by the local watch, then they should be turned back over to *Nightingale* for any discipline."

"Sir, I ..."

Villar glanced once at Ousley.

"A moment, if you please, Mister Ousley," Alexis said. "I believe it's time for you to see the cargo's well squared away while Mister Villar and I discuss what's to be done about our wayward men."

"Aye, sir."

Ousley nodded and Alexis waited until he was some distance away before speaking quietly.

"Something our bosun should not hear, Mister Villar?"

"No, sir ... well, only that I'm not sure if *you'll* wish to hear what I have to say."

"Out with it, if you please, Mister Villar." Her lips twitched. "It's not getting any tastier stewing in your skull, as Mister Ousley pointed out."

Villar smiled briefly as well, then sighed.

"Sir, I don't see how it is we'll get Ruse and Sinkey back. If they were indeed taken and not run, that is." He shrugged. "Well, even if run, they're likely in the hands of the guard by now, and the Jadiqis won't turn them back to us just for the asking."

Alexis frowned. "I don't quite understand, Mister Villar. The regulations and colonial charters are quite clear on the point. A man off a Queen's ship is not subject to the local authorities so long as a Queen's ship is in system. They're to be turned back over to the Navy for any punishment."

Villar scratched at his collar and looked away.

"That is what the charters demand," he allowed.

ONCE THE BOAT WAS LOADED, Alexis had it lift and land once more on the opposite side of the field. She and Villar made their way down the ramp to the guarded doorway, but this time the guards made no move to open it. They stared straight ahead, ignoring her.

"I wish to speak with Mister Khouri again," Alexis said to the one on the right.

"The minister is busy," the left-hand guard said, not looking at Alexis.

"Show me to the meeting room. I'll wait."

"Very busy."

"All meetings are done," the other guard said. "All business is done."

Alexis looked from one to the other. Both guards were impassive, but seemed to give off an aura of self-satisfaction.

"Sir," Villar whispered, "perhaps if we were to retire to the ship for a time and discuss what might be done."

"Ruse and Sinkey are in it up to their necks, if we're correct, Mister Villar, and may not have that sort of time."

Villar shook his head and nodded back toward the boat, out of earshot of the two guards. They moved there.

"They'll want the execution public," Villar whispered. "That's what we heard they did last time. But it's one thing to do that once we've left, when they can claim the men ran and were left behind, then committed some crime, quite another to do them harm while *Nightingale* is still in system."

"Still in system and responsible for them, as their colonial charter stipulates," Alexis agreed, nodding. "Harming them while we're in system means admitting they have them, and that ..."

"Admitting they have them means they're obligated to turn the two back to *Nightingale* for discipline, sir," Villar said.

Alexis glared at the two guards, but nodded. "So they're safe so long as *Nightingale* is in-system — as long as that may be."

Villar nodded, though Alexis could see from his face that he wasn't at all confident it would make a difference. *Nightingale* would have to leave eventually, listing Ruse and Sinkey as *run* in the muster books if Khouri refused to admit they were being detained. Once the ship transitioned, the two spacers' fate was sealed.

Even if they haven't been taken up by the Jadiqis, their fate's sealed once Nightingale *sails. Executed here or marked as deserted and hang for that later, it's much the same.*

The only hope was to somehow convince Khouri to turn them over.

"Let's away, Mister Villar, and see what we may come up with."

Alexis managed to barely contain her rage at Khouri until they were back aboard *Nightingale*. Something in her manner or the set of her jaw, which ached from her clenching it, must have warned the others aboard *Nightingale's* boat, though, for the passenger compartment was unusually still and quiet as the boat lifted and made for the ship.

"There may be nothing we can do, sir, it's the way of ..." Villar ventured midway through the flight, then broke off and turned his gaze to the bulkhead as Alexis' eyes narrowed.

They remained that way for the rest of the flight to *Nightingale*. Both staring forward at the bulkhead and cockpit hatch, Alexis' mind whirling over the problem of her missing men and her outrage at Khouri, who she'd come to see as personifying the whole of the Jadiqis, Villar attempting to draw no further attention to himself.

"He has them," Alexis said quietly as the soft *thumps* of the boat making fast to *Nightingale* sounded through the quiet compartment.

Villar nodded.

"He has them and means to kill them as soon as *Nightingale* sails." Alexis rose and made her way to the boat's hatch, unaware that the crew behind her, Villar and the bosun included, remained immobile, watching her instead of jumping into action to unload the boat as they normally would. The hatch slid open as the boat fully docked and Alexis boarded her ship.

"Not my lads, he won't."

THIRTY-FOUR

"Isom, come and look at this, will you?"

Alexis arranged the documents she wanted him to review on her tabletop and slid them to the other side.

The problem was her conflicting orders and regulations all coming home to roost here on Al Jadiq.

On the one hand, the standard clauses in colonial charters, and Al Jadiq's was no different, called for Naval personnel to be turned over to the Navy for offenses against local laws. Despite the autonomy granted to colonies in their own affairs, the Service would never accept those varied and oftentimes regressive laws being applied to its own personnel.

On the other hand, *Nightingale's* specific orders were to "provide neither offense nor insult to local laws and customs, nor to bring any dishonor upon Her Majesty or Her Naval Service".

"Not a bit of provision for how silly or barbaric those customs might be," Alexis muttered.

"Sir?"

She shook her head. "Never mind me, Isom, just look over these things." She ran her fingers over the table spreading things out. "You've a legal mind, after all. Is there a bit of this that gives clear direction?"

Isom read through what she'd laid out. "Mister Prescott's practice was in property, for the most part, sir, and I was just a clerk before I was taken up by the Press." He pursed his lips. "But I can't say as how any of this could be called clear, no."

Alexis grunted. She supposed the easy way around things would be to mark Ruse and Sinkey as *run* in *Nightingale's* muster book, then sail away. That's what other commanders might do — what Lieutenant Bensley had apparently been satisfied to do before.

Apply the fiction that I don't know full well what's happened to them, and what happens to them further after they're assumed to have run and there's no Navy ship in-system is of no concern to the Service or its honor.

Her orders were so ambiguous that they could completely justify leaving Ruse and Sinkey to their fate — or forcing the Jadiqis to turn them over.

And on the captain's head be it, when it's over and Admiralty finally weighs in.

Isom shook his head again. "Could be read either way, sir. I suppose it would be up to Admiralty to decide?"

"After the fact," Alexis agreed. "They'll confirm or disavow a captain's actions, all after the dust settles."

"If you don't mind me saying, sir, those two are no great loss."

"Ousley said as much."

"Taken up with those two miners and joined in on the —" Isom broke off, scowling.

Alexis nodded understanding. A captain's clerk was an odd position — privy to all the crew felt and said, but having the captain's ear. Being part of the crew he'd be well aware of the extortion happening aboard, but if the crew didn't want it spoken of openly, it placed him in a bad spot. If the crew found out, they might not trust him in the future.

Isom my ears and my nonexistent coxswain my fist, as it were.

She'd been dearly missing that other appendage since she'd taken the miners, Iveson and Spracklen, aboard. If anything the depredations of the original gang of extorters had grown greater along with their numbers.

Still, there was no one aboard who seemed to fit the bill — respected enough by the crew to lead her boat crew and enforce her will in the berthing spaces.

Alexis sighed. With no clear direction from her orders, she had to fall back on her own sense of duty. Ruse and Sinkey had been decent enough lads when she'd come aboard. Followers and none too quick, but they hadn't yet turned to the bad as they had after she'd brought Iveson and Spracklen on.

In a way, their actions could be my fault. If those two miners were a bad enough influence on them. She caught her lower lip between her teeth and gnawed on it. *Fault or not, they're my responsibility, though.*

Decision made, she tapped her tabletop to signal the quarterdeck. "Mister Villar?"

"Yes, sir."

"You've been signaling the Jadiqi to request another meeting with Mister Khouri?"

"Yes, sir," Villar said. "On the bell, as you ordered." He paused. "Mister Khouri is still ... 'unavailable and it is unknown when there may be time to receive you'."

"A new signal, Mister Villar. Inform the Jadiqis that we will be meeting with Mister Khouri in one hour's time regarding a matter of urgent importance." She took a deep breath. "Then assemble my boat crew, Corporal Brace, and a dozen Marines." She paused again, thinking.

"Sir?" Villar asked, perhaps sensing that her orders were not quite complete.

Alexis' eyes narrowed.

Very well, then, she thought, the exact wording of her orders running through her mind. *If Admiralty's going to leave such things to my discretion, then I'll bloody well take advantage of that.*

Her jaw clenched and she felt the now familiar sense that she was about to do something she'd regret later, but would never choose to change. Much as when she'd thrown Daviel Coalson off the back of *Marylin* — it made her sick to think of, but she felt certain she'd do it again even knowing that.

Oddly, even with that feeling and the gravity of the situation, it was as though a weight were lifted from her shoulders. At least this was a difficulty she could address directly – she could act.

"The number four port gun crew and their gun to the ship's boat as well, Mister Villar."

Turn me away, will you, Mister Khouri?

"We're going to bring our wayward *Nightingales* home."

THIRTY-FIVE

Alexis settled herself in the boat's cockpit next to the pilot. She could hear the bustle of activity from the passenger compartment as Brace and his Marines strapped in with the rest of her boat crew. There was a trio of muted *clangs,* a long pause, then a fourth. She assumed that was *Ole Sparky,* as the number four port gun crew had christened their weapon, being clamped down to the deck in the boat's hold.

"Have you ever done this before, Rasch?" she asked.

Next to her, Rasch shook his head tightly, eyes scanning the boat's controls. "Only in the simulation, when I was made pilot, sir. Been no need of it since."

Alexis patted his shoulder. She'd expected that — it was rare enough that a ship's boat was used to board another ship in normal space, much less assault a planet. Such maneuvers were for the pilots aboard the Marine transports.

"Do it just as you did then and we'll all be fine," she assured him.

"As you say, sir."

"Sir," Villar called from the passenger compartment. "All aboard and strapped in ... if you're certain this is —"

"Thank you, Mister Villar."

Alexis could well understand his concern. Khouri's earlier responses, or those of the Jadiqis saying he was unavailable, had left no reason to believe he'd change his mind and return the two spacers to *Nightingale* no matter how much she asked.

"Let's be off, Rasch," Alexis said, clapping the pilot on the shoulder.

Rasch worked the controls and the boat detached from *Nightingale* and sped toward the planet in a single motion. No adjustment of orbit or clearing maneuvers, simply an abrupt acceleration to its full speed aimed directly at the planet's spaceport.

Despite the boat's inertial compensators, Alexis felt as though she could almost feel the acceleration as the planet loomed larger and larger in the forward screen.

"Steady, Rasch," she said. "And straight in. They'll not fire on a Queen's ship, even if they have anything in the way of weapons."

Nightingale's sailing notes for Al-Jadiq made no mention of defensive systems and the colony was so young that she suspected there were none. Still, she wouldn't have suspected the presence of so many aircars, either. Al Jadiq might be young, but the colonists clearly had wealth from somewhere and there was no telling what they might have bought for themselves.

"As you say, sir." Rasch swallowed hard.

This trip down went far faster than the last. The boat burned through the atmosphere at the very limits of its tolerances and Alexis kept a close eye on the cockpit's monitors, knowing just how inexperienced Rasch was with this maneuver.

Despite that inexperience, Rasch brought the boat to ground less than ten meters from the building where she'd first met with Khouri.

Alexis was in motion before it had stopped moving, leaving the cockpit and stepping out onto the still extending ramp. Steam rose from the still muddy field and Alexis could feel the heat emanating from the boat's hull.

The same two guards from earlier stepped in front of the door to block her way, expressions both puzzled and angry. The boat's landing had kicked up the muddy surface of the field, casting dark water and soil toward them in a heavy wash. They weren't quite covered in it, but their uniforms would never pass inspection — assuming the Jadiqis had such standards.

"Corporal Brace!" she called, not stopping in her pace.

Behind her she heard the rustle as Brace and four of his Marines spread out in a line.

"Arms!" Brace bellowed.

The two guards' eyes widened.

"Aim!"

Alexis continued walking toward them. One of the guards glanced at the other, swallowed heavily, and both dove to the ground as Brace drew in a deep breath.

"Fire!"

Alexis had to work hard to keep from flinching at the *crack* of ionizing air around her. Brace's men fired high, as she'd instructed them, but after seeing the gunnery of *Nightingale*'s crew she was none too confident in that of the Marines. The Marine complement, though, was better trained and drilled than the crew at large, not having been looted by passing ships as the Naval crew had been.

Sharp *pops* echoed across the plain as the Marines' lasers struck the stone above the door. Stone cracked and pocked, shards flying off, at the sudden release of energy.

She stopped between the two prone guards. The plain was silent save for the sound of the Marines' rifles being worked to load new capacitors for another shot and a bit of a crackling noise from the cooling boat's hull.

"Bring it out, lads!"

Behind her, she heard the rumble of wheels on the boat's ramp as

Nightingale's gunner and crew manhandled a ship's gun to the hatch and pointed its crystalline barrels at the doorway.

"Gentlemen," she said, looking down at the guards who were still prostrate in the mud, "I mean to see Mister Khouri. If you wish to have a doorway left to guard, I suggest you open the sodding thing for me instanter."

ALEXIS SEATED herself in the chair she'd used during her previous visits.

"No one is available. Many hours," the aide said again. The man had an odd accent and Alexis suspected this was not his first language. She remembered reading in the sailing notes that these settlers were so insular, even before they'd left Zariah, that many families never did business outside of their enclaves, and so taught their children their own language first.

Alexis stared straight ahead, trying to project calm and determination, rather than the rage she felt building in her.

There'd been a bit of hope when the guards opened the doors at the landing field, but she couldn't have her lads trundle *Ole Sparky* down the corridor, not least because she wanted it available to protect the boat.

Instead she had Villar and only two Marines accompany her, keying her tablet to record and transmit everything around her back to the boat and then on to *Nightingale*. Despite her outward calm, there was also a bit of fear that the Jadiqis might not stop at a pair of spacers. Mightn't they also decide to keep an officer or two and respond to Admiralty's inquiries with a mild: *Mister Khouri was busy for many hours — we have no idea where your lieutenant might have got to.*

"Many manys," the man said. He looked at her expectantly. "Very manys?"

Alexis took a deep breath to steady herself, certain they'd chosen someone like this to sit with her in an attempt to further put her off. She'd expected Khouri to make himself unavailable and wasn't bothered by that, but she was bothered by the rest of her plan. It was risky, might not work, and would likely be frowned upon by Admiralty — or not. Given what she knew of Admiralty's convoluted reasoning, they might well wish the opportunity to "apologize" for Alexis' actions as a rogue captain exceeding her authority, while quietly implying there were far worse rogues than Alexis to assign to this patrol.

A pain began behind her right eye at that. She much preferred a straight-forward boarding action to the convoluted balancing act her orders and her duty to her crew had put on her these last few hours.

She took another deep breath, slowly so as to still project the calm and determination she wasn't quite feeling, and forced herself to think only about the one reason for doing this that made her forget the rest and the possible consequences.

Ruse and Sinkey were hers, and she'd, by God, get them back.

"Now, look," Alexis said, turning to the aide and pointing at Khouri's empty chair. "Khouri knows I'm here, I know Khouri knows I'm here, and I'm quite certain that he's nearby watching me say I know he knows I'm here. So, Mister Khouri," she said louder, "wherever you are, in five minutes' time I am going to return to *Nightingale's* boat ... then I am going to lift, set down in the middle of your bloody town, and my Marines and I will be knocking on random doors until I have my lads in hand."

"Quite a few manys?" the aide asked hopefully.

The far doorway opened and Khouri entered. He jerked his head at the aide, who hurriedly left as though it was the kindest thing anyone had ever done for him.

Khouri settled himself in his chair, drew a cup of tea from the samovar without offering any to Alexis, and sipped.

"I shall complain to your Admiralty of your actions," he said finally.

"I'm sure you will," Alexis said. She leaned forward and glared at him, "but don't be too quick about it, as I'm far from finished."

Khouri snorted. "What will you do? You have a tiny ship, a tiny crew —" He laughed as though suddenly quite pleased with himself. "— you are a tiny girl. We are an entire planet — and as representative of that planet, I tell you to take your tiny ship and leave now. Your business is through."

"Not nearly," Alexis said. "Your police, these Jannasari, took two of my men from the marketplace. I'll have them back now."

Khouri shook his head. "We have none of your men. This thing did not happen."

To be honest, Alexis had harbored some doubts herself. She had only Brissenden's word and he hadn't actually seen Ruse and Sinkey taken, but Khouri's attitude convinced her that he was lying. He was simply so dismissive and denied so hotly that her final doubts vanished.

"My men, Mister Khouri, will be returned to me instanter, or there will be consequences."

"What? That you will search for them?" He shrugged. "I will add this to my complaint, you will not find them, and eventually you must leave."

He was right about that, Alexis knew. No matter what she wished, *Nightingale* must eventually sail on about the remainder of her patrol and, once she did, Ruse and Sinkey would meet their fate.

Alexis steeled herself. She'd known it would come to this, but had still hoped Khouri might produce her men. Her actions might be a mistake, but with such conflicting orders to work by it really came down to only one thing — Ruse and Sinkey, whatever their faults, were *Nightingales*. They were hers and she'd not leave them.

She swiftly reached behind her to the carefully tailored pocket at the small of her back and drew the flechette pistol she'd carried since her time aboard *HMS Shrewsbury* then aimed it at Khouri, waiting for him to react.

Khouri's expression grew puzzled. He looked to either side, then behind him, then down at his lap before returning his gaze to her.

"What is it you point at?" he asked.

Alexis blinked, then looked at her hand and adjusted her grip so that the tiny flechette pistol wasn't entirely hidden in her grip.

"It is small, yet mighty, Mister Khouri, I assure you."

Khouri's expression hardened.

"You would not —"

"Yes, I would; yes, I will; no, you won't," Alexis said. "You're about say a number of things to become even more tiresome, and I'm bloody well fed up with it, so let's have those be the answers to everything you're about to say. Mister Villar!"

"Sir?"

"Will you confirm that my tablet is transmitting to the boat and thence to *Nightingale*?"

"Uh ... aye, sir, is this —"

"Kindly take Corporal Brace and his men back to the boat, Mister Villar." She fixed her gaze on Khouri. "If I have not returned in one hour's time, you are to lift and set sail for Dalthus. There you are to supply *Nightingale's* log and this recording to any and all outgoing ships for transmission to Admiralty. The message is that Al Jadiq has taken Queen's men off a Queen's ship, detained or caused harm to the commander of a Queen's ship in the performance of her duties ... and is in rebellion against the Crown."

Khouri blanched. Alexis could see the thoughts working in his head. The mere accusation of rebellion would bring a fleet to Al Jadiq. A fleet with an admiral who might or might not see things Khouri's way after a thorough investigation of these events. Would he take that risk, given the possible consequences?

If found to be in rebellion against the Crown, it would be hanging for a man.

Not that he'll be alive to see the consequences, Alexis promised herself. The penny had been rolling out a ship's gun on the landing field, now she was in for the full pound and more.

"Threaten as you will," Khouri said, but Alexis thought she could detect a sheen of sweat on his forehead. "I say I do not have these men and there is nothing you may do about —"

He cut off abruptly, jumping as flechettes cut into the chair cushion next to him. Bits of fabric and stuffing puffed into the air and the room echoed with the high-pitched *zip* of the little gun.

"Sir, I really think —"

"To the boat, Mister Villar. This is my doing and none of yours." She hadn't told Villar this would be her endgame, hoping it wouldn't come to it, but also not wanting him to be implicated in her actions.

"Aye, sir."

Alexis waited while Villar and the others left, keeping her eyes fixed on Khouri.

"I'll have my men back instanter, Mister Khouri," Alexis said, "I will have my men or I will shoot you and any who stands in my way as I search for them."

"Are you mad?" Khouri asked finally.

Alexis considered how very often she was asked that and these latest circumstances — risking her career and threatening to kill this man and more over a pair such as Ruse and Sinkey — then nodded firmly. Whatever else, they were hers.

"Yes. Quite, it seems. And now it's time for you to realize that your life is in the hands of a madwoman and act accordingly, yes?"

"THANK YOU, SIR, THANK YOU!" Ruse said as soon as the door to Khouri's audience chamber shut and they began their way down the corridor to the landing field. "Thought we was dead, I did."

Alexis fumed and let her temper get the better of her. The two men had put her in an untenable position with their actions — abandon members of her crew or offend, threaten, Al Jadiq's colonial representative. The Jadiqis might well have been looking for an opportunity to flex their power over some of *Nightingale's* crew, but, damn them, these two had willingly given them the opportunity.

More than that, she was still furious with the two for joining with Iveson, Spracklen and the others in extorting the other men. And angry with herself for bringing those two aboard. If it hadn't been for the insult to the Service and *Nightingale* in the Jadiqis actions, for her own sense of responsibility to her lads ...

"I didn't do it for you, Ruse," Alexis said, jaw tight. "Were it just you two I'd have left you there to be shortened. Damn your eyes, a bigger pair of disappointments I've never seen."

Ruse hung his head.

"It weren't but a bit of fun, sir," Sinkey said. "We never touched her nor would have, just a bit of a flirt, really. Why, she were even smilin' at us ..." He frowned. "Well, her eyes crinkled up an' looked like a smile, that being all we could see in those things they wear. What's the harm in —"

Alexis rounded on the pair, backing them up against the corridor's wall.

"Do you think I give a tinker's dam about you two chatting up some girl in the market?" She fought the urge to grab them by the ears and drag them to *Nightingale's* boat. "I'm talking about what you're up to aboard my ship."

"What —"

"Do you think I'm blind? You and your mates, Scarborough and Iveson and the others — you two've gone over to the worst of the lot."

"We're just —"

"Stealing from your mates is what you're 'just'." She stepped back and looked them up and down with disgust. "Thieving lubbers, the lot of you."

Ruse bristled at that.

"But —"

"No," Alexis said. She met both of their eyes in turn. "I'll hear no excuses and I'll not pretend to not know what's going on. Not with you two, not here, and not after pulling your sorry arses from the fire."

Ruse hung his head and Sinkey swallowed hard.

"I've read your records lads, and I expected better of you."

Sinkey frowned and his brow furrowed.

"You did?"

Alexis stared at him for a moment, straining for a thought just out of her reach.

How could he not realize that?

Nearly all of *Nightingale's* crew were performing far below her expectations. From the ship-handling to the guncrews, her crew was a lamentable mess. But what had she really done about it?

She blinked.

Nothing.

Oh, she'd ranted in her cabin where only Isom could hear her and set them to drills. Given them goals, but no real reason to strive for them. No real reason not to disappoint her.

No reason to stand with me, she thought.

More than that, she realized that Sinkey's question wasn't just that she'd expected better of him, but that she'd read his records and had any knowledge of him. Since she'd come aboard, she'd been so isolated on the quarterdeck or in her cabin that she'd not made many connections with the common crew — not like back aboard *Shrewsbury*, or even *Hermione*, where she'd known the men of her division so well. She'd spent time talking to them — oh, not some Captain Goodfellow, wanting to be liked more than obeyed, but she'd known each man, at least a little bit about him.

Her heart sank. This whole mess, right up to these two being taken by the Jadiqis wasn't only her crew's fault, but hers as well. She thought about her first commander, Captain Grantham, and how he'd walk through *Merlin's* sick berth after an action, always with a word or some personal note for every man there.

Could I do that? Is there even one thing I know about every man aboard my ship?

Her face flushed as she realized there wasn't.

No reason to stand with me, for I've not stood with them.

She flushed as she realized that, and as she realized why. The loss of *Belial* was still raw in her memory, and the loss of that crew. Knowing them, knowing the *Nightingales,* would bring them too close and open her to that kind of loss again.

Knowing them would mean knowing what she'd lost if it came to that, and she dreaded it, but she'd not get their best without it. She needed their best, needed it desperately, she thought, if enemies like the *Owl* were any indication — and, truth to tell, they deserved better of her.

They're following orders — but they're not following me.

She stepped toward them and laid a hand on each of the men's shoulders. This might be a poor pair to start with, but even they deserved better of her than she'd given.

"Lads, I need your help."

Ruse blinked.

"Sir?"

"*Nightingale's* not what she should be, you know that."

Sinkey snorted, then flushed. "Sorry, sir, but ... well, she's ..."

"A cack-handed bunch of castoffs," Alexis said and saw the two men flush. "But you're my castoffs and I'll stand by you." She nodded toward the room they'd just left. "As I did here, see?"

Ruse nodded.

"I need you to stand with me," she said. "You two are decent hands, and not so old as some of the others who've actually spent time in the Dark enough to know the way of it. The crew'll look to you. Leave off with those two bastard miners and show them what a proper Queen's man can do."

Ruse looked doubtful.

"We're not much for leading and such, sir."

Alexis knew that, but at least she saw them thinking on it.

"No, no you may not be, but, damn you, lads, if you must follow, could you not choose someone worthy of it? Someone you can admire or aspire to? Scarborough? Is that the sort of man you'd be? Or your sons, if you have them?"

They both flushed again and looked away.

Alexis thought she might have a decent chance that her words had got through to them — a start in any case.

"Come on then, lads." She jerked her head down the corridor toward the landing field. "Back aboard ship and put this behind us." She left it to them to decide if she meant their actions on Al Jadiq or the poor start of her tenure aboard *Nightingale.* "Let's get home."

And *Nightingale* was home, for a crew that spent months, or sometimes years, aboard her — home and what family they had. She caught and held each of their eyes in turn.

"And don't you dare disappoint me again, lads."

THIRTY-SIX

22 December, aboard *HMS Nightingale*, darkspace, leaving Al Jadiq System

"Bring them forward, Mister Ousley."

Alexis struggled to keep her face impassive as Ruse and Sinkey were brought forward to stand before the slightly raised platform at the fore of *Nightingale's* gundeck. Alexis, Villar, and Spindler, along with Corporal Brace and two other Marines faced the assembled crew.

The two spacers looked relieved to be back aboard *Nightingale* and no longer in whatever cell the Jadiqis had kept them in, but still worried about what was to come. She'd made it clear to them in the boat on the way up to the ship that there'd still be consequences at captain's mast for their disobeying orders and speaking to a Jadiqi woman in the marketplace.

She didn't like it — hated, in fact, this part of command, but what else was there? Discipline had to be maintained and with so much time and distance between *Nightingale* and any other Naval ship, much less a port with a Naval presence, there were few options. If consequences were weeks or months away, many men wouldn't concern themselves with them.

Despite her dislike of the lash, these were simple men, especially on the Fringe, where many colonies' educational opportunities were limited to the hours in a day not needed to put food on the table. They understood simple rules and simple consequences of the sort they'd grown up with. And that more for *Nightingale's* crew than was usual for other ships, she knew, as those who'd been troublemakers or slackers aboard other ships would be no stranger to a captain's mast.

Alexis scanned the faces of the assembled crew and realized that the men's expressions were not what she was used to seeing at captain's mast aboard other ships. Nor, she realized, were they what she herself wanted from her crew. She'd never want the fear and loathing that had been present aboard *Hermione* under the despised and cruel Captain Neals, but what she saw in *Nightingale's* crew was far too light-hearted, especially given the grave consequences if she hadn't managed to get Ruse and Sinkey back aboard.

I've set quite the wrong tone aboard this ship, in more ways than one, and it's past time it changed.

Despite her talk with them, Ruse and Sinkey themselves seemed to be more amused than chastened by the situation.

Well past time.

Alexis pulled her tablet from a pocket and read off the Articles of War one by one, placing a bit of emphasis on each the two men had violated and more on the punishments open to her under the Articles, most of which ended with:

"... *shall suffer death*" she read again, "or such other punishment, as from the nature and degree of the offense a court martial shall deem him to deserve."

When she finished the crew, and Ruse and Sinkey especially, seemed to have lost a bit of their jovial attitude, and with the formal bit out of the way it was time for her to say a thing or two about their offenses and their fate.

"You bloody, sodding, cack-brained, cunny-witted, *lubbers!*" she bellowed as loudly as she could, which was none too loud, but the shuffling and muttering ceased once she started and by the end she was yelling into dead silence. "You're an embarrassment! To the Queen, me, *Nightingale*, and even to your mates! If *Nightingale* weren't so shorthanded, I'd have left you there to be shortened by the bloody Jadiqis and called it a good bargain to be done with you!"

Alexis felt the eyes of the crew on her, but kept her own boring into Ruse and Sinkey.

"That's no bloody liberty port where they expect a bit of tomfoolery, lads." She lowered her tone and pointed aft. "But you knew that. Been here before and know they're a stick-up-the-arse religious colony and behave so anyway? What'd you show them, eh? That the Navy has no discipline, that's what. That *Nightingales* have no sense, for another." She paused and narrowed her eyes. "Almost that they can take Queen's crew off a Queen's ship and not pay for it?"

She paused, suddenly angrier than she'd been from the start of this. She'd already given Ruse and Sinkey a taste of what she thought of them, both for their actions on Al Jadiq and aboard *Nightingale*. It was, perhaps, time — past time — for the crew as a whole to know her thoughts.

"*My* crew off *my* ship? If it weren't for want of a headsman I'd shorten you two myself!"

Alexis forced herself to calm and looked around for the first time, meeting the wide eyes of the other crewmen one by one.

"I know who you are, lads, don't doubt it. Dumped off every passing ship that wanted rid of you — too old, too weak, too slow —" She eyed Ruse and Sinkey again. "— too much *bloody* trouble to keep aboard. Dregs of the Fringe, the lot of you, aye?"

She looked around again. Some expressions were angry, others resigned — a few were nodding, either the too slow of wit to realize what she'd said or self-aware enough to accept it.

"Well, you're *Nightingales* now, and we're stuck with each other, but I *will* have your best, lads. Better than the best you showed those captains who cast you off, you hear me? I'll not ask any man to do more than he's able, but I will have your very best or know the reason why!"

She turned her attention back to Ruse and Sinkey, shaking her head.

"As for you two..." She spoke quieter now. "I'll stand with you, lads — there's no tin-pot Fringe world I'll let take one of mine, but you'll bloody well stand with me as well or I'll greet your backbones once a fortnight until you do. Mister Ousley?"

"Aye sir!"

Alexis' stomach clenched and she forced herself to remain impassive. She hated what was to come, not least because she'd felt a bosun's cat herself, but saw no other choice.

"Rig a grating and fetch your cat, Mister Ousley. Two dozen each and your very best work, do you hear?"

"Aye sir!"

Alexis held Ruse's eye as Ousley set two men to rigging a grating upright between the posts that ran the length of *Nightingale's* deck, and sent a bosun's mate to fetch a cat — the short whip made from unwinding the tough thermoplastic line of the ship's rigging into nine strands. If either of the men caused trouble, it would be Ruse she suspected, especially after she announced the rest of their punishment — Sinkey would just follow along with him.

"And a month on water alone," she said coldly. "Mark that down, Mister Wileman." She ran a quick glance over the rest of the crew before she returned her gaze to Ruse. "A dozen lashes for any man who slips them a bit of a wet, as well."

"Aye sir," the purser said, wincing.

Ruse's eyes narrowed and he stared back at her. The two dozen lashes he and Sinkey were facing now would be bad, but the crew viewed such things as part of life — over, done with, and then forgotten, as she'd learned aboard her first ship. A month on ship's water, run through the recyclers — and through the crew — for months on end, without recourse to the beer, wine, or rum used to make the water palatable, would be the worst of the punishments. With the threat of a dozen lashes hanging over them, none of Ruse and Sinkey's mates would dare to slip the men a bit of their own ration either.

Alexis stared back at Ruse as his eyes narrowed further. His nostrils flared and his jaw clenched, then he seemed to come to some decision and his posture relaxed. He shrugged, took a deep breath, and raised his hands to strip off his upper jumpsuit as he turned to face the grating.

"Aye, fair enough."

THIRTY-SEVEN

from Al Jadiq to Zariah

"Pipe *Up Spirits*, Mister Ousley, we'll allow the men a bit of a wet and a rest, then exercise the guns again in the afternoon."

"Aye, sir."

Alexis turned to the navigation plot and began reviewing the results of the morning's gunnery drill.

Better, not nearly good, she thought.

She'd moved the worst of the crew, especially the cabal of four — Scarborough, Carras, Chivington, and Monks — from the guns, despite them being younger, stronger, and better able to haul shot canisters and wrestle the heavy carriages about, but the gunnery times and accuracy were still not up to Naval standards, let alone her own.

Nightingale was nearly three and a half weeks out of Al Jadiq, with two weeks left to sail before reaching Zariah again. Things aboard were better, if not entirely good. Ruse and Sinkey had, at least, left off with the miners. They'd changed messes almost immediately after their punishment and she thought well of them for that.

But the mess they'd joined was Nabb's, and that concerned her.

Despite Ousley's good opinion of the lad, he was still young and Alexis worried at the influence two hands like Ruse and Sinkey might have on him. The worry might be for nothing, as he'd likely be off the ship and back under the care of his mum on Dalthus in less than two months, but it did still bother her.

After the main deck was put to rights, guns brought inboard and bowsed against the hull, gunports closed and locked in place, and the compartment re-aired, Ousley returned.

"Deck's secure and the men're out of their vacsuits, sir," he said. "Mister Wileman's just bringing the rum up now."

Alexis nodded and closed the reports on the plot and made her way back to the main deck. Perhaps, just perhaps, there was a glimmer of hope in the current improvement. If the guncrews, as they were put together now, were willing enough, perhaps sufficient drill would bring about the necessary performance. There was still, though, what to do about the men she'd moved off the guns — they were lazy, obstinate, and, worst of all, still extortionate with the rest of the crew.

The daily rum issue remained a frustration to her, as she'd found no solution to their, along with the two miners', predations on the rest of the crew. She wished someone, anyone, would come forward and expose the six bastards for the thieves they were.

Wileman and his assistant brought the large cask — emblazoned, as Naval tradition called for with the words, "The Queen — God Bless Her" — up from storage in his offices below. Alexis took her place with Villar and Spindler on a slightly raised platform at one end of the deck. The men were already lined up, the four hard cases at the front of the line as was their wont, the two miners, Iveson and Spracklen, close behind.

The six weren't entirely together, Alexis had noted, it was only that Iveson and Spracklen had caught on to the others' game and duplicated it. There seemed to be a sort of truce to the two groups, at least while Ruse and Sinkey were with the miners, that they'd prey on the rest of the crew equally and leave each other alone.

Alexis had ordered this issue diluted, rather than neat, with the men's ration mixed into water and citrus juice. She wanted to exercise the guns again soon, she hoped the dilution would keep the crew from downing all of their ration at once. It would also, she hoped, reduce the amount those four could extort from the others. It disturbed Alexis to no end that none of the crew trusted her, her officers, or even the bosun enough to speak out against them, even after Al Jadiq, which she'd hoped might bring the crew closer to her — those four, and the miners, were a cancer eating away at her crew and she almost wished for some arrogant frigate captain to come along and demand a trade of personnel. She'd gladly pawn those six off on someone else for virtually any she could get in return.

The men were served, those four hanging about the cask still to collect their tribute. Next in line was Nabb, talking quietly with Ruse and Sinkey. That brought her concerns for the lad back to the fore of her thoughts. Ruse and Sinkey weren't truly bad sorts, just easily influenced and a bit lazy. She didn't want those traits to rub off on Nabb, no matter her intent to return him to Dalthus and his mum.

Nabb had his portion now and stepped away from the cask. Alexis clenched her jaw as Scarborough met him with a scowl. Ruse and Sinkey stepped up beside Nabb, their own full cups in hand.

Scarborough squared his shoulders, jaw outthrust, with a hard look in his eyes.

Nearby, Ousley's head came around to look at the group as though he'd sensed something — he opened his mouth to speak, but before he could the deck dissolved into chaos.

Nabb, Ruse, and Sinkey, as one, flung the contents of their cups into the faces of the four extorters, following that up with swift blows.

Scarborough doubled over as Nabb buried a fist in his gut. Ruse slammed his now empty cup into Chivington's face. Sinkey took on both Carras and Monks, driving his knee into Carras' groin while swinging his cup at the side of Monks' head.

There was a moment, just a moment, where the deck was still and silent save for the group of fighters and the sound of blows, then Ousley shouted, *"Oy! Belay that!"* and waded in, his two boson's mates at his side, pulling seldom used stunsticks from their belts. Shouts and catcalls started from the rest of the crew, some of whom took the opportunity to approach the fighters and offer a blow or two of their own — nearly all landing on the four extorters, Alexis saw.

Scarborough took more than one punch to his kidneys from behind, spinning in place to face each new attacker, but finding only a sea of blankly innocent faces. Someone in the crowd stepped forward and drove a foot into the back of Chivington's knee, collapsing his leg and giving Ruse an opportunity to put a knee in the man's face. Blood washed the deck from Chivington's nose and she could hear his cry of pain even over the shouts.

Alexis took a step back from the edge of the platform, gesturing for Villar and Spindler to do so as well. She'd let Ousley and his mates, along with the Marines, who Brace was sending into the scuffle now, settle the matter and restore order — better that than for one of her officers to be struck by mistake in the heat of the fight. With this happening right in front of her she'd have no choice but to call for Ousley and his cat once order was restored, she didn't want to have to do worse for striking an officer, even all unknowing.

The brawl ended as quickly as it began. Most of the crew moved back from the fighting as Ousley and his mates shouted and shoved their way into the mix. In short order the bosun, his mates, and the Marines had the principals separated and restrained — though Alexis noted those enforcing order seemed to take shots of their own at the much-disliked hard cases.

She stepped back to the front of the platform, Villar and Spindler beside her, with Brace and one of his Marines to either side — both of those had their own stunsticks drawn and were watching the crew carefully.

"Pack up the cask, Mister Wileman," Alexis said, "there'll be no further rum issue today. Nor tomorrow neither — *quiet down!*" Her bellow silenced the mutters from the mass of crew. "I'll have not a bit of whinging or we'll review the log and see which of you got a blow or kick in at the edges —" She nodded at the seven restrained men. "— then it'll be more than this lot at the next Mast."

She waited, eyes scanning the rest of the crew until they'd settled and seemed to accept it. If she did have to review the log's recording of the events and who'd snuck in a kick or a blow, likely half or more of the crew'd be facing the bosun's cat. Two days without the rum issue was less than they deserved, but she could well understand their urge to get in a bit of their own on those four. She turned her attention to the bosun and his captives.

"In my quarters, Mister Ousley," Alexis said, "the lot of them, and in irons."

ALEXIS USED the time Ousley needed to get the brawlers in restraints to arrange things in her quarters, and for the rest of the ship. She sent Villar and Corporal Brace to oversee the rest of the crew, trusting them to keep order along with Ousley's mates. Spindler was sent to the quarterdeck to keep the watch, a Marine along with him. In addition to the Marine outside her compartment's hatchway, she brought two inside to flank her as she sat at her table. She didn't truly expect any further trouble, either from the crew at large or the brawlers, but wanted to take no chances.

Ousley and another Marine soon entered with the seven men, hands bound. The group of four extorters, as Alexis couldn't help but think of them, were angry, jerking away when Ousley or the Marine sought to move them into place before Alexis desk, while Nabb, Ruse, and Sinkey appeared calm — curiously so, given the recent brawl and the consequences they were facing.

Of the lot, the four seemed to have gotten the worst of it. There was more than one blackened eye starting, along with Chivington's bloody and swollen nose. Carras walked hunched over, as though straightening pained him. The other three were in disarray, but appeared none the worse for wear and in good spirits.

Alexis sighed. She'd have to fight the urge to congratulate the three and go easy on them, for that's what she'd like to do. Nor could she go too hard on the four, as it was clear they hadn't started the brawl. Nor could she say a word about their extortion, for there were none among the crew who'd come forward to accuse them.

'Sole master after God,' my arse.

"Mister Ousley, were you or any of your men struck?" she asked. Though not as dire as if they'd struck an officer, landing a blow on the bosun, his mates, or one of the Marines would force her to increase the punishment for all involved.

"No, sir," Ousley answered.

"Bank?" she asked one of the Marines.

He shook his head. "Not as I know of, sir."

"I'm sure Corporal Brace would have sent word along with you if they had." Alexis ran her eyes over the seven men. "Brawling at *Spirits*. And not the first time brawling, Scarborough."

"Didn't do nuffink! I were —"

Ousley grabbed Scarborough by the collar, knocking him forward then jerking him back.

"Shut your gob while the captain talks!"

Alexis paused a moment, wishing she could do more — could address more of the problems these four were causing aboard her ship. The fight had started right in front of her, though, and she couldn't claim they were anything but the targets of an attack. She couldn't order them flogged for that, much as she might like to.

"For you four, bread and water for a fortnight — *one sound, Scarborough, and it'll be a month!*"

Scarborough shut his mouth, glaring first at her, then at Nabb, who looked on impassive, almost cheerful.

Alexis couldn't understand why he and the other two had done it — nor why they'd done it so publicly. Nabb was new, only weeks aboard ship, but Ruse and Sinkey, lazy and dense as they seemed to be at times, had been in the Service long enough to know she'd have no choice but to order the cat for the instigators. Their backs had barely had time to heal from their flogging after the events on Al Jadiq.

More than that, Nabb, Ruse, and Sinkey were among the few those four *weren't* regularly extorting; too young, strong, and willing to fight back for the bullies to cow, even outnumbered.

"Get them out of here," Alexis said, keeping her eyes fixed on Nabb as Ousley shoved the four toward the hatchway and turned them over to a mate outside.

Nabb met her gaze for a moment, then looked down at the deck, but his lips twitched.

Does he think this is a bloody joke?

Ruse and Sinkey kept their gazes downcast throughout, though they darted more than one glance at Nabb.

"As for you three," she continued once the hatch was closed and Ousley returned to stand behind them, "starting a brawl? Not even an argument to start? Just punches thrown in front of everyone?" She shook her head. "What do you have to say for yourselves?"

Nabb looked up at that and threw a quick glance at Ruse and Sinkey who nodded imperceptibly.

"Nothing to say, sir. No excuse," Nab said, squaring his shoulders. "Lost our tempers, like, is all." He took a deep breath and met Alexis' eye. "Feel bad about the rest of the crew losing two days' spirits over it ... might be they'll enjoy their *full* ration all the more when it comes, though."

Alexis frowned and glanced at Ousley who was regarding the three more thoughtfully than before. Was Nabb saying there was more to this than just a scuffle between the two groups? Did he mean to put an end to the extortion?

She'd still have to punish them appropriately. Couldn't be seen to countenance what they'd done.

"You'll have a better rein on your tempers going forward, I trust?"

This time Nabb glanced at Ousley.

"Much as needs be, I imagine, sir," he said, turning back.

Ousley snorted, then pursed his lips and nodded as he stared at Nabb, as though satisfied with something.

Alexis sighed and rubbed her face with one hand. The politics of a crew — a full crew and not the neck-or-nothing prizes she'd commanded before — were far more Byzantine than she'd ever imagined.

"A half dozen each, Mister Ousley," Alexis said. It was really the minimum she could order, given the circumstances, "and the same fortnight's bread and water as the others."

"Aye, sir."

Ruse and Sinkey looked downcast for a moment, but Nabb shoved Sinkey with his shoulder and the two joined him in saying, "Aye, sir," as well.

"That's all," Alexis said. "We'll hold a Mast this afternoon and be done with it."

Ousley herded the three to the hatchway, but Alexis made a sudden decision. It might not be the right one or the right time, but it felt so to her.

"A moment," she called, waiting for the others to turn. "Nabb ..."

She swallowed. She wanted so much to see him safely back home on Dalthus, but suddenly felt it certain he wouldn't go — that he'd determined to join the Navy as his father had, for whatever reason, and was set on that. Much as she wanted to keep him safe, if she was right about his motives for this fight, she needed such a man with her, and it did feel so right.

"I've need of a coxswain — and a proper boat crew. Would you take the position?"

Nabb nodded quickly. "Aye, sir, I would." He jerked his head toward the others. "Ruse and Sinkey'd make the start of a proper crew."

Alexis blinked. Of all the ways she could think of to describe those two, proper crew wasn't in it.

"I'll trust you to fill out the crew, Nabb," she said, trying to keep her voice clear of those doubts.

"Aye, sir."

Ousley saw them through the hatch, then turned to Alexis.

"That lad's a starter, sir. He'll make master's mate with a bit of seasoning, should he strike for it."

Alexis agreed. "More than that, I think, Mister Ousley."

Ousley glanced at the hatch, then back to her.

"If he don't stay a coxswain, that is."

"I doubt he'll do that, not once another opportunity presents itself."

Ousley frowned.

"A man'll choose what he chooses for his own reasons, sir." He nodded again. "I'll see to settling the crew after all this."

PART TWO

THIRTY-EIGHT

5 April, aboard *HMS Nightingale*, darkspace, enroute to Zariah

Isom's entry from the pantry prompted Alexis to close the latest bit of *Nightingale's* mountain of reports and dispatches.

In the nearly four months since she'd left Al Jadiq for the first time and completed her first circuit of her patrol area by returning to Zariah, everything aboard had improved — save the sheer mass of paperwork and reports required of her as commander.

The time spent on such things was made even more frustrating when she considered the lack of any information or response from Admiralty. Despite hours of work on reports and dispatches detailing *Nightingale's* actions, she'd received virtually nothing in return.

In fact, the only Admiralty message sent specifically to *Nightingale* these last few months had been in response to her dispatches on the incident at Al Jadiq and the recovery of Ruse and Sinkey. Alexis had feared there'd be repercussions from that, but the response, without even an indication of who at Admiralty had reviewed the incident, was a simple *Carry on*.

She was grateful for that, if frustrated by its brevity, as she'd fully expected a reprimand at the very least.

Grateful also for the relative peace *Nightingale* had encountered since. They'd had no further cause to run out the guns, save in exercise, encountering only a handful of smugglers amongst the merchants she'd stopped for inspection. Those had been returned to Zariah for adjudication or their cargoes seized as she thought appropriate.

If the ship's encounters had been peaceful in that time, though, the same could not be said for the crew's. There were several conflicts between the cohort of extorters and the rest of the crew in the weeks after Nabb's fight with them. All occurred below decks and out of sight of either Alexis or Ousley, thankfully, so there was no cause for her to intervene again — also all seemed to have gone Nabb's way, which cheered her further.

She turned her attention to the plate Isom slid in front of her, which contained far more food than Alexis truly needed. Garcia seemed to have made it his mission to fatten his captain up to some private standard and she'd found herself unable to finish most of what he prepared for her. This morning it was a massive proper breakfast of fried eggs, bacon, sausage, fried potatoes, mushrooms, baked beans, half a tomato, and both white and black puddings. Garcia and Isom saw to her personal stores and she wondered where they were managing to keep it all.

"This is the last of the tomatoes until we reach some system with a bit for sale," Isom said, pouring her a glass of weak ship's beer.

She didn't care for the beer at all, but liked the ship's water even less, and there was no coffee or tea to be had until *Nightingale* made her way back to Zariah or Dalthus — the outer worlds, such as Man's Fall and Al Jadiq, either couldn't grow such things at all or hadn't bothered yet.

"I could almost be thankful for that, as it means less food on the plate," Alexis said, raising an eyebrow. "One does wonder, though, where the other half of the tomato's got to."

Isom flushed which confirmed Alexis suspicion that her clerk, short as his time in the Navy might have been, had become acquainted with the custom of colluding with the cook in augmenting their own meals. It was a time-honored perquisite of the positions, after all.

"Mention to Garcia that I need a bit less food than the typical captain, if you will?"

Isom nodded. "I will, sir, but he has his ways."

Alexis sighed. She slid most of the files and other work she had open on her table to the side, knowing that Garcia's meals were long on quality as well as quantity and not wanting to be distracted from it.

"Thank you, Isom, that will be all for now."

"Aye, sir."

She smiled a bit as Isom hurried back to her pantry's hatch and what she was certain was an equally large plate of his own. Still, she wouldn't begrudge that bit to either Isom or Garcia — if nothing else aboard *Nightingale* had come easily to her, those two had at least seen to it that mealtimes were something to look forward to. She picked up her fork and was raising the first bite to her mouth when a soft *ping* interrupted her.

"Sail, sir," Villar announced over her cabin's speakers.

"Where away, Mister Villar?"

"Fine on the port bow, sir, and closer than I'd like — sails came up all of a sudden."

Alexis frowned, slid her plate to the side, and brought the navigation plot monitors up on her table. The image of the other ship was clear, and closer than it should be to have just been sighted, which must mean that it had been lying still with its particle projectors uncharged and only now set sail and turned them on.

That last was a little too close to their first encounter, with the ill-fated *Greenaway*, for Alexis to be comfortable this ship might be some innocent merchant or smuggler at worst.

"Clear for action, Mister Villar, and signal for that ship to heave-to instanter."

"NO RESPONSE, SIR."

"Running is quite the response, Creasy." Alexis studied the navigation plot. The distance was closing, but slowly. The other ship was running fully away from *Nightingale*, not making the best use of the winds, but simply pointing its bow away and turning if *Nightingale* drifted to one side or the other.

"Not running very well, though," Villar said quietly.

"No," Alexis agreed.

As a strategy, the other ship's maneuvers generally allowed *Nightingale* to gain on it, more often or not. It was as though the ship were being commanded by someone who next to nothing about sailing the Dark — much less ship-handling itself, as what maneuvers were made were executed in a slipshod manner. One warning shot alongside, along with an *Imperative* signal added to the already flashing *Heave-to* and *Inspection*, had already been ignored by the other ship and Alexis' tolerance was at an end.

"One more shot alongside, Mister Villar, and if they refuse to heave-to, then I'll have one into her."

"Aye, sir."

Villar passed the orders along and a streak of light leapt out from *Nightingale's* bowchaser, passing close alongside the other ship. Villar waited a moment, then ordered the other bowchaser fired. This one loaded with chain shot, and a wide bar leapt across the space between the ships, striking the other ship's rigging.

Alexis could see suited figures on the other ship's hull, but they didn't appear to be working at repairing the damage to the rigging — at least not successfully.

"Again," Alexis ordered, "and reload with chain in both bowchasers."

"Aye, sir."

Chainshot wasn't strictly according to New London's doctrine. The Navy preferred its captains use roundshot and fire for an enemy's hull. *Nightingale's* crew, though they'd improved greatly since Nabb and the others had begun fighting back against the extorters, were still not up to the standards Alexis expected, and though they were gaining on the other ship, Alexis wanted it slowed further.

The chase dragged on, shot after shot flashing between the two ships as the distance narrowed. All going in one direction, Alexis noted thankfully, as the other ship had yet to fire back. An occasional vacsuited figure made its way around the other ship's hull and into the rigging, but so far as Alexis could tell there was little repair work being done — at least little that was successful.

The other ship's sails became more and more ragged as *Nightingale* fired, until, finally, their azure glow went out altogether.

"Did we strike their particle projector?" Alexis asked.

Dorsett, on the tactical console, shook his head. "No, sir, it happened between shots."

"They've not struck, sir," Villar pointed out.

Alexis studied the image of the other ship. The hull was lit as one would expect still, so there was power available, but the sails were dark. The mast and hull lights used for signaling weren't doing so, however — neither the flashing code that indicated surrender nor, still, any response to *Nightingale's* signals.

"Perhaps one of our shots damaged their particle projector and it's only now failed?" Villar suggested.

"I been tracking where we struck 'em, sir," Dorsett said, "and shouldn't be any damage to a projector."

"Continue to close with them," Alexis ordered, "but be wary. I'll not have us sucked in again, as with the *Owl*."

"Aye, sir."

The closing rate increased now that the other ship's sails were dead. *Nightingale* approached rapidly, then more slowly as she took in her own sails. The chase's gunports remained closed and sails dark. What few vacsuited figures had been on her hull were no longer visible. It was as though the ship had been abandoned in mid-chase and Alexis couldn't help think of their encounter with *Greenaway*.

Apparently neither could *Nightingale's* quarterdeck crew, as Creasy muttered, "*Dutchman*," quite loudly.

"Enough, Dorsett," Alexis snapped. "We saw folk out and about on her hull."

"Not there now," Creasy muttered.

Alexis ignored that, not wanting to give credence to the spacer's fears by addressing them. Creasy and any others would see soon enough that the other ship was as normal as any and no spirits drove it through the Dark.

They closed further.

"Pass the word to the gun captains, Creasy. Watch them and fire at the first sign of treachery. I'll not see us caught flat-footed as we were by the *Owl*." Alexis kept her own eyes closely on the images of the other ship as *Nightingale* came about to pull alongside. "So much as a twitch from one of her gunports and I want our full broadside into her."

"Aye sir."

Nothing appeared amiss or out of place as *Nightingale* drew closer — no more than the disturbing lack of any activity, that is. Alexis held off on ordering her own crew, other than those working the sails, to go to the hull or boarding tubes, as she wanted every spare hand on the guns until the last moment. If they did face treachery again, she'd be as prepared as possible for it.

Up close, the damage to the other ship was more visible. Loose rigging drifted slowly, twisting until it struck something that altered its direction. The hull was pocked in multiple places where shot had struck there instead of the sails and rigging.

"One man from each gun to the hull and make us fast," she ordered finally when the two ships were close enough and at rest. "Weapons close and the gun captains to remain ready."

"Aye sir."

Nightingale slid alongside, moving a bit too quickly to come to rest directly there.

"Back sails, quarter charge," Villar said to the helmsman.

"Aye, sir."

The ships dim sails were hauled around to face the wind on her bow, then pulsed with a short particle charge to catch a bit of the winds and slow her more. Once doused again, *Nightingale* came to rest within reach of the other ship.

"Nicely done, Mister Villar," Alexis said, "and you as well Busbey." She watched the images on the navigation plot as the first lines were launched across the space between the ships, puffs of gas visible from the mouths of the launchers as bags and grapples flew from *Nightingale* to attach to the other ship. "Now we'll just —"

The other ship disappeared.

THIRTY-NINE

Zariah

"Well it can't have just gone nowhere!"

Alexis slammed her hand onto her tabletop, jarring it enough to slosh a bit of beer out of Ousley's glass. The bosun, along with the others, hurriedly grasped his glass to save the rest, and Isom appeared with a cloth to wipe up the spill.

The table's display showed nearly every angle *Nightingale's* optics had caught of the *Silver Leaf's* disappearance. Alexis and her officers had finished reviewing them, sometimes frame by frame, searching for some explanation of where the other ship had gone and how.

She rubbed her forehead, trying to calm herself.

"Gentlemen, there must be some explanation."

Ousley, Villar, and Spindler all looked at each other, then back to her.

"It did appear to be a transition event, sir," Villar said.

"And yet we are nowhere near a system, much less a Lagrangian point," Alexis pointed out. "So what do we have, gentlemen? Has someone — pirates, no less — discovered how to transition to and from *darkspace* outside of a Lagrangian point? Or is it Creasy's bloody Dutchman?"

"Might be better it *were* Creasy's Dutchman, sir," Ousley said.

"How's that?" Villar asked.

"The men might be shaken by ghosties, but a ship that can transition at will?"

Alexis nodded agreement. "Escape our fire, transition back to *darkspace* where we don't expect and rake us with fire, then disappear again before we can respond. We'd be at such a tactical disadvantage we'd have no hope of overcoming."

"If we were facing that, wouldn't the *Leaf* have done so?" Villar asked. "It's been hours since it ... well, transitioned ... surely if they had that capability they'd have come back to strike at us."

"We did them a bit of damage, perhaps they're grateful to have got away."

"And we're lucky they've not appeared off our stern to rake us."

Spindler shivered at the thought, and Alexis agreed with him. How did one fight such a foe?

Yet the *Silver Leaf* hadn't done so, she'd only used the ability to escape them. Perhaps, given the difference in distances and space between *darkspace* and normal-space, it wasn't possible. There was little in the way of theory, much less consensus, about how normal-space mapped to *darkspace*, other than the Lagrangian points and the dark matter shoals which built up around corresponding normal-space masses.

Away from a system, in the true depths of *darkspace*, there was no telling.

Or there might be a danger, in the midst of an action, of transitioning back to *darkspace* in the same place as the other ship. That thought made Alexis shudder — the whole reason for pilot boats and the convention of transitioning into and out of systems at specific Lagrangian points was to avoid just such an event. Whatever differences in physics there were in *darkspace*, the same place couldn't be occupied by two different masses — that rule held here as well, at least.

"I wish we had word back from Admiralty on those helm circuits we took off *Greenaway*." Alexis rubbed her face. Knowing what those changes to the helm did might let her understand what exactly she was facing out here. "Or that we'd kept them for ourselves to look into." She sighed.

"Perhaps we should tell the men it *is* a Dutchman," Villar said, "but we've some hocus-pocus in our shot that will do for him."

Alexis raised an eyebrow. "Hocus-pocus?"

"Fight superstition with superstition, sir."

"There aren't really Dutchmen, are there, sir?" Spindler asked, eyes wide.

"And that's why not, Mister Villar," Alexis said with a nod at Spindler. She knew, or at least suspected, that Villar had been joking, but superstitions were strong in spacers. "Encourage that, and at the next bit of bad luck we'll have talk of a Jonah aboard, or some poor landsman will find himself beaten for whistling."

"Well, that wouldn't happen at all, sir," Ousley said. "Not aboard *Nightingale*."

"You think not?"

Ousley shook his head firmly. "Tell every newcome aboard he'd best not whistle on my decks, sir. Bad joss, that."

Alexis opened her mouth to reply, but hesitated as she sought just the words to use.

"Challenge the winds like that?" Ousley went on. "Damned foolish. Why, I was on the old *Adonis* once and some damn fool whistled — with shoals to leeward, mind you — next thing we knew was a hell of a storm blowing us in on them. Hull was breached and were a full day drifting in a hulk, sippin' at our vacsuit air, afore help came." He shook his head again. "Won't risk that again, I won't. Nip that in the bud, me and my mates, don't you worry."

"So the Dutchman's right out, then, sir?" Villar asked, eyes bright.

"Indeed." Alexis stared at Ousley for a moment. "We'll tell the men this only makes *Nightingale's* gunnery that much more important — that we'll want to disable a ship quickly, before it can escape." She caught Villar's and Spindler's eye in turn. "*Escape*, mind you. Let them think that's the only capability this transitioning-anywhere gives our enemy, while we three on the quarterdeck stay alert in case they can transition back."

The others nodded.

"So keep talk of Dutchmen to a minimum, Mister Ousley."

"Aye, sir." The bosun frowned, his brow furrowed. He pointed toward the hatch to Alexis' pantry. "Have you by chance counted your wee beasty's toes, sir?"

Alexis found herself frozen in place again, mouth half-open, and unable to think of a single thing to say. Of all the things her bosun might be concerned about, the number of toes on that vile creature wasn't a thing she'd have guessed.

"It's only that he's nearly a cat, isn't he?" Ousley went on. "That's lucky, sure, but a *polydact*? Well, the lads'd be comforted by that, Dutchman or no."

Alexis shared a look with Villar, who was smothering laughter, and Spindler, who seemed puzzled.

"Thank you, Mister Ousley, I'll keep that in mind."

She drained her glass and nodded as the others did as well and took their leave.

Once the hatch was closed and she was alone, she took her beret off and ran fingers through her hair. Her head was aching.

The fight at *Up Spirits* had marked a change in *Nightingale*. Alexis had noted that the extortion of the men's spirits issue appeared to have ended entirely, and the crew as a whole seemed happier and more responsive with the new situation.

She waved a hand across her tabletop, dismissing the images of the *Silver Leaf*. Staring at the ship wouldn't tell her the truth of where or how it had gone, she could only deal with the knowledge that it had somehow.

And worry that the next ship we take action against can do more.

The men would likely do enough speculating on their own, after all.

A sudden thought occurred to her. She pondered it for a moment, grimaced, but then resigned herself. It couldn't hurt, after all.

"Isom?"

Isom stuck his head through the pantry hatchway.

"Aye, sir?"

Alexis took a deep breath. It might be silly, but with this crew and ship she'd take whatever advantage she could find.

"Do you suppose I might bother you to count the creature's toes?"

FORTY

12 April, aboard the merchantman *Drunken Hermit*, *darkspace*, enroute to Zariah

"There ain't nuffink t'find, I tell yer!"

Alexis watched as Ousley and one of his mates eased a panel aside and peered into the space behind it. The *Drunken Hermit*, a name Alexis felt more suited to some spacers' pub than a ship, was twelve days out of Eidera when it crossed *Nightingale's* path.

The captain, a sweating, bald-headed man of middle age, was anything but pleased by that happenstance and less so at Alexis' insistence that they inspect more than just the obvious cargo in his ship's hold. Something about the *Hermit* reminded her a great deal of the ship she'd traveled aboard through Hanover.

That ship, *Marylin*, was owned by an utter rogue, Avrel Dansby, and Alexis had become quite familiar with the hidey holes and spaces for less than legal goods possible.

"Nothing," Ousley called, his head fully inside the space and shining a light about.

"Ain't that what I tells you already? Yer just wasting time here!"

"Measure it," Alexis ordered, then to the ship's captain, "Captain

Manser, the inspection will be conducted to my satisfaction — if that time is wasted, I do apologize for the delay in your ship's schedule."

Alexis looked around the engineering space again. The *Hermit* was filthy and cluttered, with a buildup of grime on the control surfaces that made her want to rub her hands clean from just looking at them, but it was an odd sort of disorder. None of the clutter came near the controls themselves and the *Hermit's* ship handling had been anything but slovenly. It was just the sort of facade Dansby had shown her would make it appear the ship was a poor merchant, barely scraping by — and deter anyone from digging too deeply beneath the surface.

Ousley cursed as he shifted position and his knee slid into something not quite solid on the deck. Verley, the master's mate, coughed and drew back, hand to his mouth, as did Alexis a moment later as the smell reached her. Ousley coughed and cursed again, but kept at his work.

"Verley!" he called. "What's the space in the next one over?"

Verley moved to compartment they'd already searched and began measuring it.

"Look, now," Manser said, licking his lips. "What if we was to retire to my cabin an' —"

Alexis was saved from hearing what Manser thought they might do in his cabin, though she suspected she'd be forever haunted by the possibilities, by Ousley's shout of triumph.

"Bugger —" Manser muttered.

"What is it you've found, Mister Ousley?"

Ousley worked his way out of the compartment and stood, then held a glass jar with a screw top out to Alexis. She took it and looked it over, not quite understanding why Ousley was grinning so broadly.

"Bugger —" Manser repeated. He looked around, but then his shoulders slumped. The three Marines Alexis had with the boarding party, and the knowledge that *Nightingale's* guns were still manned, likely had something to do with that.

"What is this?" she asked, tilting the jar up to the light. It looked like nothing so much as fruit preserves. She turned to Manser. "Captain?"

Manser looked hopeful for a moment, then Ousley cleared his throat and his shoulders slumped further. He scowled at Ousley.

"Go on and tell 'er then, if yer so bloody clever."

"If I'm not mistaken, sir, that would be an Eideran viper chili jam. It's on the proscribed list."

Alexis frowned. There were innumerable plants and animals on the proscribed list, those items it was forbidden to transfer from one world to another, usually because they were too dangerous or unusually invasive in some way. The list didn't generally include prepared products though.

"It's a food?" she asked.

"Not as such," Ousley said. "The chili's addictive when mixed with sugar, you see."

"So it's a drug, then?"

Ousley shook his head. "Tasty, I'm told, but no other effects." He narrowed his eyes and stared at Manser. "No, the trick is to get someone to eat it, then they're addicted and'll pay through the nose for more. There's enough in that false compartment there that it's not just for someone aboard."

"I see." Alexis turned a cold eye to Manser as well. "Well, then, Mister Ousley, run the tests to confirm what it is, then have one of your mates take command of the *Hermit*. Three hands and two Marines along with him."

"Aye, sir."

Villar and Spindler, along with a similar number of crew and Marines were already aboard the two other ships *Nightingale* had seized for smuggling. The captains of those were simply carrying goods on which they'd tried to avoid paying the Crown's duties, and would likely face nothing more than a fine and confiscation of the goods when her little flotilla arrived at Zariah, but the *Hermit* was now a different matter. Carrying goods on the proscribed list meant

Manser's ship was liable to be seized and he'd face prison or indenture.

She motioned to one of the Marines. "Angers, see that Captain Manser is made comfortable in *Nightingale's* brig, will you?"

"Aye, sir."

"Walk with me back to *Nightingale*, Mister Ousley."

Alexis waited until they were in the docking tube, midway between the two ships before speaking again.

"Has Scarborough been found?"

Ousley shook his head. "No sign of him."

Alexis winced. The leader of the former extorters had been missing from his station when *Nightingale* went to quarters after sighting the *Drunken Hermit*. As quarters meant clearing the decks and striking all unnecessary items down into the hold, there were few places the man could be — an exhausted crewman, deep in sleep, might miss the call coming over the ship's speakers, but was unlikely to sleep through his bunk being folded up fast to the bulkhead.

The weeks since Nabb and the others had stood up to the extorters had seen many changes amongst the crew. Even the older, frailer members walked a bit straighter and taller, while Scarborough and his cohorts kept to themselves more and more. It wasn't out of the question that some of the crew might have decided to take a bit of revenge against the man, and Alexis dearly hoped that was not the case. It wasn't unheard of for a hated member of a crew to be run outside the hull and tossed off into *darkspace*. If that had happened, she'd never know — despite the ship's log recording things, there were ways a crew learned to get around the optics both inside and outside the hull.

"Run a thorough search for him once we've secured from quarters."

"Aye, sir."

"T'BOOSON, SAR!"

Alexis blinked — she wasn't sure if it was a good thing or not, but she seemed to have become used to Clanly's accent.

"Send Mister Ousley through, Clanly, thank you."

Her hatch slid open and the bosun entered.

"Found Scarborough, sir."

Ousley's face was still, as though he were carefully controlling his emotions, and a sudden chill went through Alexis. She'd already been fearing the worst. Oddly, the worst, at least for *Nightingale*, wasn't that he'd been put over the side into *darkspace*. If that was what had happened, she could assume he'd simply been lost — if he'd been found dead, though, if there'd been a murder aboard her ship, she'd have to take action against whoever'd done it.

"Is he ..."

"Ah, he's alive, sir," Ousley said. "Found him in the hold."

Alexis breathed a sigh of relief — anything short of murder she could deal with.

"Drunk? Beaten?"

Ousley's face twisted and he cocked his head to the side. "Ah ... not as such, sir, no, but poorly nonetheless. It's —" He scratched at his neck. "Best, perhaps, if me and my mates were to handle it, sir."

"Really?" She pondered that for a moment, then shook her head. If he was alive and not drunk or beaten, then he must have been hiding down there and shirking his duties. She'd had little enough opportunity to punish him and his cohorts for their actions that she'd not pass up an opportunity now. Perhaps it was unfair, but even if he were sick, "poorly", as Ousley said, she'd have a go at him.

"No, the man missed a call to quarters — and not from just over-sleeping. If he'd been found in his bunk it would be different, but hiding down in the hold, ignoring the call to quarters during an action?" She shook her head again. "I have to take notice of it, I think. I'll see him at next captain's mast, but want his explanation now — can you bring him in or is he with the surgeon?"

"Ah ... he's outside, sir, no call for Mister Poulter at all, but ..."

Ousley trailed off. Alexis had never seen the bosun at such a loss for words.

"Whatever is the matter? Bring him in."

Ousley grimaced. "Sir, I'd suggest —"

"What's got into you, Mister Ousley? Bring the man in!"

Ousley sighed. "Aye, sir."

He trudged to the hatch, slid it open and gestured. Two of Ousley's master's mates entered with Scarborough between them, but not closely held as they normally would with some malefactor. Instead they kept their distance, gesturing for him to move forward, but not shoving or guiding him.

The man was disheveled and dejected, shoulders slumped and head bowed ... as well as soaking wet.

His hair hung in wet, tangled clumps and rivulets streamed down his face. His wide eyes darted quickly in the direction of nearly every sound or movement, as though terrified. Liquid fell from him to pool on the deck. Outside her hatch, Alexis caught sight of a crewman following along behind with a mop. Clanly, the Marine, edged away from the hatch, face twisted in disgust as though ...

"Good lord, what's that smell?" Alexis exclaimed as Scarborough came to a stop and a sharp, acrid odor reached her.

Ousley cleared his throat.

"You'll want your deck scrubbed, sir," he said. "Found him in the hold, as I said ... in a, ah —"

"Sippers and gulpers after," Scarborough muttered, barely audible. His gaze was vacant.

"I thought you said he wasn't drunk?" Alexis asked.

"No, sir, but near drowned when we found him."

"Drowned?" Alexis' eyes widened. What could he have nearly drowned in that would smell so foul? Her eyes widened. "Surely they didn't dump him in a vat?"

What would the nutrient solution and growing beef do to a man? Did anyone know?

"Ah ... no, sir." Ousley looked away. "It were an empty beer vat."

"Empty? But —"

"Sippers and gulpers!" Scarborough yelled suddenly, looking around wildly. "You want your sippers and gulpers, you gets 'em after!"

"It were ... ah ... refilled, sir." Ousley looked at Scarborough sadly and shook his head in amazement. "Must've taken the lads a week or more to ... well, make the necessary, as it were."

Alexis stared at Scarborough as Ousley's words and the acrid odor suddenly making things clearer.

"Dear God —"

"Sippers and gulpers come after now, you sodding bastard!" Scarborough yelled.

"Weren't but a few centimeters' air between the lid and the ... well, afters," Ousley said, voice full of wonder.

"How ... how long do you think ..."

"No telling, sir." Ousley and his mates edged away from Scarborough as the man shuddered and more droplets fell from him. "Sometime last night — he were missing this morning, but his mates covered it, come to find out."

Last night — and his mates had covered for him, probably thinking he'd snuck off, but inadvertently keeping him from being found earlier and leaving him for hours in a vat of —

"Afters!" Scarborough yelled. "Afters for you, you bloody sot!"

— hours in a vat of ... afters, with only a few centimeters of air between the lid and —

"Oh, dear."

Alexis was torn between horror at what had been done to the man and outright laughter at the very appropriateness of it. More, she took heart that her crew had come together against a common enemy at least, even if it was one of their own — and that they'd managed it in a way that wasn't lethal.

She sighed. Still she'd have to make it clear that this should be the end of it. Scarborough and his mates would have the message that their schemes wouldn't be tolerated by the crew any longer, and the crew needed the message that she'd tolerate no further revenge.

All without actually acknowledging I know what's gone on — or I'd have to punish everyone involved.

"I'll want it made clear to the crew that they're to use the *proper* heads, no matter if there's a line, I suppose."

Ousley nodded, slowly. "Aye, sir. That's what must've happened here. Terrible long lines there are a'times. A man gets desperate, he does."

"But not again," Alexis said pointedly.

"Aye, sir." He glanced at his mates whose faces were clearly struggling between amusement and disgust at Scarborough. "And the tale of ... well ..." He jerked his head at the dripping crewman.

Alexis fixed her gaze on Scarborough, who looked back but seemed not to clearly see her.

"The danger of using an alternative in a dark hold late at night?" she suggested.

Ousley nodded. "A fall, perhaps, sir? Slipped in the dark and took a tumble into ... er ..."

"Yes, a fall." Alexis nodded. The shipboard catchall when everyone knew exactly what had occurred but daren't acknowledge it. "Isn't that what happened, Scarborough? You —"

"*Sippers and gulpers!*"

Alexis winced. "Get him cleaned up, Ousley, and take him to Mister Poulter."

"He's not hurt, sir, not a bruise on —"

"Sip the afters!"

"Take him to the surgeon, Mister Ousley. There are other sorts of hurts." She paused, eyeing the dripping, stinking crewman. Poulter had been a questioning thorn in her side since she'd taken command, with his damnable queries as to her thoughts at every opportunity. It might be petty, but ...

"In fact, now I think on it, I believe Mister Poulter should see the man instanter. No delay, do you understand?"

Ousley frowned. "Without he's, well, rinsed, as it were, sir?"

"*Afters for you, you bugger!*"

Alexis nodded. "I believe Scarborough's hurts are entirely in Mister Poulter's bailiwick and brook no delay."

"Aye, sir."

Ousley nodded to his mates, who led Scarborough from her cabin. Alexis eyed the trail of liquid left on the deck.

"I'll have a man come to scrub that down instanter, sir."

"Thank you." She paused. "And Ousley, after that vat's emptied into the recyclers ..."

"Sir?"

"Space it before our good purser somehow manages to fill it with beer again."

FORTY-ONE

21 April, aboard *HMS Nightingale*, arrival at Zariah System

Darkness and swirling shadows.

Alexis moaned, knowing what was to come. She fought to wake, to move, to scream — anything to break the ever-repeating scene which was about to unfold.

Figures formed from the shadows. Two, large and small, at the forefront, as ever. The first man she'd killed and the boy she'd failed so horribly.

The figures stepped forward, then paused at a low, chittering sound, barely heard.

Alexis frowned — there'd never been such a sound in the nightmare before, and she'd come to dread any change in it. The last change had been the addition of the smaller figure, and that had presaged Artley's death.

The figures raised their arms to point accusing fingers at her, but stopped as the sound came again, louder this time.

Alexis strained to hear and realized that something else was different.

Her neck and shoulder felt warm, and it was only then that she realized she'd always been cold in this dream. The rest of her still was, chilled and cold and as stone, but her neck and left shoulder were warm — hot even.

The chittering sound came again, along with the brush of something soft against her ear, and the figures moved back toward the shadows.

She raised a hand to her ear and the swirling shadows faded …

Alexis woke, torn between relief that the nightmare had not run its full, usual course and confusion.

Something tickled her ear and she raised her hand, encountering warm fur at her throat.

"What —"

Soft chittering near her ear and a cold, wet nose against her cheek caused her to realize what it was. The bloody creature'd escaped his cage again and curled up on her chest during the night.

"I suppose I should thank you," she murmured, stroking his fur. There was something oddly comforting about the beast, now that it wasn't rushing about the compartment like some furry Dervish. She settled a hand on him, feeling his soft fur and the warmth soaked into her neck — comforting and peaceful.

The ship's bell chimed softly over the speakers. Six times — six bells of the middle watch. In a bare hour the morning watch would start and she'd have to be up and about as the crew cleaned the ship and went to their breakfast in preparation for their expected arrival at Zariah. Her body felt a bit more sleep might be in order, but her mind dreaded the possibility of returning to sleep and risking the nightmare again.

"I can't rely on you to chitter in my ear all the time," she murmured, stroking the little beast's fur. He nestled in closer, rubbing against her neck. "Though perhaps you're not entirely awful after all."

A moment's more drowsy rest and she decided it was time to rise. She slid a hand under the beast and lifted him gently onto an empty space on the cot. Isom could put him away in his cage once the crew was awake, no sense in both their rests being disturbed.

She stood to draw on her trousers from where they hung beside the cot, then sat again to slide her feet into her boots.

Her left foot met something cold and wet.

"*Bloody —*"

Alexis reached for the beast, but it was already in motion. Turning from a loosely coiled ball of fur to a streaking blur in an instant.

She glared after it, teeth clenched, then pulled her foot from her boot, stripped off the soiled stocking, and rose to hop one-footed toward her head to wash.

"*Isom!*"

REGULAR UNIFORM, but dress boots — the only spare pair she had — made Alexis feel self-conscious as she stepped through the quarterdeck hatch. More than self-conscious, a spot on the ball of her foot still felt cold and wet, regardless of how much she'd scrubbed it in the head. She even had the half-serious fear that she could detect the odor still.

The Zariah pilot boat was in sight on the navigation plot, though still some hours away, and Alexis could sense the quarterdeck crew's anticipation. This was their third return to the system since she'd taken command and they were anxious for a chance to leave the ship for a time after the long trek through the Man's Fall, Al Jadiq, and then Eidera systems — the latter having no station, liberty was restricted to a very few vendors allowed to come up to *Nightingale*, and the two former allowing no liberty at all. Zariah's station allowed for a more controlled environment, at least so far as access was concerned, and Alexis had already announced that both watches would have a chance to leave the ship while they were here.

Moreover, a large part of the disappointment over there being no salvage money for the gallenium had passed. There were still some aboard who were disgruntled, but most had settled back into the ship's routine within a few weeks, treating the event like any number of dreams that hadn't materialized.

The three ships following *Nightingale* now, and the two she'd brought in on her previous rounds, went a long way toward that as well.

The prize money for confiscated cargoes might not be so grand as that for a hold full of gallenium, but it was surer, was paid quicker, and would get one just as drunk, at least the once.

ALEXIS' first stop was the office of the Prize Court agent. She hoped to move things along quickly and have the Court representatives take over control of the three ships soon, allowing her men on those ships to enjoy some liberty time on the station before *Nightingale* sailed again. Bramley's office was much as she remembered it, though Bramley himself was grimmer. Far grimmer.

"More smugglers, lieutenant?"

"Contraband for the two and proscribed goods for the last," Alexis said.

Bramley snorted, reviewing the reports Alexis had forwarded once *Nightingale* transitioned to normal space and could communicate with the station. "Eideran pepper jam?" He shook his head. "I see you've been busily protecting the Queen's subjects from their personal proclivities ... to your own profit, of course."

Alexis frowned. Her visits to Bramley had been cordial in the past and she couldn't account for his current attitude.

"I don't create the proscribed list, Mister Bramley, only enforce it." Bramley snorted again and Alexis found all of the possible connotations of that quite offensive. "Nor do I work for you — *Nightingale* has her orders and I intend to follow them."

"At least the ones which put coin in your purse," Bramley said.

"Whatever are you talking about?"

Bramley slid a report from his desktop to her tablet.

"Since you brought in that ore carrier some months ago," he said angrily, "the shipping factors have been compiling a list of overdue ships. We've no idea what's happened before that, as there was so little cooperation without a proper magistrate on Zariah, but since ... well, just look." Alexis did so, but Bramley went on before she could read a word. "Three additional ore ships are overdue just since you were last here. *Three.* And two general merchants, the *Silver Leaf* and the *Distant Crown.*"

Alexis scanned the report. Overdue could mean any number of things. A *darkspace* storm, issues loading cargo or waiting for a cargo — the list was long.

"Do you have images of the missing ships?" Alexis asked. "We did encounter a converted merchant being used as a pirate — presumably, as she attacked us — and it may have been one of these."

"You did?" Bramley appeared to be more pleased by this. "It would be good to tell the factors you'd done *something* more than confiscate trade goods. Was this ship taken or destroyed?"

"It was ..." Alexis knew what she was about to say sounded quite mad, but it was what had happened. "The ship transitioned as we were approaching."

Bramley frowned. "Did you not follow it to normal-space and pursue?" he asked.

"It transitioned outside a Lagrangian point, Mister Bramley. *Nightingale* was unable to follow." Bramley's look was exactly what Alexis would expect in response to such a ludicrous assertion. "I realize how that sounds, but it is what happened."

Bramley snorted. "This is not the sort of tale I intend to take to the factors, lieutenant. They have no interest in your fairy stories."

Nor Creasy's Dutchmen neither, I imagine, but it doesn't change what happened you sot.

Saying that aloud, however, would do no good. Instead she shrugged. "The events are what they are. I may not be able to explain it, but neither can I deny what every man aboard *Nightingale* saw."

"Ghosts and goblins," Bramley repeated. "Jams and, what was it, untaxed wines? An odd mixture to bring back with you, and all while you harass honest merchantmen like Captain Lounds, of the Marchant Company, no less —" His lip curled with distaste, "— and busy yourself with *jam*. We shall all, I'm sure, feel ourselves the safer for your efforts."

So, Captain Lounds has made his way back here.

Alexis bristled. She could understand his and the merchants' concerns, shared them herself, in fact, but she didn't see how she could be expected to end something she was only just now informed of. "Mister Bramley, *Nightingale* has a large patrol area and must travel all of it. If you've discovered additional missing ships, then I'll take that information into account when planning *Nightingale's* patrols, of course."

"'Of course,'" Bramley said with sneer.

"And if you have any thoughts on the matter, I should be glad to —"

"My thoughts?" Bramley glared at her. "Is it my responsibility to do your job for you, lieutenant?"

Alexis sighed and wondered what on earth Lounds had told the man to make for such a change in his demeanor. Their prior meetings had been cordial, even friendly.

"I researched you quite thoroughly after Captain Lounds informed me of your disrespect," Bramley said suddenly.

Alexis frowned, not at all certain where Bramley might be going with this or how she'd managed to offend the man to such depths.

"Oh, yes, I did," Bramley went on, "and I discovered your dirty secret. I was certain I recognized your name from somewhere."

Now Alexis blinked and stared at the man, flabbergasted. "Mister Bramley, I must say I have no idea what you think you've discovered, but —"

"Must have thought you were quite clever, didn't you? Must've been all the talk?"

"Mister Bramley! I have had enough of this!" Alexis stood preparing to leave. "Quite enough! I'll thank you to process the accounting of these ships, as is your duty, and leave whatever mysteries you think you've uncovered to your imaginations."

"Does the name *Grapple* mean a thing to you, lieutenant?"

Alexis froze, then cocked her head, puzzled.

"I see that it does," Bramley went on. "See that it might have been forgotten. But, no, I've looked into the matter. You must have quite enjoyed the attention — everyone thinking you'd taken a pirate ship by yourself, then gotten all the coin from it as a prize. I can see, though, how you muddied the records to keep it all for yourself and cut the rest of the crew out of the prize."

"That's not what —"

"Likely that's why you were transferred off so quickly to another ship. I have friends in the Navy who were kind enough to forward me those records as well. Transferred, then charges of mutiny? The trial's sealed, but I can imagine well enough what you did to get off — some clever sort of business as you used to keep all the prize money."

Alexis stared at the man in bewilderment. None of what he said was how it had happened. It was a clerical error on the part of the Prize Court here on Zariah, not some machination of Alexis', which had been the error behind her receiving the lion's share of prize money for the ship *Grapple* — and the trial, well, that was sealed to protect the reputation of the service and the ship's captain, not Alexis.

"Mister Bramley —" she began, thinking, despite her fury at the man's attitude and words, that it if she could only explain —

"Be about your *business*, lieutenant," Bramley said with a dismissive wave. "Protect us good people from jams and whatnot, but believe I see you for what you are and there'll be a reckoning." His eyes narrowed. "A reckoning, I promise you."

ALEXIS STORMED out of Bramley's office, barely able to contain the urge to return, grasp the bugger by his ears and bash his head against his desktop until there was some gleam of sense in his hooded little eyes. She stalked down the station's companionway, oblivious to those who hurriedly stepped out of her way.

"Is there some problem with the prizes again, sir?"

Alexis forced herself to relax and slow down, seeing that Villar, who must have finished his own business at the chandlery, was hurrying after her. Longer though his legs might be, he was having to work to keep up with her. There were also, she noted now, a number of spacers hopping out of her way and eyeing her warily as she passed.

She took a deep breath to calm herself, and pushed down the first thought, that a brief stop into one of the pubs for a glass of bourbon, or even tracking down an establishment that served a proper Scotch, wouldn't be amiss.

"No, they'll adjudicate the cargoes we've taken, Mister Villar. It's only that I've learned again I should never assume I've already met the most irritating man in the universe — there appears to be a vast conspiracy intent on proving me wrong each time I make that mistake."

"You didn't shoot him, did you, sir?"

Alexis stopped and spun on Villar in shock. Did he truly think that of her? Leaving aside the fantasies she'd just been having of Bramley's head and desk. Then she saw his lips twitch slightly.

Things with Villar had been steadily improving and she'd found he had a wry sense of humor she quite enjoyed. One which, she found, could lighten her mood at the worst of times, as it did now.

Bramley be damned, she thought. Her duty was to the Service and Kingdom, not some petulant agent of the Prize Court, no matter how unpleasant he'd become. More, she suddenly realized that he was partially correct. She'd been concentrating on the patrolling aspects of *Nightingale's* brief and relying on that to encounter any smuggler's or pirates. That allowed those pirates to still have free rein in their hunting, so long as *Nightingale* had moved on. A reasonable course when she'd had so little information, but that was now changed.

What she had now in the data she'd gotten from Bramley about the newly discovered missing ships might allow her to properly hunt them. If gallenium transports were the primary targets, and the number of those missing seemed to indicate that, then she thought she already knew where their hunting ground would be, and let the hunter become the hunted.

"No. No, I didn't shoot anyone," she said, quite seriously. A passing spacer glanced at her, frowned, then hurried his pace. She smiled, set off toward *Nightingale's* berth, and called back over her shoulder, "But remember, Mister Villar, the day is still young!"

FORTY-TWO

Dalthus

"Another fine meal, Isom, my compliments to Garcia," Alexis said as he cleared the table.

"Indeed," Villar agreed.

Spindler and Poulter nodded their approval as well.

"He has another odd pudding for you," Isom said. "Not sure what he's calling it, but he came back aboard at Zariah with loads of milk and he's had it on the stove all day."

Alexis raised an eyebrow. "Well, whatever it is, I'm certain it will be as delicious as the last."

When it was served, Alexis found that her prediction was correct. Rich and tooth-achingly sweet, the brown, caramely sauce — and how he'd gotten that from milk, she didn't know — was poured over pound cake.

She scraped her fork against the plate to get the last bits of it, knowing that there'd be less of this sort of thing once they were past Dalthus again and they were forced to rely on the younger colonies for resupply.

"Gentlemen, sir," Spindler said, raising his glass as Isom began clearing the last of the plates. "The Queen!"

"The Queen," Alexis and the others echoed, raising their glasses and drinking.

Isom took the opportunity presented by everyone's raised glasses to whisk the cloth off the table.

Alexis cleared her throat and keyed the table back to its working display.

"And with dinner over, gentlemen, we have a bit of business. You may consider yourself free, Mister Poulter, if you wish. This will be ship's business."

"I'd stay, if I may," Poulter said. "I may not be proper Navy, but perhaps I may contribute something."

Alexis nodded acceptance, but couldn't bring herself to agree. To date, she still hadn't warmed to Poulter, as she still felt he pestered her with questions he had no business asking.

"Very well, then," she said. "The issue, gentlemen, is the piracy — or at least overdue ships — reported by the authorities on Zariah. The pirates appear to be targeting the gallenium transports out of Dalthus, but have also taken a few common merchantmen. Your thoughts as to what we should do about it?"

She had her own thoughts, but wanted to hear from the others first. They had time yet before a course of action must be decided on and part of her role as commander was to teach the other officers. She had no delusions that she knew everything, but felt Spindler, at least, could benefit from her coaching. Villar, she thought, might have some very valid ideas that had eluded her.

"The gallenium's an obvious target," Villar said, "due to its value."

"But difficult to dispose of," Alexis said, "there are markets, but it's not a common cargo one might find a buyer for on any station."

Villar nodded. "I do hear it's been done in this area before — the sales, at least." He raised an eyebrow at Alexis.

"Yes, the illicit mining at Dalthus. The Coalsons and a few others."

"Do you suppose they're involved still?"

Alexis was glad it was Villar who'd asked the question, freeing her from the fear that she'd allowed her ... well, if she were honest about it, hatred of the family ... to color her suspicions.

"It may be possible," she allowed.

"He did seem to have a great deal of coin to throw about."

Alexis nodded. "Let's not focus too much on one possibility, though," she said, "there are others with a bit more coin than one would expect."

Villar frowned for a moment, then nodded. "The Jadiqis."

"A fleet of their own ships and far more in the way of imported goods than one would expect in such a young colony."

Villar nodded.

"Any others come to mind?" Alexis asked. "Assuming it's not some random band with no associations to anyone we've had dealings with." The others were silent. "Very well, then. Thoughts on where to find the bastards in the act?" She paused. "Mister Spindler?"

Spindler jumped. He'd been looking back and forth between Alexis and Villar and apparently hadn't expected to be singled out.

"I'm — I'm not certain, sir."

"None of us are certain, Mister Spindler, hence the need for this discussion. Think it through a moment — there's a bit of evidence for us to work from."

Spindler's brow furrowed and Alexis shared a look with Villar, whose lips twitched in a suppressed smile. Then she caught Poulter looking at her as well, and her own amusement vanished. Damn him, but the man put her on edge.

"I suppose," Spindler said tentatively, "there was that first ship we encountered, the gallenium transport they cheated us out of."

Alexis raised an eyebrow and Spindler flushed.

"Well, I suppose it wasn't cheating, but still ..."

"To this evening's point, Mister Spindler," Alexis prompted.

Spindler looked even more nervous, as he had since she'd snapped at him on Man's Fall, and Alexis regretted that incident even more. No matter her own frustrations and temper — and she was glad to admit that both had eased considerably since Nabb, Ruse, and Sinkey had begun bringing the crew around, and more since she'd made the decision to actively seek out the pirates — she must remember not to take it out on her officers, who had no real recourse. She had the extreme example of *Hermione's* Captain Neals to remind her of the dangers of that.

"What about that first ship, Mister Spindler?" she prompted.

"Well ... it was being taken and was in the Remada Straits when we came across it." He frowned. "It seems to me that would be a fine place to come across ships, were I a pirate, and particularly for traffic from Dalthus to Zariah. All that gallenium being shipped ..."

Alexis nodded. It was no more than something well-known, that *darkspace* straits and pirates went together like toast and jam, but it wouldn't hurt the lad to come to such conclusions on his own.

"But the Straits are quite large," Spindler went on. "We might be watching one side while the pirates take ships in another. We'd have to sail one end to the other and still trust to luck."

Spindler's brow furrowed.

Villar started to speak, likely to prompt the lad with a question, but Alexis signaled him to be still and he nodded understanding. Spindler was thinking things through on his own and she thought he might come to it without help.

"If I were hunting back home," Spindler said, "well, if I were following my father's hunt, I suppose he'd use a bait of some sort." He looked up at Alexis. "Pirates are sort of predators, aren't they, sir?"

Alexis nodded. "They are, indeed, Mister Spindler."

"I'm sorry to disagree, sir, but carrion eaters, more like," Villar said and Alexis once more noted the changes in their relationship that allowed him to feel comfortable expressing his own opinion. "No honor in them. Not like a proper foe."

"I'm not so certain of that," Alexis said, "Well, not that the pirates have honor, but that there's any such thing as a proper, honorable foe." She thought of Giron and the little ships destroyed in their flight from there. "War has a way of bringing out the worst in us, I think. It's quite easy to justify nearly any act at the time some other bloke's trying to kill you."

Poulter shifted in his seat, looking at her intently, but said nothing. She'd almost forgotten the surgeon was there and instantly wished he wasn't.

Likely wanting to pull out his tablet and begin taking notes on me.

"Regardless, Mister Spindler was on the hunt for these pirates. What bait might we use, Mister Spindler?"

"The gallenium transports, I suppose, they seem to be the most targeted." He frowned. "But they don't stay still, do they? So they're not at all like bait — and the pirates would still have the means to take a gallenium transport, even if we gave them all of *Nightingale's* guns. The things have so much mass they turn so poorly, all a pirate would have to do is hang off their stern and fire. The transport would never be able to bring her guns to bear." He sighed. "I'm sorry, sir, it was a poor idea."

"Hhm." Alexis shared a look with Villar. "Is it the bait that fights back when you hunt with your father, Mister Spindler?"

"Well, no, sir, it's the hunters nearby in a blind." He frowned again, brow furrowed with thought. "Perhaps if *Nightingale* ..." He shook his head. "No, that wouldn't work, would it? The pirates would see us and not attack — there aren't any blinds in *darkspace*. They could see there was another ship with the transport and simply wait for the next one, couldn't they?"

"If *Nightingale* were with the transport, you're absolutely correct," Alexis said, then waited.

"We'd have to be in order to see the pirates come. If we couldn't see them ..."

Spindler's voice trailed off and Alexis had to hold back a laugh as his forehead creased even more.

It's like a freshly plowed field up there — I could plant wheat in those furrows.

"Our optics!" Spindler fairly cried out. He began tapping rapidly on Alexis' table, then looked up, face falling. "Oh ... I'm sorry, sir, I ..."

"Do go on, Mister Spindler," she said. "Follow your thought and show us what you wish."

"Thank you, sir."

Spindler tapped for a moment, then slid two lists of ship specifications into the center of the table.

"What am I looking at, Mister Spindler?" Alexis asked. "Talk me through it, will you?"

"Aye, sir. See here?" He pointed to one list. "This is our optics and these here —" He pointed to the other. "— are civilian standards. The lenses and filtering to keep the *darkspace* radiations out affect the range, see? Ours are better, but most merchants don't like to spend so much — some don't even have this range." He paused, looking at her with wide eyes. "The pirates' ships would likely just be captured merchantmen, wouldn't they?"

"In most cases, yes," Alexis said. "You've been studying ship specifications?"

Spindler flushed. "Mister Villar's given me extra studying, sir, when I ... well ..."

"Mister Spindler has exhibited a singular lack of hygiene in the midshipmen's berth on occasion," Villar said dryly.

Alexis suppressed a smile. *Nightingale's* lack of lieutenants left it to the senior midshipman to manage the berth, consisting of the single cabin Villar and Spindler shared. She could well imagine what conflicts the close quarters might engender and was happy that Villar seemed to have it in hand without being too hard on Spindler.

"You seem to have put those studies to good use," she said. "So what advantage do you think our optics would give us in this matter?"

"Well, sir," Spindler said, "we could sort of follow the transport, do you see? A pirate finding the transport would almost have to be ahead of its course, wouldn't it? So they'd see the transport, but not us, and then we'd see them before they could see us and ..." He broke off, perhaps realizing how fast he was speaking, and looked at Alexis. Then his face fell. "I suppose the pirates might take some other transport while we were following the one. Perhaps it's not such a good plan."

"Don't be so quick to dismiss it, Mister Spindler," Alexis said. "We're only one ship, after all. There'll always be the chance, no matter what we do, that the pirates will strike elsewhere. We must simply do our best to increase our chances."

"So it's not a bad idea, sir?"

Alexis smiled and shared a look with Villar.

"Do you have any better idea, Mister Villar?"

Villar shook his head. "No, sir. It seems a decent plan."

Alexis nodded. "Very well, then, Mister Spindler. We shall do as you say."

Spindler stared at her, wide-eyed. "You mean we're going to do it, sir? My plan?"

"Indeed," she said. "And I should wish you spend our time enroute to Dalthus in further study of those ship specifications, especially those of the missing ships. The pirates may be using one of those captured merchantmen — not the transports, I imagine — as their ship now. Perhaps not, but it's possible. If they are, the more we can guess about their optics and capabilities, the better."

Spindler nodded eagerly, apparently not caring that he'd just been given even more studying to do.

"And while you're at it, calculate the maximum visibility distance for the optics on *Nightingale* and each of those ships under the conditions in the Straits." They'd recalculate those as they sailed, for conditions always changed a bit, but she'd like to know the distances involved for further planning. It would be important to know how closely they could follow a transport, while remaining hidden from a pirate, for she'd want to be able to close quickly and engage the pirate without putting the transport in undue danger.

"Aye, sir."

"Very well, gentlemen, we have a plan thanks to Mister Spindler —" She nodded to Spindler who flushed red. "— and time to flesh out the details before we reach Dalthus. I suggest we get our rest now."

"Aye, sir," Villar and Spindler said, rising.

Poulter rose as well, but paused instead of heading toward the hatch with the others.

"A moment, if you don't mind, lieutenant?"

FORTY-THREE

7 May, aboard *HMS Nightingale*, enroute Zariah to Dalthus

Alexis nodded reluctantly at Poulter's request, resisting the urge to sigh. She waited until Villar and Spindler left and the hatch was closed once more.

"Yes?"

"I only wanted to say that I've noticed you seem better rested since we left Zariah," Poulter said.

Bloody hell, is the man monitoring my sleep somehow?

She even glanced around the cabin for a moment, wondering if she might see some device he'd installed.

Now that he said it, though, she thought she might have slept better. Perhaps it was the extra work of pouring over shipping reports, and missing ship reports, to find whatever patterns there might be, or perhaps only the sense of purpose in pursuing the pirates instead of only sailing about waiting for something to cross their path.

"I have, Mister Poulter." She could allow him that, at least.

"I thought you handled the boy quite well."

Alexis' jaw clenched. "He's not a boy, he's a Queen's officer — young, he may be, but he's also that."

"I —"

"And deserves the respect his position demands, Mister Poulter. I realize you're not properly Navy, that the Sick and Hurt Board is rather outside the traditional command structure, and that a surgeon's place aboard ship is ... somewhat aside from the rest of us."

For that, she knew some ships' captains were quite friendly with their surgeons. She could understand the desire, in fact. She'd never before felt so isolated as she did aboard *Nightingale* — well, perhaps aboard the ill-fated *Hermione*. Here, though, she really had no one she could simply talk to — every interaction with the crew, even with Villar, carried the baggage of commander to crew. She might be Sole Master after God aboard a Queen's ship, but that also meant having no equal she could converse with.

"Nevertheless," she went on, "Mister Spindler must maintain the respect of the crew. Oh —" She held up a hand to stop Poulter as he began to speak. "— the hands might well refer to him as 'lad' and 'boy' amongst themselves, there's no stopping that, and the older, wiser ones, such as Mister Ousley and his mates, know it's partly their job to bring him along as an officer. But they know the way of doing so while still respecting his position."

"I see," Poulter said. "I meant no disrespect. Only that you gave him quite a feeling of accomplishment, guiding him toward that plan and then accepting it."

"I don't recall him needing so very much in the way of guidance. I, and Mister Villar, for all that, might have had the same thing in mind to start with, but Spindler came to it much on his own, I think. If he should come to the realization that the plan was known to Villar and me at the start by his own devices, that's one thing, but I don't wish it bandied about that his thoughts were less worthy than they were."

Poulter shook his head. "I assure you, lieutenant, I do not bandy." He raised an eyebrow. "In fact, I consider such conversations as this quite private." He paused. "Should you ever wish to talk about anything."

Alexis took a deep breath and clamped down on her desire to snap at the man. This was exactly what she'd been afraid of when Poulter asked to stay behind and here he was with his demands she talk about something.

Whatever is it with these surgeons and their talk? We never got that sort of thing from the surgeons aboard Merlin *or even* Shrewsbury.

Of course, those men were older and had been in the Navy quite a long time. Moreover, she supposed, she had no way of knowing what might go on between a captain and the ship's surgeon behind closed doors.

"It's sometimes helpful to say some things aloud —"

"What is it with you lot and your bloody talking!" Alexis snapped.

Poulter raised an eyebrow.

Alexis took a deep breath and closed her eyes. She'd been feeling so good about things since leaving Zariah with the intent to actively hunt down the pirates. There was work for her to do and that work drove off the memories and shadows — now Poulter's words, for she knew exactly what he, and the bloody Lieutenant Curtice before him, wanted her to talk about.

Things happened. Horrible things. But, as the men say after a flogging, "Over, done with, and forgotten." What possible use is there in dredging the bloody memories up on purpose when they come unbidden so damned often?

She opened her eyes to find Poulter staring at her calmly.

"I've upset you," he said.

Alexis took another deep breath, forcing memories and shadows away. She regretted her outburst — something she knew she was doing far too often. Not least because it likely reinforced whatever thoughts Poulter already had of her state of mind, but also because she did have to work with the man. There was no telling how long she'd command *Nightingale*, and she couldn't very well spend the entire time sending "afters"-soaked spacers to him for care ... much as she might like to.

At some point, they'd have to settle his place aboard ship, and this might be the best time. In addition, Poulter was a part of *Nightingale's* crew, and she'd determined to get to know them all better. She'd managed a start at that, she thought, with regular walks about the ship, stopping now and then to have a word with each man from time to time. She supposed she owed Poulter the same courtesy.

She sighed.

Over, done with, and forgotten — if I can manage it.

Settle it now and move on.

"I'm sorry for my outburst, Mister Poulter. Sit down, please." Alexis sat with him and caught Isom's eye. "I'll have a bourbon, Isom, and something more for Mister Poulter."

"Nothing for me, thank you."

"Just the bourbon, then, Isom."

She remained silent, watching Poulter, as Isom brought her glass and poured.

"Just leave the bottle, Isom," she said, "there's no need for you to wait on just the two of us. You can finish up with Garcia and then turn in."

"Aye, sir."

Poulter nodded at the bottle. "That helps, I suppose?"

Damn the man, but he does make it hard.

Had he no knowledge of the Navy at all? Every officer she'd ever encountered drank like a veritable fish.

"Helps with what, Mister Poulter?"

Poulter smiled, then his smile fell a bit.

"You know, I fear we got off on quite the wrong foot from the start," he said.

Alexis nodded. She could acknowledge that, at least. And that it might be more her fault than his. She'd reacted to meeting him as though he were an extension of Lieutenant Curtice back on Lesser

Ichthorpe, and there may have been nothing the man could have said to get them off on the right foot at all. That lieutenant had been tasked with evaluating her after Giron. She'd found him an insufferable prat, full of nothing but question after question about the battle at Giron and how Alexis felt about it.

"What is it you wished to speak of, Mister Poulter?"

Poulter smiled. "I suppose I should tell you that I'm acquainted with Lieutenant Curtice. I believe you know him as well."

Alexis froze. It was as though every time she took a step with Poulter, she was stepping in something very like one of the creature's messes. Speaking of the creature, in fact, she found herself suddenly wishing it might slip its cage once more and claw its way up Poulter as it had at their first dinner aboard.

She cocked her head, hopefully listening for the telltale chittering that told the creature was about, but heard nothing.

"I've made the lieutenant's acquaintance," Alexis said.

Perhaps the Jadiqis are correct. Perhaps there is a God ... and he is vengeful. I certainly must have done something horrid to deserve this.

How else to explain that the surgeon aboard her ship, out of all the ships and all the surgeons in the fleet, should be acquainted with the man who'd said she shouldn't have the command in the first place?

"How did you find Lieutenant Curtice?" Poulter asked.

"Tedious," Alexis said without thinking, then quickly, "Forgive me for speaking so of your friend, Mister Poulter, but Lieutenant Curtice and I did find ourselves at odds while on Lesser Ichthorpe and I spoke in haste."

"Nothing at all to forgive. We're acquainted and colleagues, but I wouldn't name him friend." Poulter smiled. "Far too tedious for that, I think."

Alexis took a bit of heart at that, but warily, waiting for her foot to encounter the next bit of mess.

Poulter shrugged. "I felt it was time, perhaps past time, that I told you he and I were acquainted. Certain documents come aboard ship, you understand, with transferred men and officers." He paused. "You have records on the men and your officers, of course, but some of these documents are for the ship's surgeon's-eyes only."

"Documents about me, you mean." Alexis reached for her glass, saw Poulter's eyes follow her hand, and stopped, going for the bowl of nuts left over from dinner instead.

Poulter raised an eyebrow, but nodded.

"Medical records, reports, that sort of thing."

"From Lieutenant Curtice."

"Some, yes."

Alexis sighed, she could only imagine what those reports might include.

"Curtice's notes indicated you were quite reluctant to speak about the events you've been through." He sighed. "I've tried to draw you out, but it seems that might have been the wrong way to go about it." He shrugged. "So, then, a more direct approach, yes?"

Alexis stared at him for a moment — this kept getting worse and worse, but she didn't know how she might end it without simply ordering Poulter to leave and, possibly, never speak to her again. She strained her mind, willing the little beast to appear, but, of course, the creature didn't cooperate.

"I'm truly at a loss to understand your, and Lieutenant Curtice's, fascination with my thoughts, Mister Poulter."

Poulter chuckled.

"Do you think the answers are for us, lieutenant?" He chuckled again. "No, we ask the questions, but only to suggest you think about the answers. Much like you prompted young Mister Spindler just a few minutes ago. The questions, and their answers, are meant to help you deal with the matter, not for myself or Lieutenant Curtice."

"I ask myself these questions all the time, Mister Poulter. I'm aware that this, the Navy, is a dangerous occupation and that men will die — I, myself, might die. I'm even, come to that, aware that my orders and decisions will result in those deaths."

"Well, then." Poulter rose, surprising Alexis. She'd thought he might push further. "I'll take my leave of you." He made his way to the hatchway but stopped and turned back.

"I will point out, though, lieutenant — knowing a thing and accepting it are two entirely different matters."

Alexis felt him watching her as she refilled her glass and sipped the bourbon.

"I know of the events at Giron, and I've been with the Navy long enough to imagine what wasn't in the official releases. Even a bit of your previous ship, *Hermione* — oh, the records are sealed, but I can imagine some of that, as well. There are few enough things which would bring about a judgment of 'groundless' on mutiny charges and send that ship's captain to a posting in atmosphere."

He looked at her and, for the first time, Alexis found his gaze sympathetic, rather than. He smiled and made his way to the hatch.

"Everyone takes different demons from events such as you've been through, lieutenant, and I do understand the reluctance of ... well, people, such as yourself to seek out an understanding ear, but whether with me or someone else, I do encourage you to exorcise them as best you may." He nodded at her bottle and glass. "Most find merely keeping them at bay is not nearly enough."

FORTY-FOUR

10 May, Carew Farmstead, Dalthus System

Alexis tossed her bag onto the bed. A few days at home would do her good and a bit of liberty would do her crew no harm. There were shipments of gallenium going out soon and *Nightingale* would be heading out to trail them.

She'd granted Villar a full day's leave, and he and Marie had gone off to the village, where there was a small inn, for the time *Nightingale* would be in-system, so she'd have her room to herself.

She scowled as Isom arranged the bloody creature's cage in a corner. Each time she returned home, she imagined the thing somehow being left behind, often because she'd dragged it a day's ride from the farmstead and left it there, but no matter how often she fantasized about such a thing, she somehow neglected to do so and the thing made its way back to *Nightingale* and her pantry.

Her tablet *pinged* and she pulled it from her pocket to see a new message. Her scowl grew deeper.

"Coalson or Arundel, sir?" Isom asked.

"Either. Both."

This message was from Coalson, wanting yet another meeting

361

between her and his coterie, but there'd be one from her cousin wanting the same soon enough.

Coalson and his bunch were intent on gaining more services from New London, but without giving up any sovereignty in return. For her part, Alexis had used their first meetings to feel out Coalson's still too great wealth and try to determine if he was still involved with piracy to achieve it. She'd managed to achieve exactly nothing, she felt — and hoped Coalson hadn't either. His group pressed her for commitments and agreements, which she suspected they intended to try holding New London to, as Alexis was the senior officer on station. Though she remained as noncommittal as possible, she still feared she might inadvertently give them some advantage.

It's like fencing with a waterfall — my own blows do nothing, yet any misstep on my part would spell disaster.

Her initial joy at meeting her cousin had turned to dismay after the first few visits as well. Lauryn was not only in favor of changing the inheritance laws, but was the head of an entire gaggle of what Alexis could only deem suffragettes, intent on changing not only the laws of inheritance, but the entire voting structure of the colony.

As though the shareholders would ever vote to give any power to those who hold none.

They seemed to view Alexis as some sort of symbol or figurehead, and simply assumed she agreed with them on every point.

In fact, she might, but hadn't the time to give it too much thought. Her time was too taken up with the running of *Nightingale* and the search for smugglers and pirates.

She sighed.

There was nothing she could truly do for either group, and yet they insisted in their demands for her time each visit home. When all she wanted to do in these visits was to relax, just for a time, from the duties aboard ship, and give her lads a brief respite as well.

Part of her wanted to fall into the bed that very moment and nap, but her grandfather had mentioned he had something to show her on this visit. Whatever it was, she decided to see to that first, and then relax.

She went down the stairs.

"Grandfather?" she called from the stairs, but she heard no answer, instead hearing voices from the kitchen.

Denholm's back was to her, peeling a pile of potatoes, scowling at each one before placing it in a bowl of water, while Julia stuffed a chicken with herbs. Alexis had to smile at the sight, it was so homey and comforting. She'd spent most of her childhood, she thought, sitting in this kitchen watching Julia stuff one thing or another into chickens. It was odd the sorts of things one remembered.

She paused in the doorway for a moment, watching the two. Denholm said something quietly and Julia laughed, then he caught sight of Alexis and turned his head to her, still smiling, one eyebrow raised in query.

Alexis almost said nothing, the moment had been so sweet and reminded her, oddly, of her and Delaine nudging each other as they waited in meetings before the invasion of Giron.

"You said you have something to show me?"

Denholm sobered. He seemed oddly unsure of himself, then Julia squeezed his forearm and murmured something Alexis didn't catch. He nodded toward the door.

"Come along, then."

Alexis frowned, puzzled, but followed him outside. They walked across the farmyard to the gate to the road, but instead of turning toward the village, Denholm turned away from it.

Alexis realized where he was taking her and almost stumbled. She felt a moment's dread — she'd rarely visited this place. Its residents were those she'd never really known, after all.

Past the gates the road narrowed and turned into a winding path through the trees, then up a small hill that overlooked a large pond. The village's fields were on the other side of the pond and the village itself was visible far in the distance. Atop the hill was the small clearing that served as the Carew family cemetery. The village had its own, so there were only three stones in the space — Alexis' parents and grandmother.

Or had been three, as Alexis followed her grandfather slowly toward the fourth. Plain and workmanlike as the others were.

Alexis knelt beside it and ran her fingertips over the engraving.

Sterlyn Artley.

Just the date he'd died, August twenty-second. Called the Glorious Twenty-Second in the newsfeeds by fools who could never understand the costs of such things.

"I couldn't find his birth date," Denholm whispered. "We can add it." He cleared his throat and laid a hand on the stone beside it, her grandmother's. "Your man, Isom, and I talked some that first night you were home."

Alexis flushed at the memory of bellowing drunken shanties as she was hoisted up the stairs to her bed.

"He helped me with the names. Don't rightly know it was the proper thing to do, but ..." His hand caressed his wife's headstone. "At times I've found comfort in a place to speak to those I've lost. Perhaps you'll find the same."

Alexis nodded, running her fingers down the stone. Below the date was the ship's name that still pained her.

Belial.

And then two columns of other names. Alexis read them to herself, automatically adding their rating aboard ship. She found that she remembered them all.

Bain Ades, topman.

Renfrid Lathem, gunner's mate.

Rod Morrall, able spacer.

"Your man, Isom, helped me with the names, as I said. From what he told me," Denholm said, "young Artley seemed a good lad and might ... might like the others' who were there at the end to keep him company."

"He would," Alexis said. She ran fingers over the names again.

She quite suddenly understood what Poulter had been on about with his talk of demons. "I killed them, you know."

Denholm dropped to the ground beside her and wrapped his arm around her. "Lexi —"

"I did," she insisted.

"It's a war, you can't —"

"It was my choice." Her voice broke and she took a moment to steady herself. "Captain Euell gave me *Belial* and told me to pick the men I wanted. I picked the best he had, the very best. My whole division and any others I could have." She could feel the tears streaming down her face, but couldn't stop them. "I named them, every one, and marked them to die there on that ship. They stood because I told them it was needful, and they fell because I couldn't find another way."

Denholm tried to pull her up and away, but she stayed there.

"Alexis, you couldn't know what would happen and ... I read the news of that battle, of every story you've been mentioned in since you left, but especially of that one, and I know what was at stake." He squeezed her shoulders. "They didn't die for nothing, now did they?"

Alexis sniffed. "No. No, but you should have seen them." She looked at him and smiled, eyes bright. "Not a man ran, not a man shirked ... I loved them for that." She sobbed and let Denholm pull her to him, burying her face in his chest. "I loved them, but, God forgive me, I'd take them to their deaths again if I had to, and I don't know how to bear that. Nor their memory."

"That will ease," Denholm said.

"Will it?" Alexis pulled back and stared at him. "I've seen the look in your eyes when you speak of grandmother or my parents — has the pain of their loss eased?"

"That's different, it —"

"Is it?" She shook her head and wiped her eyes. "Perhaps. There was a man, you know, while I've been away." Alexis flushed. She felt awkward saying it, especially to her grandfather, but didn't know how else to explain to him how her losses might not be different from his own. "I care for him a great deal — I may love him. I don't know exactly." She shrugged. "He may be dead as well, I don't know that either — he sailed off with Admiral Chipley's fleet in pursuit of the Hanoverese and there's been no word for —"

"I'm sorry."

"No, it's not that I'm trying to explain." She frowned. "I don't know if I love Delaine or not — the uncertainty of it, where he is, pains me. It does. But I do know I love my lads — my *Merlins*, my *Hermiones* —" She swallowed and nodded at the marker, her hand going out again to caress the cold stone. "— my *Belials*." She gave a pained chuckle. "Even my *Nightingales*, God knows why, the motley, shirking, tag-ends of the fleet that they are. They're mine and I love them with all my heart, so don't try to tell me the loss of a single one of them is made even a bit less."

Denholm merely nodded. He might not understand, but she felt he'd accept her words. He nodded to the stone.

"I was worried it should be something grander," he said quietly.

"Grand wouldn't do at all," Alexis said, with a fond smile. "The grand ships were the frigates and ships of the line in that battle." She caressed the letters spelling out the ship's name again. "She wasn't one of those at all. Just one of the tiny, little ships doing yeoman's work there that day."

She rose.

"Thank you."

She took her grandfather's arm and they made their way back to the path leading down toward the farm.

Alexis turned and turned back to look at the stones again. For a moment, her vision blurred and she staggered. In her mind, she saw not just the single stone marking *Belial*, but rows of them stretching off in all directions. The sun seemed to darken and shadows rose up beside each stone. She gasped.

"Alexis?"

She shook herself and her vision cleared. The sun, bright as before, dispelling the shadows and phantom stones both.

Demons, indeed.

She shivered.

"Memories," she said, thinking that might be a better than her grandfather thinking she was having some sort of visions. Better than her believing the fears of her nightmares were appearing in day.

"Memory's an odd thing. It's —" Denholm frowned and nodded down the hillside toward the fields around the village. "Like hedgerows around a fallow field. Newly plowed it's all raw and torn up, but step outside, leave it for a time, and when you return you've a peaceful meadow with just the best of what was before. Give it time to become that."

Alexis considered that, but wondered how it might apply when one's fields were constantly being plowed again and again.

"There's been no time, there never is. With the war there's just been one thing, one loss after another, with never a moment for it to heal. The war's still on — every new trip to Zariah brings the Gazette with stories of ships I know, crews I know, in one battle or another. They don't even bother listing the names of the common crew, you know? Only the offices. So I've no way of telling how many others of my lads are dead or injured or ..." She scrubbed at her eyes again. "I sometimes wish that I could bring them all here and hide them away so they'd be safe."

She sighed. Oddly, she did feel better — a good cry and the admission of how much guilt she felt for those who'd fallen. Not that she thought this one instance might be an end to that guilt or the nightmares that came with it, but perhaps Poulter had a point about the talking. It was something to think about, at least — but not now. She couldn't spare the time to think about that any more than she could keep her *Nightingales* from harm's way.

"But I can't, because in seven days' time a gallenium transport will be leaving for the Straits, and it's my bloody duty to take my lads off into danger again."

FORTY-FIVE

convoy in the Remada Straits

Alexis woke to a hand on her shoulder and Isom's whispered, "Mister Villar's at the hatch, sir."

Followed quickly by, "Sorry he's out again, sir. Thought the new latch would keep him penned up."

For a moment, she wondered why on earth her first officer would be kept penned up, then realized it was the vile creature Isom was talking about as he lifted it from her chest.

She sat up and rubbed her eyes. She had slept well, despite the creature's presence.

"Let him in."

"Three bells of the middle, sir, and sails sighted off to the edge of the Straits and bearing on the convoy," Villar said.

Alexis stretched. Isom was already back with her uniform. She pulled on the trousers, her tunic, then slid her arms into the jacket he held for her.

"Check my boots, please."

"Aye, sir."

With both a look and a sniff Isom gave her boots the all clear. As she was pulling the second one on, Villar's words registered.

"Sails? More than one?"

"Two, sir."

Alexis frowned. Pirates were a solitary lot and seldom worked together.

Not normally, at least, but neither do they tend to transition at will as that last one did — so perhaps they're less normal here than I should expect.

"I assume we're not yet visible to them?" Alexis asked as they left her cabin for the quarterdeck.

Villar shook his head. "Not for some hours yet."

They reached the quarterdeck and Alexis could see the truth of that on the navigation plot. The gallenium transports were sailing as nearly as they could down the middle of the Straits, keeping well away from the edges of the three systems where their rate of travel would slow and the dark matter built up into a halo of shoals.

The two unknown ships were nearer to Lesser Remada, and sailing on a course to intercept the transports.

Nightingale was also to one side of the Straits, but well behind the transports, while the two new vessels were ahead.

Each of the ships had a wide circle about it, representing, in her officers' best guesses, the range at which each ships' optics could detect the light of another's sails. The exact range would depend on how large the other ship was, how much sail she had set, and the strength of her particle projectors, as well as the current conditions in the Straits — too much dark matter being kicked up by strong winds would reduce visibility.

Even as an estimate, though, she could see that it would be some time before the other ships, even the convoy, would spot *Nightingale*. By that time, she thought she'd have them. The winds were variable, but generally more toward the Strait's center here. *Nightingale* would have the wind gauge on them, and, she hoped, superior speed.

"Call the men to an early breakfast, Mister Villar,"

HOURS PASSED.

Alexis studied the navigation plot. *Nightingale* was still out of sight of the three ships and the convoy of ore carriers. The decision of when to change that would be vital. Too soon, and she risked the pirates escaping — leave it too long, though, and they might be amongst the convoy before she could come up and stop them. The problem was made more difficult by the cycle of winds in the Straits.

The convoy was in a stream of dark energy winds traveling toward the Zariah end of the Straits. The pirates and *Nightingale* were coming in on a swirl of those winds that seemed to curve toward Lesser Remada up out of the Straits, and then back down into the center.

As she watched, the convoy, which had been signaling the oncoming ships for some time, lights on their masts and hulls flashing more and more frantically as they sought some assurance that those approaching were not what they feared, broke into disarray.

One of the ships, the one closest to the oncoming pirates, its captain apparently deciding that the time had come for every man to take his fate in his own hands, broke from even the loose formation the transports had been maintaining.

The ship turned away from the pirates, cutting across the path of another and forcing that transport to turn up into the wind to avoid a collision.

The turning ship wore around the wind and set its course back down the Straits toward Dalthus. The one which had been cut off slowed.

Nightingale was too distant for Alexis to be certain, but she imagined the transports sails would be slack and fluttering as the ship faced the wind instead of catching it on her side.

"She's in irons, certain," Villar muttered.

"Why did he run?" Spindler asked. "Wouldn't they have a better chance if they concentrated their firepower?"

"Some think only of themselves," Villar said. "No matter the cost to others, for his actions have likely doomed that ship he cut off if we can't intercede in time."

Alexis nodded to Villar. It would take that transport precious minutes to work the lines of the sails and catch the wind again, perhaps even having to take it on the front of the sails, gain some way backward, and horse the ship around to catch the winds properly — all the while with a pair of unknown ships bearing down on them. Her crew would be frantic and growing more so.

"Doomed if we weren't here," she said. "Bring the projectors to full power, Mister Villar, and beat to quarters, if you please."

"Aye, sir."

Alexis kept her eyes on the plot as the ship around her burst into action. Increasing the power to the projectors meant a corresponding increase in the ship's visibility. For both the convoy and the two pirates, it would be as though *Nightingale* had suddenly appeared where no ship had been before, like a flare suddenly burning in the night sky.

FORTY-SIX

17 MAY, ABOARD *HMS NIGHTINGALE,* DARKSPACE, THE REMADA Straits

"That's the *Owl,*" Villar said.

Alexis nodded. They were close enough now that *Nightingale's* optics could magnify the other ships enough to identify them if they'd been seen before. The ship's computers gave a ninety-three percent chance that the trailing pirate ship was the *Owl.* Villar was quite a bit more certain and Alexis agreed with him. She thought she could make out some of the spots on the hull where *Nightingale's* shot had struck, now poorly and haphazardly repaired.

It had taken the other ship's a few minutes to react to *Nightingale's* brightened sails, minutes which drew them ever closer.

The gallenium transports seemed uncertain of whether to treat Alexis' ship as a savior or yet another threat. Alexis had yet to order her colors raised — she regretted any anxiety this caused the transport captains, but, for the moment at least, the pirates were not running, and she wanted them sailing toward her as long as possible, so that they couldn't get away.

The computer's certainty that the other ship was the *Owl* changed to ninety-six percent.

"A fair bet, Mister Villar," Alexis said.

Around her, the quarterdeck was still and muted. The ship itself was, as well. On the main deck, all of the bunks had been folded up to the wall. The guns were nestled next to the still closed gunports, while their crews stood by. The deck was still aired, but all of the crew was in their vacsuits, helmets close to hand. So was the quarterdeck crew, though they'd have air throughout the battle, unless the hull was shot through.

Isom and Garcia were on the orlop with Poulter — they'd assist him with any wounded. The creature, Alexis presumed, had been safely ensconced in the hold by Isom.

For a moment, quite to her surprise, Alexis found herself missing the warm, furry comfort of the damned mongoose. She had a sudden image of wearing the bloody thing like a sort of scarf inside her helmet and chuckled.

Creasy and Dorsett shared a look. Dorsett leaned over and whispered, "Captain's got your bloody Dutchmen right where she wants 'em — see 'er laughin' at 'em."

Dorsett nodded and Alexis let them believe what they would, if it gave them heart to think she had some plan other than to drive straight for the foe, then she'd not correct them.

Alexis studied the plot for a moment more. It was time. She keyed her suit radio so that it would transmit throughout the ship. With the gunports closed, those on the guns could hear her, and the sail crews were in the locker, as well.

"Let's have them know them who they're facing, lads. Show the colors."

NIGHTINGALE'S HULL and mast shone brighter as lights lit, alternating red and white to name her a New London Naval ship.

The gallenium transports, the two not fleeing, edged up toward the wind to close with her, presumably feeling safer near the Navy..

The pirates hesitated, then began a flurry of signals.

"Any thought to what they're saying, Creasy?" Alexis asked.

"No, sir. Some sort of private code — give the computer enough of it, and some actions to match it with, maybe there's a chance to break it."

"With luck, we'll have them both in hand before that can happen."

That luck wasn't with them, though, as the signals continued. For a time, it was almost as if the two ships were arguing with each other, but eventually seemed to settle their differences.

The *Owl*, which was farther away from *Nightingale*, wore ship and fled before the wind. *Nightingale* would be able to catch it, Alexis was certain, but the leading rounded up and headed right for her.

She heard Creasy grunt.

"Something?" she asked.

"I thought to try something, sir, in amongst that exchange of signals, see?"

"Yes?"

"Well, there's some merchants don't like to keep a proper quarter-deck watch, see, so they automate things a bit."

"What sorts of things?"

"They don't like so many queries from us revenue boats, sir? So they have their signals consoles automatically send a reply. I sent out our number along with '*What ship?*', and she responded right quick just now."

"With her name?"

"Aye, sir, *Distant Crown*, for what it's worth."

Alexis frowned. That was one of the ships Bramley had said was missing — apparently taken by the pirates and without their signals console being reprogrammed.

"Well, we know her name, at least, and that's further confirmation she's crewed by pirates now."

"Aye, sir," Creasy said, "but —" He scowled as though unwilling to mention it.

"What is it, Creasy?" Alexis couldn't understand his hesitation, could he possibly still be worried about Dutchmen?

The signalman scratched at his neck. "Why would she respond at all, you see? What with them being pirates and us a Queen's ship and them all in the middle of signals to the other one? So they've something automated, at least, and maybe more." He grimaced as though afraid to voice the thought. "Some captains are cheaper than most, sir. There's a chance — just a chance, mind you."

Villar's head came up, his gaze hawkish.

"Do you think so?" he asked.

Creasy shrugged. "No tellin', sir, but if it is ..."

Alexis looked from one to the other, wondering if the two were doing this to her on purpose.

"Would it be at all convenient for one of you to fill your commander in what you're talking about?" she asked.

Creasy flushed, but Villar actually grinned.

"There's a certain class of merchant, sir, who finds there's less cost in keeping a full watch on the quarterdeck — ones who think a helmsman's enough, and him, perhaps, drowsing a bit in the deep Dark."

Alexis nodded. She could see that happening. A merchant captain would want to squeeze out every pence he could, and smaller watches meant a smaller quarterdeck crew.

"And some go further than a signals response, sir," Villar said. "So as not to irritate a revenue cutter's commander – the surly sort, I mean."

Alexis glanced at him and raised an eyebrow. Was he tweaking her?

"Not that I've encountered any such as that," Villar said, lips twitching.

"So as not to irritate those revenue captains, myself being the soul of patience," she said, "they have this automated response to identify their ship — yes, I see that, but what further..." She stopped and frowned. Her next act in approaching such a ship, though, would likely be to inspect it — and she'd be just as irritated if her next signal were ignored for any length of time. Irritated and suspicious, so what use was the first reply? Unless ...

"No," she said, "what fool would —"

"Never underestimate what a cheap and lazy man will do, sir," Villar said.

"Do you really suppose?"

NIGHTINGALE CLOSED WITH *DISTANT CROWN*, while the *Owl* continued to flee. She'd thought at first that the other captain might have meant to swing around and take *Nightingale* from another angle while she was engaged with the *Distant Crown*, but it was now clear that the *Owl* was fleeing with no intent to return.

Villar made a disgusted sound.

"No honor amongst thieves, I suppose," he said.

"No," Alexis agreed, "but why the *Crown's* not fleeing as well is curious. Do you suppose they think they can take us alone?"

"There's no telling, and I shouldn't think they'd be able to. That one's smaller than the *Owl*, and I doubt they've had time to cut and seal her hull to introduce more gunports as the *Owl* has."

"Perhaps they mean to only delay us for a time, then transition to normal-space where we can't follow." She scowled at the navigation plot. "That's a trick I'd dearly love to have from them. Admiralty would be quite interested, I think."

She'd included their encounter with the ship that transitioned away in her dispatches, but there'd been no reply to that yet. Perhaps there'd be one when next they reached Zariah.

The *Crown* was on the starboard tack, coming upwind toward

Nightingale, while Alexis drove nearly directly downwind. As the distance closed, and the *Crown* began to pass in front, though, she changed that.

"Put the wind on the starboard beam, Busbey," she ordered.

"Wind on the starboard beam, aye."

Nightingale was the faster sailor, from what Alexis could tell so far, and she wanted to keep her ship ahead of the other for what she had planned.

If it's not some phantom of Creasy's mind, like his Dutchmen.

She couldn't imagine any captain allowing his ship to be handled in the way both Creasy and Villar swore some did, but if the *Crown's* former commander was one who did such things she'd be willing to take advantage of it.

Even if he wasn't — hadn't been, she supposed, for the former captain and crew had almost certainly been killed outright by these pirates — *Nightingale* would still be well-positioned to begin the coming battle.

"He's not tacked at all," Alexis mused, watching the plot.

Villar nodded. "No course changes at all — if it weren't for the crew on the hull, I'd imagine her —" He glanced at the signals console then leaned closer and lowered his voice. "I'd imagine she had no crew, if I couldn't see those there."

Alexis watched the images of the other ship and the few — too few, she thought — figures of crewmen in vacsuits on the ship's hull. There was little active work being done on the sails, as though the captain, having set a course that would eventually bring him into contact with *Nightingale,* was unwilling to put forth the effort to change it.

Or as though they have no clear idea what to do, outside a few basic bits of sailing.

"Well, we can see those crew well enough," she whispered back, "so I'll have no talk of Dutchmen with this action."

The distance closed more. They were within range of the guns now, but Alexis waited. *Nightingale* was ahead of the *Crown,* while the other ship approached at an angle. Either ship could bring the other to bear with a bit of a turn, but neither fired.

What the other captain was thinking, Alexis didn't know, but she wanted her first, best laid broadside to have the greatest chance of damaging the other ship significantly. Her guncrews had improved, but they were still nowhere near what she could wish them to be.

The *Crown* fired first, not with a turn and a broadside, but with a bowchaser. The smaller gun at the ship's fore could bear on *Nightingale* without maneuvering.

A bolt of condensed light sprang across the space between the ships, missing low and ahead of *Nightingale*. She waited for a second bowchaser to fire, but none did.

"Take in two reefs and cut the particle projector by ten percent," Alexis ordered. Doing so would reduce *Nightingale's* speed, letting her fall back a bit and put her broadside directly in line with the other ship's bow.

"Aye, sir." Villar passed on the necessary orders to the sail crew, while Busbey adjusted the power to the projector.

As the ship slowed, the *Crown's* bowchaser fired again, the shot was high, but not high enough to miss. It flashed through *Nightingale's* sails, cutting lines and punching a round hole through the metal mesh of the sail itself.

The azure glow of the sail flashed white around the edges of the hole, but the sail held and didn't tear.

"Now," Alexis said, simply, judging the positions of the two ships.

"Signals away, sir," Creasy said, almost immediately.

Along *Nightingale's* hull and mast, lights flashed. Her number, identifying her as a Queen's ship, and the simple, common command of a revenue cutter. *Heave-to. Inspection.*

For a moment, nothing happened, and Alexis opened her mouth to order the alternative to the plan and maneuver *Nightingale* for a full broadside.

"A moment, if you please, sir," Villar whispered, watching the plot intensely.

Alexis held back.

Somewhere in the *Crown's* signals console, her former captain's orders took effect. *Nightingale's* number was recognized. A buzzer sounded on the helm — enough to wake a drowsing helmsman, alone on the quarterdeck late in the middle watch. A second buzzer sounded in the captain's cabin.

And, so as not to irritate a surly customs and revenue lieutenant should those two worthies not react quickly enough, the helm executed its preprogrammed orders.

"Bless all the lazy fools," Alexis whispered.

The *Crown's* sails went dark, projector off completely, and her rudder turned hard, bringing the ship's bow up to the wind — hove-to and waiting for inspection — directly into *Nightingale's* broadside.

"*Fire!*"

It was still a bit ragged, Alexis noted, but well-aimed directly at the other ship's bow. Light flashed across the intervening space and seemed to splash against the *Crown's* bow as thermoplastic vaporized and the shot lit the fog of particles.

Alexis counted down the seconds, willing the other ship's sails to remain dark and her target to sit, dead in space. She could well imagine the chaos on the *Crown's* quarterdeck while the captain and helmsman attempted to determine what had happened.

She could see the damage the first broadside had done to the other ship on the images splayed across her plot. The outer hatch of the bow sail locker was simply gone, shot away all entire, and she could just make out the inner hatch. It was possible that had been holed as well, or it could be only a shadow. She leaned closer to the image to see and —

"Man over!" Dorsett called.

Alexis spun to the tactical console.

"What?"

"Here, sir," Dorsett showed her the image.

Two vacsuited figures were at the ship's stern near the tall rudder. Beyond them, drifting, was another. His safety line must have been cut when the *Crown's* only hit had run through *Nightingale's* rigging. Now he was behind the ship and, though *Nightingale* was barely moving herself, he was too far away for a line to reach him.

"Ready!" came the call from the guns.

Alexis forced her thoughts away from the man. Whoever it was, she had a battle to fight still and couldn't risk the ship for one man.

"*Fire!* Then independent fire! Pour it on them, lads!" She turned again. "Keep him in sight Dorsett."

"Aye, sir."

The second broadside did for the inner hatch and Alexis suspected some of the shots had made it through entirely and run the length of the *Crown's* gundeck. That would make the deck a scene of chaos and horror. Raked like this from the bow, there'd be nothing to stop the incoming shot but bodies and the guns themselves.

"Creasy, make the stern lights bright as can be, you hear? So long as he's sight of the ship, he'll keep hope."

"Aye, sir."

Alexis hoped that would be true. Spacers hated the thought of being left behind in the Dark, with the weight of dark matter pressing in on them, unprotected by the field of gallenium in a ship's hull. They'd dump their air and suffocate themselves rather than suffer that fate, but if he could see the ship, he might keep the hope that *Nightingale* would return for him.

For a moment, she thought to drop a ship's boat. While ill-suited for any long trek through the dark, the boats did carry a small lug-sail for use in emergencies or if a ship was destroyed. But with *Nightingale* so short-handed, she couldn't spare the men to crew a boat, not with one enemy ship already engaged and another nearby. She steeled herself and hoped the man, whoever he might be, would hold on to hope until she could return for him.

Her guncrews began firing independently, shot after shot raking the *Crown*. Most struck into the bow and worked their way through the interior of the ship. A few missed, sliding along the ship's hull, and some struck the masts and rigging.

"Belay firing," Alexis ordered, seeing the *Crown's* mast shot through. It drifted and twisted, caught in its own rigging and quickly became a gnarled mess.

She looked from the navigation plot to the tactical console and cursed silently. The *Crown* was a battered hulk, not going anywhere without repairing her mast, but the *Owl* was still sailing away. She might be able to catch the other pirate, but it would be a close run chase — and not close at all if she delayed even a moment.

Alexis shared a look with Villar, wondering what decision he might make — but knew it was hers alone. Her gaze went to the retreating image of the *Owl*, then to that of the spacer who'd gone overboard. The choice was between any future victims of the *Owl* and certain death for one of her crew.

"Raise sail and charge the projector," she ordered, knowing it would allow the *Owl* to escape, but unwilling to leave any member of her crew to that fate. "We'll come about and collect our man, then board the *Distant Crown*."

FORTY-SEVEN

17 May, aboard *HMS Nightingale*, darkspace, the Remada Straits

Alexis gripped the edge of the navigation plot, knuckles white. She felt torn between conflicting duties. As *Nightingale's* commander, her place was on quarterdeck, watching over the ship. On the other hand, she was not so far removed from her time as a midshipman and lieutenant aboard a larger ship that she could shake the feeling that her place was with her lads. All of *Nightingale's* crew were her lads now, but she felt especially concerned about those in the boarding parties — she was sending them into unknown danger aboard *Distant Crown*, no matter the other ship had been battered into submission and now sat still and silent waiting for them.

What if this Distant Crown *has the same ability to transition as* Silver Leaf?

She'd been taken in by more than one ruse since boarding *Nightingale* and was determined to avoid another.

It was Spracklen, one of the miners pressed on Dalthus, who'd gone over to float behind the ship, and he'd shown not a bit of gratitude when he was brought back aboard. He was badly shaken, no doubt, but glared at Alexis as though he blamed her for the entire ordeal, and stalked off with his messmates.

After collecting him, she brought *Nightingale* about again and approached the *Crown*. The *Owl* was out of sight, but she hoped there'd be survivors aboard the *Crown* who might give her some insight into where to find the other ship.

Alexis saw that Villar was gripping the navigation plot's edge just as she was, his eyes darting to his vacsuit helmet then to her. It should be him leading the boarding party, as it would be a chance for him to distinguish himself in an action and perhaps gain some attention from Admiralty.

No, her place was on the quarterdeck. Villar's with the boarding.

Alexis took a deep breath to order him to the boarding tubes.

Bugger it.

"Mister Spindler, you have the quarterdeck — bring us alongside *Distant Crown,* maintain that position, and support the boarding as you think best."

"Wha — aye, sir!"

Alexis raised her vacsuit helmet.

"Mister Villar, you are to take the forward boarding tube, I will take the aft." She wasn't certain, but it appeared to her that Villar was suppressing a grin. "Pass the word to be careful of any ruse or trap, mind you."

"Aye, sir!"

Villar clamped his helmet over his head and nearly beat Alexis to the hatch.

———

AS THOUGH HE'D read her mind, Isom met her halfway down the companionway ladder with her weapons. She felt the *click* as he placed a holstered, chemical-propellant pistol against her vacsuit's side, the strong magnet in the holster gripping a metal plate in her suit tightly. The sword she took from him and held ready. It was a longer blade than the common crew would carry, partly to make up for her short stature and shorter reach.

She'd use that until she was aboard the other ship — and after, if *Distant Crown's* gravity had failed — it being so difficult to control a firearm without some gravity to help with it. Her flechette pistol, no matter that it would be easier to control, wouldn't work outside a ship's hull and field in *darkspace* — the radiation would interfere with the electronics, much as they did with the vacsuits' radios. With the *Crown* so holed, the main decks would be awash in it.

Her own suit's radio sounded with nothing but garbled static, already affected by the radiation allowed in by the open gunports, and she shut it off.

The guns were still manned — undermanned, as most of their crews were at the boarding tubes, ready for when Midshipman Spindler brought *Nightingale* alongside the other ship — but enough to send yet another broadside in the *Crown* if there were any attempt at treachery.

The crowd around the aft airlock and boarding tube was restless. Men worked their hands on the hilts of their weapons and shuffled from one foot to the other, impatient to be about their business.

Alexis came to the back of the crowd. She clapped a hand on the nearest man's shoulder and pressed her helmet to his.

"Make a lane!" she shouted.

The man touched his helmet to those in front of him and repeated her order. Those men did as well, parting to let her through.

The boarding crew was already armed with the heavy bladed cutlasses handed out by Corporal Brace and his men. One or two, the better trained, had firearms.

Alexis was nearly at the front of the crowd when the deck lights flashed in the signal that *Nightingale* was near enough the other ship.

She could feel the vibration of the men's shouting as they surged forward. No real sound, but it transferred right through their suits, from body to close-packed body.

This was what she lived for, this and the guns themselves. It was difficult to admit, but she'd missed being amongst the guns during an action. Missed the rasp of her breath in the vacsuit's helmet, the trickles of sweat as heat built up inside the suit, the hard, heavy work of hauling shot canisters from the garlands to the guns. Missed the boardings, as well — the feel of her lads around her, jostling for position as ships neared each other.

A part of her — distant now — knew she'd regret these feelings later, when memories of the battle came in the night. But for the moment, as she flowed along with her lads through the lock and flung herself down the boarding tube which was blasted by compressed air to extend between the ships, felt herself knocked about by arms and legs around her as the crowd forced its way through a breach in *Distant Crown's* hull — for this moment, she felt alive.

Alexis made it through the breach, felt her feet connect with the other ship's deck, raised her sword, ready to block a blow or start her own ... and froze.

No trap or resistance met them, only a few vacsuited figures still on their feet, and those standing still, arms raised in surrender.

The damage done by *Nightingale's* repeated raking of this ship was a horror. Only a third of the other ship's crew appeared to be standing, the rest were on the deck, some moving feebly, others still. The hull was stoved in all the way forward to the bow and nearly every gun showed some damage.

Nightingale's crew milled about, as though uncertain of how to proceed. Even without resistance, they should have been moving to secure the other ship's crew — the whole and healthy, at least. Those who were injured would have to wait a bit longer for care.

What gave them pause, and Alexis herself, was the nature of the *Crown's* crew.

Not the rough, hard men of a pirate ship she'd expect. The faces she could see through the enemies' vacsuit helmets were very different than that — more than half of them women, old and young, along with older men and those so young she'd call them boys.

Alexis hesitated, taking in the scene, and wondered at the sight, then she pressed her helmet to that of the *Nightingale* next to her so that her voice could be heard.

"Pass the word," she said loudly. "Round them up before they have a chance to regain their senses."

ALEXIS OPENED her eyes at the *click* of a glass being set in front of her. She and her officers, still in vacsuits, for they'd all been back and forth to the *Crown* repeatedly.

"Thank you, Isom," she said, taking the glass and a long gulp. The bourbon burned a trail down her throat and seemed to explode in her stomach. "Don't stand on ceremony, gentlemen."

The others all followed suit, even Spindler, young as he was, could stand a drink after what they'd seen aboard the other ship.

"I've never seen the like," Villar muttered.

"Never bloody heard of the like," Ousley said. He drained his glass entirely. "A pirate band of women and children and oldsters?"

He winced and eased himself in his seat. More than half the *Crown's* "crew" might have been women and children, but some had been viciously persistent, waiting, apparently passive, until a *Nightingale* came to offer assistance and then striking with whatever weapon was at hand.

Ousley had taken a sword thrust to the thigh from a boy younger than Spindler.

Their rescue efforts had turned less gentle after that, moving to ensure that each person aboard the *Crown* was disarmed and well-bound before bringing them across to be treated by Poulter or locked in a hold compartment they'd chosen as a makeshift brig.

Once the *Crown* was somewhat repaired, they'd move the captured crew back to that ship and put a prize crew aboard.

"Any word on what was done to the helm?" Alexis asked.

Ousley shook his head. "Verley and Nabb are looking at it."

"Nabb?"

Ousley nodded. "Lad's a dab hand with the electronics."

They'd had to breach the quarterdeck hatch, as its occupants had locked it up tight. There were only two men on the quarterdeck, one dead, the other nearly so, and apparently by each other's hand.

The helm showed similar modifications as those on the gallenium transport they'd encountered, and Alexis wanted to see what her crew could make of those themselves, rather than simply forwarding them to Admiralty as she had at the start.

If the pirates did have a way of transitioning outside of a Lagrangian point, she'd need that capability to pursue the *Owl*. Why the *Crown* hadn't, and why the two men on the quarterdeck had fought each other, was still a mystery.

"I left word with Mister Poulter that you wanted the quarterdeck survivor here and conscious instanter," Villar said. "He was displeased."

"My concern for Mister Poulter's displeasure is less than I imagine he could wish," Alexis said. "I want answers and I'm certain someone who was on the *Crown's* quarterdeck will be the one to supply them — lord knows we've had no luck with the others."

"An idea of where they're from, at least?" Alexis asked.

Ousley grunted.

The most they'd gotten out of many of the survivors was a curse or a bit of spittle.

"Never seen the like," Ousley muttered.

"Cooksun, sar!" Clanley called from the hatchway.

Alexis stared at Nabb standing in the opening and laughed aloud. She knew it was more the aftereffects of the battle and not the Marine's accent that made it seem so funny, but she couldn't help herself.

"Come in, Nabb."

"Aye, sir," Nabb said, coming to stand near the table.

"Did you and Verley find anything in the helm?"

Nabb nodded. "Nothing good, sir, but we found it and made sense of it, I think."

"Nothing good? So is this method of transitioning not something we could duplicate?"

Nabb's eyes grew wide. "I should bloody well hope not —"

"Watch your tongue with the captain!" Ousley barked.

Nabb rolled his eyes at the bosun, but addressed Alexis more calmly.

"All it does, sir, is turn off the safeties. There's no more to it than that."

Villar frowned. "There has to be more to it."

Nabb shook his head. "Not a bit, sir. It's wired up to transition anywhere, but that don't mean, well, that you'd wind up *anywhere*, if you take my meaning."

"Well what's the use of that?" Villar asked. "There must be some point to it."

Nabb shrugged. "Point would be the ship and crew'd go to wherever such things go, sir. But it don't seem there's any coming back."

Alexis took another drink and pondered it for a moment. She felt she was missing something important, but there was too much noise, too many possibilities, for her to see the truth clearly.

Pirates taking gallenium shipments, which were valuable but not the easiest thing to dispose of, ships that were modified to transition in such a way as to effectively destroy themselves, the Coalsons and Jadiqis with more coin than seemed right — none of it made sense. And now the *Crown* with a crew half made up of women and children, all of whom seemed to hate their captors with a viciousness that drove them to strike even when horribly injured themselves. Some of those things might not be related at all, but what were the pieces she needed?

"Bloody fanatics," Ousley muttered, wincing again.

Alexis frowned. "What did you say?"

"Well, sir, it's one thing to go a'pirating, but this lot takes it too far. To strike at those trying to pull you off a wrecked ship? Ain't right."

"We've been looking at this all wrong," Alexis said, rising. "With me to the Orlop, gentlemen, I want our mysterious quarterdeck-man awake instanter."

"I DO THIS UNDER PROTEST," Poulter said, holding an injector to the arm of the man on a cot. "This man was stabbed — he needs rest."

The orlop was crowded, with nearly every cot occupied, most by those off the *Crown*, but three by *Nightingales* who'd been injured before they'd realized the *Crowns* intended them harm even as they surrendered.

"He was stabbed by one of his own, Mister Poulter, and we need answers." Alexis nodded for him to continue.

Poulter injected him and the man's eyes sprang open.

He blinked, looking around wildly, and jerked his arms which were bound to the cot.

Alexis leaned close. The drugs would make the man somewhat malleable and willing to answer questions. She was about to speak when the man spat in her face.

"Devil's whore!"

Ousley drove his fist into the man's side, just above the stab wound. "Watch it, you!"

"You can't —" Poulter protested, but Alexis nodded to Corporal Brace who inserted himself between Poulter and the group around the cot, neatly edging the surgeon back.

"Easy, Mister Ousley." Alexis wiped the spittle from her face. "It was original, at least."

"Bitch!" The man spat again, but Alexis had stood and it missed her.

And we're back to that again.

She sighed and stared at the man for a moment, wondering how to proceed. What might anger him enough to get him talking and give something away? Perhaps knowing that he'd failed in his aim to take the transports and that his cohort had abandoned him?

"The *Owl* fled," she said. "The gallenium transports are all safe and on their way. I saw to that."

The man shook his head from side to side, clearly disoriented and savagely angry.

"Defilers!"

"What's he babbling on about?" Ousley asked.

"Ssh," Alexis said, then focused her attention on the man, speaking quietly to him. "Why didn't you transition away? What stopped you?"

"Would have! Would have taken you with us, too!" The man was speaking in quick, disjointed sentences, the result of the drugs Poulter'd given him. They'd do the man no good, but would loosen his tongue. "But that coward! He betrayed the faith and stopped me — afraid to die." His eyes focused on Alexis and he sneered. "We'll be free of you lot soon — my brothers and sisters'll see to that."

Alexis frowned, not sure why he'd want to have taken *Nightingale* along if he'd managed to transition — and he seemed to be saying that the other man on the *Crown's* quarterdeck had stopped him, had been afraid to die. Did that mean the other man had wanted to surrender? That didn't ring true — nothing about these pirates rang true, in fact. They were so different from those she'd encountered before, especially with this talk of faith and unbelievers. She suspected the Jadiqis of being behind this for profit, what with the amount goods they imported, but none of the *Crown's* crew, this man included, looked like the Jadiqis she'd seen.

"Where are you based? Where is the *Owl* going now?" Alexis asked.

"Smash the unbelievers, they brought this on us. Started it. Now they'll suffer themselves, then the heretics who did nothing to stop it," the man said. He coughed, winced in pain, and a bit of bloody froth appeared on his lips.

"Is that where the *Owl*'s going?" Alexis asked. "To smash the unbelievers?"

The man nodded. "Once they're gone, it'll stop."

"What will stop?" Villar asked.

Alexis held up her hand to keep him quiet. She thought she saw it now.

"The ships will stop coming once the unbelievers are gone?" she asked.

"Left us alone 'til they came," the man muttered, his eyelids drooping. "Then the ships never stopped."

"Lieutenant Carew," Poulter said forcefully. He pushed Corporal Brace to the side. "This man is a prisoner; he needs to be still — you're killing him."

He wouldn't be the first.

Alexis regarded the man for a moment, she wanted to know more, but felt she had enough. Unbelievers. Unbelievers held to blame for the arrival of ships? Merchant ships? That she'd heard before.

An "internal matter", my arse.

She nodded to Poulter, then to the others. Piracy was bad enough, but if the *Owl* was about what she now suspected, the consequences for two colonies would be dire.

"Let's put the *Crown* to rights, gentlemen, we sail for Al Jadiq instanter."

FORTY-EIGHT

It wasn't instanter — not by any measure.

The *Crown* was too damaged to sail and her surviving crew too numerous to keep aboard *Nightingale* all the way to Al Jadiq. Alexis chafed at the delay, hating that the *Owl* was getting more and more of a lead with every moment, but also unwilling to abandon the *Crown's* crew aboard their derelict vessel. They'd either die there or set their ship to rights and return to their predations — neither was acceptable, and *Nightingale* had no space to keep so many secure. Instead, the ship was repaired so that it would at least hold air and sail, most of the survivors were locked in the hold, and she put Villar aboard with a prize crew to bring the hulk along.

It was possible they might be able to run some sort of ruse on the *Owl*, convincing them that it was the *Crown* which had taken *Nightingale* and luring the other ship in.

An accounting of those survivors came to twenty-eight, less than half those who'd been aboard, with more than half of those left too injured in the action to even stand. A few of them, after the initial shock wore off, were willing to talk, and confirmed that they were from Man's Fall, had somehow split from the main beliefs there, and, with one or two exceptions, still believed it was their mission to rid *darkspace* of trespassers.

They also blamed Al Jadiq for the increase in visits to Man's Fall, thinking that without that colony, if Man's Fall were still the farthest out on the Fringe, they'd have had no visitors at all and could have had the idyllic life they wished.

That would never work, she knew. Humanity was constantly expanding. What was an unspoiled new world, alone at the very edges of settled space, within a few generations became a thriving colony surrounded by others equally populated. And even their own people wouldn't remain the same forever — though it might be settled with those who held the same beliefs, each new generation would have some who would rebel against the strictures set by the founders.

The Jadiqis themselves had discovered that more than once, settling first on Abhatian, then Zariah, then Al Jadiq, having to move ever outward to maintain the isolation they wished.

Those on Man's Fall should have seen that, or perhaps the majority did and it was only the smaller group of fanatics who thought they could hold back change.

One can't remain isolated when one is surrounded — and our history of expansion shows you eventually will be.

She still, though, had no idea what they thought one ship could accomplish until Creasy managed to make the discovery of the *Owl's* intent. Working with the *Crown's* signals console, he was able to unlock the code the pirates used and brought word to Alexis.

More than gallenium, the pirates had taken mining charges off a transport bound for Dalthus. The low-yield nuclear devices were designed to split stubborn asteroids, exposing the ore within.

Nightingale's transition from *darkspace* to Al Jadiq was quite different than previous visits. No sooner had the stars appeared and the ship's monitors woken to begin scanning the system than alarms began sounding on the quarterdeck.

Dorsett jumped at the tactical station, startled into action, and began reporting. Alexis merely closed her eyes for a moment, realizing she was too late once again.

"Debris tracks in orbit, sir! Two ... three ... no, two hulls broken up, a third's intact, somewhat." He ran fingers over his monitors. "Fusion radiation in orbit."

"Repeating signal from orbit, sir," Creasy interrupted. "Ship in distress. Require assistance. It's the *Dark Gale*, sir."

Alexis nodded, not sure why she wasn't surprised to find Captain Lounds and his Marchant Company ship still tied up in this mess somehow.

"Best speed for orbit," she ordered. "Creasy, contact the *Dark Gale* and determine what they need. Dorsett, keep a close lookout — whoever was responsible for this may still be in system."

"Aye, sir."

As they made their way toward the planet, more and more of the damage became clear.

"*Dark Gale's* badly damaged, sir," Villar pointed out.

Alexis nodded. There were at least two, possibly three, other ships which had been destroyed outright in orbit. The *Gale* had, at least, an intact hull, though that hull was stripped of virtually all fittings. The remains of her masts were twisted into tortured shapes, sails and rigging missing entirely. Moreover, the ship itself was in a tumbling, rapidly decaying orbit.

"Tell them we're coming, Creasy."

"Aye, sir." He paused. "Still no direct contact, though, only the repeating signal."

"They may be able to receive our message, but unable to respond. Hearing help is on the way could make the difference."

She turned her attention back to the navigation plot and images of the planet itself. As time dragged on, even under *Nightingale's* full power to the conventional drive, she began to see the full extent of the damage here, if not what might have caused it, and cursed herself for not transitioning at the closer L1 point. It might have even made sense to return to *darkspace* immediately and sail to that point, but now that *Nightingale* was in transit it would take too long to reverse course.

And lives may be lost for me not seeing that.

The primary port of Al Jadiq was visible now, images brought in by the ship's optics, through a light cloud cover. She supposed it would be quite a lovely day on the surface, if not for the three massive columns of thick, dark smoke rising from the city. Those columns were each over half a kilometer across and she could make out the devastation of flattened buildings on the upwind side.

"The mining charges, do you suppose?" Villar asked.

Alexis nodded. Her first ship, *Merlin*, had been on the receiving end of one of those, though in space where the blast area was less. She shuddered at the effects of one in atmosphere. They were designed to break up large asteroids into more manageable pieces, or to expose ore seams embedded deep within. Here they'd been put to quite another purpose.

"Why?" Villar's voice was rough.

"For being in league with the devil, I suppose, much as we ourselves are." Alexis swallowed hard. "A full explanation will have to wait until we catch up with them." She sighed. "Understanding, perhaps, a bit longer."

She stared at the images for a time, silently willing *Nightingale* to faster speed, then shook herself. There were preparations they could make, rather than remaining idle.

"When we reach orbit, Mister Villar, you shall take a boat and crew to the surface. See what aid you might render." She supposed it was her place, as commander, to make that contact, but given the Jadiqi attitudes it was probably best to send Villar. "Mister Khouri ... or whoever may be left in charge will likely accept aid from you easier than from me." Villar nodded. "Now is not the time to push back against their prejudices."

"HANDSOMELY, NOW, BUSBEY," Alexis murmured to helmsman who was hunched over his console, shoulders tense and with sweat beading his face despite the cool air of the quarterdeck. "Handsomely."

"Aye ... aye, sir."

She couldn't blame him for his nervousness. The *Dark Gale* was in a bizarre tumble at the very edges of Al Jadiq's atmosphere, and sinking further. So deep, in fact, that there was some, small though it might be yet, effect on the other ship's course as both gravity and the thinnest bit of atmosphere worked on the slowly tumbling craft.

Busbey's task, with the help of *Nightingale's* computer, was to match that course and tumble, placing *Nightingale* alongside.

There was still no word from the other ship, but with so much damage to the hull and fittings, they might have no way to transmit anything but the automated distress beacon *Nightingale* had already detected. But ships were tough, Alexis knew. So long as the inertial compensators were active, those inside the *Gale* would be as unaffected by the tumble as she herself was on *Nightingale's* quarterdeck. Once the tumble was matched, they'd be able to extend a boarding tube and cut through the other ship's hull, hopefully freeing any survivors.

It was something neither Busbey nor any other helmsman could have done alone, but the ship's computers were the equal to the task ... if only barely.

"This is the best there may be, sir," Busbey said finally.

Beside her, Ousley grunted, watching the operation and examining his own calculations on a tablet.

"Too much torque for the tubes, sir, it's not steady enough. Have to be done by lines, I think."

Alexis grimaced. An aired boarding tube would be best, for there was no guarantee those aboard the *Gale* would be in vacsuits. But if the other ship's tumble couldn't be matched closely enough, then they'd have to string lines across, leaving enough slack to make up the difference, and bring the *Gale's* crew over in vacuum.

"We've bags enough, I think," Ousley said, causing Alexis to grimace again.

None of the *Gale's* crew, merchantmen though they might be, would relish the idea of being dragged through space in a rescue bag. Or they might, in fact, once they realized the alternative was to go down into Al Jadiq's atmosphere with their ship.

"Be about it, Mister Ousley."

THE NEXT SEVERAL hours consisted of what Alexis thought was one of the worst parts of command — standing idly by while the men who looked to her went off into danger on her orders.

"Stand down, Busbey," she said quietly, squeezing the helmsman's shoulder. "Let Audley have a turn."

"Aye, sir."

Busbey moved aside and Audley, the port-watch helmsman, took his place. Alexis had the two, from port and starboard watches, changing off every fifteen or twenty minutes to keep them fresh. The constant adjustments necessary to keep *Nightingale* orbiting around the tumbling *Gale* wore on the men quickly.

More wearing was the work of Ousley and the men with him.

The bosun, three of his mates, and six of *Nightingale's* most experienced hands — most experienced with working outside the hull, that is — had the unenviable task of moving between the two ships.

While the helmsmen attempted to keep the ship as stable as possible in relation to the *Gale*, Ousley and his mates fired lines across the intervening space, then slid along those first, tenuous connections to the *Gale's* hull. They made the lines fast and set up a breaching chamber on the damaged ship's hull.

The lines made the helmsman's job even more difficult, for there was now less leeway in the necessary station keeping. The lines had some slack, and there were two master's mates on *Nightingale's* hull to let out and manage the lines, so that they didn't snap when

Nightingale drifted farther away, but now the helmsmen had to ensure that they didn't become twisted with each other or tangled up in what was left of the *Gale's* rigging.

Ousley and his crew breached the *Gale's* hull and entered.

From the images sent back from their suits, Alexis found the other ship's interior a nightmare scene. Lights flickered in smoke-filled compartments as Ousley and his men moved throughout the ship, locating and checking each figure they came across. Few of the *Gale's* crew were in vacsuits, telling Alexis that whatever had befallen the ship had come as a surprise.

Some sections of the ship's hull had been breached, venting atmosphere and killing those within. Others of the crew were unconscious from whatever damage had been inflicted. Consoles and electronics everywhere had short-circuited, filling the ship with an acrid smoke. The ship's environmental systems were either unable to keep up with the smoke or had been damaged themselves.

Soon enough the *Gale's* crew began making the trip to *Nightingale*. Those who could locate a vacsuit and were uninjured came across on their own, safety line clipped to the tether between the two ships and pulling themselves along as quickly as they could. Those without suits or those who were too injured to make the journey on their own were sealed into the heavy rescue bags and pulled across by one of their mates or one of the *Nightingales*.

Captain Lounds was one of these.

His cabin had been breached and he was unable to retrieve his suit, leaving him trapped on the *Gale's* quarterdeck, surrounded by dead and useless equipment which must have frustrated him to no end.

To his credit, once aboard *Nightingale*, he shed himself of the rescue bag and stayed by the airlock, helping pull aboard each of his crewmen and seeing to their needs.

When the last of these was aboard, Ousley and his mates back inside after casting loose the tethers, Alexis gave the weary, sweat-soaked Busbey a nod.

"Take us up to a more sane orbit, Busbey."

"Aye, sir."

"Then you and Audley see the purser for a bit of a wet," Alexis said. "Lord knows you've earned it."

"Aye, sir — thank you, sir," the two men said in unison.

"A DRINK, CAPTAIN LOUNDS?" Alexis asked.

The man looked at her, glassy-eyed. His face was sheened in sweat-streaked soot where the smoke from ruined components covered him. Beneath that soot, a bruise covered the left side of his face and Alexis felt certain there were others elsewhere.

"My crew ..." he said, voice trailing off.

"They're safe aboard *Nightingale*, sir," Alexis reminded him. "Our surgeon is seeing to them."

"*Nightingale* ..." Lounds frowned. "You're that lieutenant."

"I am, sir. Can you tell me what happened here?"

Isom arrived with a bottle of bourbon and glass. He poured and held it out to Lounds who downed it in one go. Isom refilled without having to be told.

"My crew ..."

"Safe aboard," Alexis repeated again. *What's left of them.* A merchantman the size of the *Gale* had a crew of over one hundred — forty-six, Lounds included, had been pulled off the hulk.

"My ship ..."

"What happened to her, captain?" Alexis prompted.

Lounds drained his glass again and some sense of where he was seemed to come him.

"My crew's aboard, you say?"

Alexis nodded. "All who ..." She trailed off, unsure if the man could handle knowledge of the full butcher's bill.

Lounds winced, but then took a deep breath. "How many?"

"Forty-six are aboard," Alexis said, simply. The large merchantman's crew had been more than that, but there was no easy way to break it to him.

"Is there —"

"Our bosun saw to every compartment himself." Ousley had insisted, not wanting to chance a single man being left behind, as the *Gale's* orbit was rapidly decaying. "He's an experienced hand," she assured Lounds.

He took another glass from Isom, but this time only downed half of it at a go.

"What happened?"

"Two ships came in … looked like common merchants." Lounds coughed, took a sip, then stared at the glass for a moment. Alexis wondered if his mind had wandered again when he went on. "Two ships. Looked to take up an orbit. Perfectly ordinary … not a thing to suspect … my first officer was on the quarterdeck, you understand, not me, but even were I there." He frowned. "Perfectly ordinary, merchants coming in system, you see."

Alexis nodded, though inside she was puzzled. Was there yet another pirate ship out there which had joined up with the *Owl*?

"They dropped four boats before they reached orbit, which seemed odd, but … ragtag merchants like that — always in a hurry, yes?"

Alexis nodded again. It was though the man was seeking reassurance from her — reassurance that there was nothing he should have seen, nothing else he should have done to avoid what happened to his ship.

"Three boats headed for the surface, one for us. They called and said … said they had a Marchant representative aboard. That's when my first officer called me? Unusual, that — for a Marchant man to be traveling on such a ragtag bit, but not impossible."

He looked down and swallowed hard.

"By the time I reached the quarterdeck they were close … too close …"

He trailed off and Alexis waited for a time, wanting to let him tell it in his own time, but finally, "Sir?"

Lounds jerked as though struck and looked at her wide-eyed.

"One of the ships — not the boats, but one of the two ships — was near those two the Jadiqis had in high orbit. The ones they thought to build a merchant fleet of their own with?"

Alexis nodded.

"It ... it just exploded. I thought, at first, it was an accident — the fusion plant, I supposed — but then ... I saw it then. The boat heading for us, I mean." He shook his head. "A Marchant man would have come on a Marchant ship; we have couriers for just that." He looked down. "Too late." He drained his glass. "Not an accident at all."

"The boat, sir? What happened?"

Lounds laughed. "How the bloody hell would I know? Next I remember I'm waking up on a quarterdeck with every console dead as ..."

He trailed off, perhaps remembering just how many dead there were.

Alexis nodded. She'd heard enough to fill in the other pieces herself. If the pirates ... no, she couldn't rightly call them that. They were something other than pirates, something worse. Pirates would take a man's goods and leave him in a ship's boat along some shipping lane. They'd give a crew at least a chance to live, so long as they didn't resist. These, though ...

A ship to the Jadiqi's "fleet" and then a breach of their fusion plant would destroy all three and account for the debris in system. A boat with a mining charge or two aboard would do for the Gale. *And the other three boats ...*

Her mind filled with images of the Jadiqi city, three columns of black smoke rising from the flattened buildings.

But the crew of that ship and those boats ...

She shook her head.

What drives a man to that, much less women and children?

"I think ..." Lounds began, paused, and then took a deep breath to steady himself. "I think I should like to see my crew, lieutenant."

FORTY-NINE

Villar soon returned to the ship, having offered what aid the small boat crew could in the face of the destruction on Al Jadiq. He also carried with him the Jadiqi government's formal request for aid from their former brethren on Zariah and the Kingdom at large.

Alexis was faced with a difficult decision. Sail for Zariah, leaving the *Owl,* for she was certain that was the ship which had not sacrificed itself to destroy the Jadiqi shipping, to wreak further havoc on Man's Fall, delay sailing for Zariah in order to deal with the *Owl,* or split her crew, sending the captured ship for Zariah while she and *Nightingale* sailed after the *Owl.*

Captain Lounds and the surviving crew of *Dark Gale* did give her another option, if only she could convince the man.

"No."

Alexis regarded Lounds levelly. He'd cleaned himself up quickly after visiting his surviving crew, though his face still showed bruises and cuts and his uniform was torn in places, he'd put himself into as much order as he could. He'd also recovered his composure, something Alexis found herself regretting.

"Absolutely not."

Sad to say, but I much preferred him when he was despondent over the loss of his ship.

She winced at how unkind a thought that was, but there was no getting around it. Worse than his recovery was that the *Gale* had, against all expectations, not yet sunk into Al Jadiq's atmosphere and burned up. The hulk's orbit was still decaying, but something about its tumble must have settled it on a slower fate.

"Captain Lounds —" she began again.

"I will not take your ... your little *rowboat,*" Lounds spat, "to Zariah for you." He shook his head emphatically. "In fact, I demand your assistance in reboarding the *Gale* and returning her to service!"

"Your ship is surely lost, sir, I'll not risk *Nightingale* or any of our boats in returning to her."

Lounds' face reddened. He opened his mouth to speak, but was cut off by the Marine at her hatch.

"Farst ossifer, sar!"

"Come through," Alexis said, grateful for the interruption, and the support. She'd thought to speak with Lounds about her plan before the others arrived, but that had clearly been a mistake.

Villar, Spindler, Ousley, and Poulter entered, arranging themselves around her table. Villar and Ousley both looked at Lounds and narrowed their eyes — whether they'd heard his demand through the hatch or merely sensed the tension in the compartment, Alexis couldn't say. Poulter looked from Lounds to Alexis and raised his brows questioningly.

"This will be a working meeting, gentlemen," Alexis said, as Isom began pouring wine. "We'll speak as you're being served."

"You're wasting time, Carew," Lounds said, his voice hoarse. "Time the *Gale* doesn't have."

"The *Gale*?" Ousley asked. His brow furrowed. "Beggin' your pardon, sir, but if it's salvaging aught off the *Gale* this is about, you'd best leave off."

"No, that's not what —"

"I'll do no such thing!" Lounds barked, cutting Alexis off again. "You are all wasting time. The *Gale* had power when we left her — a repair crew may restore power to the engines and thence to a more stable orbit where full repairs may be made." He glared at Alexis. "I fail to see why you are sabotaging the chance of recovering my ship, and the Marchant Company won't stand for it!"

Alexis and Ousley shared a glance. She could empathize with Lounds, certainly, but the man refused to face reality.

"Captain Lounds, sir," Villar said gently, edging his seat closer to the man and leaning forward. "The damage to your ship is quite —" He reached for the table's top then glanced at Alexis. "May I, sir?"

Alexis nodded.

Villar tapped for a moment and brought up imagery of the *Gale*.

"I've seen the damage," Lounds said. "The masts and rigging can be repaired once in a stable orbit. The hull fittings can be replaced. We've a full shop aboard — could build a whole other ship from it, for god's sake!"

"Look at her stern, sir," Villar said, voice soft.

The *Gale's* stern was a twisted mess. Her long, wide rudder and planes were warped and cracked from the mining charge's blast. That was repairable, and they weren't needed in normal-space any more than the sails, but what Villar pointed out next was not. The nozzles of the *Gale's* conventional drive were equally damaged — knocked askew, covered by the misshapen rudder, and even missing altogether.

"She's a few hours left at most," Ousley said every bit as softly as Villar had. "Remarkable she's not gone down as it is, but there's not time enough to repair that."

Lounds' shoulders slumped and his expression went dead.

"You have two ships here," he said, looking up at Alexis, his voice as flat as his expression. "A tow to higher orbit ... give her time ..."

Ousley shook his head. "She's too large, sir, we've not the power, even with the prize added in. You can see that."

Lounds swallowed heavily and his eyes fell.

Alexis ran a hand absently over the edge of her table, almost a caress, as she sometimes did the navigation plot on the quarterdeck. She could see the other captain's pain and knew it. The loss of *Belial* still stung her to the core ... and the thought of losing *Nightingale*.

"If there were any way, Captain Lounds," she said, wishing she'd treated the man more kindly at the start of this meeting. Perhaps he'd have been more receptive to her — or perhaps he'd needed to hear it from Villar and Ousley, men he could respect, a feeling she suspected he didn't feel for her.

Lounds looked up and met her eyes. She tried to communicate her understanding and let the man know she knew how he felt about his ship. It was likely harder for him, she suspected, for he wasn't Navy. Whatever Alexis felt for her ship, for her crew even, always had to be secondary to her duty — much as she might love them, they were tools toward that end. There was never time to mourn their loss in the heat of things.

Lounds closed his eyes, took a deep breath, and nodded.

"Very well, then," Alexis said. "Captain Lounds, you and a third of your crew, those who are whole, that is, will take *Distant Crown* and sail for Zariah instanter — the worst of your wounded with you, as well, as many as may be safely transported in the *Crown,* and the bulk of the prisoners from that ship." Alexis paused. That was as far as she'd got with Lounds in describing her plan before he began objecting, and she felt he might again. "One third of those remaining should stay here on Al Jadiq to assist with the recovery efforts in the meantime. The *Crown* is much smaller than the *Gale* ... was —" She felt her own heart twinge in sympathy at Lounds' expression. "— and the smaller crew will allow you to get your wounded to the best care on Zariah all the quicker." She took a deep breath. "The remaining third of the *Gale's* crew, especially those with any experience on the guns, I plan to take aboard *Nightingale.*"

Lounds' nostrils flared. He opened his mouth, then clamped it shut.

"We'll give your lads some opportunity to strike back at those who did this to you."

"You plan to hunt down that ship, then?" Lounds asked, eyes narrowed. "Do you know where the pirates base themselves?"

"Not pirates — not in the traditional sense, at least," Alexis said. "They're —" How to phrase it? "They're some sort of extremist sect from Man's Fall. They —"

Alexis broke off as she saw Lounds' face react to her words. His eyes widened and color drained from his face as his jaw slackened.

She thought quickly. Lounds and his insistence that colonies had no rights to restrict trade, her certainty that the *Dark Gale* was one of those ships Stoltzfus had complained about visiting Man's Fall, Lounds' talk of opening up new markets — all those combined with his reaction, far more than anyone should have at the news of an extremist sect on an already religious colony world ...

"You bloody fool," she whispered, "you've been trading with them, haven't you?"

"I —" Lounds licked his lips and hesitated.

"Say it man!" Alexis barked. She could sense him steeling himself to deny or put off anything he'd done and didn't want him to have the chance.

Villar was staring at him as well, then glanced over at Alexis. He seemed to sense what she suspected and what she wanted.

"Tell us now," he said. "It'll come out and your one chance to convince us you didn't know you were trading with pirates is now."

"I didn't!" Lounds said. "They ... they wanted goods! Is it my place to say they can't have them?"

"What goods?" Alexis asked. "And what did they pay you with? Man's Fall has no exports."

"It —"

"Bloody hell," Villar said. "You took gallenium in payment?"

"A bit!" Lounds said, his eyes were wide and panicked. "They said they'd found a single source on the planet! A bar or two each visit, no more, it seemed —"

"It seemed plausible because you wished it to be, not thinking that gallenium that accessible would be noted on the survey report and no religious commune would be able to afford the bloody system!"

"What did they buy?" Alexis asked. She had a chilling suspicion she knew. The niggling feeling that the crew of *Distant Crown* hadn't been speaking of Al Jadiq when they talked of heretics grew. Unbelievers, yes, but heretics was something else, wasn't it?

Lounds drew a deep breath and closed his eyes.

"Arms," he said softly, then louder as though trying to convince himself, "Nothing proscribed! Laser rifles, flechettes — the sorts of thing any sane colony would have already to protect themselves and for hunting!"

"Or to take a visiting ship," Villar muttered.

"I didn't know!"

"How many?" Alexis asked.

Lounds frowned. "I don't know."

"Bollocks," Alexis said. "I'd wager you know every bit of cargo comes on and off your ship, Captain Lounds." She narrowed her eyes, recalling that when she'd searched the *Gale* there'd been no mention of weapons or gallenium in his records. "Whether it's on the manifests or not."

Lounds flushed.

"What have you delivered to them in the way of weapons, captain?"

"I ..." His shoulders slumped. "Four dozen crates of flechette pistols. Near the same of laser rifles. Nothing, really."

Alexis ran the numbers in her head. If all of the ships she'd encountered had crews similar to that of the *Distant Crown*, then it was more than enough to arm them thrice over. And if she was correct, if the destruction of "heretics" meant not the Jadiqis, but those who opposed them in their own faith, then there were more than enough for what she feared as well.

"You'll be sailing for Zariah with a *quarter* of your surviving crew,

Captain Lounds, and I'll be taking the rest aboard *Nightingale*." She glared at him as he started to speak and he bowed his head. "Get them aboard, Mister Villar, we sail for Man's Fall instanter." She ground her teeth together. "Damn me, but we're dragging along behind yet again."

FIFTY

"This is *not* an 'internal matter', Mister Stoltzfus, and never was — you *must* tell me what you know."

"We have —"

Alexis cut him off. The man was determined to remain blind to the possible consequences and she couldn't let him. It was past time he faced the facts. *Nightingale* had beaten the *Owl* back to Man's Fall, assuming she was correct in the remaining ship's destination, but she felt there was little time before it arrived.

She had the boat land just outside of the port town, instead of the far off landing field, then she, Spindler, her boat crew, and two Marines had marched into town and demanded the whereabouts of Stoltzfus. Villar was left in command of *Nightingale* instead of Spindler, because she wanted an experienced officer on the quarterdeck should anything happen while she was away.

"Piracy, Mister Stoltzfus, murder and piracy. Add to that planetary attacks —"

"We will not accuse any of the attacks on our farmsteads."

"Not on Man's Fall, you bloody fool! The attacks on Al Jadiq!"

Stoltzfus stared at her open mouthed. It was, perhaps, the first time she'd manage to stop his never-ending mantra of "internal matter".

"You hadn't heard about those? Two of their ships destroyed in orbit and three mining charges set off in the city itself. Men, women, and *children* slaughtered — and not your children here on Man's Fall, who you're apparently quite willing to sacrifice to keep this madness quiet, but children who're wholly innocent of whatever it is you've harbored here."

Alexis was happy to see Stoltzfus wince at that.

"That's a declaration of war against the Jadiqis, sir, and the Crown won't stand for it. Harboring the pirates was bad —"

"We haven't —"

"*For god's sake shut your mouth and listen, man!* A Marchant Company ship was destroyed at Al Jadiq. Surely you're not so far removed here that you've forgotten what their influence is like? What you say no longer matters; it's what the Crown suspects! I believe you — I believe you've not actively aided them, at least, but it won't be me making the ruling, will it? They're based here, I know that for a certainty, and what do you think the odds are of some coreward admiral sent to investigate and believing you've not been in on it from the start? Piracy loses you your charter, Mister Stoltzfus, but attacking another colony? Sir, that condemns you all — the least you could hope for your people would be a term of indenture to make reparations to the Jadiqis ..." Alexis leaned forward, hoping the man was hearing her. "For you and the other elders of your church, it'll be the noose. All of that assuming these ... whoever they are ... don't kill you themselves. Those we captured spoke of eliminating the heretics, and just who do you suppose the candidates for that might be?"

Stoltzfus' head drooped. His shoulders began to shake. Alexis gave him a moment and when he finally looked up there were tears in his eyes.

"The merchants wouldn't stop," he whispered.

Alexis wasn't at all sure what that had to do with anything, but she remained silent, face impassive and staring at Stoltzfus, willing him to go on. Once he started telling it, she felt, it would all come out and make some sense of this mess.

"They wouldn't. We told them to stay away ... we asked your Navy to keep them away." His look was accusing, then he shook his head. "Well, when we first arrived here, no one came, but after the Jadiqis settled? They bought so much and the merchants thought we should as well, since they were coming this way then. We told them no, but they kept coming. All we wanted was to live here in peace as God wills."

Alexis ground her teeth, willing him to get to the meat of it, but held her tongue.

"There are those among us who still feel anger at the transgressions of those not of our faith — they have difficulty accepting that everyone must follow their own path. The merchants came ... tempting us, testing us, with the devil's wares. Tempting our children away to sail with them, as well. We're a small community, lieutenant — and young people, everywhere, are ... impatient. Some left with those merchants and it was difficult for us. Both because they were gone and because of where they went."

Stoltzfus frowned.

"You're young, yourself, lieutenant, and have no children, I expect?"

Alexis shook her head.

"And no faith, you've said." He held up his hand. "I mean nothing derogatory by that, lieutenant, we each have our own path. Is there something, though, that you hold dear? Something larger than yourself which you'd sacrifice for?"

It surprised Alexis a bit that the first thing she thought of at Stoltzfus' words were not her family lands on Dalthus. Oh, she loved her grandfather and those lands, and the people on them, as well, but what sprang to her mind at the question was an image of the Navy — not the admirals and captains she reported to, or the ships and fleets, but of the crews she'd served with and had the honor to command.

The *Merlins* who'd welcomed her into their world and taught her so much. The *Hermiones* who'd stood by her after the mutiny and their captivity — even the mutineers themselves. The *Belials* who'd stood with her against such horrible odds, even at the cost of their own lives, because she'd told them it was needful. Even the *Nightingales*, motley flotsam of the fleet that they were, for they'd begun to show themselves quite well, now that she had their measure and stopped coddling them.

The Navy had changed her, no doubt. Perhaps it had revealed to her the larger picture than just those lands and people on Dalthus — that there were others, equally in need of someone to stand between them and those who'd prey on them. Why that should be her, she didn't know, but she did feel, having stood with such men once, she couldn't bear to leave them to it alone.

"Yes," Stoltzfus said, dragging her from her thoughts, "I see that there is." His face hardened a bit. "Now imagine if you will that someone tempted those you love the most into the greatest evil you can imagine."

He sighed.

"I and the other elders believe those men, the merchants, were the tools of God, sent to test our faith. Others thought they were tools of the devil sent to tempt us. A fine distinction for one not of our teachings to understand, perhaps, but an important one. To fail a test means we are not yet ready ... to fall into temptation means we are lost."

Stoltzfus straightened his shoulders as though bracing himself.

"Not everyone in our fold was born to the faith — some came to it later in life. Some of those, not the most faithful, perhaps, have been part of your Navy."

Alexis nodded. She could understand that. For someone who'd been aboard ship in the war, with shot flying and splintering about, shards of laser blasts puncturing suits, comrades falling all around — the call of such a faith might resonate. She frowned. With such a lack of technology, though, it might also be a place to hide. Somewhere that there'd be no constant use of tablets and recorded transactions to show one's identity. Men with a past or men who'd run.

"There is no one who feels the need to prove himself so much as the convert, nor any so zealous. Overzealous, I suppose would be the better description.

"I swear to you, lieutenant, that neither I nor any of the elders knew what these men planned. Perhaps they didn't know themselves, they simply acted." He sighed again. "The next time a merchant landed — right there in our town square, mind you, not even in the distant field — and spread their wares out ... technology, labor-saving, power generators ... everything we'd chosen to leave behind."

Alexis winced, picturing it.

"They rushed them and took the boat, then the ship."

"The crew?" Alexis prompted. "The merchant crew? What happened to them?"

Stoltzfus closed his eyes.

"These men felt they should not ... could not allow for witnesses to their acts."

"And you did nothing to stop them," Alexis said.

"We are a peaceful people, lieutenant, we do not believe in violence. There was nothing we could —"

"These were men of your peaceful, non-violent community, Mister Stoltzfus, murdering a merchant crew in your own system. Right in your bloody town square, if I'm hearing you properly." She took a deep breath to control her temper. "And you stood by and did nothing."

"Our community does not believe in confrontation, lieutenant, but neither do we blindly accept transgressions of that nature." He looked down, paused for a long time, then met her eyes again. "Sadly, I can see now that our ways only ..." He frowned. "Not encouraged, but perhaps forced these men farther along their path. We responded to their acts of violence by removing them from our community."

"If you don't believe in force, then how did you get them to leave?"

"They quickly found that no one would trade with them, there was no help for their farmsteads, save from others who had participated in the attack, no communication from the rest of us, even." He shrugged. "It is usually an effective method of bringing someone back to the faith, lieutenant. To be isolated and alone is not the natural state of man — we long for our community and the knowledge that we are not alone.

"As I said, in this case our ways were not effective. There were too many, I think, involved at the start, and so by removing them from our community we simply forced them to create their own. They traded amongst themselves, assisted each other, and held their own services at which their zealousness only grew.

"I suppose if history shows us there is anyone more zealous than the convert ... it is the reformer. They determined that God means for us not merely to eschew these things, but to actively oppose them. To attack and destroy the means for man's trespass upon the face of Heaven. One of these men was a technician in your Navy and understood the machines you use to move yourselves to Heaven and back."

"The gallenium," Alexis said, finally understanding. The targeting of gallenium shipments, but no evidence of them being sold elsewhere, along with the damage to the helm on that first ore carrier *Nightingale* had encountered and the disappearance of the *Silver Leaf*. "He'd worked on repairing those consoles, so knew how to turn off the safeguards. Not discovered some way to transition away from a Lagrangian point, but how to force a ship to transition outside of a Lagrangian point." She swallowed hard and shuddered, wondering if it was the whole crew of the ship who'd been willing to take that act instead of being captured, or if there'd been just one fanatic on the quarterdeck who'd taken them all Dutchman with him. "Their goal was never to profit from taking the ore, it was to destroy it."

Stoltzfus nodded.

"And the crews, man? If they sent those ships to transitioning outside of ... what did they do with the crews?"

Alexis fumed as Stoltzfus closed his eyes and bowed his head.

"No one knows what happens to a ship that transitions outside a Lagrangian point." No one might know for certain, but the spacers who sailed the Dark certainly feared such a fate. Going overboard and left behind in *darkspace* was terrifying enough, they'd dump their air and suffocate rather than feel their blood and thoughts slow as the dark matter pressed in around them — the mystery of transitioning like that, though, they'd not even speak of that. Simply whisper 'Dutchman' and say no more of it. "How could you stand by?"

"We did what we could."

"It wasn't enough. Not nearly enough —" So many ships gone missing — maybe more than even she knew or suspected — perhaps hundreds of crew. "Where are they?"

"I don't know."

"Enough of your nonsense, Mister Stoltzfus! Quite enough!"

"I don't know, I tell you! Somewhere on the planet, we don't know where. They have ships' boats, several of them, and attack our settlements without warning to take what food they want. We don't have any means of tracking them."

"How many ships did they take? And how many of them are there?"

"Three, I think, perhaps four, here on Man's Fall — I've no idea how many elsewhere." He grimaced. "Two hundred eighty-four of our number went with them when they left. Not all by choice, I think — there were families in that number, women and children."

Alexis nodded and ran the numbers in her head. There'd been a crew of forty-three aboard *Distant Crown*, perhaps the same aboard *Silver Leaf*, though they'd never know. So perhaps *Lively Owl* and one other ship left, with similar numbers — they'd not have the numbers to crew more than that, and surely there'd be some left behind at whatever base they kept here on Man's Fall.

"There were women and children aboard *Distant Crown* when we took her, Mister Stoltzfus. They fought us as well."

Stoltzfus closed his eyes and his lips moved silently. Alexis assumed he was praying, though for what she couldn't imagine. She left him to it, nonetheless — once past his initial objections, he'd been forthcoming and she wanted to encourage that.

Alexis was interrupted by a *ping* from her tablet. She pulled it from her pocket to find an urgent request from Villar.

"Yes, Mister Villar?"

"Sir! A ship's entered the system — it's the *Lively Owl*, sir!"

Alexis stood, glancing at Stoltzfus.

"Which Lagrangian point?"

"L4, sir. She's burning hard for the planet."

There was that, at least — the *Owl* wasn't right on top of them, as it would be if they'd used the L1 point closest to the planet. Alexis quickly considered options. The *Owl* might have a few former Navy men aboard, but most of the crew would be recruits from Man's Fall, hastily trained in the shipboard systems. On the other hand, *Nightingale's* crew might have improved, but they'd not trained at all in fighting while in normal-space. What concerned Alexis the most was that the *Owl* might have some unknown number of ship's boats loaded with mining charges as they'd used on Al Jadiq. The closer she allowed that ship to the planet, the greater the risk one of the boats would make it past *Nightingale* and be able to strike the port town.

Damn me, but I should be aboard —

The time, though, to reach the ship's boat, even if she had it move from the edge of town to pick her up, and then to return and dock with *Nightingale*.

"Mister Villar," she said, making her decision. "You are to command *Nightingale* toward the *Owl* immediately and take or destroy her. Priority to any boats she drops along the way, please."

"Aye, sir."

Alexis heard him order *Nightingale* to quarters and instruct the helmsman to break orbit and head toward the others ship.

"Sir," Villar said finally, "are you certain you won't take the boat up to meet us?"

"The risk is too great, I think." Alexis was glad that he'd set her orders in motion before asking questions. "A single boat with a mining charge would devastate this town, it's so much smaller than the Jadiqi's. I want you to keep that ship and her boats well away from the planet."

"Aye, sir."

Alexis turned her attention back to Stoltzfus.

"And when we're done with them, we'll turn our attention to whatever's left of their band on planet, Mister Stoltzfus, your sensibilities notwithstanding. Had you been honest with me from the first, a great many people would still be alive."

Stoltzfus opened his mouth, perhaps to argue again, but then seemed to deflate. His shoulders slumped, his eyes fell, and he nodded slowly.

Alexis sat for a time, somewhat at a loss. She wanted to contact Villar and see what might be happening, but knew the two ships were still too far apart for an action — *Nightingale's* guns were too small to bother engaging at any great distance, even a converted merchantman's hull would shrug off the dispersed energy.

No, it would, she thought, twenty minutes or more before the first engagement took place. In that time, Villar would likely be reviewing just how one went about attacking in normal-space, as he'd be making use of *Nightingale's* computer for aiming — something not possible in *darkspace* and seldom practiced by ships so small as *Nightingale*. He surely didn't need her jogging his elbow at every turn and pestering him with questions.

It surprised her then, when her tablet *pinged* again so soon.

"Sir —" Villar was saying.

"Yes?"

"The *Owl's* turned about. She was headed in-system from L4 when we circled around in our orbit and spotted her, but now she's had time to see us and she's headed back to the Lagrangian point."

Though she muttered a string of oaths that would make her bosun cover his ears, Alexis' mind stayed on the problem. The outburst was more a way to release the stress of the decision she instantly knew was a result of her previous one — and that the first had been a mistake.

She'd assumed the *Owl*'s commander would be determined to fight through to the "heretics" in some self-sacrificial last attack, not run as he had before.

And now I've made the options even worse.

If she'd gone back aboard at the first, it would have slowed *Nightingale*, but not nearly so much as it would now. Her boat couldn't accelerate fast enough to match the velocity *Nightingale* had built up. The ship would have to slow, even considering that she'd eventually have to do so anyway to transition at the Lagrangian point.

But if the *Owl* were allowed to reach that Lagrangian point and transition to *darkspace* with too much of a lead — well, once her sails were set and charged, she might be well away by the time *Nightingale* could transition and follow.

We'll lose her again. She glanced at Stoltzfus. *And she'll be free to come back here and finish things.*

No matter that she knew the *Owl* would be back, *Nightingale* would have to leave eventually, if for no other reason than to protect the shipping the *Owl* might prey on in the meantime.

"There's no time to retrieve me, Mister Villar," she said. "By the time my boat's caught up with *Nightingale*, the *Owl* will have transitioned and be on her way in *darkspace*. It will be a hard to task to catch them as it is." Alexis clenched her jaw, hating what she had to do, but knowing how important it was to stop the *Owl* from escaping to further prey upon the shipping lanes. "The *Owl* must be stopped before yet another merchant crew's condemned to whatever awaits them in a failed transition. Mister Villar, your orders are to take *Nightingale* in pursuit of the *Lively Owl*. You are to take or destroy her as you see fit or are able, and such pursuit is to continue so long as the ship and crew are in a condition to do so. I will remain here on Man's Fall until you've taken her and returned. Is that clear?"

"Sir, I —" Villar looked confused and unsure.

"The crew are not the only ones to have improved greatly since I came aboard, Mister Villar. I'm entrusting you with my ship and my lads, and I have no reservations."

Villar looked at her for a moment. "Thank you, sir, I'll —" His shoulders squared and his jaw firmed. "Aye, sir. I'll not disappoint you."

Alexis ended her communication with Villar, though she kept the link to *Nightingale* open. At least she'd be able to follow her ship's progress to the Lagrangian point. She glanced up and found Stoltzfus looking at her oddly.

"I'm sorry, Mister Stoltzfus, but the *Owl* and those aboard her must be stopped."

She expected him to object, to make some further plea, but instead he simply nodded.

"Such is your path," he said, simply.

———

ALEXIS WAITED IN STOLTZFUS' office. The two of them seemed to be waiting for whatever happened next before their conversation would continue. Whatever Stoltzfus was thinking, Alexis was wishing that she was aboard *Nightingale*. She watched the two ships' positions, transmitted to her tablet by *Nightingale*, and saw the moment the *Owl* disappeared from normal-space just before Villar contacted her to report it.

"Sir," Villar said. "The *Owl's* just transitioned and we're closing on the Lagrangian point ourselves, a bare ten minutes behind them, I think. There was a transmission, though, just as the *Owl* transitioned."

Alexis waited out a brief pause, knowing that she'd only be talking over Villar's next words due to the brief but noticeable transmission lag given *Nightingale's* distance from the planet.

"It was encrypted," Villar went on, "but poorly, and the signal's console made short work of it." He frowned. "Only two words and not much sense to it, just: *Attack now*. We've seen no signs of other ships in-system, what do you suppose it means?"

Alexis glanced at Stoltzfus and saw that he too suspected the message's meaning. The pirates, rebels against Man's Fall, call them what you will, might have crewed three or four ships, but they also had a settlement on the planet itself. It appeared the commander of the *Owl* had decided if he couldn't finish off the heretics, then his comrades should.

"I believe we understand that message, Mister Villar," she said. "Carry on and take the *Owl* — it appears I'll not be so idle as I thought while you do so."

FIFTY-ONE

Alexis rushed back to the boat, collecting Spindler, Nabb, and her Marines along the way. Her mind worked furiously. In the worst case the pirates would have mining charges at their base here on Man's Fall, not just aboard the *Owl*. If those charges were aboard ship's boats and even now speeding toward the port town in response to the *Owl's* orders, then there was little she could do about it.

She thought of calling Rasch with her tablet and ordering the pilot to take the boat up and intercept anything coming toward the city, but the other possibility, that the pirates had boats, more than one, but without any charges, meant there'd be a ground battle in the town itself, and her boat crew, other than the two Marines, was currently weaponless.

There were weapons aboard the boat itself, but secured in an arms locker which would open only for Alexis or one of her officers — none of whom were with the boat.

The delay grated on her nerves, as she felt with every moment a pirate boat filled with explosives or murderous fanatics must be drawing ever closer, despite Rasch's repeated reports that the boat's sensors detected nothing in the air or space nearby.

She reached the boat, keyed the arms locker with her thumb and code, and had her boat crew empty it. There were more arms than they needed, but if it came to a fight in the city she hoped she might convince some of the residents to give over their claims of pacifism and defend themselves.

That done, she stepped into the cockpit and laid a hand on Rasch's shoulder.

"I want you to take the boat up — you'll gain sensor range with altitude."

Rasch nodded.

"Copy your sensor plot to my tablet. If you see anything, anything at all in the air, don't wait for my orders. According to Stoltzfus, there are no legitimate air transports on the planet — anything flying is the enemy."

"Aye, sir."

Alexis thought Rasch looked nervous and understood he had reason to be. Ship's boats had little in the way of weapons. They were never used in *darkspace*, since they lacked any propulsion that would work there — well, they each had a small lug-sail for use as a last resort if a ship were damaged or destroyed, but they were useless in an action.

In normal-space they might be used to stand off a surrendered ship's bow or stern during boarding, but such actions in normal space were rare and seldom practiced.

Rasch would have control of two small guns in the boat's bow, should he need to engage another boat. They were powerful, being tied directly to the boat's fusion plant since there was no need for gallenium protected capacitors as in a *darkspace* action. The guns could fire almost continuously and with enough force to eventually breach a ship's hull, but he'd be facing more maneuverable boats and not a stationary ship.

"It's a job more suited to the Marine's landing and support craft, I know," she said, squeezing his shoulder, "but those coming — if they come at all — have no more experience with this sort of thing than you, and less than you in flying the boat, yes?"

Rasch nodded, but didn't look entirely convinced.

"Do your best for me, Rasch, that's all I ask. If they come and have mining charges ..."

"Aye, sir," Rasch said, swallowing. "I'll do my best."

Alexis squeezed his shoulder again and hurried aft. Nabb and the Marines had completed handing out weapons to her boat crew. The extras were bundled for carrying and distribution to those in the city who'd take them up to assist in their defense.

Most of the arms used chemical propellants for use in *darkspace*, though there were several flechette rifles and a few laser rifles. The latter came with bandoleers of capacitors, each capable of a handful of shots before needing to be replaced.

Alexis took one of those to supplement her tiny flechette pistol. She eyed the rack of short, chopping blades more commonly used in *darkspace*.

"Do you suppose we'll need those, Connelly?" she asked.

The Marine shook his head. "Imagine if it comes to hand-to-hand we're in the shitter sure ... begging your pardon, sir."

Alexis grinned at him, though she did wish she'd brought more of *Nightingale's* Marines and Corporal Brace along instead of only her boat crew.

"I could wish Corporal Brace and the rest of the lads were down here with us," Connelly said, echoing her thoughts.

Alexis nodded. She hoped neither she nor Connelly nor Villar would have cause to regret her mistake further. Brace and the Marines would likely do Villar little good in his pursuit of the *Owl*, while they'd be far better suited to the sort of fighting she thought would soon occur here.

There were belts with medical kits as well, which she saw passed out, leaving the pouches of vacsuit patches behind — they'd not need those in this battle.

"Have you any experience with land battles?" she asked.

Connelly shook his head. "I've only ever served aboard ships, and small ones at that." He shrugged. "A bit of the basics, I suppose — but that more for attacking. How to clear off the transport without getting yourself knackered on the ramp and such."

"Well we'll have to muddle through as best we can. I can rely on you to speak up if you have aught to say on the matter?"

"Aye, sir, I will."

"Good."

They closed up the boat and signaled Rasch that he could lift, then watched for a moment as the boat rose — slowly at first, then more swiftly until it was out of sight above them.

Alexis checked her tablet and ensured that the boat's sensor suite was relaying to her. Nothing else showed in the air and she had a moment's worry that she might be about to storm into Man's Fall's town with a dozen armed men, two dozen more weapons, to no purpose at all.

She pushed that thought aside, though.

The hatred the captured crew of the *Distant Crown* had expressed and the *Owl's* last message made her certain that the fanatics, for want of a better name, intended to wipe out those they considered heretics as some sort of vicious last act.

If the arrival and departure of a ship's boat so close to their town wasn't enough to draw out every resident, it seemed that marching a troop of armed men through to the town square sufficed. By the time Alexis arrived there, the square was crowded. Stoltzfus stood to one side with a half dozen older men Alexis assumed were the other leaders of the colony.

Fortunately, the crowd parted easily before her group and she didn't have to force a path through to confront them.

"Your ship landing here wasn't enough?" one of the men asked, glaring at her. "Now you bring your vile weapons to our world?"

"Hush, Samuel," Stoltzfus said, then to Alexis, "I assume you mean some sort of defense against this attack you warned me of?"

Alexis nodded. "I have weapons for two dozen more."

"We have our own guns," the man who'd first spoken, Samuel, said. "Meant for hunting or defense against beasts, not men."

"Well, you're about to be attacked by men, not beasts," Alexis said. "I've sent *Nightingale's* boat aloft to detect, and perhaps intercept, them, but we'd best prepare here. Perhaps evacuate the town, in case they use mining charges as they did on Al Jadiq?"

"It is in God's hands," Samuel said. "There is nothing to prepare."

Stoltzfus nodded. "I do wish you would take your crew back to the landing field, lieutenant, or even outside of our town. We wish no violence here."

Alexis stared at the two men for a moment, not quite believing what she was hearing. Her tablet pinged and she shouldered her rifle to pull it out.

It appeared her fears were well-founded and an attack was underway. Worse, she'd underestimated the force involved, for four ship's boats had been detected closing on the town. They were still more than an hour away, and Rasch already had *Nightingale's* boat closing on them, but the number was more than she'd expected.

They must have stripped boats from their captures. Planning for this? Or for attacks on farmsteads?

It didn't matter now, though. She looked around at her little band of crew. Merchant boats were smaller than her own from *Nightingale*, but with four inbound there could be as many as a hundred men or even more on their way.

"Violence is coming whether you will it or no, Mister Stoltzfus," she said. "The only question is how you'll meet it."

"GET TO YOUR PLACE, MAN," Nabb said, "they'll be here soon."

"Aye, they will, and why's that our worry, eh?"

Nabb's jaw tightened and his eyes narrowed. Alexis laid a hand on his arm. They were still at the town square, now all but deserted, but centrally located. Since they had no idea where the pirates …

Pirates? Rebels? Zealots?

Regardless of what she called them, she had no idea where their boats would land, so the central square offered the place they could most easily deploy from. Connelly agreed, saying they could move forward once they knew where the enemy's boats would come to ground.

The residents of Man's Fall had left the square quickly once it was known the four boats were incoming. Some returned to their homes, others to the large, central structure Alexis assumed was their house of worship. None had stayed to fight, which was the crux of Nabb's argument with Arington, one of Alexis' boat crew.

"They run like sheep!" Arington said. "Why's my neck on the line fer 'em then?"

"You took the Queen's shilling and you man a Queen's ship, Arington," Alexis said. "These are the Queen's subjects in danger, think of them what you will, and you'll stand for them."

"Well, we ain't on no ship, are we?" He shook his head. "Didn't sign for this, I didn't."

Alexis looked around at the others of the boat crew and found several of them wavering as well. They didn't think much of the Man's Fall colonists, not with their refusal to fight for themselves. She felt Nabb tense and squeezed his arm again — it wouldn't do to simply order the men, not this time. If they were unsure they might break at the first moment that offered itself.

"These men mean to wipe out what they see as heresy, Arington. Not just sack the town, not just take it — wipe it out, root and branch. The women and children here'll be left widowed and orphaned, or worse. Would you stand by and see that happen?"

"I've a wife and children of my own, sir."

"And who might stand for them one day, if you won't stand for these?"

Arington paused at that.

"Aye, they may be sheep," Alexis allowed. To be truthful, she had a low opinion of the colonists herself. She thought it was one thing to abjure violence, quite another to stand quietly and take it. Perhaps if she'd been raised in their faith she might feel differently, but there it was. Regardless, she knew there were those who wouldn't or couldn't defend themselves for whatever reason. "But with the wolves coming, will you stand by idly and see them put to the slaughter?"

Arington seemed to consider that and Alexis turned to the others.

"This is why you joined, then, lads, isn't it?" she called out, louder than she needed to for addressing such a small group, but she felt they needed to hear it loud. "We *Nightingales* may have had other work 'til now, but did you join to collect the Queen's taxes? Did you, Arington?"

"Not rightly, no."

"Did you join to stop some fool shipping bloody *jam* from Eidera, lads?"

Some, a few, but enough, she thought, called back, "No!"

"Did you take the shilling to chase drunken miners off some Fringe world?"

"No!"

The shouts were more and louder now, and followed by:

"No, but I'll make a bloody spacer-man of one if it kills him!"

That from one of the lads set to train Iveson and Spracklen.

Alexis laughed with the rest. Then, quieter than before, so that they drew closer to hear her:

"Did you join to stand at the fore, lads? To be the Queen's strong arm between Her subjects and the evils that ply the Dark?"

"Aye!" several shouted.

"I were pressed!" sounded one voice, and there were more laughter.

Alexis grinned, then sobered.

"So will you stand with me now, lads? Between these folk and those who'd do them harm? Sheep they may be, but you're not are you?"

"No!"

"The bloody wolf's at the door, will you stand with me?"

"*Aye!*"

She looked out over them, seeing their confident expressions, the surety that they had the right and right would prevail. At Nabb, looking so much like his father and already a sure, steady force she could rely on, at Spindler, who'd shouted along with the rest and had the glint of glory in his eyes that she knew only too well, and she wondered which she'd see the next morning — or which she'd next see in her dreams.

FIFTY-TWO

Rasch was the first to fall, as part of her had known would be the case.

Alexis watched on her tablet as his boat transmitted his position and those of the oncoming enemy. She saw him turn in toward the approaching boats, knew, even as he did it, that it was the wrong time — too soon — but before she could key her tablet to call out to him, it was over.

He'd turned in, firing, and managed to take down one of the oncoming boats, but the maneuver left him in the sights of the rear-most enemy and her tablet went blank as though neither *Nightingale's* boat nor Rasch had ever existed at all.

After that it was all waiting.

She crouched in the shadow of one of the buildings bordering the town square, blind now that Rasch and the boat were gone, and not knowing where the enemy would land or strike. She supposed, if they had mining charges and were willing to use them, despite Stoltzfus' confidence that they wouldn't, that she'd never really know when they arrived — she'd simply cease to exist, along with all her lads.

She thought to send out scouts to other areas of the town, but had too few men, and Connelly agreed. Against a force which was almost certainly larger, she had to keep her own men together. It seemed likely that they wouldn't be able to defeat the oncoming force, but perhaps they could do enough damage to drive them away.

There was a screeching roar and a ship's boat crashed into the town square. It had too much momentum, likely the result of an inexperienced pilot, and there was the further screech of metal on stone as its landing gear slid across the cobbles. Its bow struck a building on the far side, and Alexis offered a silent prayer of gratitude that she'd hadn't been waiting there as the building collapsed to cover the adjacent street.

"Wait for it, lads," Connelly called out. "Wait for my word!"

Alexis had turned the specifics of the battle over to the more experienced Marine. Firing before the boat's hatches opened would be pointless, as their arms would never penetrate the boat's hull. Connelly was waiting for the hatches to open and those on board to leave its cover before firing.

Two of the boat's hatches opened, the starboard side being covered in rubble from the collapsed building. Figures streamed out from its port and rear. Alexis counted silently to herself, reaching twenty before Connelly apparently judged the exiting figures were becoming too dispersed.

He fired, shouting, *"Fire!"* at the same time, and an instant later Alexis' men fired. She raised her own weapon, sighted on a figure rushing down the boat's ramp, and pulled the trigger.

Light flashed from her rifle and she heard the *crack* of ionized air mixed with the louder *cracks* of chemical rifles and the soft whine of flechettes.

One after another, the figures in the square fell. Some stopped, apparently confused. Alexis sighted on one of those and fired again — she missed, but adjusted her aim and the figure fell, whether struck by her own shot or another's, she didn't know.

Those exiting the boat could tell now where the shots were

coming from and rushed for the side of the square Alexis' troops were on. She had half of her men in each of two streets on the north side of the square and the boat had crashed opposite them.

Lasers and flechettes struck the walls around her and she retreated back down the street with Connelly, Nabb, and a few others. Spindler had command of those in the other street and she hoped he had the sense to retreat also.

She fired back again and another figure fell, but she felt the butt of her rifle vibrate in the signal that its capacitor was discharged. She didn't think she'd taken so many shots, but must have.

She pressed the button next to the weapon's trigger and the spent capacitor dropped to the street — she'd worry about collecting those later, if she was still alive — and pulled a fresh one from her bandoleer. It snapped into place with a satisfying *click*, and she took aim again.

The square was littered with bodies from the initial ambush and the mad rush across the open space. There were only, perhaps, a dozen still rushing her position, and some of those fell as she watched.

It was only as she had him in her sights that she noted the size of her next target and his beardless face — she hesitated, realizing that the attacker rushing her was a boy no older than Spindler.

The boy fired his own rifle and the flash of light struck a spacer next to Alexis. She had no time to see who it was or how badly he was hurt, only knew that it was one of her own lads the running boy had struck and fired her own weapon.

She shrugged off the initial horror of what she'd just done, forcing herself to think only of her own *Nightingales* and the innocent towns-people. Whoever got off the attacking boats, misguided as they might be, they'd chosen this fight — and the alternative was for more of her own to die.

She fired again, then searched for a new target, but there were no more running figures in the square.

"Forward!" Connelly yelled. "Check 'em close, lads!"

Alexis moved forward with the others, keeping her rifle on the nearest body while she approached, kicking whatever weapons there were away, and seeing if the figure was dead or only injured.

Most of them were dead, shot through with lasers which struck true or flechette rifles which did such horrible damage that there was little chance of survival.

A few were still alive and Alexis ordered them dragged to the square's edge, well away from their weapons.

She marveled as their own injured were brought there as well. Only three. Both Spindler and Nabb were hale and she closed her eyes for a moment, both resting and giving thanks.

"Take a rest here, Arington," Connelly was saying. "There's some townsfolk coming to offer aid."

"Bugger off, lobster," Arington said, "I'll follow the captain well enough with one leg."

Alexis opened her eyes. Arington was limping, but held his rifle squarely and glared at the Marine as if daring him to question his fitness to go on.

"Your bloody leg's shot through," Connelly said. "Sit for a time."

The silence of the square was broken by the distant *cracks* of lasers and whines of flechettes. Connelly looked up.

"To the east and west, sir, I'd say the other two boats came in to either side of the town and are working their way inward."

Alexis nodded.

"Spindler!" she called. "With me, lad! Connelly, take half the men and head east, I'll go west."

"Aye, sir."

Connelly rushed off to gather the men. Alexis spared a glance for Spindler as he rushed over — the boy's eyes were glassy, as though his mind were somewhere else entirely, and Alexis understood the look all too well. She eyed Arlington, whose left leg wouldn't hold his weight. The cloth of his jumpsuit was charred where a laser had struck and burned through.

"Are you hale, Arington?" she asked, hating herself, for she knew

434

what his answer would be and what it should be instead. But she needed every man and every gun. "Will you stand with me?"

"Aye, sir!" Arington limped forward.

The sound of more shots echoed through the square, closer now, and Alexis could hear screams as well. Wherever the other two boats had come down, they were working their way through the town and people were dying.

"With me, then, to the west, man." She clapped a hand on his shoulder. "You'll not disappoint me, will you?"

Arington shook his head. "Never, sir!"

Alexis strode off to the west, Spindler, Nabb, Arington, and others along behind her. She followed the sounds of shots and screams through the streets.

The shots and the screams grew louder.

Alexis peeked around a corner and spotted a group exiting a house, weapons in hand. The group crossed the street to another door and shot at the lock, but Alexis motioned her little band forward quickly.

She shot, catching a woman in Man's Fall dress, long skirts and an odd, lacy cap, as she moved toward the now open doorway — a woman no different from those Alexis thought to defend, save for the rifle she carried and fired through the broken doorway. The woman fell, her weapon clattering on the cobbles so that Alexis heard it in an odd moment of silence.

More shots rang out.

Alexis felt a burning sensation in her left arm and there was a brush of wind near her right ear.

She glanced down and saw her uniform sleeve with a charred hole in the left arm. Her hand felt numb, but it moved when she commanded it, so she raised her rifle and fired again.

She heard no crack, saw no flash, and realized that her capacitor had been spent without her noticing.

Others rushed by her as she stopped to pull a fresh capacitor from her bandoleer. She slapped it into her rifle, not even remembering that she'd ejected the empty one, and rushed forward. She had no thought in her mind other than her lads were rushing into danger and she wasn't at the fore.

One of her lads fell in the rush, injured or dead, she couldn't tell, but she rushed on. She fired — more of the enemy fell — and her group overran them.

She paused, gasping for breath.

Spindler was at her side. His head cocked to the side.

"I heard a shot down there!" he cried, pointing.

Alexis hadn't heard it, but she nodded and rushed toward the side street he'd pointed at and listened herself.

"There, sir, do you hear it?"

Alexis hadn't, which made her wonder if it was his younger ears that could detect the sounds.

Then a scream echoed down the street and she caught the scent of something burning.

"This way!" she called to the others.

Spindler dashed off ahead of her.

Alexis followed and the passageway between buildings became hazy with smoke. She could see flames in the buildings to either side and residents were streaming into the street, rushing past them. She thought one of the boats must have landed near here, perhaps harder than the others, and set the town on fire.

The smoke grew heavier as they followed the *crack* of lasers and the whine of flechettes. They were also following the sound of screams, but Alexis tried to block the source of those out of her mind.

"There they are!" Spindler shouted. He raised his rifle to fire and rushed forward, the buildings on either side afire.

Alexis lost sight of him in the smoke, called out to him to come back.

Nabb rushed past her, through the intersection and down the path Spindler had taken, just as there was a loud groan and the buildings to either side, as though choreographed, collapsed into the street ahead.

ALEXIS STARED in horror at the way ahead of her. It was a mass of inflamed timbers from the collapsed buildings.

"Where, sir?" Arington asked, almost shouting to be heard over the roar of the flames.

For a moment, Alexis couldn't answer. All she could do was stare ahead, willing Spindler and Nabb to somehow emerge from the smoke and flames. Finally, she shook herself — the whole of this was more important than any two men, no matter what she felt.

She listened, heard the sounds of shots, and dashed to her left.

People were in the streets now, fleeing from both the flames and the sound of shots. Most turned and chose another street as they saw Alexis' band, not knowing which group of armed invaders was which.

Over to the next street, turn, and she saw an armed group backing out of a building and crossing the street. She raised her rifle, sighted, and fired just as they saw her as well.

Beside her someone raised his own rifle, then ran his shoulder into her, knocking her aside. She heard the *whish* of flechettes passing nearby as her hip hit the cobbles hard, but her unarmed training with the Marines took over and flung her forearm out to break her fall. It hurt, but not as much as if her head had hit.

Alexis scrambled to her feet and found Ruse writhing in pain on the street. His left side, from knee to shoulder was raw where tiny darts of thermoplastic had torn into him.

She looked around for Sinkey, didn't see him, and feared he'd fallen too, as the two men were so inseparable.

"Arington!" she called out, pulling patches from her medical pouch. They'd stick over the wounds, stopping the bleeding and most of the pain. "Help me with him!"

They slapped more patches on him, Ruse crying out, then sighing with relief as the pain killers took effect, and dragged him to the side of the street and propped him against a building that wasn't afire.

Alexis knelt beside him. His eyes were glassy from the pain killers. She squeezed his uninjured shoulder gently.

"Did I do for the bastard?" he asked.

Alexis nodded. "I think you did — or one of your mates. They're all down, I think."

Ruse grunted. "Weren't but a girl, I think." He grinned at her. "Not that a girl can't be a right bastard in a fight, eh, sir?"

"We do our best."

He looked around at the smoke. Flames from the next street over cast eerie shadows.

"Bloody stupid way to fight," he muttered, eyes rolling a bit. "I'll take a good vacsuit and a long-nine to fire, me."

His voice trailed off and Alexis rose. She hated to leave him, since she needed all her men with her if she was to finish this. There were more shots sounding in the distance. If they could finish it quickly, they could then get Ruse more help.

The shooters down the street were all down or fled, so Alexis took a moment to look around. She counted her band — they were all panting or coughing from the growing smoke, covered in soot, with red-rimmed eyes, but they were all still with her, save Nabb, Spindler, and Sinkey she saw.

She pushed aside the thought that she knew too well where Nabb and Spindler were. There'd be time enough for that later.

"Where's Sinkey? Did he fall?"

Arington shook his head and pointed.

"Ducked low and run that way." He pointed toward where the enemy had been firing from. "Run right past the bastards and 'round the corner."

Alexis frowned. Past the enemy and around the block back toward the street that was afire. Why would he do that? She had little time to think, though, as she heard more shots in the distance.

"Come on, lads, let's after them and finish this!" she called.

The few men who'd sat down or leaned against a building to rest rose to their feet.

There was a crash and a tower of sparks billowed into the sky above the buildings. Smoke roiled and flowed around the intersection ahead.

Out of it, figures emerged, shadowy and indistinct at first, but clearly armed. Alexis raised her rifle, as did her men.

She shook off the feeling that this image, roiling smoke and shadowy figures, was so much like her nightmares. There was no fire in those visions, but the similarities sent a chill down her spine none-theless.

She took aim. Three of them — perhaps, hopefully, all that was left of the enemy forces at this side of town — rushing forward, two larger and almost dragging a third.

"*Night —*"

There was a *crack* as one of her men fired. The oncoming figures threw themselves to lie prone on the cobbles.

"*Nightingale!* Belay that you sodding bugger!"

Alexis had never been so glad for those of her crew who were still horrible marksmen as she was as Sinkey and Nabb rose and dragged Spindler to his feet between them.

FIFTY-THREE

The aftermath of the battle was almost as arduous as the fight itself.

Without the sound of shots to follow, Alexis assumed the zealots on her side of the town were defeated and made her way back to the town square to meet up with Connelly and his group. The fires were spreading behind them, but there was little she and her men could do alone – with Man's Fall's objection to modern materials, most of the buildings were of wood, some of the smaller ones even had thatch roofs, and burned readily.

As she reached the town square and saw Connelly, she also saw groups of the townspeople mobilizing now that the sounds of shooting were done. She might think ill of them for that, as she knew her men still did – that they'd been unwilling to defend themselves – but they certainly weren't cowards in the face of the fires.

Brigades of bucket carriers formed, with men and women taking turns at hand pumps to fill them and send them in a long, sloshing line towards the flames. Alexis and the *Nightingales* joined in this, working until long after dark to battle the blaze.

With daylight and an end to the fires came a more gruesome task – clearing the bodies of both the attackers and their victims.

The looks on her men's faces as they helped carry the bodies from streets and houses made her suspect that she wasn't the only one who'd have nightmares from this business. She saw more than one man step away from the prone form of one of the attackers, perhaps a young boy or girl, no more than a child, in the streets, lean his fore-head against a nearby wall, and take deep, wracking breaths. Then a mate would clap him on the shoulder, speak a word, and, with a nod, they'd get back to it.

She knew each man was wondering, as she did, what could have driven them – and wondering, as well, whether it was he who'd shot them down the day before. Hard as that was, though, it was difficult to feel too much for the children with guns when the home they'd just come out of held a family slaughtered as they huddled over their own children.

The townsfolk of Man's Fall were sobered by the scene as well, but no more inclined toward Alexis and her crew than they had been before. Despite the gruesome examples of what awaited them at the hands of the zealots, there were few thanks for having been saved. To their credit, she supposed, they did offer thanks for the *Nightingales'* assistance in the recovery.

Alexis could only give thanks that none of her own, save Rasch, had fallen in the battle. Ruse and Spindler were the worst injured – Ruse with his flechette wounds and Spindler with burns – but they'd recover quickly, even with the limited treatments available to them on the planet, and quicker once *Nightingale* returned.

That led Alexis to her worries over her ship and the rest of her crew. Worries which were short-lived, as *Nightingale* returned to the system that very day, sending a *ping* to her tablet along with news that the *Owl* was destroyed, *Nightingale* whole, and her crew safe, save for one man.

It struck her odd that both her group and the ship had come through with so little damage – only one man lost from each. That thought was put aside, though, as she returned to assisting the town and waited for *Nightingale* to make orbit.

ALEXIS SETTLED into her chair and smiled at Isom as he slid a glass before her and Villar. She waited until he'd poured the wine, gesturing for Villar to sit.

"Anxious as I am to hear of your action with the *Owl*, Mister Villar, have you a written report of it as yet?"

Villar shook his head. "Some notes, sir, and I updated the log, of course, but I assumed you'd write the reports for dispatch to Admiralty."

They drank, Alexis finding the wine soothing to her smoke seared throat. She'd likely have to avoid the bourbon for a time, as she thought that might sting.

"I think that report should come from you," she said. "You fought the action, after all."

"Thank you, sir."

His name on the report of a successful action might gain him some attention at Admiralty, and could possibly hasten a promotion to lieutenant.

"Will you tell me, then? And then be about writing it?"

"Aye, sir." Villar settled into his chair and took another sip of wine.

Before he could begin his recount of the action, though, there was a rustling noise from under the table and a streak of brown fur rushed past her legs, circled the cabin, and darted back.

"Damn," Alexis muttered. "Isom! The damnable creature's loose again, will you come see to it, please? I'm sorry, Mister Villar, but he must have slipped his cage again and – "

Villar flushed and Isom stood frozen in the pantry's hatchway, not meeting her eye.

"What is it, the both of you?"

Villar reached into a pocket and pulled something out. He went to place it on the table, but before his hand was over its surface a blur of brown fur appeared on the tabletop and resolved into the damned mongoose. The creature sat on its hindquarters at the table's edge, glanced once at Alexis, then stared intently at Villar's hand.

"It's ... well, sir, it's that we've had Boots rather free of his –"

"'Boots', is it?" Alexis asked. Were even her officers on the vile creature's side?

Villar cleared his throat, then extended his hand to the creature. He had a small piece of ship's beef between his fingers, which the creature took eagerly and began nibbling on.

"It's only that the crew, sir, were feeling a bit bad for him being locked up."

"Indeed."

"Especially so after the *Owl*, sir," Isom added.

Alexis raised an eyebrow. "What would the *Owl* have to do with the creature?"

Isom ducked his head and darted into the pantry. "Perhaps it's best Mister Villar explained, sir."

She turned her attention Villar, who was watching the creature with an amused smile on his face He quickly sobered and straightened in his chair.

"The tale, Mister Villar? And that of the *Owl* itself, if you please?"

"They're rather one and the same, sir."

"How's that?"

"Ah ... perhaps if I were to tell it from the beginning?" The creature finished the small piece of beef and was looking at Villar expectantly. Villar nodded to it and patted his pocket. "But if I may first?"

"Very well, but then let's hear it."

Villar nodded, withdrew another piece of beef, this one larger, and gave it to the creature. Alexis wondered at what must have happened to result in a Naval officer being willing to put vat-grown beef in his uniform pockets – the smell in the midshipmen's berth must be horrendous.

"We were some distance behind the *Owl* when we transitioned, sir," Villar began, "but *Nightingale* wasn't damaged as she was in our last encounter. I saw fairly soon that we were the faster.

"As we closed, I had Oswell and Mares laying the bowchasers – they did fine work and laid the shot well. Put more than one right through the *Owl's* sails and into her stern as well."

Alexis nodded, acknowledging it and making a note to single the two men out in her own report to Admiralty.

"I kept the gundeck aired until we closed further, wanting the men to have time without their helmets," Villar went on, "but when I did call for vacuum, there was ... well, a commotion."

Villar glanced at the creature and Alexis followed his gaze with a glare.

"A commotion which, I presume, delayed vacuum long enough to round up this thing?" She supposed she'd have done the same – much as she might like to be rid of the creature, she didn't think she'd go so far as to space it deliberately if she had the choice.

"Yes, sir. Boots ... that is ... " Villar pointed at the creature who gazed back impassively. "He ... it? Well, he was rushing about the gundeck like he was crazed by something. All of the hands chasing him about, some shot went off the garlands and rolled about loose. They were all rushing about, trying to catch him, and no one was willing to put the deck into vacuum, what with him being loose."

Alexis took a deep breath, but nodded.

"Then, all at once, he stopped his mad dashes and climbed up on the number six gun -- Garbett's crew. I'd reached the gundeck myself at that point, to see what the commotion was about, and he –" Villar pointed at the creature again. "—the mongoose, I mean. Well, he'd gone up on the gun itself and was rubbing his face on the barrel, then he crawled down into the breech itself." Villar shook his head. "Old Garbett pulled him out – Isom arrived and took him back to his cage in the hold."

"Swear I don't know how wee Boots manages the latch, sir!" Isom called from the pantry.

Alexis winced as he named the vile thing again, but supposed she was going to have to get used to it if the crew had taken to the beast, which it was sounding as though they had.

"And the crew's taken to the creature over that?" Alexis asked.

"That ... and what happened later, sir."

"Later?"

Villar nodded. "We closed with the *Owl* further, sir. The gundeck was in vacuum, guns run out. Mares and Oswell sent several more shots into them from the bowchasers. The *Owl* tried to maneuver away – they seem to have had no stomach for a straight up fight. Not one where they hadn't got in the first broadside by surprise, at least.

"Given our speed, I felt we could well-afford to come off the pace and present our broadside a time or two. We put two broadsides into her stern – well-laid, I'll say of the men – and I think the *Owl* was then prepared to turn and face us. They'd taken some damage, though their rudder and planes were whole and working, and we'd shown that *Nightingale* could keep up and harry them from astern at will, you see?"

Alexis nodded. No captain could stand to allow that for very long, eventually, *Nightingale's* broadsides would have damaged the *Owl's* vulnerable rudder or planes, rendering her less able to maneuver and an even easier target.

"Just as I'd determined that the *Owl's* captain must certainly fall off the winds to meet us with his own broadside, she did start to make the turn. I ordered Busbey to put the helm over hard and bring our own broadside to bear once more, hoping to get in one last strike at their stern, you see?"

"As I would do," Alexis allowed. One last blow where the enemy was most vulnerable before *Nightingale* would have to take a blow herself.

Villar paused, raised his glass, and drained it. He glanced at the creature, who'd stopped gnawing on its beef and sat with its head cocked at Alexis. She looked from it to Villar.

"And then?"

Villar cleared his throat, raised his glass to his lips, and set it down as he found it empty. He took a deep breath, as though steeling himself to speak.

"All of the guns fired, sir, and struck the *Owl* squarely on the stern." He glanced at her, then back to the creature. "All but the number six, that is."

It took Alexis a moment to make the connection and realize why Villar kept glancing at the creature. What had it done to the number six gun? It had gotten into the breech – if that wasn't cleaned enough, any shed fur might interfere with the shot's transfer from the lasing tubes in the canister to the guns barrel. Enough, and the gun itself might burst.

"Is that what happened?" she asked. She knew from Villar's initial message that one man had died in the action, but not yet who or how. "Did the gun burst?"

Villar shook his head. "No, it was … I know how this will sound, sir, but I reviewed the log, so I was able to see what happened and not rely on the crew's account alone."

"And what was it?"

"Well, sir, it's … as the broadside fired, all but number six, old Garbett slipped. He went to one knee on the deck, his head and body hit the gun and knocked it askew – altered his aim, how he'd already laid the gun, by a bit, you understand?"

Alexis nodded warily.

"Garbett reached out a hand to the gun's top – to steady himself or pull himself up, one – I can't be certain which – but as he did so, his hand came down on the firing button." Villar swallowed and shrugged. "The gun fired and old Garbett went down flat to the deck. Dead, sir."

"Dead? From a mere slip?"

"Mister Poulter says it was the blow to his head, sir, even through the helmet. The men aren't so certain."

Alexis shook her head, bewildered. "They'll not take the surgeon's word for it? What do they think –" She broke off as she saw Villar staring at the creature again. "What is it, Mister Villar, I fear there's a great deal more to this."

Villar nodded. "It's the shot, sir – that last shot from number six, you see? The one Garbett set off before he died."

"And?"

"Well, sir, Dancy says he saw it clear as day – I reviewed the quarterdeck logs, the images of the *Owl*, but I couldn't be certain. Dancy swears he saw it though, and Wooldridge as well ..."

"Saw *what*, Mister Villar? Out with it!"

"The *Owl* just exploded, sir. Fusion plant went up all at once. Dancy swears it was that last shot. Says he saw it clear as day – go through a small breech in the stern made by that last broadside." He shrugged. "Must have, in fact, to strike her fusion plant and breech that."

Isom chose that moment to return and refill their glasses.

Alexis took a sip. It was certainly an astounding feat, if what Dancy had seen was true. A lucky shot, indeed. "A lucky slip," she said. "For *Nightingale*, if not for Garbett. I'd not have lost him so."

"Not to hear the crew talk, sir," Villar said.

"Not what? Lucky for the ship or unlucky for Garbett?"

"Oh! Lucky for the ship, sir, certainly – but the talk of old Garbett is more ... well, there's *why* Garbett slipped, you see?"

Alexis followed Villar's gaze back to the creature.

"No," she breathed in realization. Her jaw clenched in anger as she realized what Villar meant. It was one thing for the creature's proclivities to soil her boots, quite another for it to have caused the death of one of *Nightingale's* crew. She was amazed, frankly, that the thing was still alive and hadn't been spaced by the ship's crew immediately after they'd discovered it. "Damn. Well, we'll see the thing well dealt-with, I assure you, Mister Villar – and assure the crew as well." She glared at the thing, but it merely gazed back calmly, sharp teeth ripping another shred off of the length of beef it held – and why Villar might be feeding it after what it had caused, she couldn't fathom. "Well dealt-with, indeed."

She blinked as Isom came to the table and hovered over the creature protectively.

"You're mistaking it, sir," he said, "the men aren't angry with Boots, not at all. They say he's lucky."

Alexis stared at him in shock, then at Villar who was nodding agreement. That certainly made no sense to her.

"Lucky? A man's dead!"

"Well, and it was Garbett, after all," Isom said. "He was a dour bastard, come to that."

"But –"

"It's that the *Owl* did still outgun *Nightingale*, sir," Villar said. "In both weight and number. The men knew they'd face a fight – a hard one – and some of them would fall. But Boots, see, made that unnecessary."

"Took out that ship with one shot," Isom said.

"It did not!" Alexis stared at the two for a moment. "You said yourself, Mister Villar, that you'd put more than one broadside into their stern! If their hull was breached, any shot of the next broadside might have done the same!"

"As may be," Isom said, "but it's what the men think – the *Owl* was turning to fight, remember, and we'd likely not get another chance at her stern."

"And Garbett? They'll just forgive that – for the 'luck' of it?"

Villar scratched his neck and grimaced. "To tell the truth, sir, they're talking of Garbett as more of a ... well, sacrifice, I suppose. Not as a victim."

"*What?*" Alexis stared at him in disbelief. "What utter nonsense!"

"A willing sacrifice," Isom said, "for what it's worth. His mates took him out of the suit after and said old Garbett had a smile on his face for the first they'd known him to."

Villar nodded. "I did see it myself." He shrugged. "Garbett did love his gun, but he was getting on in years. Likely be put in atmosphere one day soon."

"His mates're sure he have rather gone as he did," Isom said. "Putting one last shot up a pirates arse and taking the lot to hell with him." He flushed. "As they said, sir."

Alexis sat back in her chair and took a deep breath, held it for a moment, then exhaled.

"What utter rubbish." She stared at the creature, which swallowed the last of its beef and began licking its forepaws. "So they've settled it in their minds that the thing's lucky, have they?"

"Most."

"Most? Well, at least some have some sense." She sighed.

Villar held up a hand and winced. "As to the others, sir ..."

"What? They have a lick of sense and want the creature spaced?" That wouldn't be good – if part of the crew thought the creature lucky and the others blamed him for Garbett's death, then she'd anger some no matter what she did with the thing.

"Not exactly, sir. There's ... talk. Not a great deal, but some."

"What sort of talk?"

"It was Creasy said it first, I think, sir," Isom said.

Alexis closed her eyes. Creasy and his talk of Dutchmen, which she thought they might finally have settled. Now what had the man come up with? She closed her eyes and waved for the two to continue. Whatever came next was best over quickly, she thought.

"Well, there're more uncanny things than Dutchmen said to inhabit the Dark, sir," Villar said, "and with the talk of Garbett as a, well, sacrifice ..."

"Dear lord." Alexis opened her eyes and stared at the creature. Was it her imagination, or did the furry little shoulders square and did its eyes contain a glint of challenge? "They think it's some pagan god?" Perhaps she could leave it, and those of the crew who'd follow it, behind on Man's Fall. It would serve the colonists right to have a mongoose-worshipping sect set up shop next door.

"Oh, no, sir!" Isom said. "That would be foolishness. No better than those Man's Fall fellows, to believe that."

"Thank –"

"Creasy says there's only spirits in the Dark – no gods at all."

Alexis closed her eyes again, counted ten, then glanced at the creature. She shook her head slowly, carefully stood, and made her way to the hatch without looking back.

"I'm returning to the planet to see about the last of the rebuilding assistance, gentlemen." She shook her head. "I feel I need some ... time."

FIFTY-FOUR

The sound of saws and hammers echoed through ...

Alexis paused in her walk, realizing that she didn't know what Man's Fall's port town was called, if anything. She'd have to make a point of asking Stoltzfus before *Nightingale* sailed.

Regardless, *Nightingale's* crew was happy-- most of them, as she'd brought more down from the ship to assist and she'd come to an accommodation with Stoltzfus and the other elders to allow them some liberty on Man's Fall while they assisted with the rebuilding. That did make it seem less a reward to some, though — as well that those repairs were being performed with hand tools only, and that the town had no pubs or taverns. Not a drop of alcohol to be found, come to that, much to the chagrin of the *Nightingales*.

Still, she was happy that her crew took the limitations with good grace.

Perhaps it was the extent of the destruction itself, or the bare dirt of so many fresh graves in the town's cemetery that kept them sober and reserved. She knew the battle and its aftermath would have an effect on her for a long time to come.

She shook her head in bewilderment as she did every time she thought of it. All of this made no sense to her still. These colonists had arrived on Man's Fall as one — one community with one set of beliefs — yet they'd turned on each other with such ferocity and hatred.

Poulter tried to explain it to her, but she still couldn't accept how such things could happen.

He, Poulter, also tried to get Alexis to talk about the fight itself — her and all the men who'd been on Man's Fall. She thought the whole of the crew's opinion could be best summed up by Ruse, who'd stared at the surgeon for a moment, his left side still covered in medical patches as his wounds healed, then simply said, "It was needful. Now bugger off and let me drink, will you?"

Alexis still wondered if she might have done something differently and avoided so much in the way of bloodshed. Perhaps pressed Stoltzfus more strongly about his "internal matter" on her first visit, or seen sooner that the "piracy" was something quite different.

For today, though, she thought, eyeing the bright sky with gratitude, she'd simply be thankful that her lads were alive.

All of them, save Garbett and Rasch -- but she pushed that thought aside, as it would force her to think of what to do with the creature as well. That bit of foolishness she didn't want to deal with just yet.

She took another bite of the dense, sweet pie she carried. Man's Fall did have some skill with sweets, though, and the town's residents were perfectly willing to part with some in exchange for the crew's labor. She started walking again — Isom, several boxes of additional pies for the crew still aboard *Nightingale* weighing him down, followed close behind.

A horse-drawn wagon loaded with boards passed her, likely headed for the reliquary and the construction there. Alexis followed it with her eyes and noticed a woman and young girl of perhaps eight or nine on the wooden walkway across the dirt street. The girl was pointing at Alexis and the mother was bent over, speaking and glancing at Alexis as well.

Likely the trousers, Alexis thought wryly, looking away and moving on.

Her crew, even in their ship's jumpsuits, fit in well enough with the men of Man's Fall — at least until the subject of one's proper behavior came up, at least — but Alexis stuck out. Her uniform was different in every possible way from the long, full skirts and round caps or shawls the women here wore. She shrugged and took another bite of pie. She could tolerate the odd looks for the time it took to finish *Nightingale's* repairs and move on. When her patrol brought her back this way, they'd be back to meeting Stoltzfus at the remote landing field and not mingling with the world's settlers.

"Sarah!"

Alexis looked jerked her head around, heart leaping in her chest for a moment as the girl darted across the street, dodging around the horses pulling another wagon. The woman, Alexis assumed the mother, came after her, but had to stop as the wagon kept moving.

"You ..." the girl said, gasping as she dashed up to Alexis. "You're ... the girl who ... stopped the bad men." She took a deep breath and her eyes scrunched up. "How did you do that? You're not very big."

Alexis had to smile. She knelt down to look the girl in the eye.

"I did have a number of friends with me at the time — that's quite important."

The girl nodded, but her face grew somber.

"My friend was Samuel Yoder," she said, "the bad men made him dead and I can't play with him anymore."

Alexis' heart twisted at the thought of the Yoder farmstead and the state she'd found it in on her first visit to Man's Fall.

"I'm glad you stopped them," the girl went on.

"Sarah!" The girl's mother made it around the wagon and rushed up to them. "I'm sorry, miss, if she's bothering you. Sarah Graber, you must *not* rush off like that. Whatever were you thinking?"

"I'm not bothered," Alexis assured the mother, then to Sarah, "I'm glad I stopped them, too."

"Do you know for certain you stopped the ones who killed Samuel?"

"Sarah, come along, now!"

"I want to know!"

"I'm sorry," the mother said again, "she's a willful thing when she sets her mind to something."

Alexis had to smile at that.

"I'm as certain as I can be," she said, then rose to speak with the mother. "It's all right — I was much the same at her age, if my grandfather's to be believed."

"I'm sure," the woman said, "but I'd not have her turn out the same as you."

Alexis froze, stunned at the stiff tone in the woman's voice. Before she could think to answer, the woman grabbed the girl's hand and pulled her along down the street. Alexis looked after them, both hurt and angry. People from this world had been the cause of the trouble — slaughtering crews, attacking innocents, all for their beliefs. Then she'd risked herself and her own crew to protect this town. Some of the residents did seem to appreciate that, now that the fight was over, there were still some who were almost offended by it. She shook her head in bewilderment.

"Sarah!"

The girl was free again and dashing toward them. Alexis knelt down instinctively to greet her and found Sarah suddenly wrapped in her arms.

"I don't think it's right," Sarah whispered. "My mother says it's wrong to fight back, but I don't think it's right that Samuel should've had to stand there and be killed without fighting back. It's not right."

Alexis was a bit shocked by the fervor in the girl's words. The mother was stalking toward them now, her face angry. She had a sudden thought — it might not be the right one, nor her place to do so, but she felt it was right. It was one thing for a people to have their beliefs and live by them, it was quite another to force those beliefs on others, even their own children. Teach them, yes; encourage them even; but Man's Fall — and Al Jadiq, come to that — kept their people so isolated that there was no option, no opportunity to even learn about something else.

"Would you fight them, then, if they came again?" Alexis asked.

"Yes. I wouldn't just stand there and let them hurt someone. It hurt when Samuel died and I don't want anyone to feel that if I can stop it."

That decided Alexis — if the girl meant only to defend herself, that might be different, but something in the words spoke to her.

She glanced at the approaching mother.

"You think about that and be sure of it, then when you're older — fifteen and not a day younger, mind you — if you see someone in a uniform like mine here in town or more likely at the big field to the south, you know the one?"

Sarah nodded.

"You go there and you find someone in a uniform like mine, then you tell them that you want to be a midshipman, and you say those words, just like you did now.

Sarah nodded again and pulled away from Alexis. "Thank you."

"You be sure, though," Alexis said. "There're some decisions one can't come back from."

"Sarah!" The girl's mother was there again, taking her arm and pulling her away.

Alexis watched her go, wondering if she'd ever make that decision and what would happen to her if she did. She shuddered at the thought of that girl floating dead in the airless hulk of some ship as Sterlyn Artley had aboard *Belial*. Still, there were darker things than the Dark itself in the souls of some men, and the defenseless of the Kingdom had need of those who'd protect them.

She found Isom looking at her oddly.

"What?"

Isom shrugged. "May be trouble from that, some'd call it inter-fering and all."

"Perhaps it's time someone did. Past time with some colonies." She watched the pair walk away, mother now tightly clutching the girl's arm. When did a desire to be left alone, to follow one's beliefs, become a thing she should oppose — perhaps when the choice of doing so was denied to others. "I don't understand it at all. We stand between them and danger, yet they despise us for it."

"Not all," Isom said, nodding to the pie.

True, the baker had taken no payment for them, simply smiling and shaking his head. It was odd, then, how one woman's disdain could sour so much. Alexis handed her plate to Isom, the pie she held no longer appealing to her.

"Not all," she agreed, "but enough to sting." She took a deep breath. "Let's get back aboard ship, Isom, I feel the need of a few days at home."

EPILOGUE

The farmyard was bustling with activity and celebration. In addition to the farm workers, most of the village had come up and Alexis had half her crew present. The other half were still aboard *Nightingale* anxiously awaiting their turn.

The fall air was cool and crisp, scented with wood smoke and grilling meat from the turning spits. Her grandfather had spared nothing and she watched tolerantly as crewmen from *Nightingale* jostled back into line for another serving of real beef or pork. Tables fairly groaned under weight of other dishes and she could see that her lads found the hard cider being served not at all a bad replacement for the weak beer and diluted spirits aboard ship. She could also see that Ousley and his mates were keeping a close watch on them to ensure that no one got too drunk and caused a scene.

The families of *Hermione's* men were still clustered to one side, as though unsure of their acceptance, but there were inroads being made. A few groups of both *Hermiones* and villagers formed and chatted together, and she felt that it would not be so long before they felt like they were at home here on Dalthus.

Home, she thought fondly as she felt her grandfather's arm go around her shoulders.

"Thank you for this," she said. "The lads needed a bit of comfort after Man's Fall."

"And you?"

She nodded. "Aye. A bit and more."

Julia appeared at her other side carrying a tray laden with full plates. "Come on then," she said, nodding to a nearby table that had seats free. "You've, neither of you, had a bite all morning. Come and sit."

They did and Alexis found just how hungry she was. She tucked into the food with a will.

"The Conclave's set to be held in four months' time," her grandfather said. "Will you be able to attend?"

Alexis frowned. "I'll try. I've a great deal of leeway with *Nightingale*'s sailing and I'll try to be back at Dalthus at that time, but if there's trouble elsewhere I can't ignore it."

"I understand," Denholm said. "But I've heard from more than one that they'd like you there to speak to the inheritance vote."

Alexis chuckled. That was a far cry from when she'd first left Dalthus, so that her presence wouldn't remind others of her "reputation" and spoil the chances of changing that law.

Denholm nodded. "Word's spread of what happened on Man's Fall, but I think there's more to it than is published in the Gazette."

Alexis flushed. The Naval Gazette had painted the story of Man's Fall in quite a different light than its reality. According to the official reports, a brave, small band of New London's spacers, outnumbered four or even five to one, had triumphed over religious zealots bent on slaughter not only against their own colony, but their neighbors as well. That the zealots were mostly young men, women, and children with no training wasn't reported.

For Alexis' part, she was glad that she'd stopped the slaughter of the Man's Fall colonists, glad the zealots were no longer a threat, but horrified at the cost. No matter *Nightingale* had seen so few casualties, there was still a cost. She could see it in her crew's eyes and sometimes haunted expressions.

It was so pointless, she thought, and worse that it was painted as some great victory by those who hadn't been there.

She couldn't tell her grandfather the truth, though. She both didn't want him to know the full story of what she'd done and didn't want to distract from the story the Navy had chosen to make of it — surely they had some point in doing so.

"I'll try my best to return, grandfather," Alexis said, turning the subject — the last thing she wanted was credit for those events, "but the Conclave lasts a full month and I can't keep *Nightingale* here all that time."

"Do what you can. I'll see to the schedule and try to accommodate your patrols."

Alexis took a long drink of cider, letting the burn of it hide her reaction to talk of Man's Fall and the feelings it brought.

Her tablet *pinged* for attention and she pulled it out frowning. There should be nothing aboard *Nightingale* that she was needed for until it was time for the port watch to come down for their celebration.

A sudden chill ran through her as she saw the first message: that a ship had transitioned into Dalthus space. She half rose, ready to call her lads to the boat and return to *Nightingale* when the second message made her relax.

It was simply a fast packet dropped in-system to transfer mail. Then her tablet *pinged* yet again as the mail was delivered and she saw that she'd gotten news and orders from Admiralty itself.

She read them, first almost shouting with excitement at the first news, then falling into despair as she read the rest.

"Damn them! Damn them to bloody hell!"

"Alexis?"

She looked up to find Julia and her grandfather watching her with concern.

"What is it?"

"It's ..." She trailed off, unsure how to explain or why she was upset. "It's peace. Peace with Hanover — or a cease fire, at least — but ..."

Julia smiled. "Well, that's good, isn't? For the war to be over?" She half rose, smiling wider, as though to tell the others and celebrate, but then she frowned at the look on Alexis' face and sat. "What else?"

"It's a peace in-place," Alexis said. Her eyes burned and her chest was tight as she looked back to the orders, trying to make sense of it. "No concessions from Hanover at all. It means they've ... they've abandoned the worlds of the Berry March ... just left Giron and the rest of them to Hanover." She paused, still not believing it. She looked across the yard to where Marie and Villar were laughing together — she'd have to tell the girl, tell her that she and the other refugees would likely never see their home world again. "It was all for nothing."

She reread the rest of the orders, those for her and for *Nightingale*, and shook her head, anger growing with every word.

A peace in-place. The Berry March abandoned and Delaine still who-knows-where in Hanover. And Nightingale *declared "surplus to requirements" and to be laid up in ordinary here at Dalthus. The crew to be paid off here, all of them light-years from their homes, save for the few who hold warrants and will live aboard until she's required again.*

"Alexis?"

She looked up to see her grandfather and Julia watching her closely. Saw the hope in Julia's eyes as she asked, "What does that mean for you?"

Alexis caught her lip between her teeth, the last bit of her orders echoing in her head.

Lieutenant Alexis Arleen Carew ordered to Reserve and Half-Pay, to await upon the Future Requirements of Her Majesty and Her Majesty's Naval Service.

She looked between them, trying to keep her own feelings off her face so as not dampen the growing hope she saw on theirs.

How could she explain it to them? How could she explain that with the Conclave prepared to vote and some signs pointing toward them changing the laws so that she'd be able to inherit, that the peace meant she'd be free of the Navy and free to take her place here on Dalthus ... how could she explain to them that she felt as though what she wanted most in her life had suddenly been snatched away? How could they understand when she barely did herself?

Alexis forced a smile and blinked to clear her eyes.

"It means I can come home."

Her tablet *pinged* again with one more incoming message and she frowned. What more could there be?

She frowned more when she opened it, from confusion at first, and then further anger at someone who made so free with the Navy's communications systems and must have found it quite humorous to send her a message ostensibly from herself with all of *Nightingale's* security headers properly in place.

Malcome bloody *Eades*, she thought.

A single word.

Wait.

AUTHOR'S NOTE

Thank you for reading *HMS Nightingale*. I hope you enjoyed it as much as I enjoyed writing it — and, yes, though there's no timeframe I'm prepared to announce at this writing, Alexis' story will continue in book five, tentatively titled *Privateer*.

If you did like it and would like to further support the series, please consider leaving a review on the purchase site or a review/rating on Goodreads. Reviews are the lifeblood of independent authors and let other readers know if a book might be to their liking.

In the previous two books, *Mutineer* and *The Little Ships*, I used historical events as the basis for at least part of the plot. That's a habit I intend to continue in the series, but *Nightingale* doesn't have a historical basis, so those of you looking for one can stop now. :)

Unless you count the mongoose.

One might wonder where Dansby, at the end of *Little Ships*, would have found a mongoose to give Alexis. Curiously, many of the island colonies in our history did import them.[1] The theory was that they would control vermin and snakes in the colonies.

Sadly, the mongoose was also partial to both chickens and eggs, so that didn't work out -- but centuries later, it's not inconceivable that colonists in Alexis' time would make the same mistake and bring a few along.

I'd also, on a far more serious note, like to comment on Alexis' nightmares.

As several readers have noted in reviews of the series, Alexis' experiences have brought on post-traumatic stress disorder (PTSD), as evidenced by her feelings of guilt, nightmares, increased drinking, and the shortening of an already abbreviated temper. This is an area I wanted to address in her character, because I've always felt the effects of combat were glossed over in much military scifi. Massive battles with huge numbers of casualties seem to have little real impact on the characters once the obligatory funeral scene is done.

Despite not having served myself, I have a great deal of respect for those who have, and, especially as current conflicts seem set to drag on into the "Oceania has always been at war with Eastasia" phase, I think glossing over that very real impact does a disservice to those military scifi should honor.

I hope that those who have real experience with PTSD will feel I've dealt with it in Alexis so far with the respect and empathy I hoped to.

J.A. Sutherland
   September 6, 2016
   Saint Thomas, USVI

Contact J.A. Sutherland:

www.alexiscarew.com
sutherland@alexiscarew.com

ALSO BY J.A. SUTHERLAND

To be notified when new releases are available, follow J.A. Sutherland on Facebook (https://www.facebook.com/alexiscarewbooks), Twitter (https://twitter.com/JASutherlandBks), or subscribe to the author's newsletter (http://www.alexiscarew.com/list).

Alexis Carew

Into the Dark

Mutineer

The Little Ships

HMS Nightingale

Privateer

Dark Artifice

Of Dubious Intent

coming early 2018

ABOUT THE AUTHOR

J.A. Sutherland spends his time sailing the Bahamas on a 43' 1925 John G. Alden sailboat called Little Bit ...

Yeah ... no. In his dreams.

Reality is a townhouse in Orlando with a 90 pound huskie-wolf mix who won't let him take naps.

When not reading or writing, he spends his time on roadtrips around the Southeast US searching for good barbeque.

Mailing List: http://www.alexiscarew.com/list

To contact the author:

www.alexiscarew.com
sutherland@alexiscarew.com

DARKSPACE

Darkspace

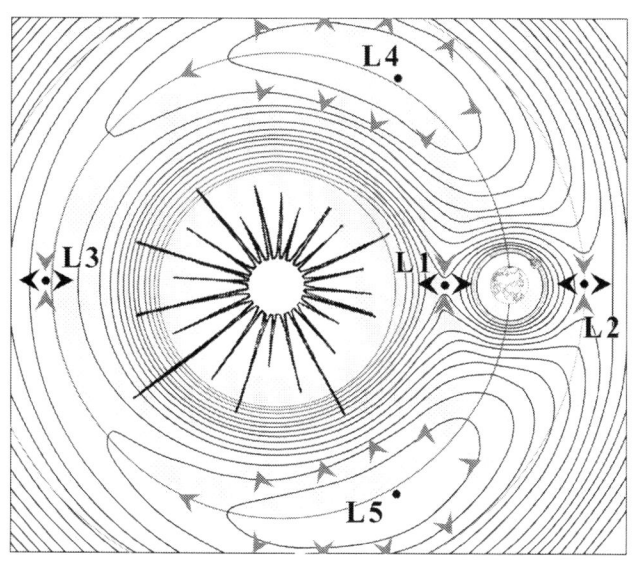

The perplexing problem dated back centuries, to when mankind was still planet-bound on Earth. Scientists, theorizing about the origin of the universe, recognized that the universe was expanding, but made the proposal that the force that had started that expansion would eventually dissipate, causing the universe to then begin contracting again. When they measured this, however, they discovered something very odd — not only was the expansion of the universe not slowing, but it was actually increasing.

This meant that something, something unseen, was continuing to apply energy to the universe's expansion. More energy than could be accounted for by what their instruments could detect. At the same time, they noticed that there seemed to be more gravitational force than could be accounted for by the observable masses of stars, planets, and other objects.

There seemed to be quite a bit of the universe that simply couldn't be seen. Over ninety percent of the energy and matter that had to make up the universe, in fact.

They called these dark energy and dark matter, for want of a better term.

Then, as humanity began serious utilization of near-Earth space, they made another discovery.

Lagrangian points were well-known in orbital mechanics. With any two bodies where one is orbiting around the other, such as a planet and a moon, there are five points in space where the gravitational effects of the two bodies provide precisely the centripetal force required to keep an object, if not stationary, then relatively so.

Humanity first used these points to build a space station at L_1, the Lagrangian point situated midway between Earth and the Moon, thus providing a convenient stopover for further exploration of the Moon. This was quickly followed by a station at L_2, the point on the far side of the moon, roughly the same distance from it as L_1. Both of these stations began reporting odd radiation signatures. Radiation that had no discernible source, but seemed to spring into existence from within the Lagrangian points themselves.

Further research into this odd radiation began taking place at the L4 and L5 points, which led and trailed the Moon in its orbit by about sixty degrees. More commonly referred to as Trojan Points, L4 and L5 are much larger in area than L1 and L2 and, it was discovered, the unknown radiation was much more intense.

More experimentation, including several probes that simply disappeared when their hulls were charged with certain high-energy particles, eventually led to one of those probes reappearing — and the discovery of darkspace, along with the missing ninety-five percent of the universe.

Dark energy that moved through it like winds. Usually blowing directly toward a star system from all directions, pushing those systems farther and farther apart, but sometimes coming in storms that could drive a ship far off course. Dark matter that permeated the space, slowing anything, even light, outside of a ship's hull and field.

Printed in Great Britain
by Amazon

80195148R00273